PUSHKIN PRESS

Her Side of the Story

Looking back over her life, Alessandra Corteggiani recalls her youth during the rise of fascism in 1930s Rome. A sensitive child, she was always alert to the loneliness and dissatisfaction of her mother and the other women in their crowded apartment block. Observing how their lives were weighed down by housework and unfulfilled romantic longing, she became determined to seek another future for herself.

This conviction will lead her to rebel against the expectations of her family, rail against the unjust treatment of women and seek to build a life with an anti-fascist professor. As her independence grows, so too does resistance against it – even from those closest to her.

Set against the dramatic backdrop of the partisan struggle in the Second World War, *Her Side of the Story* is a profound, devastating story of one woman's determination to carve her own path.

ALBA DE CÉSPEDES (1911–97) was a bestselling Italian-Cuban novelist, poet and screenwriter. The granddaughter of the first President of Cuba, de Céspedes was raised in Rome. Married at 15 and a mother by 16, she began her writing career after her divorce at the age of 20. She worked as a journalist throughout the 1930s while also taking an active part in the Italian partisan struggle, and she was twice jailed for her anti-fascist activities. After the fall of fascism, she founded the literary journal *Mercurio* and went on to become one of Italy's most successful and most widely translated authors. *Forbidden Notebook* is also published by Pushkin Press.

JILL FOULSTON has translated novels by Erri de Luca, Marco Balzano, Augusto de Angelis, and Piero Chiara. In 2020, she was shortlisted for the Italian Prose in Translation Award. A former editor at Penguin and Virago, she lives in London.

Her Side of the Story

ALBA DE CÉSPEDES

TRANSLATED FROM THE ITALIAN
BY JILL FOULSTON

WITH AN AFTERWORD
BY ELENA FERRANTE

PUSHKIN PRESS

Pushkin Press
Somerset House, Strand
London WC2R 1LA

Original text © 1949 Arnoldo Mondadori S.p.A., Milano
© 2015 Mondadori Libri S.p.A., Milano

English translation © 2024 Jill Foulston

Afterword copyright © 2003 by Elena Ferrante
Afterword translation copyright © 2016 by Ann Goldstein

Her Side of the Story was first published as
Dalla parte di lei by Mondadori in Milan, 1949

First published by Pushkin Press in 2024

1 3 5 7 9 8 6 4 2

ISBN 13: 978-1-78227-758-3

Offset by Tetragon, London

Printed and bound in the United Kingdom by Clays Ltd, Elcograf S.p.A.

www.pushkinpress.com

From childhood's hour I have not been
As others were; I have not seen
As others saw; I could not bring
My passions from a common spring.
From the same source I have not taken
My sorrow; I could not awaken
My heart to joy at the same tone;
And all I loved, I loved alone.

—*Alone*, Edgar Allan Poe (1875)

Her Side
of the Story

A NOTE FROM THE TRANSLATOR

B Y THE TIME she wrote *Her Side of the Story* (*Dalla parte di lei*), Alba de Céspedes was already an extremely successful writer, but she struggled with the ambitious novel she originally hoped to call *Confessione di una donna*, or *Confessions of a Woman*. She wanted to astonish the critics with her style—though not at the cost of diluting her message. For, as Melania Mazzucco points out in her introduction to the Italian edition, de Céspedes intended to act as the defender of women. Like Flaubert, she could say proudly of her protagonist: *Alessandra, sono io*, I am Alessandra.

The first Italian edition was published in August 1949. Later, finding the novel "too rich" and considering the American public "very simple," de Céspedes rigorously edited the Italian text for the English-language translation by Frances Frenaye. There were then further cuts (by de Céspedes herself and several editors at different imprints) before the book finally appeared in 1952, in shortened form, under the title *The Best of Husbands*. In Italy, the original version was only superseded in 1994, when Mondadori published an edition that reflected the first edit De Cespedes had undertaken. It is that version, shorter than the original Italian edition, but much longer than Frenaye's English translation, that is translated here for the first time.

The novel opens around 1939, although perhaps because very few dates appear, and because it is such an intensely personal narrative, it can be difficult to correlate the plot with historical events. In June 1940, under the fascist dictator Benito Mussolini, Italy joined the Second World War as one of the Axis powers allied with Germany. The war dominates the second half of the novel, and although Mussolini is never mentioned by name, the "arrogant voice" that is frequently to be heard on the radio is his.

During the first three years of the war, Italy was fighting alongside Germany and pursuing its own imperialistic ambitions in the Mediterranean and Africa. Following the Allied invasion of Sicily in July 1943, Rome came under attack, and the novel's heroine and narrator, Alessandra, witnesses the aftermath of the Allied bombardment of July 19 that left horse carcasses littering the pavements of Rome's San Lorenzo neighborhood. A few days later, Mussolini was arrested by order of King Victor Emmanuel III. Alessandra recalls, "Even though I was pleased not to be afraid anymore, I burst into tears, humiliated to think that the arrogant voice had truly been the voice of my time and my era."

But the war was not over. In September 1943, Italy signed an Armistice with the Allies, and Germany occupied most of the north and center of the country. Italy then declared war on Germany, initiating what was in effect a civil war within Italy itself, much of it conducted by partisans against the German occupiers. Rome was finally liberated by American forces in June of 1944, and in April of 1945 Mussolini was killed by partisans. Italy's long-awaited freedom was achieved, but the country had now fallen within the American sphere of influence, something to which de Céspedes, with her Cuban ancestry, reacted with anger and regret. Speaking of Italy's new relationship with the United States, she protested, "I can't . . . understand how a nation could reduce itself to being a branch of a supermarket."

A FEW NOTES on terminology. Early in the novel, Lydia and the Captain meet in a *latteria* and later Tullio waits in a *latteria* for Alessandra and Tomaso. A *latteria* was a small neighborhood shop selling milk and other dairy products, and it also offered coffee and light meals. Although there is no direct equivalent, the nearest term in English would be a milk bar.

The word *babbo* is an alternative to *papà*, the latter essentially French in origin and much used in the north. Historically, the upper classes preferred to use *papà* while the rest of the population— particularly in Tuscany—preferred *babbo*. Both words are now widely used by children, with *babbo* being marginally more popular in the south.

As an Anglo-American, Hervey would more typically have spelled his name with an "a," as Harvey. Hervey is actually the phonetic representation of the Italian pronunciation of Harvey, and for this edition the author's original spelling has been preserved.

—Jill Foulston
London, March 2023

I MET FRANCESCO MINELLI for the first time in Rome, on October 20, 1941. I was working on my dissertation, and my father had been nearly blind for a year because of a cataract. We were living in one of the new apartment blocks on the Lungotevere Flaminio, where we'd found a place soon after my mother's death. I considered myself an only child, even though before my birth my brother had come into the world, revealed himself to be a boy wonder, and drowned at the age of three. There were pictures of him all over the house: many of them showed him nearly naked, protected only by a white undershirt sliding off his bare rounded shoulders; in another portrait he was lying on his stomach on a bearskin. My mother's favorite was a small picture in which he was standing, one hand reaching for a piano keyboard. She maintained that had he lived he would have been a great composer, another Mozart. His name was Alessandro, and when I was born, a few months after his death, I was burdened with the name Alessandra in order to perpetuate his memory, and in the hope that some of the virtues that had left an indelible memory of him would show up in me. This connection with my dead brother was a heavy burden during my early childhood years. I could never shake it off: when I was scolded, it was to point out how, despite my name, I'd betrayed the hopes invested in me, not to mention that Alessandro would never have dared act in such a way. Even when I got good grades at school or demonstrated diligence and loyalty, the implication was that half the credit should be given to Alessandro, who was expressing himself through me. This suppression of my personality made me grow up reserved and unsociable, and I later mistook as faith in my own gifts what was really only my parents' fading memory of Alessandro.

I, however, attributed an evil power to the spiritual presence of my brother. My mother communicated with him by means of a three-legged table and a medium called Ottavia. I had no doubt that he had found a home in me but—contrary to my parents' belief—only in order to suggest unacceptable deeds, wicked thoughts, and unwholesome desires.

So I gave in, concluding it was useless to fight them. Alessandro represented what for other children my age was the devil or an evil spirit. *There he is*, I'd think. *He's in charge.* I thought he might take control of me as he did the little table.

I was often left alone at home in the care of an old servant, Sista. My father was at the office, and my mother went out every day for hours. She was a piano teacher, and I realized later that she could have shown considerable talent if she'd been able to direct it towards art instead of the requirements and tastes of the wealthy middle classes, whose children she had to teach. Before leaving she'd prepare some diversion to amuse me while she was out. She knew I didn't like loud, violent games, so she had me sit in a wicker chair just my size, and on a low table beside me she set out scraps of cloth, shells, and daisies to thread into bracelets or necklaces, along with some books. Under her affectionate guidance, I soon learned to read and write quite well; yet, as if to spite me, even this precocity was attributed to the influence of Alessandro. In fact, I thought and expressed myself like someone twice my age, and my mother wasn't at all surprised, because she mentally replaced my age with what Alessandro's would have been, and let me read books suited to more mature girls. Yet I now see that it was an excellent choice of books and informed by a sound education.

After kissing me fiercely, as if we were going to be apart for a long time, she would go out and leave me by myself. A clattering of plates came from the kitchen; Sista's thin shadow moved along the hallway. At dusk Sista would shut herself in her room in the dark, and I'd hear her saying the rosary. That's when I'd leave my books, shells, and daisy chains and go off to explore the house, knowing I wouldn't be caught.

I wasn't allowed to turn on any lights because we lived in the strictest economy. I'd start by wandering around in the half-light, proceeding slowly and holding my arms out like a sleepwalker. I'd go up to the furniture, solid, old pieces which at that hour seemed to rise up from their quiet stillness to become mysterious presences. Spurred on by a feverish curiosity, I'd open doors, rummage through drawers, and finally, seeing the light retreat from the dark rooms, I'd crouch down in a corner, giddy with fear and delight.

In the summer, I'd go and sit on the balcony overlooking the communal courtyard, or I'd stand on a little bench and look out the window. I never chose the window facing the street: I preferred the one opening onto the small wisteria-clad courtyard that separated our house from a convent. The swallows swooped gladly into the shade of the courtyard and, with the first screech, I'd get up as if called and run to the window. I'd stay there watching the birds, the clouds' shifting patterns, and the life of that secret community of women filtered through lighted windows. The nuns walked quickly, throwing large Chinese shadows on the white blinds at the convent windows. The swallows' cruel shrieks were lashings that stirred my imagination. In my corner at the dark window, I quietly plundered everything around me. I defined this ineffable state of mind as "Alessandro."

I would then take refuge with Sista, who sat near the stove in the kitchen, flushed by the burning coals. My mother would come back and turn on the light: the old servant and I would emerge from the shadows, stupefied by darkness and silence. My mute conversations with the piano and the swallows were so tiring they gave me dark circles under my eyes. Taking me in her arms and apologizing for her absence, my mother would tell me about the young daughters of a princess, Donna Chiara and Donna Dorotea, to whom she'd been teaching music for years without results.

My father came home fairly late, as southerners do. We'd hear his key turn in the lock—a long, thin key that was always sticking out of his vest pocket—and then the sharp click of the light switch. We'd be in the kitchen, where my mother was helping Sista prepare supper: but as soon as she heard the sound of the lock, before her husband even entered the house, she'd hurriedly smooth her hair and go through to the dining room, sitting down with me on a hard sofa. She'd pick up a book and pretend to be engrossed in it. Then she'd ask, "Is that you, Ariberto?," her bright voice expressing joyful surprise. During my early years, my mother put on this little comedy every night, and for a long time it was incomprehensible to me. I couldn't understand why she frantically opened a book if she couldn't keep on reading it. All the same, I remained fascinated by her call ringing through the house harmoniously every evening, making my father's ugly name sound romantic.

My father was a strong, tall man with a crew cut. When I was an adult I came across some pictures of him in his youth, and I could see how he might have been successful with women. He had deep-set, very black eyes, and full, sensual lips. He always wore dark clothes, maybe because he was in the civil service. He spoke little, contenting himself with a disapproving shake of his head, while my mother spoke animatedly. She'd describe things she'd seen or heard in the street, spicing the story with clever observations, and enriching it with her imagination. My father would look at her and shake his head.

They often argued, but there were no scenes or noisy quarrels. They spoke quietly, skillfully launching sharp, biting verbal blows. I'd watch them, dismayed, though I didn't understand what they were arguing about. If it hadn't been for their angry expressions, I wouldn't even have known they were fighting.

When this happened, Sista, who was always listening behind the door, would come and get me. She'd take me to the kitchen and force me to recite the rosary or the litany. Sometimes, to distract me, she'd tell me the story of the Madonna of Lourdes, who appears to the shepherdess Bernadette, or the one in Loreto who travels in a house carried by angels.

MEANWHILE, MY PARENTS went to their bedroom and shut the door. The silence thickened around me and our old servant. I worried that I'd see, in the doorway, one of those spirits summoned by Ottavia on Fridays, which my childish imagination pictured as creaking white skeletons.

"Sista, I'm frightened!" I'd say, and Sista would ask, "Of what?" But her voice was uncertain, and she kept looking towards my mother's room, as if she, too, were frightened.

They spoke softly, and I couldn't hear a single word. Silence was a sign of the storm, spreading along the dark hallway and into the four rooms of our house: an ambiguous silence that seeped out from under the closed door and saturated the air, insidious as a gas leak. Sista, hands trembling, let her knitting fall to her knees. At last, showing signs of impatience and anxiety, she'd take me to my room, as if dragging me to safety, and begin hurriedly undressing me, tucking me under the sheets. I obeyed, mutely letting her turn out the lamp, defeated by the silence coming from the master bedroom.

Often after these distressing evenings, my mother would tiptoe into my room at night, kneel beside my bed, and frantically clasp me to her. She didn't turn on the light, but in the dark I made out her white nightgown. I threw my arms around her neck and kissed her. It was an instant: she would soon escape and I'd close my eyes, exhausted.

My mother's name was Eleonora. I inherited my blond hair from her. She was so blond that when she sat against the light from the window, her hair seemed white, and I was astonished to see it, as if I'd had a vision of her future old age. Her blue eyes and her transparent skin came from her Austrian mother, a fairly well-known actress who had abandoned the stage to marry my Italian grandfather, an artillery officer. In fact, my mother had been given that name to remind my grandmother of playing Nora in Ibsen's *A Doll's House,* which she performed on gala evenings. Two or three times a year, on the rare afternoons she took off, my mother would have me sit beside her and she'd open the big box labeled "photographs" to show me pictures of my grandmother. She looked extremely elegant in her costumes, wearing large hats adorned with feathers or strings of pearls in her loose hair. I could hardly believe she was really my grandmother, our relative, and could have come to visit us, entering through the front door of the building, which was forever ringing with the sound of the hammer of the porter, who was also a shoemaker. I knew the titles of the plays she'd been in by heart, and the names of the characters she'd played. My mother wanted me to have some knowledge of the theater, so she told me the stories of all the tragedies, read the most important scenes to me, and was cheered when I remembered the names of the characters as if they were family members. Those were wonderful times. Sista listened to these tales from her seat in the corner, hands under her apron, as if she wanted to vouch for the truth of such marvelous stories with her presence.

In the same box there were photos of my father's relatives, small landowners from Abruzzo, little more than peasants. Women with ample, tightly corseted bosoms, hair parted and combed into two heavy curls falling on either side of a solid face. There was also a picture of my paternal grandfather in a dark jacket and floppy bow tie.

"They're good people," my mother said, "country folk." They often sent us sacks of flour or baskets of tasty stuffed figs; but none of my aunts was named Ophelia or Desdemona or Juliet, and I wasn't such a glutton that I preferred an almond tart to Shakespeare's romantic tragedies. So, in tacit agreement with my mother, I looked down on our Abruzzese relatives. We opened their baskets, covered in rough canvas and sewn shut, with no interest and in fact with something like tolerance, despite our poverty. Sista was the only one who appreciated the contents, jealously stashing them away.

Sista was absolutely, if nervously, devoted to my mother. She was used to serving in poor homes where the women used coarse, vulgar language and confined their interests to their larders and kitchens, so she had instantly fallen for her new mistress. When my father wasn't there, she followed her around the house and returned to her own work at night to make up for lost time. If she heard her playing the piano, she quickly abandoned everything else, pulled off her apron, and ran to the living room; she'd listen to scales, études, and exercises just as she would sonatas.

She liked sitting quietly in the shadows: throughout my childhood, the darkness was always brightened by the shining eyes of this woman from Nuoro. She didn't say much—I don't think I ever heard her talk at length—and seemed bound to our house by the irresistible attraction my mother's person exercised over her, revealing to her a world she'd never known, not even in her brief youth. So although she was very religious, she stayed with us despite the fact that my mother never went to mass and didn't raise me according to a strict Catholic morality. I think she felt that living with us was sinful; she may even have confessed it and promised to end it, but she found herself increasingly mired in this habitual sin. When my mother wasn't there, she must have felt the house like a vein drained of blood: the long, lonely hours of the afternoon went by wearily. If her mistress was even slightly late, she instantly began to worry that, distracted and absent-minded as she was, she'd been run over by a tram or a carriage: she'd imagine her body lying inert on the paving stones, her forehead pale, hair slick with blood. I knew that a painful yelp was stuck in her throat as she sat still and silent, fingering her rosary beads or warming her hands at the brazier. Yet an unlikely sense of decorum stopped her from waiting for my mother at the window. At such times, I, too, was seized by a chilling, irrational fear and clung to Sista's side. Maybe she thought she would have to go back to working for fat ladies, excellent housewives, and I would be sent to my grandmother in Abruzzo. The light fell gradually, drowning us in waves of darkness. Those were exceptionally sad moments. At last Mamma would return, announcing, "Here I am!" from the doorway as if responding to our desperate call.

Sista also served my father loyally and meekly. She served him and respected him: he was a man, the head of the house. In fact, if she needed anything, she found it easier to ask him, because she recognized him as her own kind: humble, inferior. I discovered later that she was aware of his sordid affairs—given the thousands of clues—but they didn't really bother her since she had seen so many married men act like that, first in her village and then in the city.

At first, I couldn't understand why my parents got married, nor did I ever learn how they met. My father was no different from the standard-issue petty bourgeois husband, the mediocre father, mediocre employee who repairs electrical switches in his free time on Sundays or devises clever gadgets for saving gas. His conversation was always the same: inadequate and spiteful. He often criticized the government or the bureaucracy with scant evidence, and he complained about office quarrels in the usual jargon. There was nothing spiritual in his physical appearance, either. He was tall and heavy, and his broad shoulders made him physically overbearing. His typically Mediterranean black eyes were sweet and moist, like September figs. His hands alone were uncommonly lovely—he wore a gold serpent ring on his right—and their shape and color recalled some noble, ancient race. His soft, smooth skin burned as if it held rich blood captive. It was this secret heat that revealed to me, embarrassingly, what had propelled my mother towards him. Their room adjoined mine and sometimes in the evening I'd stay up, alert, kneeling on my bed with my ear against the wall. I was consumed by jealousy, and it seemed that "Alessandro" really was behind my base actions.

Once, when I was very small, not yet ten years old, I surprised my parents embracing in the dining room. They were facing the window, with their backs to me. One of my father's hands was resting on my mother's hip, stroking it hungrily. She was wearing a thin dress and she surely felt the dry heat of his skin. But it didn't bother her, that was clear. All of a sudden he placed his lips on the side of her neck, at the top of her shoulder. I imagined that his lips must burn like his hands: my mother's neck was long, white, and very delicate, and it would have been easy to leave a red mark on it. I expected her to resist, to react

impulsively, and yet she stayed beside him, becoming lazy, slow, voracious. I turned to leave and bumped into a chair. At the noise my parents
turned and looked at me in surprise. My face was tense and angry.
"What's the matter, Sandi?" my mother asked. But she didn't come
to me, didn't hold me; we didn't run off together. On the contrary, she
let out a hollow, forced laugh. "Are you jealous?" she joked. "Are you
jealous?" I didn't reply. I stared at her, suffering bitterly.

I went back to my room, consumed with silent rancor. I could still
see my father's face: he was smiling mischievously, complicit with
Mamma. For the first time, I felt he'd invaded our cozy feminine world
like an insidious enemy. Before that, he'd seemed like a creature of
another breed entrusted to us, his needs exclusively material. That was
in fact all that seemed to interest him: we often ate leftovers from the
previous meal while he had a steak: his clothes were frequently ironed,
while we hung ours outside on the balcony to rid them of their most obvious wrinkles. I was therefore convinced that he lived in a different
world, where the things my mother had by her example taught me to
disparage had pride of place.

Around that time, I began to consider suicide, believing my mother
to have betrayed our secret understanding. From then on, the idea
returned countless times to tempt me, whenever I feared I'd be unable
to get through a difficult moment or simply a night of uncertainty or
anxiety.

The inadequacy of my religious education has always kept me from
resigning myself to an unhappy life with the thought that it's only
transitory. The thought of suicide, however, which I clung to as a last
resort, was a great help during difficult times. Thanks to that thought,
I managed to appear cheerful and carefree even in the depths of despair.
As a child, I'd imagined committing suicide by hanging myself from
my window, which had a grate over it. Sometimes, though, I thought
it would be enough to run away from home, leaving at night and walking, walking, until I fell down exhausted and lifeless. In any event,

that wasn't feasible since my father locked the door every night before going to bed: three turns of the key.

Sleep calmed my desperation and my intentions. Nevertheless, during that period I often begged Sista to take me to church. I was like my mother, with her sudden impulses; sometimes for three or four days in a row she, too, would go to church at dusk, kneeling and singing, captivated by the music. But I prayed to the Lord to let me die. Nor did I consider my invocation a sacrilege: in our huge apartment block, God was called on to defend the most unspeakable cases. Years later, word got around that the lover of the woman on the second floor had pneumonia and was close to death. We also heard that the woman had urgently requested from the nearby parish a triduum, three days of prayer, "according to her intent," which by now everyone knew very well: that her lover should live, become strong again, so that she could go on betraying her husband with him. All the women in the building attended the triduum. The woman from the second floor knelt in the front pew, her face hidden in her hands. The others refrained from crowding around her, in order to show respect for her modesty, her reputation, and her secret: they came to the service as if they'd just wandered in, one near the holy water stoup, another in front of a side altar. All of them, however, addressed God with the same fervor, indignant that he should continue to make the poor woman suffer.

I'd leave the house towards evening, hanging on to Sista's hand. I felt serious and contrite as I walked, as if nursing a vow of holiness instead of some reprehensible desire. Passing through the gray streets of our neighborhood, we headed for the church, rising sleek and white between the large apartment buildings along the Tiber. It was the outer limit of our walks, as if the river marked the boundary of our domain and, with it, our freedom.

On the Lungotevere in the happy season, the plane trees were crowded with sparrows, and at sunset, as they flitted around capriciously looking for the best branch to sleep on, the old trees hummed like beehives and quivered with the birds' short, restless flights. I wished I could linger and look at the trees, but instead, arm in arm with Sista, I plunged into the dark cavern of the church. The greasy smell of human bodies and the oily aroma of incense stagnated in the aisles, and the shadow to which Sista and I were sentenced by my mother's absence loomed over us. I barely knew the first prayers of our religion, but that reddish half-light, the hymns, and the strange scent immediately awakened my faith, igniting it like a flame.

I watched my hands tremble in the light from the candles. I stared at them intently, hoping to discover the blood of the stigmata; I felt my face growing thinner, like Santa Teresa's on a statue my mother liked. Little by little, I lost the weight of my flesh and rose into the pure air of heaven, stars sparkling between my fingers. A sweet, raging river of words flooded my breast along with the organ music. They were the words my grandmother had recited in the theatre, the most beautiful words I knew, and with them I addressed God. He responded in the same language, and from then on I learned to recognize him in words of love rather than in altarpieces.

Everyone in the church looked serious and sad. They felt no joy in prayer or song. I loved them and wanted them to be happy, and I knew that all they needed was to be taught how to pray in the language of love. I could have saved them, but I didn't dare: I was held back by the thought of Sista, who considered me merely Alessandra, a child. Everyone thought of me as only a child. But when the service was over and the last notes of the organ propelled us along the Tiber, the swallows recognized me and greeted me joyfully, as they greeted God.

WE LIVED ON Via Paolo Emilio, in a large apartment block built during the reign of King Umberto I. The entrance was narrow and dark and collected dirt, because the porter, as I mentioned, was busy working as a shoemaker, and his wife was lazy.

The gray spiral staircase was lit only by a skylight high overhead. Despite the secretive, somewhat disreputable appearance of the entrance and the stairs, the large block was inhabited by middle-class people of modest means. One rarely saw men during the day: they were almost all at work. Dispirited by the constant struggle to make ends meet, they left early and came home at fixed times, a newspaper tucked in their pocket or under their arm.

The large block, therefore, seemed to be inhabited by women only. It was in fact their undisputed territory, they went up and down the dark staircase innumerable times throughout the day, with their shopping bags empty, full, with a bottle of milk wrapped in newspaper, taking children to school with their baskets and lunchboxes, bringing them home, their blue smocks peeking out from under coats that were too short. They climbed the stairs, never looking around; they knew the writing on the walls by heart, and the wood on the bannister was bright with the constant polishing of their hands. Only girls went down quickly, drawn by the fresh air, their shoes clattering over the steps like hail against a window. I don't remember much about the boys who lived in the building. Early on, they were rough kids who spent the entire day in the street and played soccer in the parish garden; then, when still very young, they were taken on by their father's employer. And soon they assumed their father's appearance, schedule, and habits.

Yet although the building looked sad and abandoned from the outside, it inhaled through its large inner courtyard as if through a generous lung. Narrow walkways with rusty railings ran past the internal windows, their arrangement revealing the age and situation of the inhabitants. Some piled up old furniture out there, others kept chicken coops or toys. Ours was adorned with plants.

The women felt at ease in the courtyard, with the familiarity that unites people in a boarding school or a prison. That sort of confidence, however, sprang not so much from living under a common roof as from shared knowledge of the harsh lives they lived: though unaware of it, they felt bound by an affectionate tolerance born of difficulty, depriva- tion, and habit. Away from the male gaze, they were able to demonstrate who they really were, with no need to play out some tedious farce.

Like a convent bell, the first slap of the shutters signaled the beginning of the day. With the dawn of the new day, they all resignedly accepted the burden of struggles renewed. They took comfort in the idea that every quotidian action was echoed by a similar action on the floor below, by another woman wrapped in yet another faded housecoat. No one dared stop, for fear of arresting the motion of some precision mech- anism. Instead, everything that contributed to their lives as housewives unconsciously drew attention to its inherent, if modest, poetic value. The clothesline that ran from one balcony to the next, making it easier to hang the sheets, was like a hand reaching out solicitously. Baskets went up and down from one floor to another with a borrowed utensil, something suddenly needed. Nevertheless, the women didn't talk much in the course of a morning. During a quiet moment, someone might come and lean on the railing to look at the sky. "The sun is so beautiful today!" In the afternoon, though, the courtyard was empty and silent. One knew instinctively that behind the windows, rooms and kitchens were being tidied. A few old ladies sat on the balcony sewing, and maids shelled peas or peeled potatoes, tossing them into a pot on the ground beside them. Towards evening, they, too, went back inside to do their chores, and that was when I was alone in the courtyard, as if it were mine by right.

In summer, after supper, the men, too, would often sit on the bal- cony in shirtsleeves or even pajamas; you could see their cigarettes pulsing like red fireflies in the dark. But the women barely said "Good night" to one another, and their talk was different. Sometimes they spoke about their children's illnesses. But everyone, bored, went in early, closing their shutters, and a great black emptiness fell over the balconies.

My mother rarely appeared in the courtyard and only, as I said, to water the flowers. This reserve, annoying though it was to the residents, earned their admiration. So even if we were very poor, our family enjoyed special consideration because of my mother's delicate beauty, her elegant bearing, and her unfailingly calm and serene mood.

There was no lack of pretty and confident women in the building; some even had a bit of culture, having been teachers or office employees before they married. Yet my mother exchanged nothing with them but a brisk "Good morning," or a passing comment on the weather or the market. The only exception to this was Lydia, who lived on the floor above ours.

My mother often took me to her apartment so I could play with Fulvia, her little girl. They'd leave us alone in her room, which was always cluttered with toys, or on an internal balcony that was also used for storage. The two of them would lie on the bed, talking quietly yet so animatedly that if we interrupted them to ask for a shawl to play with, a piece of paper or a pen, they'd give us their instant permission so we'd leave them in peace. At first I didn't understand why my mother was friends with a woman with whom she had nothing in common. But I noticed that I, too, was coming under the influence of her daughter, my only friend from then on. She seemed older than I was, though she was actually a few months younger. She was pretty, with dark hair and lively, dramatic features. She was already so developed at twelve or thirteen that men would watch her go by when we went out with Sista. She looked like her mother, who was attractive, somewhat plump, and spirited, and favored shiny low-cut silk dresses that showed off her cleavage.

Mother and daughter were almost always alone because Signor Celanti was a travelling salesman. When he came home, they felt they were hosting a stranger, and they didn't hesitate to let him know how inconvenient it was to have him around, interrupting their usual rhythms: they ate quickly, went to bed early, were short on the phone;

one would pretend to have long-lasting migraines while the other wouldn't stop playing irritating and tiresome children's games. Their house, a frequent destination for visits from the neighbors, was abandoned the minute Lydia announced, "Domenico is back." Ultimately, both of them—perhaps without meaning to—rendered the house so inhospitable, so untidy, and so dull that Signor Celanti soon took off again with his suitcase, but not before praising the advantages of hotel life and the cooking in northern cities.

As soon as he left, Lydia and Fulvia would become their usual selves and go back to living as they always did. Lydia resumed her endless phone calls and went out in the afternoons, trailing the pungent scent of cloves, like a scarf, all the way down the stairs.

She'd go to the Captain. It was this captain she whispered about with my mother. Fulvia and I were well aware of it. She only ever used his title: *the Captain says . . . the Captain likes . . .* as if she didn't know his name or surname. But it didn't seem strange to me at the time: other women in the building had the Engineer or the Lawyer, and we didn't know anything else about them, either.

Lydia talked about their romantic trysts, their long walks, and the letters a young servant brought her. My mother's heart beat faster just listening to her. When I was a little older, I realized that the visits to her friend often followed evenings when she and my father were shut in their room, and silence spread through the house.

My mother had met Lydia when she was asked to give Fulvia piano lessons. Lydia came to knock on our door, and—as often happens in such buildings, where you worried that, showing up unexpectedly, you'd find the apartment a mess and people half dressed—she refused to come in, saying what she had to say at the door. Her visit caused some astonishment: no one had ever come to see us, not even for the usual and very widespread habit of asking to borrow a little salt or a few leaves of basil. My mother really wanted her to come into the living room, a dark room that was never aired out. Lydia admitted later that she'd come only in

order to see my mother up close, since her beauty and her reserve provoked gossip and rumors. It was an immediate success: Lydia, fragrant
with talcum powder, was cheerful, lively and colorful, like a just watered
plant. My mother was lethargic and small-breasted. She was attracted
to Lydia's full, lush bosom, which seemed to have its own, independent
animal life. After a few lessons, which Fulvia took reluctantly, content
with learning enough to pick out the popular songs, they became friends.
My mother would go to them at a set time, as she did with her other
pupils. But the moment she got there, Lydia called from her room: "Come
in here, Eleonora." She'd immediately start talking, unfolding her vivid
stories and offering cigarettes. And so the hours went by.

I became jealous, with the vehemence that proves the authenticity
of all my feelings. One evening, encouraged by Sista, I risked going up
to ask my mother to come home. It was the first time I'd taken the stairs
farther than our landing: I felt I was in another world. I hesitated. Sista
prodded me from below: "Be brave!" and I knocked.

"Tell my mother it's very late," I said with a stern frown.

Lydia smiled. "Come in," she invited me, and when I appeared
uncertain, she repeated it. "Come in and tell her yourself."

I had hardly ever been in anyone else's house, so I was instantly
overcome with curiosity to see how they lived, what their rooms and
beds were like, what objects they had on their furniture. Lydia closed
the door behind me and I stood, ecstatic, in front of some prints of myth-
ological subjects: nymphs dancing in a meadow.

"I'd like you to meet Fulvia. You'll be friends." It was summer. Fulvia was in her room, half naked in a long voile dress of her mother's.
Her hair was up and she had lipstick on.

"I'm Gloria Swanson," she said, and when I didn't understand, she
initiated me into the game. "Come here," she said, undoing my braids.
"I'll dress you up like Lillian Gish."

Fulvia, in short, attached herself to me as Lydia had to my mother.
It was due largely to our naïveté, which goaded them on, and to their

perhaps unconscious desire to destroy our sense of order. Excited by the amazement they awakened in us, they unveiled the secret life of the large building we'd lived in for years. When seen through Lydia and Fulvia's tales, all those women we met every day, grazing elbows as we climbed the stairs, appeared larger than life, with romantic histories like the characters Grandmother had played onstage. We finally understood the reason for the silence that fell over the deserted courtyard every afternoon. Released from their thankless tasks and making a brave stand against the dull life they had to live, the women fled the dark rooms, the gray kitchens, the courtyard that, as darkness fell, awaited the inevitable death of another day of pointless youth. The old women, bent over their sewing, stayed behind like pillars, guarding those neat, silent houses. They didn't betray the young women: rather, they helped them, as if they were members of the same congregation. They were bound by a silent and long-standing scorn for men's lives, for their cruel and selfish ways, in a repressed bitterness that was handed down from one generation to the next. Every morning when they got up, men would find their coffee ready and their clothes ironed, and they'd walk out into the crisp air giving no thought to the house or their children. They left behind rooms musty with sleep, unmade beds, and cups stained with milky coffee. They always came home at a specific time, occasionally in small groups like students, having run into each other on the tram or on the Cavour Bridge, and they'd continue together, chatting. In the summer, they'd fan themselves with their hats. As soon as they came in, they'd ask, "Is supper ready?," taking off their jackets and revealing worn suspenders. "The pasta is overcooked," "The rice isn't done yet," and with comments like these they spread ill humor. Then they'd sit down in the only armchair in the coolest room to read the newspaper. They only ever gleaned news of disasters from their reading: the price of bread is rising, salaries are falling, and they always ended up saying, "We'll have to economize." They never found anything good in the papers. Soon they went out again. You'd hear the door slam behind them just as a minute before or a minute after you'd hear doors slamming on the other floors. They came home when the house was dark, the children asleep, and the day over—spent, finished. Once more they took off their jackets, sat down by the radio, and listened to political debates. They never had a thing to say to the women, not even "How are you feeling? Tired? What a pretty dress you're wearing." They never told stories, didn't enjoy conversation or jokes, and hardly ever smiled. When a man spoke to his wife, he'd say, "You all do . . . ," "You all say . . ." lumping her with his children, his mother-in-law, the maid—all of them lazy, spendthrift, ungrateful people.

Yet they had been engaged for a long time, as was traditional with middle-class southerners. The young men had waited hours and hours just to see their beloved come to the window, or to follow when she went for a walk with her mother. They'd written passionate letters. It was not uncommon for girls to wait many years before getting married, since it was difficult to find a secure job and save enough money to buy furniture. They would wait, preparing their trousseau, and trusting in the hope of love and happiness. Instead, they found life draining—the kitchen, the house, the swelling and flattening of their bodies as they brought children into the world. Gradually, beneath an appearance of resignation, the women began to feel angry and resentful about the trap they'd been lured into.

Nevertheless, they usually got by in their onerous daily existence without complaining, and they didn't keep reminding their husbands about the young women they'd been or how they'd been promised a peaceful, happy life. In the beginning, they'd tried: they'd spent many nights crying, their husbands asleep beside them. They'd flattered and tricked, pretended to faint. The most sophisticated had tried to interest their companions in music, novels, taken them to gardens they'd strolled in when they were in love—hoping they'd understand and mend their ways. But all they did was destroy their cherished memories of those places, because there, where they'd uttered the first anxious words or exchanged the first kisses, still infused with unsatisfied desire and curiosity, their husbands couldn't find anything to say that wasn't trite or unfeeling. During the first years of marriage, a number of women had nervous breakdowns or crying fits. Lydia said one had tried to poison herself with veronal. Ultimately some accepted that they were just too old, or had lost all their charm and appeal. But they were the ones who were newly married, or who felt constrained by a solid Catholic faith. By now, most of the others waited every afternoon for a husband to say, "I'm off," as he slammed the door shut. Those who had grown-up girls waited for them to leave as well, with friends their own age. They'd carefully prepare a snack, put it in a bag, and send the younger children to the park with the maid. All the others went out to do what they wanted or what interested them. No one asked the women, "And what will you do?" They were left with piles of laundry to mend and baskets of clothes to iron, stuck in their miserable routine.

Life was more bearable, Fulvia said, in winter. The women, grown lazy with the cold, would sit next to a brazier or in the kitchen, watching the rain slide down the windows and caring attentively for children with seasonal illnesses. In winter, they might find some bitter reward in that snug domestic life, and at night would fall, exhausted, into a dull, obliterating sleep.

The approach of spring dotted the trees on Prati's bleak streets with red buds, and the mimosas and honeysuckle pressed against the gates, spreading their strong scent in the air; it reached right into our old courtyard. The women would throw open the windows to hear the swallows calling as they flew back and forth with shrill invitations. Unable to hold out any longer, they broke away from worries and sorrows as if from hateful constraints. "Jesus, forgive me!" they'd say as they passed the picture of the Sacred Heart in the hall and shut themselves up in their rooms. A short time later, they emerged transformed. They all liked dresses with floral patterns on a black background, wide hats that shaded their faces. They put on lipstick, scent, and powder, sheer gloves, and presented themselves like this to the older women at the windows, who barely looked at them: they recognized the perfume, the determined voice saying, "I'm going out." And even if she happened to be their son's wife, they didn't dare say anything, bound by a solidarity stronger than kinship.

Their lovers, Fulvia told me—sometimes I managed to catch a glimpse of them from the window—were waiting on the street corner. It was an unnecessary precaution, since everyone in the neighborhood knew who they were. Often they were younger men of a slightly higher class. I imagined a lover would be a fairly attractive man, well dressed, romantic-looking. I was amazed to see that almost none of them were like that. But it all became clear when Fulvia told me that the lover of a mature lady on the third floor, a lawyer, always called her Baby.

My mother and I were perturbed by these stories and the mysterious presence of those men besieging our house from a distance. We'd go downstairs in silence, dreamy and distracted, and make our way back into our dark apartment, among the heavy furniture, the books, and the piano. I immediately went to lie down; my mother would turn out the light and sit on my bed. If my father called her during those moments, her answer was curt and resentful. Meanwhile, Alessandro surfaced in me, asking obscene questions and stirring up a tumult of new and unmentionable feelings. The letters Fulvia had told me about were blank as they passed before my eyes: love letters, handed on by young servant girls and the old doorman. I wished I could steal them and read them all.

My mother stayed quietly with me on my bed, and finally left without kissing me. I watched her slender figure go through the door. Not long afterwards, Sista came in and shook me out of my drowsy state.

"You've been with *them*. Say the Act of Contrition and the Ave Maria."

THEN TWO NOTABLE events took place: my mother met the Pierce family and had her first sessions with the medium, Ottavia.

The Pierces were a family of English origin who had moved from Florence to Rome that year. The mother, an American, was very rich, yet unlike many of her compatriots she didn't waste her money on balls and frivolous parties, using it instead to buy art and aid young musicians. The Pierces lived on the Janiculum in a villa surrounded by large trees and tall palms. The view from there was enchanting: Rome's cupolas were framed by the windows like family portraits, and you could see the Tiber flowing under the bridges like a ribbon through lace. My mother would often suggest the Janiculum Hill for our Sunday walks so my father and I could admire the villa's grounds from a distance. Actually, we sometimes pressed on, all the way to the side gates. Then she'd let me climb up on the wall, and she'd point to the three large windows on the first floor which belonged to the music room: inside was a grand piano Mrs. Pierce had had sent from America, her harp, and an ultra-modern gramophone that changed records automatically.

It was a very beautiful villa in the classical style, with dense vegetation that made the garden impassable. I saw large, elegant dogs go by, and my mother assured me that there were also white peacocks on the lawn, though I never did see them. We were both fascinated by that mansion, but my father didn't share our enthusiasm. Maybe he felt the instinctive dislike of the poor for conspicuous wealth. He'd hurry us along, impatient to get to a nearby trattoria and drink a lemon soda.

Every Sunday evening, he took us to a café. I always loved gelato. But having seen the grounds of the Pierces' villa from a distance, I was brooding and distracted; I fiddled with my spoon and left most of my gelato to melt into a yellow puddle. My mother did the same: this tendency of ours to become lost in thought irritated my father beyond words. He mistakenly saw it as contempt for our situation and his inability to earn much money.

Yet neither my mother nor I ever gave a thought to the way we lived. She had worn the same dresses for years, and although she occasionally freshened them with a buckle or a ribbon—or perhaps because of this—they were now so out of fashion that wearing them seemed an ostentatious eccentricity. She didn't own a fur coat, only a shabby black one with which to face the rigors of winter. Her beautiful hair—still long and gathered in a bun on her neck—was humbled under modest hats an older woman would have rejected. Our café was extremely cheap, and our fun was limited to those Sunday walks. The two of us studied the villa for some time, if only because we were drawn to the large trees planted in groups or in couples like people, and we realized what a privilege and a delight it must be for the Pierce family to look at them. Nor was it their only privilege. My mother considered them fortunate partly because, thanks to their money, they could follow their natural spiritual inclinations without worrying about day-to-day needs.

Absorbed in these thoughts, we sat at a small iron table on a pavement crowded with more tables and people like us: mother, father, and children. From their windows in tall gray apartment blocks, residents eyed our gelato resentfully until it disappeared from our bowls. The tram grazed the pavement as it passed and each time a harsh screech of metal drowned out our listless conversation. I couldn't stop thinking about the ivy- and moss-covered trees behind the grand gate, the damp green lawns where white peacocks walked (though I hadn't seen them), the three tall, gabled windows, the grand piano and the harp alone in the shadows.

That piano held a great allure for my mother, and this was due not only to its beautiful sound but also to the fact that she didn't use it for teaching scales, exercises, or tedious sonatinas. She could play it freely, as if she were in her own home. The reason she had been called to the Pierces' villa was rather unusual. The first day she went there, the mistress of the house had not received her in a rush, like other women, who'd present her with a new student and leave after a few minutes; she had invited my mother to tea, and she spoke about her art collection, her travels, and, finally, her family. Her husband was an industrialist who collected Brazilian butterflies in his spare time, and she had a married daughter in London as well as two younger children living with her, Hervey and Arletta. The former—who wasn't well, she said quickly—often travelled.

It was Arletta my mother was to concern herself with, not to teach her the piano but to awaken in her an interest in music, as other teachers were trying to interest her in painting and poetry. The girl had not an ounce of artistic sensibility, her mother quietly confided. She explained how painful that was for the other family members, who lived almost exclusively for such things. Hervey was often away from Rome in part for that very reason. In fact, he'd left only a short time ago and would be gone for about a year. Arletta's personality had become so intrusive that it couldn't be ignored in the daily life of the house. She flaunted her preference for popular songs over chamber music, pulp novels over the classics of literature, and it would be necessary to educate her tastes gradually. She was very young, and willing, so perhaps she was curable.

Soon afterwards Arletta came in, and, given that she could have guessed what had just been said about her, my mother felt some embarrassment when shaking her hand. She told me she had imagined her differently: lively, cheeky, prone to argument and sarcasm. But she was my age, a little chubby, and rather homely. Arletta immediately offered to take my mother to the music room, and the way she turned the gilded handle revealed the reverential fear the room aroused in her.

The vast room was in shadow. Delicate branches were intertwined outside the windows, and the afternoon sun coming through the leaves of trees that reached up to the window sills turned the room the color of the deep sea, giving it the murky aspect of an aquarium. The dark bulk of the piano rose like an island in a corner, and the harp's subtle gold, touched by shafts of sunlight, shone through the motes of dust. There was no furniture in the large space apart from some Empire-style chairs softened by lyre-shaped backrests and two deep sofas. Near the window, four tall music stands for violins threw huge, transparent, skeleton-like shadows over the white wall. My mother and Arletta tiptoed, afraid of disturbing all that silence and order. When she reached the center of the room Arletta stopped abruptly: in the light from the window, her white arms and white dress made her look like a large jellyfish.

"Signora," she said, "I'm afraid. My brother doesn't want me to come in here." She seemed truly intimidated. "He feels that I'm resistant to music," she added. "In fact hostile to it. It's not my fault. I don't understand it. Hervey's right. He'll travel a long way just to hear a pianist, and when he's in Rome you might say that he lives alone in here with his records and his violin. I know very well that he doesn't want me to come in here, because he's afraid I'll leave something in the air to disturb him even when I'm not around. It's painful for me, Signora—it's as if I had some secret illness and were contagious. You must cure me. It might be best to start with easy things, for children. I must get better," she said determinedly. And added softly, "Because I love my brother Hervey more than anything."

My mother took her hands and thanked her for being frank. She opened the windows in order to dispel the room's mysterious atmosphere, and the branch of a fir tree reached into the room like an animal that had been lying in wait. Despite that, the large room remained stubbornly impenetrable and secret, the musical instruments like characters with thoughts and feelings.

"It's Hervey," Arletta repeated, looking around fearfully, and my mother also began to feel uneasy. "My mother doesn't even dare to come in and play when he's not here." Arletta pointed to a white satin chair next to the harp. "When my mother plays, Hervey lies on the sofa and closes his eyes to listen."

"And you?"

"I stay in my room, or go for a walk in the garden. At some distance, so he can't see me from the windows."

Arletta spiritedly defended her brother when my mother boldly expressed disapproval of such bizarre behavior. "Oh, no, Signora! Hervey is an artist. He plays the violin, or he'll sit at the piano and improvise. Mother says the pieces are wonderful. No," she said, "it's really my fault." She added sadly, "Lady Randall, my sister Shirley who lives in London, plays the piano beautifully."

.   .   .

TO MAKE SPACE for her new student, my mother had to give up others, since she was at Villa Pierce twice a week for nearly an entire afternoon. Unaware of the special nature of these lessons, my father had advised her against this: he worried that once she lost the students who had been studying with her for years, it would be difficult to find others if the Pierce family should suddenly disappear, and the new source of income with them.

However, she showed herself not only determined but obstinate. On days when she went to Arletta, she was restless from the start, as anxious as if she were going to a party. Given my nature and my feelings for her, I would have been jealous of the new student if my mother, on her return, hadn't been demonstrably warmer than usual. In fact, after spending several hours at Villa Pierce, she seemed animated by a new enthusiasm. When she came home, her quick, light step shook our gloomy, somnolent rooms.

She often brought back sweets, a bag of sugared almonds she'd received as a gift. This irritated my father, and I myself ate them reluctantly. Maybe he feared that, in becoming acquainted with a way of life so different from ours, his wife might regret the life she led during the rest of the week. Indeed, most of my mother's previous students were from the middle class, girls who were studying to become teachers so they could in turn make a living. Thus my mother got no personal satisfaction from her work and never met anyone the least bit interesting or notable. It was only to help my father provide for our needs that she had to go out whatever the weather and squeeze into the tram, climb up and down staircases like ours, enter sordid little apartments that smelled of the food eaten that morning and evening. It cheered me that afternoons at Villa Pierce offered her a pleasant holiday, and I willingly helped Sista relieve my mother of the burden of her household jobs. I even learned to mend, work I didn't mind doing because I could sit silently by my favorite window while my thoughts ran free.

Those thoughts were not a little disturbed by my acquaintance—
through Ottavia, the medium—with the mysterious and terrifying
characters who lived in the sky, where I watched the swallows darting
at sunset.

Ottavia had been going to the Celantis' house for some time, and
Fulvia had often spoken of her when we were alone in her room or
chatting on the terrace. I once caught sight of her on the stairs: a sturdy
middle-aged woman, her gray hair cut like a man's. She always carried
a large purse stuffed with sacred images, medals on red ribbons, lucky
charms made of coral, and packets of herbs against the evil eye, and
she was followed by a young boy whom she introduced as her nephew,
a kid of about fifteen whose head was shaved even in the harshest
months of winter. There was something wrong with her left leg and
she limped, but she didn't struggle or show embarrassment: every step
was an arrogant thump, a statement. Enea, the boy, followed her at
a distance, and, as far as I can remember, he was always dressed in
black, with black gloves and black socks that gave him the look of a
young priest. He had clear, olive skin, and his eyes—dark, soft, long-
lashed—were like my father's.

According to the Celantis, Ottavia had been going up and down
the dark staircase in our building for years. She had a special way of
announcing her arrival, rapping three times carefully and precisely
to make sure the men were not at home; if they were, she'd pretend
she was on the wrong floor. This took place on Fridays, the day most
propitious for seances. On that day, starting in the morning, a heavy
aroma of incense filled the stairway. On the landings, the doors were
left half open, and girls went warily from one apartment to another,
borrowing a white cloth, a small table. In short, a thinly disguised
excitement brightened the whole day.

From morning onwards, the dead all returned to live in their houses.
Hearing a noise in the next room, Fulvia said calmly, "That's Uncle
Quintino." The women got up early and worked hard at their chores,

perhaps so the dead would remember what a bitter thing life was. They'd head for the spot the dead had occupied for years, and speak harshly, sarcastically, blaming them for their death as if for a betrayal, a cunning escape. Now and again they'd sigh, staring at the empty chair, once their mother's or grandmother's. Then slowly, delicately, they'd dust off the back, as if arranging a shawl. From the empty chair that day, eyes watched them, unflinching, resigned. Even though I was excluded from the seances at first, I, too, was aware of an invisible presence. All it took was a creaking sound to make me turn around, drenched in sweat, my heart racing. *Alessandro,* I whispered, afraid. I realized that he wasn't resigned, like the others, to being a silent shadow. He wanted to play a part in our lives, using me to do so.

My mother, on the other hand, seemed uninterested in these activities, and didn't believe in prophetic revelations. She wasn't, in any case, curious about the future, since at the time she had no hope that our monotonous life would ever change. My father would keep his government job until he retired; she would go on teaching until she was old. And the dreams she sometimes confided—the possibility of becoming a famous pianist, the country house we might have had—lasted no longer than the time it took her to recount them.

After she started going to the Pierces' villa, however, she began to show more interest in those sessions. She laughed despite herself when Lydia told her that the spirits' predictions always came true. And yet it was only when Lydia hinted at the possibility of communicating with Alessandro through Ottavia's automatic writing that she showed some hesitation. Still, she put off the invitation once again: "We'll see."

AS I SAID, my brother Alessandro drowned to death. It's very rare for a child of that age to drown in the Tiber, a river both confined and defended by high walls. It was all because of a babysitter's negligence, and that's why my mother never had one for me. She preferred to leave me at home for entire afternoons, suggesting that I go out and get fresh air on the balcony, rather than hand me over to someone she didn't know. She gave in to my going as far as the church with Sista, but unwillingly.

Alessandro had been entrusted—as the poor used to do—to a girl barely older than thirteen who had just arrived in Rome from the country. The stunted trees and dusty gravel of the city parks held no appeal for her; she was used to feeling fresh, damp grass under her bare feet. The tall apartment blocks and noisy streets truly frightened her, and she spent long hours crying in her windowless room, miserable about being so far from the meadows and the river. That's why every day, disobeying her mistress, she'd walk some distance, carrying the child, to get to the banks of the Tiber just beyond the Risorgimento bridge. At the time it was an undeveloped wasteland called the Piazza d'Armi. Once there, she climbed down to the riverbed, took off her socks and shoes and my brother's, too. She lay down happily on the green shore, under the vast sky, listening to birdsong and the water's gurgling as she had in her village. The child played next to her, making mud pies and running among the reeds along the river's edge. After the accident, she insisted that Alessandro had been happy at those times, and confessed she had persuaded him to become more confident in the water. She said it had all happened in the blink of an eye. She was lying on the grass in the shade of the reeds, eyes closed, arms under her head. She heard a splash, a short cry instantly muffled. She jumped to her feet just in time to see a little hand waving in the water like a flag. Then: nothing. The water was smooth and clear. She didn't call for help; she stood there, bewildered and unhappy, as if the river had carried off her handkerchief.

She went back home: "The river has taken the boy." A crowd rushed to the spot and though the boatmen searched and shoveled, the little body never surfaced. For years my mother recoiled from looking at the river; she stared straight ahead when she crossed the bridges and wouldn't even talk about it. But every year, on the twelfth of July, the three of us left the house: my mother dressed in black, me with a black bow at my waist or in my hair, and we'd walk silently to the bridge and cautiously descend the bank. The sad spot was still marked by a large cluster of rustling reeds. My mother would walk to the water's edge and stand there, watching the water as intently as if it were her child's face. Then she'd throw the flowers she'd brought into the river: always large white daisies. She threw them slowly, one by one, and they lay just on the surface of the water, spinning away with the current. In the evening she'd call us into the living room and play Bach.

To her free and unbridled imagination, this son, stolen by the water, seemed to have been destined for extraordinary things. Though she always loved me dearly, I felt that her love for Alessandro was of a different kind. She found in me the character she'd inherited from her mother: the same dangerous sensitivity. In fact, I'd often catch her staring at me with a gaze that was full of love but imbued with such genuine pity that I felt like crying without knowing why. My preference for solitude and long hours at the window and my love of poetry did not escape her. The discovery of our affinities sometimes elicited an unexpected and impulsive tenderness in her, yet sometimes so alarmed her that suddenly, as if threatened by an unseen danger, she'd pull me away from the window or my solitary games and order me sharply: "Get away from there. Go upstairs and see Fulvia. Don't sit around in this house. Go and play with girls your age. Get some fresh air. Go!"

My mother was convinced that Alessandro would have been different from us. She maintained that he would have gained everything she had lost in life: he would even have become a great pianist. She imagined the trips we would have taken, accompanying him to the great European cities: she described Paris, Vienna, the bridges on the Seine and the Danube, Buda and Margaret Island. She had never been abroad, but she knew those cities by heart because her mother had described them to her in every detail. It seemed almost impossible that so many wonderful things should exist, and sometimes I suspected her of making them up: she spoke of the people we'd meet, rulers, princes, and artists whose names we read on the covers of musical scores. She described the women Alessandro would have known: some would actually cross oceans to meet him. I felt they would all have been beautiful and unhappy like Ophelia and Desdemona, and I listened, enthralled. At such times, the resentment I harbored towards Alessandro would dissipate. My mother would fall silent but remain rapt, her eyes staring. I imagined her seeing the dark throat of the bridge and the Tiber flowing rapidly and insidiously, because, turning pale, she covered her face with her hands.

IT WAS A Friday morning when Ottavia came to our house for the first time. My mother, Sista, and I stood by the open door, as if expecting the priest's blessing at Easter. Fulvia and her mother were waiting with us.

Ottavia entered and immediately asked for a brazier with a small fire going. When she got it, she threw on it a handful of incense taken from a large packet in her purse. She handed the brazier to the boy who was trailing her and ordered my mother to give her a tour of the house. We stopped in every room, and while Enea religiously waved the brazier in every corner, leaving a thick cloud of scent, Ottavia stood still, eyes lowered, reciting prayers for the dead. Then she'd start walking again, her gait uneven but strong.

When we'd visited every corner of the house she stopped and asked, "Where?"

"Best in the living room," Lydia replied, glancing at my mother for her approval.

We went in and shut the door. It was a room we rarely entered—only when my mother invited us to the piano—and it held the most somber furniture in the house. Even the air struggled to get in, choked by heavy curtains, provincial and outdated. Ottavia wanted the windows to stay shut, the curtains drawn. Sista watched us, her forehead creased with reproach. Swiftly and confidently, Ottavia placed on the table the green-shaded lamp my mother used for the piano at night and around it she threw talismans threaded on a red ribbon. She took out paper and pencil and asked us to gather around as she prepared to write.

I sat between Fulvia and Enea; Fulvia appeared excited and intrigued while Enea stared at me so insistently that every few minutes I had to turn to respond to the summons of his gaze: this young man who dared to share the daily company of spirits made me uneasy. My mother took a spot next to the medium and put her hands on the table, face up. In the circle of light, she once again seemed different, different from all other women in the world, and it bothered me to see her next to Lydia, who could stay nonchalant even at moments like this. The medium's hand began to quiver over the white paper. Fulvia whispered, "He's here."

I was scared. I must have turned pale, like my mother, and Enea's constant scrutiny made me even more uncomfortable. All this time, Ottavia was writing, and she read as the syllables formed themselves: "Bles-sings-on-all-who-are-gath-ered-here."

Lydia glanced at the paper with the help of a lorgnette. Then, as if recognizing the writing of a relative: "It's Cola." Ottavia nodded.

Cola was a spirit guide. Ottavia explained later that he had to work off his sentence, which meant remaining bound to our world, through her human life, until such time as he could ascend to the higher spheres. She spoke of Cola as she would a living person, an old lunatic relative who had lived as her lodger for many years. She described his character, tastes, even his quirks. She told us that when Cola wanted to communicate with her and didn't find her ready to write, he'd often persist, making her drop whatever she had in her hand or hiding something from her—irritable, like someone who's lost patience—until she took a piece of paper and a pencil and began to write. She told us she had even seen him a few times, but in the evening, by the light of the candle stubs she kept burning. He was tall and stooped, perhaps sad or worried. She had seen his face only once, for a moment: his features were not well defined, and yet he expressed a profound melancholy. When he appeared, Ottavia said, it was a sign that he needed an intercession said for him.

On that first day with Ottavia, it wasn't possible to communicate with Alessandro. When Ottavia asked Cola about him, my mother clung to the table, stunned.

I'll go and see, Cola wrote, and he left us as if retiring to an adjacent room, with the gait Ottavia had described. I didn't understand how he could walk on clouds or in the air. He came back and wrote, *He's busy right now. He can't come. It will happen next Friday.*

My mother bowed her head when she heard this message about the appointment. I started to tremble, and Enea took my hand to give me courage. His hand was dry and hot like my father's. I shivered at his touch, not daring to pull away, whether because my nerves were already shaken or on account of the smell and the dark. But certainly I felt an impetuous desire to move closer to him, detecting in his dry warmth a secret and unmentionable attraction.

Cola, meanwhile, was dictating rapidly. He said he could see events in my mother's future that would change the course of her life.

"Why?" she asked, leaning over the table, with a naïve and surprised look.

The writing stopped for a while. The pencil would approach the paper, then hesitate and pull away. Suddenly Cola started writing so quickly and unevenly that Ottavia could barely keep up.

After the spirit had dictated to her, she remained thoughtful for a moment, not revealing his message. Her hand was still trembling. At last, she looked up at my mother with a grave expression. She looked in my direction, perhaps questioning whether she could speak freely. My mother gave her a quick nod.

Unable to contain her curiosity, Lydia leaned over the paper and read through her lorgnette, and then lowered the lenses. She, too, began staring at my mother.

Alarmed, my mother asked, "Say something! Is it bad news?"

Ottavia shook her head and looked at her with deference. "He says you will have a great love," she announced.

Astonished, my mother did not reply but blushed like a newlywed. Lydia shook her out of it by patting her arm gleefully. "Oh my dear, my dear!," all the while giving her knowing looks and smiling suggestively. The medium smiled, too, pleased to have discovered, despite her natural modesty, this wonderful, unexpected quality. Hesitant, but persuaded by the others, my mother returned the smile. Then she looked at me, stunned.

I jumped up and ran to embrace her, upsetting the calm in the room.

ALL THIS HAPPENED a year before my mother's death, so I must have been around sixteen. I was already taller than my peers, but still had my hair in two braids that hung down to my chest. I had no womanly curves; the white blouses I wore could have concealed the lithe and slender bust of a boy. And since my face, which had a northern character, fairly regular and composed, didn't allow for either dimples or charming creases when I smiled, I feared for a long time that my masculine appearance was due to Alessandro's diabolical incarnation in me.

I spent most of the day by myself. At school, being at the top of my class soon isolated me in a circle of cold suspicion, and I made no effort to leave it. School life didn't interest me much, and my success at my studies was attributable only to my inability to do anything carelessly or halfheartedly. On the other hand, I was troubled by my classmates' apathy and vulgar behavior. Making fun of the teachers—who were, as I recall, kind and fair—responding with sarcasm and humiliating remarks to people who dedicated their time to teaching and improving us seemed to express a rude, vulgar character. I couldn't ignore the fact that the person I loved more than anyone in the world—my mother—was a teacher, and so I couldn't bear the idea that she, too, might be treated poorly by her students; nor did I consider it clever to parade ignorance or bad grades, showing not the slightest interest in what served to refine and elevate the spirit.

Naturally, my schoolmates made fun of me. I pretended not to be upset, which only increased their insistent derision. Yet something happened one day that almost got me expelled from school, and which seems worth recounting. One of the classmates I sometimes talked to was a girl called Natalia Donati. She wasn't very pretty, mostly because of her thick glasses, and she wasn't all that intelligent, but she was sweet and sensitive, and readily affectionate. She was rumored to have a crush on an older boy called Andreani, who was in his second year of high school. In fact, she couldn't see him go by without blushing. As we walked home together, she confessed that simply exchanging a few words with him during recess made her feel weak. She was always watching him, and she probably made a nuisance of herself trying to join, uninvited, the groups he was in.

Her actions did not escape her shrewder classmates, who took advantage of them to play a tasteless joke. Natalia confided to me that she'd received an affectionate letter from Andreani followed by a declaration of love. He begged her in both not to reveal or to betray the secret of their love to anyone, during recess, in order to avoid malicious comments.

She read me the letters in a public park, the only green space in the middle of all those gloomy, identical houses in Prati. Natalia had wanted to go there because "I don't like reading his letters on the street with people going by." It seemed a sensitive reaction. She sat on the edge of a bench and got choked up when she repeated the passionate words of her beloved. Yet as I witnessed her emotional confusion and the importance she attached to his words, and contrasted the writing with the total indifference he normally showed her, it occurred to me that the letters might have been faked, and were the cause of the hilarity that had started spreading through the classroom every time Natalia stood up to answer a question.

I finally discovered that the letters had been drafted by Magini, an older boy who was repeating a year. He'd written them with the approval and advice of a few other bold, unscrupulous classmates. I didn't dare reveal my discovery to Natalia. We often walked home together, perhaps because I was the only one who knew about the secret. When we parted, she would kiss me on both cheeks and promise to go on confiding in me all the emotions her secret aroused.

Another letter arrived, and again Natalia read it to me on the bench in the public park. The phrases, so cleverly constructed, caused me unspeakable pain. I felt I ought to reveal the truth, yet I didn't want to be the one to hurt her. I must have looked distressed, because she watched me for a moment and then embraced me, saying that I mustn't lose heart: soon I, too, would have a devoted lover.

We walked home arm in arm. Natalia spoke with such enthusiasm that I almost believed that her story was true. But when we said good-bye and I saw her go off looking radiant as she blew me a kiss, she appeared so pitiful in her little green coat and thick glasses that I decided to do something to defend her.

The next day, I confronted Magini after the final bell. I grabbed his arm as he was crossing the courtyard and whispered to him hurriedly.

I didn't know him very well, but since he was older it seemed better to speak to him frankly. I told him about Natalia's enthusiasm, about her sensitivity and the importance she gave to those letters. He was pleased to discover this, and said that the joke had worked. He patted his pocket and confided that there was a new letter for Natalia, an invitation to come to the Giardino del Lago the next Sunday, where, instead of Andreani, Natalia would find her classmates waiting to laugh at her.

I turned pale and pleaded with Magini not to go through with his plan. He laughed and shook his head. I turned to him in all seriousness and, overcoming my instinctive reserve, tried to help him understand how important romantic feelings are to a woman, and that it was criminal to joke about them. He kept laughing, and then he started laughing about love itself, not just about Natalia. I looked him straight in the eyes and tried once more to dissuade him. My plea was heartfelt and emotional. He replied that the letter would be delivered the next day, and said that if I wanted to, I could come with them to the Giardino del Lago.

I was flooded with savage, whirling rage. Magini was in front of me, and he gave me a sly smile in parting. In a flash, I raised my arm and hit him in the forehead with my heavy case of compasses.

He was a tall boy, and he fell full length in the entrance hall. His friends gathered around as the blood gushed from his head and congealed in his bushy eyebrows.

I was marched off to the headmaster's office and left there. I could still see the thick, scarlet drops falling from the boy's forehead onto his white shirt. I couldn't bear the sight of blood—or of two people who resort to violence when arguing. I couldn't understand how I'd got involved in a situation like this. The headmaster finally arrived. He was already an old man and he knew me well, since I'd been at his school for some years. Before then, I'd been to his office only in order to be praised. He spoke to me kindly, inviting me to explain the reason for my deplorable act. I held out, looking straight at him and wondering if an old man could understand the importance of a love story or if he would laugh like Magini. Confronted with my silence, he started to interrogate me, advancing a few hypotheses. I remained silent. Finally, he took my hands and suggested that perhaps Magini had allowed himself certain liberties and I'd acted in self-defense. So I spoke, asking him to keep it secret. I told him that afterwards I'd been horrified by the blood, but in the moment I'd wanted Magini to fall down dead. He looked at me, worried, but said, "I understand." Then he spoke to Magini and his classmates. Thanks to my habitual good conduct, I wasn't expelled from school. It was said that we had quarreled over a book. However, Natalia now considered me violent and vindictive, and I lost her friendship.

I told my mother what had happened that same day.

I led her to the window overlooking the nuns' garden: it seemed easier to talk there, where we had spent so many hours in sweet confidence. I stood in front of her and told her the whole story, in detail and at length. I wasn't trying to justify my part in it so much as to help her understand, maybe so I myself would understand, how it all could have happened.

Her look intimidated me; I thought she must consider me a child still because of my braids and my slim body. She listened to me attentively, her cheek resting on one hand. She didn't interrupt when I confessed that I'd hit him in the head and he'd fallen down, or when I talked about the blood that flowed from his temple onto his white shirt. Although startled, she didn't scold me; she stayed and listened until I finished.

She then got up slowly, took me by the shoulders, and, looking into my eyes, asked, as if she were speaking to a grown woman, "So love is very important for you, too, isn't it Sandi?"

I stared at her and nodded a frenetic *yes* before bursting into a flood of tears, which had nothing to do with what I'd done. I felt a wistful emptiness opening up inside, given a name by my mother's unexpected question. I clung to her, frightened, as I had when I was a child.

We looked through the window, holding each other close, cheek to cheek. Outside—how well I remember it—were low clouds, and the wind blew fiercely before giving way to rain. With the storm coming, the nuns had carefully closed each window, and the convent wall looked impenetrable. The weakest leaves had fallen from the branches and were twirling in furious gusts of wind.

Consoled by the warmth of my mother's arms, I felt a bitter peace settle in me. But suddenly I started. "What about Papa?"

"We won't say anything to Papa," she replied. After a brief pause, she said quietly, "We can't tell him everything. Men don't understand these things, Sandi. They don't weigh every word or gesture; they look for concrete facts. And women are always in the wrong when they come up against concrete facts. It's not their fault. We're on two different planets; and each one rotates on its own axis—inevitably. There are a few brief encounters—seconds, perhaps—after which each person returns to shut him- or herself away in solitude."

The wind hissed through the cracks, making me shiver.

"You're almost as tall as I am," said my mother. "You're a woman now, not an adolescent."

I recall having a sense at that moment that she wouldn't be with me for long: her words came from a faraway place, as if she were already speaking across some vast space or through water. I held her as if to keep her there, and didn't dare look in her face for fear of seeing some sign of farewell.

"That's why I wished you were a boy," she went on. "Men don't have all the subtle reasons for unhappiness that we do. Men adapt. They're lucky. And I wanted to leave behind a lucky person. My mother tried everything to get me to give up music, novels, poetry. She wanted me to enjoy myself, to be stronger than she was. When I was still young, she used to tell me gloomy and painful love stories, hoping to arouse an instinct for self-preservation. They were dark, terrible, and shocking tales, and she told them in a low, tragic voice that revealed her training as an actress. I couldn't listen to her. I would cry and try to get away, but she held me by the wrists. She was a peculiar woman, and she showed a sort of determination in this, a cruel, Germanic determination. I used to get up at night to read poetry in German or *Werther*, which was really difficult. I practiced the piano with such intensity that I once had a nervous breakdown. She stopped treating me like that, but one day as she parted my hair over my forehead, a habit of hers, she said, 'It's too bad! I wanted you to be happy.'"

"Was Grandmother happy?"

My mother paused for a moment. "I don't think so. Maybe before she was married, when she lived out a great love story every night on the stage. Then . . . No, she definitely wasn't happy then. Hers was a marriage of passion, but up close it seemed like any other. There was nothing left of the overwhelming emotion that had driven her to leave the theatre: absolutely nothing. They actually seemed bored living together. Neither had much patience, and my mother was a tempestuous woman. She died fairly young, so I don't have many memories of her. But I remember a few things very well. In the summer, for example, she would take me on vacation to Tyrol. We would walk beside fields of grain, in the high mountains that amplified our voices, every word we said. She walked quickly, one hand holding up her long skirt, and the other pulling me behind her, all the while reciting bits of some play. She recited in German, which I didn't understand very well. And that voice was so different from her usual voice that I began to suspect she was inhabited by a secret creature who showed up only at those moments. Someone who continued living onstage in her stead, with the scent of powder, dust, and wax, in a dressing room bedecked with tall baskets of flowers, where every evening she found a fabulous love story hanging in the wardrobe along with her costume and her wig." After a short pause, she added, "No, she really wasn't happy. I remember the desperate way she used to hold me and kiss me."

My mother held me as she spoke. She didn't know it, of course, but hers, too, was a desperate embrace. I shivered, lost in sudden pity for myself as a woman. It seemed to me that we were a gentle and unlucky species. I felt weighed down—through my mother and her mother, the women in plays and novels, the ones looking out on the courtyard as if from behind bars, and others I met in the street, with sad eyes and enormous bellies—by a centuries-old unhappiness, an inconsolable solitude.

"Mamma," I asked in desperation, "can one ever be happy in love?"

"Oh, yes! I think so. You just have to wait. Sometimes," she added quietly, "you wait your whole life."

•   •   •

THAT CONVERSATION CHANGED the relationship between my
mother and me. From that day on, though she made no reference to it,
she stopped babying me and began confiding in me like a sister. She
paid less attention to how I spent my days, knowing I was alone for long
periods, and of course she understood that that was how I would come
to a greater understanding of myself, and ask myself all the questions
one does at that age.

So she spent entire afternoons at Villa Pierce without remorse.
She'd come home and say, "My arm hurts. I played for hours without stopping." She threw herself on the bed and called me to her in
the pale twilight. Her hands looked colorless on the dark bedcover of the
marital bed; a happy excitement coursed beneath her skin, tinging
her cheeks a delicate vermillion that made her look younger. I hadn't
often seen her rendered so pretty by those colors: only when she talked
about her childhood or told stories from Shakespeare and seemed to be
feverish.

Something, however, was troubling her, and it was Hervey's hidden
presence that both people and things in the grand villa seemed to obey.
Her tone was nervous and mildly irritated when she spoke of this
Hervey.

"They arrange flowers the way he likes them, buy paintings by his
favorite artists, and sometimes in the afternoons I hear violent strokes
from the axe as the trees he dislikes are felled, executed. *No, no*, I am
always telling Arletta: *you need to fight back*. When I stop playing to
rest, and we go for a short walk around the garden or have tea, she
immediately starts talking to me about her brother."

"And what does she say?" I asked, curious.

"Oh, I don't know," she replied casually. "I hardly listen to her."

But I knew that wasn't true.

I once saw her go downstairs when the Pierces' car, which came for
her every day, stopped at the entrance. She went down quickly, like girls

who have recently left adolescence behind and are longing to get down to the street to see how they look to men, and test their feminine powers. No one would have expected that only an empty car awaited her.

But it wasn't empty. From then on, Hervey waited inside for her. There weren't any photographs of him in the rooms at the villa, but on the piano lay wax molds of his hands: white, severed at the wrist, and separated, because, as Arletta explained, they had served as models for a statue of St. Sebastian.

"I touched them once when Arletta left the room," she said. "They aren't cold, you know. Wax has a delicate human warmth." She told me she'd put one on her arm. When I was by myself, I put a hand on my arm, then on my neck, to feel the same sensation. It was disturbing.

One evening I asked my mother why Hervey didn't live at Villa Pierce.

"He's sick," she replied, but in an odd tone, surely the one Arletta used, and even the servants, when they spoke of Signor Hervey. No one, however, ever gave the illness a definite name. Maybe it was the fact of his being different that led them to blame some physical anomaly for his different ways of speaking, feeling, and living.

And yet, Arletta confirmed, as a boy Hervey had sometimes even played soccer. He had built toy gliders, and considered becoming an engineer. The gliders were often discussed when Hervey wasn't there. It was in fact one of the first things my mother learned about him.

"And then what happened?" it occurred to her to ask. And they began to speak in that submissive, hushed tone. Then war broke out: Hervey was fifteen, Shirley nine, and Arletta a newborn. The Pierces had been living in Brussels in a villa similar to the one in Rome, but the gates faced a grand city boulevard, where many people passed by. As evening approached, Hervey would leave his study and go sit behind the gate. You no longer saw the placid middle classes slowly making their way home for dinner but lots of young men already in military uniform, with rifles on their shoulders, pistols or bayonet at their hips. Weapons, in other words. The soldiers held no appeal for Hervey, as they usually do for boys; he felt instead a sort of repugnance. He'd make an excuse to stop them and call them over to the gate. He looked at their uniforms, the regimental insignia, and tried to see the faces under the berets. Then he'd say, "Don't go to war. You shouldn't shoot people who've done nothing wrong." The soldiers were astonished to hear a young boy speaking like that. He went on.

"Throw away your uniform. Escape! Escape to the countryside and hide." Small groups of curious onlookers formed near the gate. Unnerved by the attention he had aroused, Hervey ran to the safety of his room.

It was then that he stopped building gliders. In fact, if he heard the dark hum of an airplane overhead his face paled. He had sudden and inexplicable fevers, and in his delirium he spoke of men buried alive in a submarine that couldn't rise off the seabed. "They must be saved!" he'd say. "Save them! Free them! They like a calm sea. They're sailors— fishermen." He dreamed of swimming in the distant depths of the sea, amid coral reefs and pearl banks. He ranted in his delirium: "I'm knocking at the hull: *knock-knock-knock*. No one's answering anymore!" Famous doctors came to examine him and Hervey looked at them, flushed with fever. "No one's responding anymore," he repeated, eyes wide with terror. "No one's responding anymore." The doctors visited, and Violet Pierce trailed after them, waiting for some word.

Afterwards, while washing their hands, turning the soap calmly between their fingers, they said to Hervey's mother, who hadn't stopped looking at them for a moment, "He's a very healthy boy, Signora."

"What about his fever?"

They remained silent, carefully drying their hands, every finger, every nail. And she waited.

"Nerves, Signora, nerves. A bit of neurasthenia."

Hervey didn't go to the big park anymore, nor did his parents urge him to do so. He didn't want to see the large advertisements for war bonds on the city walls, showing men with their chests ripped open by horrendous wounds, their uniforms stained with blood. "It's not necessary to fight wars." He was pale as he looked through the bars of the gate.

By now, people knew the boy. Some actually waited for him to appear just to pelt him with curses or insults. He was tall and blond. "German!" they yelled when they saw him. "*Boche.*"

He would reply, "I'm not German. But would it matter if I were?"

And they hissed, "*Boche! Sale boche!*" They threw stones; a rock hit him on the cheek. The youngest climbed up high on the bars of the gate to mock him from there.

"We shouldn't hurt anyone," Hervey said, with no ill will. "We should love one another, even the Germans. Every man is a world created by God."

They kept railing at him. "Protestant!" they yelled. "Spy! *Boche!*" They threw stones at his legs. Hervey turned and calmly walked back to the house, blood dripping onto his clothes. His mother fainted when she saw his injuries. The next day three or four people came to the house and asked the Pierces to set off at once, to leave Belgium, because they were foreigners. For their own safety, it was said. "For safety," they also searched Harold Pierce's drawers.

The Pierces went back to England. When the war was over, they came to live in Italy because Hervey wanted to study music.

"That's how it all started," Arletta concluded, shaking her head. "With his hatred of war. As I've told you, he even thought at first that he might become an engineer. I would have liked an engineer for a brother, someone who built bridges and houses. But Hervey doesn't like houses. He never looks out at our lovely view, you know. The belvedere is right at the top of the villa, and from there you can see cupolas and houses, all the houses in Rome, pink, red, and yellow. So different from the sad houses in London. A vast panorama like the one you see from the Janiculum. My father and I are the only ones who go up there to enjoy it. My mother doesn't approve of our taste. But believe me, Signora, it's really beautiful up there in the evening. You can see the city trams flashing, big neon signs, all the lights . . . From Hervey's window all you can see is a tall cedar of Lebanon, which is very old. My brother always tells the story of that tree. I don't know how to tell it, and it's rather long. If I told you, it would lose all its flavor: I don't have his storytelling talent, which makes everything extraordinary. But, anyway, apparently there's a horse locked in that tree. At night, when the branches are rustling, Hervey hears it neighing."

In repeating all this, my mother's voice grew warm and subdued like Ottavia's when she read the spirits' messages. The gloomy furniture stood out in the faint light of the room like dark rocks. My father had wanted a large photo of his parents on the wall opposite the bed. They were shown half length, shoulders touching, eyes staring gravely at the photographer. They were wearing dark clothes, and, against the milky white backdrop of the enlargement, they, too, were solid rocks, cliffs.

"Mamma," I said quietly, "I don't believe Arletta's brother is ill. You remember how Papa puts a finger to his forehead and acts like he's twisting a screw? He says we're ill."

"Is that what he says?" She turned to look at me, hoping perhaps to discover in my eyes the real significance of my allusion. Then she hugged me, and we sat there, in a silent embrace on the tall bed. Surely, inwardly she called me "my baby," "Sandi," "sweetheart, sweetheart," but I had to guess everything and ask nothing; to understand this from her desperate way of embracing, which had also been, she said, her own mother's way. And I felt that in no other way would I, one day, be able to hold the woman who was my daughter.

THE FOLLOWING YEAR, Arletta started playing the piano. Every day, all winter long, my mother went to Villa Pierce, leaving me on my own. It was a sad, rainy winter, or maybe it only seemed so because I was lonely. But certainly when I look back on those days I have the scent of wet earth in my nostrils, and through the windows I see the sky white with clouds.

Left by ourselves, my father and I often had the opportunity to talk. In fact, he seemed to want to be close to me, not because he took any interest in my education or in knowing me better but to while away the time by chatting. He'd sit beside me, hoping I'd be willing to pass on gossip or information about the girls in the building, whom he knew from having seen them go by on the stairs. He didn't know what to do with himself when he wasn't in the office and had finished reading the paper. He read it diligently, including the classifieds—even though he never bought or sold a thing—and the most inconsequential provincial news. In his view, it was right and proper to read the paper, while reading books was wasting time. And he was uniquely occupied in wasting it: he sat in an armchair filing his nails, looked out the window, went down to have a coffee at the café on the corner. Twice a year he went to Abruzzo to see nonna, and came back with the proceeds from selling olives and dried figs.

We all went to the station together—Mamma, Sista, and I—to help him carry two huge baskets full of provisions from the train to the tram. We were unused to the noisy, crowded streets of the center, and at the station our eyes widened at the sight of so many people coming and going, heading for unknown towns. My mind went back to my mother's descriptions of the wonderful cities where her mother used to act. Our heads in the clouds, we took off, suspended on the gray smoke puffing from the smokestacks as if on the tail of a comet. The hissing of the pistons set our hearts racing wildly.

Mamma said, "These are the tracks that go to Vienna," and we squinted in an effort to follow them all the way there.

Sista called us. "The train is here," and her serious tone and stern appearance—black dress, black kerchief knotted under her chin—brought us back to our dreary routine. Still dreaming, we stepped back, frightened of being run over by the wheels of a locomotive. At last, the sight of a basket draped with a white cloth sitting next to a window told us that my father had arrived.

As he hugged us, he announced, "I've brought caciotta and capocollo."
He liked to eat well. He had the look of a gourmand, and his way of
dressing was entirely fitting for an older man who wants to please the
ladies. He always carried a comb with him, and a case containing a few
light cigarettes, even though he rarely smoked. On Saturday afternoons
before he went out he would put brilliantine in his hair and mustache,
and a sharp scent lingered in the rooms after he closed the door behind
him. It really bothered me, and I would open doors and windows to get
rid of it; I didn't feel that I was really alone until it had completely
vanished. I didn't love my father. I always felt like answering him
curtly or harshly, though I was habitually courteous with everyone,
no matter who.

Sometimes he would sidle up to me while I was sitting in my corner
by the window. His presence disturbed me so much that I acted hostile
and rebellious.

"What are you doing?" he would ask, interrupting my reading.

"Can't you see?" I answered sharply.

"Right. What's it about?"

Begrudgingly, I showed him the title page.

"You like reading, eh?" He added, "You're like your mother."

His tone was subtly veined with contempt, and he always assumed
that tone when he said, "your mother" instead of "Mamma."

"What do you mean?"

"Well, you're not like other women. They like going to the cinema,
sitting in cafés, and sewing or working or tidying the house when they're
at home. You two are princesses."

He often resorted to that word, letting the noble title sum up our
laziness, indolence, and taste for useless, refined things. Though
trembling with rage, I maintained an icy calm so as to exclude him
from the intimacy of my resentment.

"Why do you say that?" I asked, not looking at him and proceeding
to cut the pages of my book. "Is it because we spend too much money?"

"Oh, no, not really."

"Is the house a mess? Do you not like the food?"

"On the contrary."

"Do we ask for expensive clothes or entertainment?"

"No, definitely not."

"Well?" I asked, finally looking at him with great antipathy. "Well?"

"Well, I don't know, but you are different from other women, I can tell you that. Maybe it's because of the books. But there's something not quite right about you two."

He put his index finger to his temple and pretended to be turning a screw. This gesture of his, often repeated, had the power to exasperate me. I felt the urge to hit him, but with a great effort I lowered my eyes to my book instead and resumed reading. He stayed in his chair, since he had nothing to do; he cleaned his nails with my paper cutter, all the while observing me as if I were anyone, a girl sitting next to him on the tram. When he looked at me like that, I instinctively felt like pulling my skirt over my knees.

There were long, embarrassing silences. Then he finished his lengthy examination of my person.

"You're thin," he said. "At your age girls already have a bust."

I flushed as if I'd been slapped, and a humiliating sense of discomfort spread through me, under my skin. I did not acknowledge his right to speak to me about such intimate things, far beyond what was allowable in a fatherly relationship.

"You're like your mother."

"My mother is a beautiful woman," I protested vigorously.

"Yes" was his calm response. "But she has no bust." He got up to read the paper and listen to the radio, leaving me defeated.

My father's temperament and his weakness in the face of beautiful feminine figures had not escaped Fulvia, who told me, "Your father really likes women. I see it in the way he looks at me. A few days ago he stopped me on the stairs and said, 'You're Alessandra's friend, aren't you?' I nodded and got away. He wanted to start right in. But married men disgust me."

Many years later, Fulvia told me that, around that time, my father often waited for her in the stairwell. He didn't make declarations of love or try to kiss her: he just wanted to touch her a certain way. She also said that despite the revulsion his hands roused in her, she'd never dared defend herself, restrained by a sense of subjection to an older man, the husband of one of her mother's friends. So she let him touch her, pretending that she didn't yet know the significance of those gestures, that it was just playful behavior.

Fulvia was very pretty then, or maybe pretty isn't the right word. She was attractive and provocative, like many Roman middle-class girls her age. She had shiny black hair, always carefully styled, and a voluptuous bosom, which she didn't bother to hide. If someone whispered a compliment while we were out together, she would answer aloud, with a spirited retort, ignoring my timidity and blushes. She wrote regularly to a boy who lived in the building opposite ours and used sign language to speak to him from her window; and with another, a classmate, she would go walking in the country instead of going to class. In any case, she didn't have to lie, because she was free all day; Lydia often spent the entire afternoon with the Captain.

When it came down to it, Fulvia was careful with that freedom. When her mother went out, she'd sit at the dressing table and amuse herself by painting her lips and her eyes and trying out various hairstyles—a low bun at her neck, gathered in a wave over her forehead—she'd seen in movie magazines, which she read avidly. Like almost all the girls in the building, she wore shabby clothes at home: ugly cotton housedresses, faded and shrunken after too many washes and torn under the arms; old shoes for slippers. In summer she'd actually go around naked under a short floral dressing gown belted tightly at the waist. When she was on her own, she spread olive oil over her face and then put slices of potato and lemon juice on it, even though her skin was very clear. In fact her skin—fine, transparent, and velvety—was the most beautiful thing about her. Whenever we were by ourselves I wanted to ask, "Can I touch it?" But I never dared.

I, on the other hand, was becoming more and more solitary and reserved. If it hadn't been for Fulvia, I would have spent entire days by myself. I sensed that my new age was transforming me, and I felt a dismayed fascination. What had happened at school with Magini certainly hadn't done anything to make me popular. The words I exchanged with the teachers were often the only ones I uttered all morning. My classmates showed no interest in me. "She's stuck-up, not nice," I heard one day. Another time: "She's ugly."

Even Fulvia would often ignore me for days. And then she would suddenly call me from the courtyard. "Come on up," she would order. As soon as she called me, I would shut my book and climb the stairs two at a time.

I would find the door half open, and in that silent, empty house Fulvia would be busy with some grooming, which didn't stop just because I had arrived. On late summer evenings, we would sit talking on the little balcony, so high over the city it seemed as if the big building we lived in were holding us aloft in triumph. From there you could see only deserted terraces, red rooftops, and a bell tower that sheltered swallows. We made a seat by placing a narrow wooden plank over two large empty pots. Sometimes Fulvia would lie down on the plank, leaving only a small space for me at her feet. Her robe opened to reveal her shoulders, her breasts, and her legs, which I studied with avid curiosity.

"I'm hot. Fan me," she would say, interrupting our chat.

I obeyed, allowing her to treat me like a servant. I felt that Alessandro was in love with her and wanted to consume her with his eyes, and I was too innocent to be able to accept these impulses consciously. I got pleasure from looking at her while she talked. She had a brusque way of speaking, almost impudent. For her, love was something quick, petty, a little dirty. She had started spending a lot of time with classmates who used bad language, told off-color stories, and smoked. Fulvia behaved like a man with them; with all except for Dario. Dario was the guy who lived in the building opposite. He went to university, and when exam time came there was a light in his window until late at night. He took his books along even when he went to the country with Fulvia: he would sit down, lean against a tree, and study while she sunbathed.

"I often take off my blouse," she admitted.

"And what do you have on underneath?"

"Under that? Nothing. I'm brown all over," she said, opening up her top at the neckline.

"What about Dario?"

"Dario studies and acts as lookout. He warns me. He'll go, 'Cover up! Someone's coming,' and if my eyes are closed he throws pebbles at me to wake me up. When he gets tired of studying, he'll come and lie on the grass beside me."

I glanced at the door, worrying that my mother might surprise us talking. Then I turned back to Fulvia. Blushing, I asked her, "Tell me. Tell me again. Explain." I wanted her to tell me about Dario. "Do you love him?" I asked. She replied that she didn't and said she felt nothing about their letters or meetings. I didn't understand why she did all that, so one time I broke through my habitual reserve and timidly questioned her about it.

She gave me a serious look. "What am I supposed to do? I'm not worth much. It's not like I'm you."

I interrupted, protesting vigorously. I didn't think a woman should ever resign herself to such bitterness.

One evening as dusk was falling—she was lying on the plank and I was sitting at her feet—she told me how babies are made.

•　　•　　•

BETWEEN FULVIA'S STORIES and the seances, it was difficult for me to sleep at night. When my parents retired to their room and my mother's voice was silent behind the closed door, I felt alone, abandoned to the countless dangers hiding in the shadows and in my own thoughts.

In her presence, I made light of my young friend's recent explanations, but they kept me awake and troubled for hours. I rarely went to church to confess, and until then I'd had little awareness of guilt. But suddenly I understood what sin really was, and I felt its misery as well as its dark and irresistible power. And yet it seemed that only in blind obedience to love could you be persuaded to agree to those acts, perhaps paying for them with your life, like Desdemona or Francesca. Fulvia had said, though, "It has nothing to do with love." When I objected, she added, "Dario says the same thing." But I couldn't believe it. I worried that she was trying to trick me with her habitual cynicism and indifference.

In bed in the dark, my agitated mind would go through the couples I knew, their lives and feelings. It seemed incredible that those men, who couldn't spare a single loving word for their companions during the day, suddenly expected them to be ready for those dreadful embraces at night. In the morning, the women seemed to carry in their eyes the memory of an exhausting humiliation as they returned to their chores.

Once I began to imagine those things, I felt a sort of tender compassion for my female neighbors. I was alone on the balcony, curled up in a corner like a dog. And they were alone in their movements, which, seen from afar, seemed like acts of folly: vigorously shaking a rag, repeatedly beating a carpet with a stick. Each of us alone in her world, a black dot on the map: Europe, Italy, Rome, Via Paolo Emilio 30, apartment 6, apartment 4, apartment 1. Like a dog, I would have welcomed a gesture of affection from anyone; they received a quick approach from a man who, for an hour, held them in the warmth of his life.

I knew it wasn't easy to resist. During the seances Enea would sit beside me and take my arm with his warm, dry hand. I didn't dare move away, won over by the novelty of that contact, which was also odious to me. He came to the house once to say that Ottavia was ill. He walked through the door and looked around as he spoke: the door was still open and I was leaning against it, my hand trembling.

"Are you alone, Alessandra?" he asked. I nodded and he gently pushed the door closed. I had never met him outside of the seances, and he seemed to bring with him the odor of incense; spirits fluttered around his arms. "I've been wanting to find you alone for a while now," Enea said, coming closer as I backed up against the wall. He was already grown up. His gaze fell on me and wherever it fell, my flesh became soft, as if the bones beneath it were collapsing. "I'm in love with you. Do you know that?" He drew near, bringing with him all the heat of his body.

Maybe I'll be disgusted, I thought. *If he comes any closer I might be sick.*

When he brought his mouth to mine I dodged to get away from his breath. Luckily I was disgusted, disgusted. I threw open the door, and a cold wind rushed in. "Get out of here now," I said quietly but harshly. "Leave."

The stairway was dark. If he had tried again to approach me I would have defended myself: I thought of the scissors lying open on the work he had interrupted. I didn't want him to touch me. And in my eyes he read such a strong aversion that he left, murmuring, "You're an idiot."

I went back to my corner and threw myself into an armchair. Enea seemed still to be swirling invisibly through the house like the spirits after those sessions. I was afraid my mother would notice something when she came home.

"How do you know?" she asked when I told her that Ottavia wouldn't come the next day.

"She sent Enea to tell us," I replied. I sat opposite my mother and stared at her, silently commanding her: *Look at me carefully, Mamma. Look into my thoughts.*

Once, surprised by the intensity of my gaze, she asked, "What's wrong, Sandi?"

"Nothing," I answered, but I wished she wouldn't believe me.

But she always believed me. It was probably my fault, since I hadn't been open with anyone for some time. My mother walked by me, her movements graceful and pure, unaware that my mind was populated by unhealthy curiosity, horrible thoughts.

"Good night, Sandi," she said with a caress.

"Good night, Mamma," I replied, but inside I was calling her desperately. *Don't leave me! Help me!* My mother didn't understand, and, if my mother didn't understand, no one would ever understand. Maybe it was this icy solitude she wanted to keep from me when she seemed to want to stop me from growing up and becoming an adult. I clung to the thought of her. *Mamma, I'm afraid!* I shouted, and even though I couldn't find my voice, surely she would hear me like this, too, as she had till now. But she no longer heard me, and without her help I was weak, sinful. Seeing me turned towards her, my mother caressed my hair and smiled, calling me "My baby." Afraid of being alone with my thoughts, I had Sista sit by my bed until it was late.

"Sista," I once asked suddenly, "have you ever been in love?"

"No," she replied.

"Really? Never ever?"

"Never."

I looked at her even features, her clear forehead: she must have been pretty once.

"Why not? Didn't anyone from your village ever court you?"

"Oh, yes! when I was young."

"And what happened?"

She hesitated a little before replying quietly, "Men are pigs, Alessandra."

I sat up in the bed, furious. "Go," I said. "Go to bed, go on." Then I turned to the wall; my mother was sleeping on the other side of it, her

hand under her cheek as usual. And I hoped that in the silence of the
night she could hear me crying, calling desperately for her help.

AT THE TIME, I knew very few men, and I can say that their ways and
their voices were more or less mysterious to me. As soon as my father
noticed that I was becoming fairly attractive, he hurried to make me
leave the co-ed school and enrolled me in an all-girls' high school headed
by an old maid whose face was half hidden by an irregular, violet-colored
birthmark.

So my awareness of being a woman brought with it a sense of guilt.
I was ashamed to find every sign on my body that revealed this condition, making it obvious not only to me but also to others.

If I happened to brush past a man on the stairs at home, I instantly
reddened and hurried by, as if to hide. And yet when I was alone, I
couldn't overcome my unhealthy curiosity. In the tram I watched men's
gestures attentively, the way they took their wallets from their pockets
and counted their money; I looked at their fingers, yellowed with nico-
tine. Whenever I was crushed in a crowd, I'd put my face to a raincoat
or an officer's coat and breathe in the strong odors of tobacco and leather,
the scent of a different breed.

Now and again, my father would announce a visit from one of his
colleagues. He loved receiving his friends in the dining room and insisted
on offering them a glass of wine, something my mother did not approve.
All afternoon I was curious, wound up at the thought of the evening's
visit. When the bell rang, I had to calm myself in order not to show the
apprehension that gripped me at the thought of introducing myself to a
man, shaking his hand and talking to him.

My father and his friend were on the other side of the table; on our
side my mother and I sat gracefully, watching them as if from a box at
the theatre. We had so many pleasant and interesting things to say, and
I wished I could talk about some of the books I'd read, my mother perhaps about music. But they never asked us any questions.

They would say I had grown and act amazed—as if growing were a choice, a liberty I'd taken. My father would immediately add that he was getting old, and the other would say, "Yes, yes," but they laughed knowingly, suggestively. Then, in a few sentences, they would quickly switch to talking about the office, and would seem more at ease.

We found it incredible that even at night they enjoyed returning to the petty problems of the office, reliving the misery they endured for the better part of their daily lives. And yet they worried whether they'd be granted the day off as a holiday approached. "They have to give it to us," they'd say. "They will." And they would laugh heartily, crudely, showing how certain they were that the government was afraid of them.

As it happened, my father knew nothing about politics. The only thing he gained from reading the newspapers was a sort of dull, irritated sarcasm, chiefly where it concerned state employees' salaries. When they were granted a minor pay raise or a bonus, he would show us the press release in the daily paper, pat us on the back, and wink, as if it were the result of some personal maneuvering on his part. He felt no solidarity with the state, only the suspicion he would have felt towards someone who was always on the verge of cheating him and whom he wished he could outsmart. He frequently mentioned his little tricks for doing as little work as possible, and sometimes he'd talk with his friends about an overzealous superior they'd nicknamed Codino. Just hearing his name entertained them. "Did you see Codino?" they'd say, laughing blithely. It seemed that from the bathroom window in the summer you could see the female treasury employees taking off their black aprons before they went out. My father and his friend accused each other of being regulars in the lavatory at that hour. I blushed and Mamma did, too, but she didn't turn to me, so as not to have to see me looking at her. I stared at my father as he carried on contentedly, and it bothered me that he had stooped to my schoolmates' level. I tried to feel sorry for him, but I couldn't. It seemed to me that the tenderness you might feel for a man shouldn't spring from pity. I didn't want to pity a man.

"Did you see that we're closed on Thursday? They had to give us the day off." They spent the holiday like this. This was their way of resting, of enjoying themselves: sitting in front of a glass of wine, waiting for the office to open again the next morning. But it was a paid holiday, and therefore they had put one over on the state, even if it cost them hours of boredom and monotony. On holidays, my father would ask, "What time is it?" like someone at the station waiting for a night train.

"You are the state," I remember my mother once saying.

"We are?" my father replied, feigning ironic surprise. "Us?" he repeated. "Him and me?"

"You, too, like everyone."

Those two started laughing again. "Ha, ha!" and they leaned back in their chairs. "If we were the State, we'd show you."

"All I'd need is a year," the other one said with unexpected and slightly threatening seriousness.

"What are you saying?" my father replied. "A month, a week." They finally settled on twenty-four hours as the time they would need to ensure the good of the country, and tossed back another glass of wine.

"First of all," my father said, "I'd like to see Codino scrub the toilets."

I didn't dare believe that these were truly "men." Books had taught me very different things about them. I knew they weren't like that. I knew it with such conviction that I sometimes felt a furious desire to get away from them, to chase them away, so that my dream of a man like Devushkin, in *Poor Folk,* wouldn't die. At the time, reading the novel had fascinated and moved me. *No, no*, I said to myself, and maybe I shook my head—*no, no*—because Mamma took my hand under the table and squeezed it hard.

WE OFTEN TALKED about men at Fulvia's house. In fact, I would say we rarely spoke about anything else. In the evening, mostly in spring and summer, several girls gathered on the terrace she used as her sitting room. Some of them lived in the same building; others were schoolmates or neighbors.

These gatherings revolved around Fulvia: she had great power over her contemporaries, who, like me, went there in order to obey her. She often treated them harshly, actually ordering them to "Go and get me a glass of water from the kitchen." Or she'd say, "I'm hungry now. I'm going to eat." And, with an indelicacy that made me blush, she would bite into some bread dipped in oil or a nice piece of fruit, in front of all those greedy eyes.

If her mother was out, Fulvia dared to smoke two or three cigarettes. "They're the Captain's," she said. We widened our nostrils, intoxicated, as the blue smoke rose in front of us. "Those are nice," Aida said. "My brother smokes Nazionali."

"They're Egyptian," Fulvia explained, and the mysterious Captain's taste for exotic goods heightened our fascination with him. "He's on inspection today," Fulvia sometimes confided. Lydia stayed home on those days, and gave us a remote smile, like a young widow. Her lush bosom, to which she sometimes pinned a flower, seemed bursting with unrestrained passion. We imagined the Captain confined to his barracks like a patriot in exile.

Fulvia often read us her letters from Dario or notes classmates had put in her exercise books. One of her classmates, Rita, said that even the teacher, a thirty-year-old man, was smitten with Fulvia.

"Yes, and then he gives me only a pass," replied Fulvia.

"But he should have failed you!"

We laughed, knowing it was true. Maddalena, a soft, rosy blonde in the same class, claimed that her brother, too, had fallen in love with Fulvia. Since then, she assured us, Giovanni had turned into the most caring and attentive brother. "He even comes to pick me up at the gates," she laughed. It was clear that she would have been happy if Giovanni had become engaged to Fulvia (at the time, and at our age, we used the word "engaged" for any little crush). Maybe he had enlisted her to act as a skilled go-between and she found she had a taste for it.

"Come with me to Villa Borghese tomorrow. Giovanni will be there. When it gets dark, I'll leave you on a bench by yourselves."

"Go!" the others urged. "Go, Fulvia!" It was as if they were all wait-ing in the shadow of the villa.

I watched her earnestly, wishing I could hold her back by the arm.

"I don't like your brother," Fulvia replied. "He calls me 'Signorina.' He must be stupid." She often repeated that just to humiliate Mad-dalena, and Maddalena bridled at the insinuation, as if the standing of her entire family were compromised by her friend's facile sarcasm.

One day, when we were all gathered on the balcony, Fulvia said to Maddalena, "I never see your brother anymore. What's he up to? Did he enter a seminary?"

Everyone started laughing, making fun of him. Aping a priest's ges-tures and casting a sidelong glance, Aida recited the rosary in a fake whine.

Maddalena watched with suppressed rage. "Laugh, yes, laugh," she said. "Go ahead and laugh. If only you knew what I found in my brother's drawer . . ."

"What!" everyone asked, suddenly curious.

Not answering, Maddalena said, "Laugh, go ahead and laugh at Giovanni."

"What did you find? Love letters from Greta Garbo?" Fulvia asked scornfully.

"I found a photo of a woman, completely naked, with her face in her hands. A really beautiful woman."

Silence fell. The girls went quiet and looked first at Maddalena admiringly, because she had a secret, and then at Fulvia, who they thought would be humiliated and defeated. But she sprang to her feet.

"More beautiful than me?" she said, dropping her bathrobe and standing naked against the gray water tank. The girls looked at her and squealed. I instantly looked away, even before making out the shape of her body, and ran away. Through the kitchen, the dark corridor. My hand was on the latch when Fulvia caught up with me.

She was still naked, but she was clutching her robe in an effort to cover up. She pounced on me, cornering me at the door to her house. I saw her face and shoulders as a confusion of white.

"You despise me, right?" she said, pressing against me so I couldn't escape.

I had no strength. "Leave me alone," I murmured.

"You despise me, right?" she repeated, caressing my face. "You're right," she mumbled. "Forgive me. Go on. Leave, Alessandra. Get out of here."

She stroked my hair and kissed me as tenderly as you would a little sister. Then she opened the door and pushed me out. I heard her saying on her way back to the balcony, "That stupid girl ran away."

IT WAS NEARLY a month before I saw her again. Still, my instinct was to go straight back to her and beg her forgiveness. I could hear her singing and laughing and it tortured me. I felt that I was the one in the wrong, I who carried my body around like a sin. I wished I could tell her about Alessandro's presence in me, but I didn't dare: I was afraid she'd treat it like a birth defect, as if my shoe concealed a cloven hoof. During those hot days, I read in the paper about a girl of twenty who discovered she was a man. I cut out the article and hid it in a book. I couldn't believe I was a girl just like everyone else. Above all, I felt there was more honesty in my friends' sincerity than in my false reserve.

ONE DAY, I was sitting on the balcony carefully mending some of my father's old socks when Fulvia called me.

"Alessandra!"

I looked up to see her looking concerned.

"Come here," she said, relying on feminine solidarity, and not referring to what had happened on the balcony. "Aida's brother was arrested," she explained as soon as I entered the apartment. Taking my arm, she led me to her room as if we'd only said goodbye an hour before.

Aida was sitting on the bed, looking serious. The others sat around her; Maddalena had a doll on her knees.

"What did he do?" I asked.

Instead of answering the others looked at me hesitantly. I thought it must have been something shameful that no one wanted to mention.

"Did he steal something?" I asked quietly.

I'd never seen Aida's brother. I knew his name was Antonio and he was training to be a typographer. I knew his tastes, his flaws, his personality, as I did those of all my classmates' brothers. Sisters talked carelessly, since kinship made them incapable of seeing the least charm in their brothers. But Antonio, whom Aida had described as reserved, introverted, and a great reader, had always sparked my interest. It upset me to imagine him surrendering to petty greed and theft.

"No," Aida said. She stared at me, hoping I'd guess. Everyone else stared at me, worried.

I lowered my voice to ask, "What, then?"

Aida finally answered. "He was arrested with the communists."

My hand flew to my mouth in a gesture of terror, and I dropped into a chair beside Fulvia.

None of us knew exactly what that word meant, and yet we had never dared to utter it. Like a dirty or obscene word, it didn't belong in our vocabulary. We all looked at Aida, and I took her hand and stroked it to comfort her.

"But how did it happen?"

"The police went to the typographer's and then they came to take him away. We were at home alone. I was the one who opened the door."

"You? What happened next?" asked Fulvia.

"They came in and looked around. I'm not sure how, but I knew immediately that something awful would come of that visit. I knew it, and yet when they asked, 'Antonio Sassetti?' I told them, 'My brother is in his room.' That's exactly what I said."

"And then what?"

"He was lying on his bed as if he were waiting for them. I went in first, hoping to be able to warn him, but they were right behind me. One of them started searching his books and took a stack of them. My brother got up, put on his raincoat and went away with them. He stopped to kiss me at the door.

"'Ciao, Aida,' he said. 'Tell Mamma I'll be back soon—maybe tomorrow.' But I knew very well that he didn't believe it. My throat felt tight. I couldn't even say goodbye. I stayed there listening to the steps on the stairs, his and the others. Then I went back to his room. The lingering smell of his Nazionali cigarettes made me burst into tears."

"Have they written anything about him in the paper?" Maddalena asked.

"No, nothing. Papa went to the police station. First they wouldn't say anything, and then they said he was a communist. No one has come to our house since, and when we go by the porter gives us a mean look through his window. Papa heard that they're all young like Antonio. There are quite a few students, too."

"What do communists do?" Maddalena whispered.

"I don't know," Aida replied. "I really don't know. They're not happy. Antonio was never happy. Friends often came to see him and they seemed unhappy, too. They were never lighthearted like other young men his age. I'd open the door, and every time it seemed like they'd just had bad news. They came to Antonio and read. We thought Antonio was hoping to educate himself so he could leave typography behind, and his friends wanted the same thing. It's odd, but, thinking back, I remember that when it got dark and I went to Antonio's room to close the shutters, they would look up from their books, their eyes full of sadness.

God! What sad expressions they had! They never saw me as a young girl to joke around and have fun with. I thought it was because of the window, which was high up, so that very little light got into the room. But Antonio had that look during the day, too."

All at once I felt a rush of admiration for Antonio. Aida said he looked like her, with black hair and brown eyes. I felt it was truly noble to allow yourself to be taken away and imprisoned because you're unhappy.

"We're not happy, either," Fulvia said, looking at the window behind which Dario studied, locked in his bad mood. "We're never happy, and I can't understand why. It's like something's suffocating us, something from which we'd like to free ourselves."

She was leaning against the windowsill, looking sideways towards Dario's window. I wasn't sure whether she was questioning or challenging him. She looked really beautiful standing there like that, dressed in a simple blouse, her hair done naturally.

"We think we want to free ourselves of old prejudices, or of our families, or of some of the principles they want to impose on us," Fulvia went on. "But maybe not. Maybe it's the silence around certain things that's suffocating, that gets us *here*." She brought her hands to her throat. "We're unhappy, right? and we believe it's . . ." She didn't dare say the word. ". . . that it's . . ."

"For love," I suggested quietly.

"Right," she said. And she paused. "But maybe not only that. It seems that men actually know the truth but hide it from us, just as we hide bad news from children."

"Antonio knew it, I think," Aida said, "and that's why he looked at me in such a melancholy way."

I hesitated before asking, "Did Antonio have a girlfriend?"

"I don't know," Aida replied. "He never talked about himself. He'd say 'Good morning' and 'Good night,' smoking his Nazionali one after another, but not saying anything."

Maddalena was silent. She had brought her doll with her, a habit that made her seem a child, still, in her relatives' eyes, and maybe in her own. It was a pretty cloth doll dressed in pink, its mouth half-open in a smile and its lively eyes crystalline blue. Maddalena gouged out an eye while we talked, digging at the cloth with her nail. Now it was on the floor staring at us. Little by little, she got the other eye out, too, and slowly tore off the doll's hair with the cold cruelty of a scalper. She squashed the nose and then, using the tip of her finger, pushed it back into the face, which—bald and eyeless—suddenly seemed like a skull with red-painted cheeks.

Maddalena then dropped her chin to her chest and began to cry. "My doll," she said, "my doll . . . ," staring at its horrible face.

As if summoned by her crying, Lydia appeared, and she consoled her, telling her she was too big now for that kind of toy; it wasn't right at her age. She gave her a red flowered silk scarf of hers to calm her down.

"They're still children, just children," she said to my mother that evening. And she told her how Maddalena had cried over her ragdoll.

IT OCCURS TO me sometimes that I'm going on too long about what happened before my marriage to Francesco. But surely no one would know anything about me, about my character, and who I am, if I silently skipped over the way I lived and what I felt then. However dark and uncomfortable it was, that time now seems truly to have been a time of perfect happiness, the more so because I was privileged to live beside the extraordinary being who was my mother. She may not have been perfect according to contemporary morals, but her imperfections, her weaknesses, and the warm compassion behind her every action were the features that spoke of her, so alive and present, a poetic legend. My mother was distant, like a character in a book, one of those women you would like to be but never quite manage to be. If I were to lose my memory of my childhood and of her, I would have lost everything that was important to me and gave me joy, along with my life story, since even today, thanks to these memories, it's easy for me to enrich the long hours of solitary meditation that make up my monotonous days. After all, I learned as a child to be happy in my own company. We were poor, and the poor are accustomed to entertaining themselves with their own thoughts. Our poverty and my early preference for being alone, a habit that led me to focus my attention on myself and my feelings, turned out to be my only asset. But I have to admit that the overwhelming importance I always gave all that and my natural tendency to live in a committed and responsible way were in large part the cause of my present situation.

Maybe I wasn't like the other girls I knew: in me, everything was transformed, became magic, produced an echo. I was attached to everything around me with yearning affection. For example, the plants on the balcony: their leaves and petals were so wholly a part of me I seemed to nourish them with my own blood. As soon as I got up in the morning, I would run to the balcony to greet them. I'm not embarrassed to confess that if it was cold I would kneel to warm them with my breath.

At that time, I became aware of happiness as a living presence. It visited me when I sat with my mother by the window. We got into the habit, the two of us, of staying home on Sunday afternoons, spending our time embroidering and sewing. Sista sat behind us mending her black clothes. On the terrace opposite the nuns, too, enjoyed their Sunday rest, and were giddy with the fresh air; sometimes they'd join hands and move in a circle, laughing innocently, their skirts opening in dark whorls.

I sewed in silence, but I was full of plans. I dreamed of becoming a professional seamstress, working calmly with white linens on my lap, my horizons limited to the soft, bright sky I saw arching over the courtyard. The nuns' modest laughter and the squeak of my mother's needle through cloth convinced me that I belonged to a kind and pleasant world. Behind me, Sista whispered the rosary. I felt so pious and devout that I wanted to imitate her, but it didn't seem necessary. At such times, my very life was a prayer.

My mother worked quickly. I was moved by the sight of her slender neck, bent over her work, her gentle profile, the gossamer mass of her hair; and the effort she put into her sewing recalled the way she played the piano in the evening. Something in her had been awakened since she'd started going to Villa Pierce: as she embroidered, she invented fanciful arabesques and flowers no one had ever seen before.

Those were the long evenings of spring. Heavy clusters of wisteria spilled over from the nuns' garden, its scent bringing a glow of sweat to our temples. In the chapel, the candles were lit behind the red stained-glass windows.

"It's impossible to see anymore," my mother said. "Your papa will be back soon."

At first, he had protested our decision to stay home on Sundays. Then he started warming to his freedom and finally took control of it. He'd go out right after breakfast and come back at lunchtime. He'd go to the bathroom to wash his hands and mustache before joining us at the table.

Once, when Sista had gone off to prepare the meal and we were alone, my mother said in a flat, hushed tone, "You must wonder why I married him . . ."

She had never spoken to me about those things before that moment, just as she'd never let me see her undressed.

"I don't think it would be easy for you to understand," she went on, "and these days it seems absurd to me, too. Incomprehensible. But then . . ."

"Yes. I do understand. I understand very well . . ." I quickly cut her off and she looked down and didn't continue. She didn't imagine me to be an expert on life at that point—she was surprised and a little dismayed, as when I'd confessed to having injured Magini at school a few years before. It was true that her marriage had raised many questions in my mind, but that was before I started conjuring up Enea's imaginary presence at night.

Before, I'd often asked myself how my mother could be intimate with a man who acted like an irritating stranger all day long. When I was still a child, she'd stick her head in my door to wish me good night, and I wanted to pull her in and keep her there. Through the opening in the door, which she kept narrow, I could see my father taking off his shoes.

The mirror on the wardrobe reflected their high, imposing bed, covered in white, a bed that had come from Abruzzo and in which one of my father's sisters had died, or so they told me. The wallpaper was the color of iron. I was afraid that my mother, so slender and fair, might never leave that gloomy room. I watched her, holding my thin arms out to her.

"Come and sleep with me, Mamma," I called out, my voice breaking with sobs.

My mother shook her head, gently pushing me away. "Don't be afraid," she said. "A night goes by quickly: tomorrow we'll be together again." She closed the door slowly. There followed a terrible silence, not interrupted by word or whisper. Standing on my bed, I pressed my ear desperately against the wall to reassure myself that she was still alive. But I didn't hear anything. When I was older, I imagined Enea's steps approaching my bed in that silence.

"Yes, I understand," I said, cutting her off when she tried to explain the reasons for her marriage.

My father had said that theirs had been a short engagement. My mother was very young; she had only just turned seventeen.

"On Sundays we went out in a boat on the river, do you remember, Eleonora?" Saying this, he thrust out his chest and sat back in his chair, as if he could boast of those excursions as glorious and heroic acts. "Do you remember?" he persisted, and he searched her with his eyes, forcing her to turn and say, "Yes, yes, I remember." Then he began to joke around, saying that my mother sat at the other end of the boat to put some distance between them. He described her as pale, frightened, and worried about losing her hat. "Her face was extremely pale," he said laughing. He enjoyed teasing her and describing her timidity. "She tried to get away from me, you know that, Alessandra? She acted hard to get. She'd go, 'No, I'm not coming on Sunday; I have things to do.' And then she'd come anyway. I didn't have to beg too hard. She always came, right, Eleonora?" Tears welling up in my eyes, I ran to hug my mother. "We'd get out on the riverbank and have a snack in a meadow. Do you remember that meadow?" He went on interrogating her in order to direct her thoughts and force her to revisit various details.

"Yes," she said. "Yes, I remember all of it."

"We'd come back towards evening and you'd gotten some color, right, Eleonora? Right?" If she didn't answer, he immediately repeated himself. "You'd gotten some color, right?" He wouldn't take his eyes off her during his interrogation. His bright eyes slid over her until she finally replied, almost breathlessly, as if she'd been running, "Yes, of course. My face got red from all the fresh air and sun." He laughed and laughed at her answer. With a look, my mother begged him to stop so I wouldn't understand. But I understood very well, and I hoped I wouldn't fall into the same trap that had taken away her youthful innocence.

MY MOTHER HAD been going to Villa Pierce for almost a year now, and the afternoons spent with Arletta, the information the girl gave her about Hervey, the flowering of the hydrangeas and the acacias— everything that happened up there had now become our sole means of entertainment. I say "ours" because, when she got back, she relayed every detail with such accuracy that I had the illusion I'd been there, too. Her tales, enlivened as they were by the spell of her voice and the grace of her gestures, thrilled me so much that as evening approached and, with it, the time of her return, I was overcome with impatience. If she was late, I felt she was cheating me of some benefit, mine by right.

As soon as she entered the house, I'd ask, "So?" It was like reading a beautiful novel in installments.

Of course, it seemed impossible that that life really existed. In fact, between Arletta's stories about her brother and the ones my mother told me every evening, sometimes even my mother got confused. She'd draw her hand across her forehead. "No, maybe that's not how it went," she said, searching her memory for some point of reference. She was so unnerved that she was afraid of Hervey's next visit, as if it represented an abuse or threat.

"I won't go back if he returns. I really won't!" she exclaimed. Arletta had given her the piano scores for his favorite pieces and begged her to perform them, watching my mother's hands as they moved over the keyboard.

"I'd like to play the way you do," she said, staring at my mother with repressed envy. My mother was almost afraid. "I could play for my brother and stay in this room with him for hours and hours. But I can't. You can, though," Arletta announced. A hungry look lit up her chubby, good-natured face. "You can accompany him while he plays the violin. Hervey will stand here, beside you. Here, let's try it," she said, moving a music stand. "Here."

The air around the music stand shifted, forming an eerie space. My mother tried to smile; she said playfully, "That's enough now." But Arletta persisted. "Let's try." She asked why my mother always dressed in black. "I wish . . ." she began, and then she drew near and touched the fabric of my mother's jacket at the shoulders. "If you weren't so tall, I could lend you one of my dresses."

While my mother reported all this, you could read her face like a book. We were in her room, she was lying on the bed, and, since spring was advancing, we left the window open. From the courtyard you could hear a woman's harsh voice scolding her child, the child crying, the spiteful slamming of shutters. You could hear oil sizzling in the pan, and the room filled with the unpleasant smell of onions. Ashamed, I went to close the window. And yet as I closed it I held the entire court-yard in an embrace. It was as if we were living people, and those in Villa Pierce angels: unapproachable. Had it not been for the extraordinary fear animating her gaze I would have believed my mother was dream-ing the evening she came back and said quietly, "I met Hervey."

From that day on, everything changed for us. Or maybe everything had already changed the first time she skipped swiftly, lightly, down the stairs and the big car took her away.

Maybe I should have felt abandoned, or judged her harshly. Instead—I remember it so well—a gentle peace spread through me: I was happy. Only, I didn't ask her, as I had on other evenings, "So?" urg-ing her to tell me what had happened. I sensed it would have been tactless. Now, I, too, would stay out of the music room, outside the gates, like everything that belonged to the courtyard. But I didn't suffer. And since the event suddenly seemed to have been predictable for some time, I was amazed that only now did she have that expression of fear in her eyes. She asked if Papa had come home, and when I said no, she drew a sigh of relief. She headed for her room, and I imagined that she wouldn't ask me in as usual in the evening. In fact, she didn't. I stood in the dark corridor a little while and then went into the kitchen and sank into a chair. Sista watched me for a moment.

"She met Arletta's brother, didn't she?" she asked, and I nodded.

Nevertheless, for several weeks my mother didn't mention Hervey again. She became unusually reserved and distracted. If Papa said something to her at the table, I had to touch her arm gently to get her attention. She often went up to the Celantis to telephone to rearrange lessons. She scheduled almost all of them in the morning. I'd hear her get up in the dark, very early, and speak quietly to Sista, trying to make up for the time she spent at Villa Pierce.

She went there every afternoon. Before she left, she'd look into the dining room where my father sat by the radio. "Well, I'm going," she'd say. Sometimes she'd suddenly turn back and embrace him as if she were leaving on a trip. When she came back in the evening, she'd sit by me at the window. She no longer told me anything. But her silence was the first story about Villa Pierce that seemed true.

At sunset, the nuns could be seen walking on the terrace during a brief period of recreation. They walked in pairs or in affectionate groups, skirts rustling. Sometimes the young sisters chased each other, making small, prudish, bashful movements, and they were all so pretty and feminine they seemed to have put on that severe garment in play. Spring definitely transformed them. You could actually see the season bursting forth everywhere with arrogance: on the convent wall, the new leaves of wisteria went from a timid green to a bold and lively green in a matter of days. Tufts of grass pushed up between the old stones like crests: crazily, whimsically. Everything participated in my mother's love, and it seemed to me as if the season were renewing itself for her.

Soon, the gold of the first stars appeared on the delicate veil of sky. The trees turned gray, then black, striped with the night's shadows.

"Come here," Mamma said, inviting me to sit with her in her chair.

My father pulled us out of the darkness, suddenly turning on the light. "What are you doing here?" Dinner was ready, the house tidied. I thought I could feel his regret when he couldn't find a reason to scold us. "Insane!" he said to himself, tapping his forehead with his index finger. "Insane!" And then he looked at us for a long time, studying us, trying to work out the reasons for our different nature.

"You're both pale," he remarked. Then he turned to my mother. "You look ill.' And as a matter of fact the pink tint that was always blooming on her prominent, angular cheekbones had disappeared. Her skin had gone white, like wheat that grows in a dark cellar.

"Eleonora, you're becoming ugly," my father said to her one day.

We were still at the table. My father was the only one who had coffee and on rare occasions he would light a cigarette. Unused to smoking, he held the cigarette in a pretentious way, balanced between his index and middle fingers. He'd bring it to his waiting lips and exhale long, thick mouthfuls. She looked up, staring at him with a combination of spite and sarcasm. Perhaps she expected him to say, *I was joking.*

But "You're ugly," he repeated. "I've noticed: you became ugly some time ago."

My mother looked at him another moment or two before she burst out laughing. I'd never seen her laugh like that, throwing her head back against the chair. She wasn't vain; I've already mentioned that she always dressed in a hurry and put her hat on without even looking in the mirror. So I was surprised by her confident laugh and the way she sat upright.

Suddenly, she stood up and practically flew around the table, disappearing into the gloomy sitting room, where we heard her start playing passionately: a pastoral motif recalling green meadows, the freedom of morning. Gradually it became intense, diabolical, and ran wild in happy arpeggios, festive silvery ringing. She played with an arrogant look, as if she were still laughing, with her head thrown back the way it had been at the table. I wanted to run to her—"Mamma!"—admonishing her—"Mamma!"—so she'd stop. It seemed as if she'd lost all control, and was unconsciously displaying her most intimate feelings. But my father's gaze kept me in my seat.

When she finished, she came back to the dining room, stood next to the table and leaned towards us, smiling triumphantly. Her cheeks were lit with deep color.

"Do you know what that was?" she said, referring to the piece she'd just played. And not waiting for our reply: "Sinding's *Rustle of Spring*," she said. "There's not much to it, right? But it's like running a race on the lawn in the early morning." She started twirling happily, dancing around the table, repeating the notes of the motif: "*Da dah, dee dah, da, da dah da,*" she sang in her glass-like voice. "*Do do, da dah, da.*" It seemed to me that grass and hyacinths should grow under her feet, and springs bubble up, cheerful bodies of water . . . "*Dee dee, da dah.*" Maybe the window would open and she would fly away like a swallow. Sista sat

still, watching her, her hands folded on her lap. My father looked serious. I adored her and wanted to kiss the hem of her dress. *"Da dah,
dee dee."*

All at once she stopped, panting, and stood with her back against
the credenza. "I'm going to play that at a big concert," she said. "It will
take place in a few days at Villa Pierce. You are invited."

MY MOTHER HAD always dreamed of giving a concert. My father
would counter that it was expensive to do so and we didn't know anyone who would be able to afford tickets. Paying no heed, she continued
to discuss the music she would want to play, the resounding success she
would have. Cheered by her descriptions, she walked back and forth animatedly across the room in an attempt to dispel her husband's
objections, voicing the hope that our situation would improve. Maybe
she, too, knew that it wouldn't happen. Yet she asked only for approval,
for hope that would allow her to cultivate such dreams. "Right?" she'd
ask him, smiling. And he'd shake his head, saying he couldn't see how
this concert could take place.

I watched my father and the bitterness hidden in my gaze was so
aggressive that I hoped it would reach him and hurt him. No, no, he
shook his head. And all my mother's dreams slipped away.

But now, maybe because winter was over, it seemed that the sad,
dark period of her life was coming to an end, like a season. I had never
thought her old, as children so often do, and in any case she was then
barely thirty-nine. After the meeting with Hervey, she seemed to have
become a girl again. When we went out together people would turn to
look at her even though she was dressed modestly, not wearing anything
extravagant or flamboyant. Yet it was difficult to find another woman
with such grace, such innate harmony. She bore me on her arm as a
tree bears a branch. She'd pause before crossing a street, apparently
worried about being struck, but I knew that she saw nothing: carriages,
cars and bicycles slid past her like a river.

I caught her acting equally distracted at home, standing in front of a wardrobe or a drawer she'd opened without remembering why. Sometimes she would linger in the armchair by my window, looking outside, her head inclined slightly to one side. God, how young my mother was then! Her cheeks, I noticed, still had the freshness of a child's, and all her gestures seemed to become even more modest and chaste, as if she were not a married woman, had never known a man's desire, and hadn't given birth to me. Her love for Hervey, which others would have judged guilty, in my eyes enveloped her in a magic veil of innocence, and a word, a laugh, or a gesture could sully it. I know that at such moments my mother felt very close to God and those teachings of his that inspire one to be good, pure, and honest. She was so thin that her dress seemed to contain only breath. Yes, my mother in love was the sweetest thing I'd ever seen.

"Let's go," I whispered to Sista, and we left her alone at the window.

We went to sit quietly in the kitchen. I almost held my breath so that in the silence of the house my mother would feel guarded and protected, as if by a shell. I sewed busily, pricking my finger with the needle to punish and humiliate myself. I was unhappy. I felt that the vile curiosity awakened in me by Enea was preventing me from being like my mother. So I often turned my thoughts to Antonio, Aida's brother. He wasn't happy, either, Aida had said, but, rather than give in to the cause of his discontent, he'd allowed himself to be taken to prison. I envied him his ability to be strong, even though it generated such profound melancholy. He would have been able to defend me, to free me from Enea. And although I had never seen him, I promised myself to him, intending to wait months for him, even years, and telling myself, *I'm his girlfriend.* I tried to reassure myself with that thought, indifferent to the fond sympathy that veiled his unknown eyes. In my imagination, we would be married. I would go and pick him up at the prison gates. But it was another city, another prison; I was an adult, serious, wearing an old raincoat. I leaned against a gatepost and waited for a long time. When Antonio finally came out and I saw him for the first time, his appearance was already familiar to me: he had a downcast face beneath brown hair, a pointed chin, sunken eyes. He was holding a package and I instantly offered to carry it, but he didn't want me to, so we set out walking in silence, the bundle between us. We had the air of poor people. I pondered the fact that this was my first romantic encounter, and I remembered how brisk and lively my mother's step was after she met Hervey. I, on the other hand, walked with difficulty next to Antonio, who was burdened with that large package, and I vainly hoped we'd come across a garden or a lovely, tree-lined boulevard: a bit of green, in other words. We walked next to a factory wall blackened with smoke. It was on the outskirts of a big city, with chimney pots thick against the sky and in the distance the sea: leaden and flat beyond a dark beach.

Antonio, I called out. And I wanted to say something loving, to smile, to shine even in the midst of that desolation. But when he turned his melancholy eyes on me I said, *Let me carry that package for you.* He shook his head—*no, no*—and we went on walking in silence.

So I carried two secrets inside: the vile impulses suggested to me by Alessandro and a desire to rebel against cowardice, as Antonio had done. These feelings fought within me, making me even less sociable. From the window I watched people passing in the street and tried to guess their secrets. Maybe everyone had an unmentionable struggle going on inside, a shameful flaw. My mother, though, carried Hervey proudly in her gait, and in the bold tone of the piano.

FOR HER CONCERT, my mother had a new dress made for me in black-and-white checked taffeta. Proud of my dress, I asked her, "What color will yours be, Mamma?"

Momentarily perplexed, she said, "I'll wear one of my usual dresses, Alessandra."

A little later, however, I surprised her in front of the open wardrobe, fingering her dresses one by one. They were all in neutral colors: sand, gray, and two or three were made of raw silk, saddened by a white lace collar: dresses for an older person. Troubled at having been caught in indecision, she seemed to ask my advice with a look. Her dresses hung limp on the hangers.

I said quietly, "They're like so many dead women, Mamma . . ."

We held one another, trembling. Then all at once she let me go, went to her chest of drawers, and took out a large box that I had never seen. The box was tied up with old twine and Mamma tore it open at once. When she took off the lid, pink and blue veils appeared, feathers, satin ribbons. I had no idea she possessed such a treasure, so I looked at her in amazement, and she in turn looked up at her mother's portrait. I realized that these were Juliet's veils, or Ophelia's, and I touched the silk in veneration.

"How can we use them?" she asked me, uncertain. We knew absolutely nothing about the demands of fashion—we were lost before all those lengths of voile.

"We'll have to ask someone, Mamma."

She put the veils and the silk back and took my hand. Clutching the box under her arm, she walked to the front door, where she met Sista coming back from the market.

"Sista, I'm going to have a new dress!" Mamma told her, caressing her shoulders as she passed.

"A dress made from Juliet's and Desdemona's veils," I added, showing off.

We shut the door before her astonished eyes and went straight upstairs to the Celantis' house. I knocked cheerfully so they'd hurry to open the door. Fulvia arrived right away, wearing her percale dressing gown.

"We have to make a dress for Mamma with Ophelia's veils!" I exclaimed, hugging her. Lydia came toward us shaking her hands to dry her nail polish. They joined in at once, not asking a single question.

"In my bedroom, there's a mirror."

Though it was almost midday, the room was still dark and untidy. A small lamp was burning on the nightstand near the unmade bed. Socks and underclothes lay in a heap on the chair and shoes were strewn here and there over the carpet. The stuffy smell of a closed room mingled with the cloying scent of nail polish.

"May we?" my mother asked hesitantly.

But Lydia was ushering her in. "Come in, come in," not bothering to straighten the bed or pick up the underwear. She opened the window and in the sunny morning air the room's slovenliness was all the more evident.

She opened the box with cries of enthusiasm. I laughed with childish excitement and hugged my mother, who was smiling, bewildered. Fulvia meanwhile had taken off her dressing gown and was running around draped in one of the silks, which was perfectly suited to being a dress, while Lydia was wrapping her head in a veil like an Indian.

Amused, my mother watched their creations before asking shyly, "Do you think it would be possible to make a dress for me out of these fabrics?"

"An evening gown?" Fulvia asked.

"Oh, no. A dress—how can I put it? I'd like to wear it on the day of the concert."

"Let's see," said Lydia. "Take off your clothes."

My mother hesitated for a moment. She put her hands to her neck, where the long row of buttons that fastened her dress began. I'd never seen her undressed in all these years. Never had I seen her go around the house in her nightgown, like the other women in the building, in the extreme August heat.

"Take off your clothes," Lydia repeated. "What, are you embarrassed? We're all women, aren't we?" Fulvia laughed.

Already each was brandishing her favorite fabric.

"Come on, Eleonora, come on," they insisted. My mother began to take off her clothes, revealing her white, extremely fine skin, her thin, elegant arms: the slight swelling of her chest barely lifted her slip.

"You look like a girl," Lydia said.

"A bride," Fulvia added. "We're dressing a bride."

I urged them on. My mother's face was completely red. Busying themselves happily around her, as if to violate her hidden grace and modesty, Lydia and Fulvia wrapped her in a light blue silk that left her arms free and crossed at her décolletage.

"That's it, without a doubt," Fulvia pronounced.

"Let's think about this carefully. Go out and then come back in," said Lydia.

"What?" Mamma hesitated.

"Yes, come through the door. Let's see you."

My mother went out. For a moment the doorway was empty. I heard my heart thumping and I was afraid she wouldn't come back, leaving us with only the memory of that light blue dress. Dismayed, I was about to call her when I saw her hand pull the faded velvet curtain aside. She entered lightly, a shy smile on her lips. She looked beautiful.

Fulvia and I applauded her enthusiastically. "That one!" we shouted, "that one!"

Lydia applauded along with us, but suddenly she signaled us to stop and said seriously, "Wait a minute. Are you sure he likes light blue?"

Stunned, we girls became uncertain, in a silence veined with apprehension. My mother hesitated before replying, "I don't know."

"Perhaps he's said something about your other clothes . . ."

"We've never talked about my clothes, and anyhow I don't have any colorful dresses."

"But it's very important. The Captain, for example, can't stand green. All men have a color that bothers them or irritates them. The

Mariani woman, you know, on the first floor? She told me he never allows her to wear red."

My mother had sat down and was contemplating the lovely light blue fabric in her lap. "I don't know," she repeated. "I really don't know." She didn't know how to navigate these questions with ease, and she felt lost.

"Have you ever noticed whether he wears a blue tie?"

"He almost never wears a tie. He wears a white shirt, open at the chest, and he rolls his sleeves up to his elbow."

Her head was resting against the wall and she looked toward the window. Beyond the empty balconies of our neighborhood, you could see the green of the park on the Pincio. She spoke quietly, hands on her lap in the folds of gauze, and we listened attentively, as we did when my brother spoke to us through Ottavia.

"The curtains in his study are white. The sofa is pale, too—gray. It's a large room, and he's always in there, like gypsies in their cara-van. On the walls are tall shelves packed with books, and paintings that depict shells, extraordinary shells from the Caribbean Sea, painted by a Mexican artist. He told me that the painter dives underwater to fish. He blinds the fish with light, and when they're dazed they rush around and bump into his mask. And then there are photographs: of gazelles, chamois, puma. And photos of trees, framed as if they were portraits of friends." She paused before continuing. "No. I really can't imagine what his favorite color is. He might not notice the color of a dress. I don't think dresses are very important to him. And yet . . ."

". . . And yet?"

"Every time I arrive and he looks at me, I want to be as beautiful as a woman in a painting." She got up and ran to embrace Lydia, Ful-via, and then me. She nearly flew to the mirror and stopped in front of it, studying herself. "Make me beautiful!" she said, clasping her hands to her heart. "Make me beautiful."

.   .   .

I WOULD LIKE the absolute innocence and genuine candor with which my mother spoke about Hervey to be clear.

At the time, they hadn't yet uttered a single word of love that might have made her feel guilty about their relationship. And I myself, by continually questioning her about him, reinforced her conviction that she wasn't doing anything wrong, since their friendship could be understood by a girl my age, and, what's more, her daughter.

When she talked to me about their encounters, it was as if she were reciting a poem, and so I understood that hers was truly love as I'd always imagined it should be: anxious, fabulous, enchanted, and yet unyielding in its terrible majesty. In fact, my mother's life had changed with its appearance: she became even more intelligent, as if everything up to now had appeared to her behind a veil. When she returned from Villa Pierce in the evenings, she would tell me about walks in the park, breaks in the music room: my mother at the piano accompanying Hervey on the violin.

Sometimes I asked, "What about Arletta?" and she avoided giving me an answer. Then one day she told me that Arletta had gone with her governess to spend some time in England with her older sister. Once my mother said, "When I go into the music room I always feel she's coming towards me in her white dress." Then she hid her head in her hands, and I stroked her hair, gently encouraging her to feel no remorse if one day all she could remember of me, too, was a profile framed by her favorite window.

It may seem that these stories were cruel to me, showing as they do that Hervey was her constant preoccupation and the greatest concern of her life, unless one considers that she had never been in love before, and—having missed the life of a girl and a woman—couldn't be satisfied by being only a mother.

I could reproach her for having subjected me to that climate of perpetual exaltation, which, above all, made me completely devoted to the myth of the Great Love and thus unintentionally led to the painful situation I find myself in today. I could reproach her, perhaps, if she hadn't already paid for her ambitions. And now that I'm forced to write about her and look into the most intimate and dramatic moments of our life together, it's not really to accuse her of having made me what I am but to explain those of my actions which would otherwise be clear only to me.

My current situation is helpful, since it allows me to examine myself harshly and to acknowledge thoughts and actions I would at other times have avoided revealing to anyone. That's why I believe no man has the right to judge a woman without knowing what different material women are made of. I consider it unjust, for example, that a tribunal composed exclusively of men should decide whether a woman is guilty or not. For if there is a single morality respected by both men and women, how can a man ever really understand the subtle reasoning that drives a woman to passion or despair, and which is innate, part of her from birth?

A man may not be able to understand how love governed everything in the large building we lived in; not even the men who lived with us noticed. They thought love was a brief fairytale for their companions, a brief passion necessary for a woman to secure the right to be mistress of her own house, have children, and dedicate her entire life to the problems of shopping and the kitchen. Yes, they actually believed that the smell of food, a heavy shopping bag hanging from her arm, hours of patient mending and standing over children with the rod could replace the romantic love that had led to their meeting. They knew so little of women they believed that this was really their life's plan, its ideal. *She's frigid*, they'd confide to their friends with a sigh. *She does nothing but keep house and look after the children*. And, with these facile conclusions, they refused to acknowledge a problem for which they accepted no obligation or responsibility. All they would have had to do was listen to women's private discussions, which they broke off when men came around, the way children do when their parents approach; or look at the books on the nightstands in bedrooms where one or two babies were often sleeping with them; or notice how women opened the windows after supper, sighing quietly. *They're tired*, they'd say, not bothering to question why they were tired. They might go as far as thinking, *They're women*, but not a single one asked himself what being a woman meant. And none of them grasped that behind every gesture, every bit of self-denial, all that feminine bravery was a secret desire for love.

To our eyes my mother in love was endowed with an extraordinary privilege. Even though she wasn't close to anyone apart from Lydia and Fulvia Celanti, the curiosity elicited by the big American car and a few indiscretions on Ottavia's and our friends' part brought the other inhabitants of the building up to date on the love affair. Often, one of them would call my name as I passed by, pay me some compliment, and take the opportunity to ask me an innocent question about my mother, and I felt cheered by the warmth of increased affection around me.

The spring of 1939 was dazzling, or at least it seemed so, owing to my state of mind. Actually, as I recall, the sky had never been so blue nor the air so mild. Yet I must admit that in addition to the sweet restlessness of the season there was the turmoil brought on by my romantic image of Hervey. He had disrupted not only my mother's life but as a consequence mine as well, and the Celantis'. Because of him, Fulvia and I had become sarcastic and contemptuous with our young male friends, and we didn't find the same pleasure in their conversation. And he certainly had something to do with a few of the disagreements between Lydia and the Captain at the time. Once when I was going into a *latteria* on Via Fabio Massimo, I saw them sitting silently before two empty glasses stained with whipped cream.

No one had ever seen the Pierces' villa, and I myself couldn't say exactly where it was. Yet when I talked about it I embellished it with attractive details. I talked about peacocks and white greyhounds. I'd read about orchids growing wild in trees in the West Indies, and I credited the great oaks at Villa Pierce with those splendid parasites. I went as far as describing a pond rippled by the placid gliding of black swans, where my mother and Hervey ventured out in a gondola. I'm not sure Fulvia always believed me, but she liked listening to me.

"Tell me more!" she would demand. Ultimately, in speaking of Hervey I was speaking only of myself. I attributed to him my desires, my impulses, and in conversation I lent him the speech of my monologues at the window. It seemed to me, therefore, that I was the one accompanying my mother on those romantic walks, I the one sitting with her at the piano. And it was to join me that she would fly down the stairs.

We would fall silent. Fulvia sometimes tried to recover herself, with a mocking, petulant laugh. We would walk together arm in arm: these were late summer evenings, forlorn, and a desolate peace hung over the streets.

Mamma insisted that we should not go beyond the bridge that marked the boundary between our neighborhood and the rest of the city. It was a sort of affectionate obsession with her, as if she could in some way stop me from growing up. Fulvia urged me to break my promise, proposing that I lie when I got back.

"No," I replied. "I don't like misleading people," and she was surprised by my abhorrence of lies, taking it for cowardice.

"But your mother would never know," she reassured me.

"It's not for her," I explained, "it's for myself. You think I'm really good, but it's not true. I'm tempted by the devil every day."

"You believe in the devil?" she asked sarcastically.

"Yes, I believe the devil is the sum of the temptations, the traps that we constantly set for ourselves. There are days when I just can't take it anymore and I'm hanging by a thread. If I learned to lie as well, I'd be lost."

"What is it that tempts you?"

I was silent for a moment. We were sitting in a public garden near Castel Sant'Angelo, like two soldiers on leave, as people went by and children played tag.

I looked down to confess: "Everything."

Fulvia turned to look at me, surprised by my confidence, then looked again into the distance. Suddenly thoughtful, she said, "It's really difficult, isn't it? I feel I could easily become a saint, or just as easily one of those women men pay. Maybe you won't understand and you won't respect me anymore."

"On the contrary, I understand completely," I said quietly. And after a pause I continued. "There's only one thing, besides my difficulty telling lies, that helps me: it kind of disgusts me when men get too close. The other day, at Maddalena's, when some boys came and we were dancing together, you all thought I was standing aside because I wasn't a very good dancer. But it was actually because I couldn't stand having a stranger's hand on my back—it burns through a thin dress. The next morning the dress will still smell strongly of smoke and of a man, which irks me. Do you understand?"

"Yes, I do. I understand." She was thoughtful for a moment. "I understand that you like men more than I do."

"Why would you think that?" I said sharply.

"Because that's how it is. Dario's mouth on mine doesn't bother me a bit. I just dry my lips, go right back to the room where everyone's dancing and start flirting with someone else. You saw that, right?"

"I did."

"I can't justify what I'm always reading in books—a woman's need or the instinct she feels to defend herself, her doubts before she gives in to a man or even before kissing him." She went on, "Last year I went to the beach at Fregene with Dario and others in the group. Sometimes I went just with Dario. We'd take a boat and push it out into the water, where we'd dive in and then take off our bathing suits."

"In the water?"

"Yes. We threw them in the boat—it was gorgeous. My hair stuck to my cheeks, with the thrilling cold. The sea was green, pale blue, and we brushed past each other swimming under water. Our white bodies looked like fish in an aquarium. I was happy, the way fish are, or seaweed . . ."

I laughed to hide my discomfort. "What if the boat had gone off with your bathing suits?"

She shrugged. "It was anchored. Sometimes Dario's hand would lightly brush me, but it was a watery hand, and it made me laugh. I wish I'd been unsettled, you know? I wish I'd protested, or else enjoyed the audaciousness of what I was doing. Nothing. Nothing. I'd like to feel at least once what you feel when a man gets close to you."

We were walking along the Tiber in the Borgo neighborhood, under the changing shade of the plane trees and the banter of sparrows nesting in the branches, chittering loud enough to drown out our conversation. At that hour, many priests were hurrying by, caught out by the first Ave Maria.

"Shall we cross?" Fulvia asked with a smile. She gave me a slight shove when we went by bridges.

"No, no," I pleaded.

"You are so innocent!" she said tenderly.

I hung my head, perplexed by my betraying her like that. By now I'd realized that my constant inhibitions and my struggles only served to restrain an overly passionate nature. My body was my defense: thin, plain, still childish. Men passed me by without noticing me.

"You're innocent," Fulvia continued. "That's what attracted me to you the first day I noticed you on the stairs. You were going past with your mother and she was holding your hand. That's it! I've finally realized what one feels, looking at you: the irresistible desire to take you by the hand and have you enter their life for good. Lots of men will ask you to marry them, I know it. It's not possible, after seeing you, to resign oneself to having you for only an hour. You're like your mother."

No one had ever spoken to me before about how I was or how I appeared. Little by little, I took shape from the keen interest Fulvia took in me: I was no longer a jumble of desires, uncertainties, and aspirations but someone fully formed, with a defined appearance. Until that moment, I'd believed that others had not the slightest opinion about me. Which is why, hearing Fulvia talk, it was as if I were seeing myself in the mirror for the first time. I clung to her arm, her fine skin, her warmth.

"Antonio's in there," I said as we walked by the huge building.

We leaned against the parapet beside the river, looking at the windows protected by grating and the writing on the façade: "Penitentiary."

"No, he's on an island now," Fulvia said, lowering her voice.

"But what has he done?" I felt impatient.

"No one knows."

The answer was always the same. We hardly spoke of Antonio now, and I was convinced that it was true that no one knew. My father, irritated by my repeated questions, had forbidden me to get involved with those things. Aida said her brother had been accused of printing flyers.

"What did they say?" I immediately asked.

And Aida, too, said, "Nobody knows."

I stared at the prison windows, and within myself I called to Antonio so insistently that I suddenly thought I saw his face appear behind the bars. In his desolate glance you could read his bewilderment, which the others expressed in those two words: "Nobody knows." I remember what Aida said on the first day, which was that Antonio and his friends weren't happy. From then on, my awareness of their painful condition was a constant rebuke to me.

In the gray light of dusk, many people passed between us and the prison, talking, reading the paper, laughing. Two women went by in a carriage, one of them powdering her nose. They seemed very busy doing everything possible so that they wouldn't have to think, so that their day as well as mine seemed like a whirlwind of incessant activities, their firm intention to thwart an examination of conscience. Perhaps if they'd been able to ask themselves, they all would have discovered that they weren't happy.

"It's terrible," I said quietly.

"It is," Fulvia repeated. "It's terrible to be locked up in there when it's such a lovely time of year out here."

She looked around eagerly. The last of the evening sunlight was gently tinting with pink the rooftops and the luxuriant treetops on the Janiculum behind the prison. "Villa Pierce is up there, isn't it?" she asked.

I nodded.

"Can't we see it from here?"

"No," I replied brusquely. "You can't see it from here or from anywhere. It's hidden by trees. It's never visible."

We started walking again in silence.

"You know what," she said abruptly, "sometimes it seems as if Villa Pierce doesn't exist, or Hervey, either."

"Why?"

"I don't know. It's just my impression. I remember reading a story in a book about a wayfarer who was crossing the forest at night, hungry and exhausted. He despaired of holding out against the cold and his own fatigue. Suddenly in the distance he saw a light from a house. He went in and found what he needed to eat and drink, warmed himself at a big fire. An elegant old man and an elderly woman welcomed him, treating him with courtesy and a thoughtfulness he had never known till then. They took him to bed, tucked him in, and he fell into the most pleasurable sleep of his life. But the next morning he woke up lying on the ground at the edge of the forest, near the main road. The house and the elderly couple had vanished.

"Oh!" I exclaimed. "And who were they?"

"His parents, whom he'd lost as a child. It was really them, as if they'd grown old somewhere else, far away from him. Isn't it a beautiful story?"

"Yes. But you were saying . . ."

"Right. That's how Villa Pierce seems to me. I feel there's something ghostly about Hervey, too, and Eleonora. You know, sometimes I also have the feeling that she must be about to disappear and not come back, as you fear."

"Be quiet," I said, trembling, as we came to the neat chessboard of streets near our house. We walked arm in arm, huddled close in the unexpected cold, and I held my mother's life in my hands just as we dangle a lovely colored globe, suspended in the airy freedom of the sky and bound to us by the fragile complicity of a thread.

THE DAY OF the concert, my father and I had lunch by ourselves. Mamma had been invited to Villa Pierce. It was the first time we had eaten alone, across from each other, as we later did for many years. I recall that it felt like a bad omen, but, out of instinctive solidarity with my mother, I decided to pretend I was entirely comfortable. I was still feeling excited after helping her put on her light blue dress. I thought it had turned out really elegant. Lydia had insisted on a seamstress with a good reputation, and, in order to pay the bill, Sista had had to make her first trip to the pawnbrokers at Monte di Pietà, taking with her a gold brooch that had belonged to Nonna. My mother looked beautiful in her light blue dress. Swelling over her breasts and hips, the silk softened her thin figure and its color matched her eyes. The sight of her, ready, in the rooms where I usually saw her going about modestly in her dark clothes, brought my hands to my mouth to stifle a cry of surprise.

She came towards us, holding out her dress like a girl at her first dance. That light step would have made it easy for her to leave, but with the air of doing nothing very serious. I stared at her with intense love for a long moment before waving goodbye and bursting into tears. I clung to Sista, hiding my head in the hollow of her shoulder and breathing in the sour smell of cooking and black clothes that was the backdrop to my solitary days.

My mother stopped, perplexed. "Why are you two crying? Sandi, why the tears? Dear God, what have I done?"

We couldn't explain it. Sista and I had a secret understanding, similar to the fear that enveloped us when we sat in the kitchen waiting for her and, with every moment that passed, marked by the big hands of the clock, the worry grew that we would never see her again. She couldn't understand that her presence was the only good thing in our lives. We smiled at her through our tears. And then she, too, smiled and embraced us, moved to see us sharing her joy so intensely.

"I'm a bit scared," she said, hesitating at the door. She added, "I'm really scared." But she soon overcame her fears. She started down the stairs quickly, every now and then leaning over the bannister to look at us once more.

"Goodbye!" she called out, throwing us a kiss, and the squalid stairwell lit up with her smile.

THE CAR RETURNED later to pick us up. I'd been ready for some time, and as soon as I heard the horn my heart began beating wildly.

My father said, "Just a moment," and pretended to read something important in the paper. We descended the stairs slowly, one behind the other, and I walked in the odious scent of brilliantine.

We sat apart from each other in the car, fidgeting. My father displayed indifference, even boredom, but I knew he was proud to be driven by a uniformed chauffeur in an expensive car. I was thinking about how Mamma went to Villa Pierce from here every day. And surely her dreary daily life slid away from her during the drive: behind her, the street we lived on, the large apartment block, the dark rooms, my father, Lydia, Sista—all of it subsided without a sound. Ah: maybe it was when driving down the grand leafy avenue on the Janiculum that she forgot me, too.

The gate was open, and the car entered, crushing the gravel, which responded with the noise of oars scudding through water. In the entrance hall, Violet Pierce, her white hair tinted violet, received her guests. We were welcomed as enthusiastically as if she'd been standing there waiting for us to arrive.

"Do you play the piano, too?" she asked me distractedly.

Intimidated, my father and I sat at the back of the room. On the seats there were small programs announcing the "Concert given by the pianist Eleonora Corteggiani." The pianist Eleonora Corteggiani was Mamma: Corteggiani was my father's surname, the name I used at school. Yet it seemed to me that she wasn't part of our family, and that she went by that name because it was the same as hers. I looked around, but didn't recognize the music room she had described to me.

Many of the guests spoke English, and we were very uncomfortable, like people who have ended up on their own in a foreign country with an unfamiliar language and customs. I looked around for Hervey and instantly felt sure he wasn't there. To pluck up my courage I stared at the piano, where I'd soon see my mother's cherished figure.

It was a grand piano, extremely long and shiny, very different from the old Pleyel upright we had at home. My father looked at it with distaste, and in that moment I couldn't help but feel bound to him by our common discomfort: our house, Sista sitting in the kitchen, the voices from the courtyard, the dark and dusty stairways seemed more suited to us, even more welcoming. *Let's leave*, I was about to say to Papa, *let's go home*, when we saw the liveried servants close the door. Signora Pierce put her hand up to ask for silence, and, from a small side door, my mother appeared.

She stepped lightly over to the piano. She then stopped and placed a hand on the music stand, and at that moment the audience applauded. It wasn't just respect but something elicited by her presence, like a cry.

She was very pale, and the Ophelia gown made from veils, which had seemed so remarkable within our own walls, looked old-fashioned here.

"Your mother's too thin," my father said. "I'm going to get her to take a restorative cure."

I turned to look at her. With those words, he pretended not to notice that his wife was an extraordinary woman. He enjoyed testing his right to criticize her and make her respect his decisions. I wanted to respond harshly and sarcastically, but at that moment my mother began playing a Bach prelude and fugue.

I'd heard that piece and the ones that followed countless times. But those, too, seemed different there. Maybe because she was hidden by the music stand, I began to doubt that it was really my mother playing them. The touch was that of a very strong, brave person, different from the one we usually heard speaking in a submissive, yielding tone, complying meekly with her husband's orders.

The audience applauded enthusiastically after every piece. My mother did not stand up to thank them but bowed her head instead, demonstrating her confusion. During the pauses Violet Pierce sailed between guests, surely whispering something flattering about my mother, because she looked towards the platform and smiled. She glided close to us, too, pausing for a moment to say, "Isn't she wonderful? *Non è maravigliosa?*" She must have forgotten who we were.

Then she stopped next to an armchair in the first row and started talking rapidly in English. Although I didn't understand anything she was saying, I could tell from the look on her face that she was addressing Hervey, and I felt a sudden stirring of emotion. It was easy to guess that she was trying to persuade him to do something. At last my mother, who'd kept her eyes on the keyboard all this time, turned to look at him, in invitation. Immediately, Hervey climbed onto the platform.

My mother had never described him to me, and all I knew was that he was very tall and had blond hair. Nevertheless, from the very first moment, his appearance matched the idea I'd formed of him. He took up his violin and began tuning it, facing my mother and getting ready to perform with her, not giving a thought to the audience. Even though I couldn't see his face, I recognized signs of a distant affinity between us, as there is between plants in the same family. Maybe because of his slim figure, or because of the nape of his neck, which, curved over his violin, was similar to that of a horse, everything I liked in life seemed to be united in him—beautiful animals, beautiful trees—and not just what I liked in a man.

He began playing. I didn't know the music. It revolved around a pastoral theme, the kind my mother said he preferred, and, instead of accompanying him, the piano made a fitting reply to his every phrase: the violin called, the piano gave a hushed response, in peaceful dialogue. Yet, little by little, the tone and the intensity grew, as if the questions were becoming quicker and more insistent. It seemed with the final beats that the piano was trying to flee, and the violin was running after it.

When the music stopped, we all had our hearts in our throats, as if we'd been following them in their chase. There was a moment of silence before the audience recovered and began to applaud. My father remained silent, pale in his dark suit.

I clapped my hands, struggling to contain the cries of joy echoing inside me. The audience applauded frenetically. Violet Pierce climbed onto the platform to congratulate the performers. It was over. My mother, blushing, stood up from the piano and made as if to escape, but Hervey took her arm and held her back. They looked at one another and smiled, bewildered at having manifested a feeling they believed themselves to be unaware of. Still smiling, they turned towards us.

I was too moved to keep clapping: I looked at them, lost in thought, as the tears filled my eyes. I felt proud and tender towards her, as if I were her mother and she my daughter. Through that veil of bright and trembling tears, I watched my mother and Hervey leave the earth, holding hands and rising, rising, her light blue dress lifting them like a cloud. And through that veil of tears I couldn't distinguish their features; they seemed to be the same sex, neither man nor woman: angels. In fact, they were both tall, and looked like brother and sister, perhaps because of the color of their hair. The confusion lingered in my mind for a moment, leaving me awed and uncertain. I couldn't explain their mysterious resemblance, the harmony that breathed through them. Detached from the earth, they quivered in the opalescent aquarium of my eyes, and my mother smiled as she had when she turned to say good-bye before disappearing down the stairs.

At last, at the audience's request, she sat down again at the piano and started playing *Rustle of Spring*, which she had performed the evening she told us about the concert. Once again, we heard her laugh through the music. Many in the crowd were on their feet.

"Let's go," my father said, putting his arm through mine. We crossed the large empty rooms, pursued by festive peals and the rippling notes of the piano. It was still light outside, but the huge trees were cloaked in shadow. The music followed us from the windows, gently pushing us along. We hastened our steps, eager to get away: once outside the gate we could no longer hear the piano.

My father leaned on me, relying on me. Later, when he went blind and I took him out for walks, I recognized his way of leaning from that evening. His face suddenly looked older and weaker, something that often happens in moments of weariness to faces that have long maintained a youthful aspect. He didn't comment on the concert, nor did he dare repeat that my mother was thin. Instead he broke down, leaning on my arm and dragging his feet, incapable of expressing his emotions except through some immediate physical reaction. And rather than feeling compassion for him and for a life that had deteriorated after generating mine—which I perceived as strong and young—I was, I must confess, cheered by his collapse. I felt that Mamma and I had the secret of eternal youth: the same things would bring us joy and excitement today and for many years to come; we would rise above time and physical decline, give ourselves over to pleasures my father had never known. I felt I was carrying all that is fleeting in our lives, in this person hanging on to my arm: flesh that ages and one day decays. I was disgusted, and I felt the loathing and aversion I'd felt when Enea tried to push me against the wall so I would feel his body. My mother was my father's only bridge to the poetry of life. She had stayed with him for years, inviting him to follow her. Now she was gone and he was alone.

I led him home slowly through the alleyways of the Borgo. The voices and the smells of the street rose up to greet us. This was our neighborhood, these were our people, and my mother seemed to have ended up there by mistake.

I looked at my father. Without realizing it, he had entrusted himself to a young girl like me, whose thoughts and habits he'd often ridiculed. The scent of his brilliantine brought back the sight of him sitting at the table, the paper open and his gold ring on his finger, studying us and shaking his head sarcastically.

Moved to pity by that memory, I said, "Come, come on, Papa," and helped him cross the street.

As soon as we got home, my father asked Sista if supper was ready, and though it was early, wanted her to serve it. Sista didn't dare ask a thing. She put the soup tureen in the center of the table and then stood dumbfounded, hands crossed on her black apron, staring at the place where the *signora* usually sat. My mother had a habit of folding her napkin into the shape of a rabbit. At that moment, the sight of it moved me like the sight of Alessandro's toys, which she devotedly kept in a drawer. Outside the window, the precious shadows of twilight were falling, the ones we awaited together sometimes; and now I was alone. I surprised myself by filling in for her, doing the things she always did in the evening: I prepared Sista's plate and I used the same words when I gave it to her, the same affectionate tones.

At the sound of my voice, Papa looked up from his plate and noticed that I was now a woman. Because I was so similar to my mother in looks and movements, he immediately took me as an adversary. Sista sat in a corner nibbling on a piece of bread, and the silence between us was an icy region no one dared to explore. Soon, however, we heard a hurried step on the stairs. I jumped up, radiant, ran to the door, and flung it open.

I'd say that even today, after all these years, when I think back to my mother I often see her as she was at that moment, clutching a huge bouquet of roses to her chest, the edges of her light blue dress peeking out from under her coat, as if she could no longer resume her humble daily appearance. Her hair was disheveled, her rosy face attractive. She leaned against the wall, as if to support herself after a sudden bout of dizziness.

"Oh, Sandi!" she whispered, and I felt that she'd never said my name so sweetly. "Oh, Sandi!" she repeated, closing her eyes. She was very beautiful. I wanted her to lie on my bed in Ophelia's gown and tell me the story of her day as she'd told me stories from Shakespeare when I was a child.

Our happy intimacy was abruptly interrupted by my father's voice from the dining room. It was a voice with enormous hands and thick black hair, the voice of a fairytale ogre.

"Eleonora," he called. "Eleonora!" he repeated loudly, when she was slow to reply.

He appeared in the entrance hall, and my mother, wholly unafraid, welcomed him with a smile. She was so happy she could delude herself that he shared her joy, at least for that evening. I felt that she wanted to meet with him, cordially, and talk about Hervey, in hopes that he'd listen and share her contentment. Nor am I ashamed to admit that it seemed completely natural to me, since I saw no connection between what united my parents and the feelings that bound her to Hervey.

"Come with me," he ordered, heading for the hall.

Mortified, my mother immediately followed. She seemed so young, maybe because of that coat, which barely covered her gown—a girl surprised on returning from a ball she'd gone to secretly.

Before entering her room she dropped the roses, and I hurriedly gathered them up, pricking my fingers. She closed the gray door behind her without looking at me.

I sat there on the red brick floor, pressing my ear to the crack. Sista tried to pull me away, but then she crouched down next to me. At first there was silence, but finally we heard my father's voice, full of a biting hatred I hadn't credited him with.

"That is the last time you'll go to Villa Pierce," he said. We guessed that he then took her arm and squeezed it hard, because there was a suppressed moan.

My mother spoke quietly—we couldn't hear what she was saying. He replied in the same tone. They both seemed to be ashamed of what they were saying to each other. Their harsh dispute frightened me, just like the silence that had once accompanied their evenings of intimacy and serenity, and my thoughts went back to those moments when I experienced, for the first time, the bitter loneliness of a daughter faced with her parents' troubling collusion. I discovered how shocking it always is, what happens between a man and a woman when they're alone, and I called to mind what Fulvia had told me about the way babies are made. It wasn't a bright, happy act or an honest one, as the act that gives life should be. And in fact darkness and the secrecy of night was the chosen time in which to do it. All the misery of that intimacy established between a man and a woman was contained in the acrimonious voices I heard on the other side of the gray door. Even their way of loving each other—for all I knew—seemed terrible and vulgar, like the battle I was witnessing.

"I'll lock you up in here," he was saying. "In here. Do you understand? Here."

I squeezed Sista's hand, upset. I pictured my mother caged in the big iron bed where Aunt Caterina had died, the large chest of drawers with the dark marble top. I pictured her delicate body crushed by that gloomy furniture.

"Please, Ariberto, please." The tone of her voice was imploring, distressed. "I beg you, I beg you." It was as if she were crawling on her knees; she, so soft, proud, as if she were truly abasing herself before the same man I had dutifully led home on my arm.

Terrified, I turned to Sista. "We have to save her, do something. Save her!"

Sista didn't answer. In the dim light of the lamp halfway down the hall, I saw her slender shadow leaning on the doorframe. Her face was as still as wax. I'd often seen her worried by a short delay on my mother's part, afraid she wouldn't come back, and it amazed me that at such a serious moment she could maintain such a rigid impassivity.

"We have to save her," I repeated. She kept quiet. I shook her by the arm several times, asking, "What can we do? Tell me! Come on! What?" until she finally said, never altering her stony expression, "What are you going to do? He's her husband."

AFTER THAT FEARFUL evening, our lives went back to being the way they always had been, and my parents never guessed that I had heard everything that went on between them. So they continued to treat each other just as they had in the days before the concert.

Yet there had been a change: I knew now what happened when they went into their bedroom, so the friendly tone they used to speak to one another seemed to me an intolerable fiction. From that day on, however, my mother stopped telling me the story of her days at Villa Pierce, and the fact that I didn't interrogate her anxiously on her return as I'd done before proved that I'd intuited the reasons for her reticence and her silence. A large number of the events I will relate from now on (and which didn't take place in my presence or in our house), I learned after her death from Lydia's accounts and from a small notebook I found hidden in the piano, where Mamma put down her thoughts. So it was relatively easy for me to reconstruct the facts.

A few days after the concert, Hervey declared his love to my mother. It must have been on the twenty-first of May, because in her notebook the date was underlined twice and everywhere on that page it said in her handwriting, tall and supple as a ribbon, *Ti amo, Eleonora.*

After that date, she noted their romantic walks: "Villa Celimontana," "saw an almond tree on the Palatine Hill," "Hadrian's Villa," "irises on the Appian Way." A petal from one of the irises was pressed between the pages and I wore it around my neck in one of Nonna Editta's reliquaries.

It was the only jewelry of hers I had left. My mother had abandoned almost all her pupils and from the moment she met Hervey, I discovered later, she had no further desire to be paid by the Pierce family. At the end of each month she gave her husband an envelope, as she had for years: it was the price of her freedom during the day. She paid it punctually, perhaps with some scorn.

"Here's the money, Ariberto." Sista made many trips to the Monte di Pietà, and when my father opened his wife's drawers after her death, he found her red silk pouch and in it, apart from the reliquary, only a stack of pawn tickets held together by a pin.

AT THE END of June, my mother spoke to me plainly about her plans.

It was a hot Saturday. Papa had gone out dressed entirely in white with a light blue bow tie.

I was reading by the window, and my mother was sitting beside me in an armchair. She had recently let me read some novels and she had gradually started recommending them herself, sketching out a sort of ideal program for me.

I remember the day well. I was reading the story of Emma Bovary, a book my mother must have read several times, because it looked very worn and there were several underlined passages. Sometimes those passages revealed impulses and feelings she would never have dared reveal to me despite our confidence. Coming across those involuntary confessions as I followed the twists of the plot made me uneasy, and I was afraid I'd committed some serious indiscretion. Apart from anything else, I had not a shred of sympathy for Madame Bovary, even though my mother loved the character, and I didn't want to know the vague affinities she found in her, just as I didn't want to know what had led her to marry my father.

I was turning these thoughts over when my mother said, "I'm not going out today, Sandi. I need to speak to you."

Gratified, I turned to her. "Shall we stay here by the window?"

"Yes, of course." She smiled.

I pulled my chair over to hers and we stayed there, content and silent. I didn't even ask myself what she had in mind to tell me, although I had been surprised by the seriousness of her tone. I was pleased to be with her, in the circle of her gaze. I felt happiness running through me like a peaceful river. It was that way with Francesco when we first met.

After a while my mother looked outside and asked, "Sandi, would you like to leave here?"

A painful knot constricted my throat and my heart began to beat rapidly. I was afraid she wanted to send me away from her and was cajoling me with the idea of a trip.

"With you?" I instantly demanded.

"Of course with me."

"Oh, yes, Mamma, yes!" I exclaimed. And I quietly added, "Let's go away," as if urging her to perform some rash or wicked deed.

She didn't immediately reply, nor did she turn around. Her eyes reflected the sky visible through the open window.

Then she repeated it, whispering, "Let's go away!" From her tone of voice I realized that these words were her constant thought, an obsession, that she repeated the phrase at every moment: when she was awake at night in the big bed, when she went about the house. It lay behind every other thought, every other word she uttered. "Let's go away." In vain she shook her head to chase the words away, but they encircled her, buzzed around her, enveloped her; they were the very air she breathed: "Let's go away."

It must have been a relief to utter them aloud at last. It was like freeing herself, accepting them. "We'll cross the border, yes? to Switzerland, perhaps."

She seemed to be inventing a game, the way she did when I was a child, pretending to take me to the foreign cities where Nonna had performed.

"We'll live in the country, far from the city and the big apartment blocks, the crowded streets and trams that clatter all night. The minute we leave the house, there will be grass under our feet. And I'll have a grand piano, a whole room for the piano."

I played along with her. I liked throwing all my hopes—those I thought I'd never fulfill—into this plan for our future life.

"I'll go out for a walk," I told her, "and come back home through the woods, guided by the sound of your piano as if by the Star of Bethlehem."

She nodded. "That's right. And in the winter, everything will be buried in snow, our house, too. We'll stay inside with the piano and our books and we'll light a big fire in the fireplace."

She went on speaking quietly. Landscapes and days unfolded in my imagination as at the theatre. And I thought maliciously of Papa's coming home on the evening of our escape. He would call out for us in his sarcastic and impatient way, saying, *I'm hungry*, and asking *Is it ready?* But he'd be greeted by a silence that would amplify his words. *Eleonora!* he'd call, *Alessandra!* I heard his voice, first vexed, then angry, and finally anguished. I saw him throwing open the door of the rooms where the dark furniture was waiting to suffocate and oppress him as it had my mother for so many years.

"Sandi . . ."

"Mamma . . ."

We fell silent. Then she turned and gave me a serious look, inviting me to step out of the fantasy world those images had created around us.

"Sandi," she said, "we won't be alone."

"Oh, Mamma!" I replied with a smile. "I never thought we'd leave without him."

Her hand covered mine and squeezed it hard, as if she wanted to let me into her feelings and problems.

"It's a very serious matter," she said.

"You can't live here," I protested eagerly, "you've got to—"

She interrupted me. "It's a very serious matter," she repeated. "I want you to understand that. It's something a mother should never dare speak to her own daughter about, to a girl. But the truth is (and maybe this is one of my faults), I have never thought of you as a daughter, and I don't believe I've ever treated you like one. I've always treated you as a woman, from the moment you were born, and I've been with you day by day, consoling you, encouraging you, knowing, myself, how difficult it is to be a woman, since a woman never really has a childhood. She's already a woman from the time she's a few years old and barely knows how to speak. Maybe I've done wrong. I'm afraid I have, because with my having done this, you've grown up weak and defenseless like me. When you were very small, I liked to imagine that you were a boy, like Alessandro, and then . . . Then one day I saw you sitting here by the window. You were only a few years old and I asked you what you were doing, if you weren't bored there all alone. 'No,' you replied, 'I'm very happy.' And then I remembered a window I used to sit at for hours when I lived with my mamma and papa in Belluno. I understood the meaning of early solitude. I knew you would suffer, that many things would hurt you, but that—oh!—others would be a source of pride. Because in you, as there is in every woman, there was a chance to show yourself to be a remarkable, marvelous being, a thing of grace and harmony, like a beautiful tree or a star. In other words, a woman. A woman, Sandi, is the entire universe, has the whole world in her, in her womb: the sun and the seasons, and the sky that spans the fields and cities . . ." She paused before continuing. "I don't know how we came to be talking about all this . . . What was I just saying? My mind is muddled . . ."

"You were saying that we were going to leave soon," I prompted.

Suddenly, my mother got up. I watched her walk back and forth in the room, seemingly unable to contain her impatience. She wrung her hands, looked at the walls, the furniture, the signs of her monotonous life, her uneventful days. "Away . . . away . . ." she murmured, already feeling safe from the snare these rooms had represented for years, their inexorable grip like quicksand. "Away . . . away . . ." She opened the door of the living room, letting out the stale odor the armchairs from Abruzzo had never lost. "Away!" She shouted it like an insult into the empty darkness of the room. She began to twirl around lightly. "Away!" she said in a singing voice. "Away! . . ." All of a sudden she stopped. "And Sista?" She stood there, uncertain. Finally she decided. "Quick, go and call her."

I found her in the kitchen doing the mending.

"Come," I whispered, taking her by the arm. "Come, come."

My mother went up to her animatedly. "Listen," she said, "we're leaving, and you're coming with us."

"Where?" she asked, dumbfounded.

"What does it matter to you where? You're coming with us."

"It's a lovely place," I said. "With trees, cows, pastures. You'll see. We're going there, do you understand? The three of us . . . We're going away, away, away!"

Intoxicated, my mother once more began to twirl gracefully around the room, her hands opening and closing, softly waving goodbye. She turned to us and held us in an embrace.

"Oh, my dears," she murmured, "my dears, my . . ." She then confided that we'd be leaving very soon.

FOR TWO WEEKS, my mother made no reference to our escape plan. But I noticed that, as she was leaving, she embraced me even more tenderly than usual in reassurance. "I'll be back soon, sweetheart," she said in an affectionate and excited tone, as if she meant "Be patient just a little longer."

This secret anticipation kept me in a constant state of excitement, which I found difficult to control. I was afraid someone would notice my unusual chattiness, or the uncharacteristic liveliness animating my every gesture, although the summer, the long days, and vacations had rendered the other inhabitants of our building newly euphoric. In the courtyard, the plants had flowered, and the laundry hanging out to dry, stirred by a keen wind, was fluttering, snapping, and waving cheerfully. Curtains swelled like sails at open windows. Winter clothes had been beaten spitefully and buried in trunks. Women, cheered by new dresses, spoke in brighter tones, their confidence revived. Our gray apartment block grew lively and loud, and in the afternoons it breathed through its open windows. The shoemaker's hammer pounded quickly and with renewed vigor, and the porter's wife sat contentedly at the entrance while the tenants' little girls played around her with earrings made of cherries.

Fulvia and I often went out together, our steps matching in a brisk, youthful rhythm. We had intimate talks, whispering in each other's ears, laughing at little or nothing at all. In summer the whole neighborhood was pierced by the sound of swallows—no other neighborhood in Rome knows their voice as well as Prati. Very early, just after sunrise, they begin chasing each other, swooping high, joyfully. They shriek, daring us to join them in the hazy blue of the sky. In the evening, though, they plunge down to the streets, grazing windows and squawking in desperate voices, trying to avoid the dangers of night. Then, when it gets dark, they suddenly fall silent, like the instruments in an orchestra at a sign from the conductor. That's when Fulvia and I would hurry back to our big building, where many families were already eating supper, at dusk, to save on lighting.

Dario often came with us. We never set an exact time. *Are you going out?* he'd signal to Fulvia from the window opposite. *Yes*, she'd reply. We'd go out, but we couldn't see Dario. Soon, however, we'd find him on our street, and in a different spot every day. He would wait for us on the sidewalk, smoking, and watch us approach with slow, indifferent glances.

"Ciao," Fulvia would say. And he would start walking with us.

He was a thin young man with a fox's sharp chin. His features were fairly common, but deep blue eyes ennobled his broad forehead. He walked beside us quietly, often running his hand nervously through his straight, untidy hair in a vain attempt to smooth it. His silence annoyed Fulvia, who had been looking forward to a pleasant and cheerful afternoon. So she'd talk on a wide variety of subjects, trying to rouse some interest in the young man, often with little success. At first I didn't understand what pleasure she derived from being with him. Yet as time went on it seemed to me, too, that Dario's moody silence was preferable to the empty swagger of other boys our age. They seemed determined to discover who they really were and pretended, through various strange behaviors, to have unique personalities. And yet they were all so alike it was truly staggering: they dressed the same way and used a jargon when they spoke, like soldiers or sailors. I found it difficult to get used to this language, but Fulvia was an expert.

From time to time I'd ask someone, "What are you going to do when you grow up?" They all answered sarcastically, and I felt uncomfortable, as I had when my classmates at the co-ed school made fun of me for getting high grades.

"We're all going to kick the bucket," they said to me once. "Even you, with your A in Latin."

"You're girls," Dario said with an affectionate look, instead of his usual apathy. "You can't understand all this. It's not easy to talk about these things with you."

"Why?" I asked him, offended by the difference he was trying to establish between us.

"What does he know?" Fulvia said. "What does he know about *why*?"

They all seemed lost, sad and lonely. But, instead of complaining about it, they feigned self-sufficiency and claimed to need no support, whether from friendship or love. They pretended a cold cynicism, a pointless cruelty, and all of it was fake. One bragged that he had plucked the feathers off a live goldfinch his sister kept in a cage. Everyone laughed, even Fulvia, and sweet, plump Maddalena. I shuddered, and protested against his stupid maliciousness.

"Why did you do that?" I asked vehemently. "Aren't you ashamed of yourself? You disgust me."

The others laughed and kept on walking, but I realized that they were embarrassed and they moved off, leaving us alone. Claudio (that was the boy's name) was still attempting a feeble laugh.

"How could you do that?" I insisted. It was gradually growing darker. The others could no longer hear us. We were walking down a wide boulevard in the Monte Mario neighborhood and you could hear the birds singing.

"What else should I do?" Claudio finally answered, irritated. I sensed that he wanted to let out his anger, his secret powerlessness. "I'm vile enough to take it out on those who are weaker than me."

"What's going on?" I asked affectionately. "What's wrong?"

He turned to look at me, amazed by my interest in him. He seemed to be taking the measure of me for a moment, wondering if he could trust me.

"I don't know," he said. Then, fearing I'd mistake his reticence for a lack of sincerity, he added, "I really don't know, Alessandra." He repeated it, taking my arm. His was thin, rough, and knobbly, and his hands were too big for his height. He was wearing a white mesh shirt with a jacket over his shoulders. An acrid odor of sweat and skin that probably wasn't very clean came from him, as it did from all the boys we knew. I supposed that in a hurry to leave the house he barely washed in the morning. Instead of putting me off, that smell endeared him to me, mixed as it was with the bitter scent of his cheap cigarettes.

"You're not happy, are you?" I asked quietly, looking into the distance as I did when silently speaking to Antonio.

"No," he replied in the same quiet, controlled voice. "How can a person be happy?" There was nothing wrong with what we were saying, and yet I noticed Claudio looking around. On our right, a bed of reeds rose tall and straight; the leaves, moved by the wind, rustled as if some-one were hidden in there, listening. On our left were large workers' housing blocks; the windows on the yellow façades were close together and the clothes hanging out to dry were touching, so that the residents of every floor were allied with one another.

"How can we be happy?" he asked. "You can't talk to anyone. This is the first time I've spoken, Alessandra, and already I feel better, as though a weight has been lifted. Maybe you can only talk openly with a woman. I can't take it anymore."

I lowered my voice again and leaned against him as we walked. But it was actually he who was leaning against me, as my father had leaned on me the night of the concert. Claudio was three years older and already looked like a man. His was my first friendship with a person of the opposite sex. I wished I could rest with him, hand over the weight of my doubts and uncertainties, be consoled by him. But he got there before me, and it was no longer possible. It was never, ever possible to be weak, my God, not even for a moment. From that moment on, I had to learn to be the shoulder to lean on, the hand that supports, the voice that consoles. Only here, today, have I found rest; yet I feared I'd never be able to rest again.

So we were walking side by side, and Claudio was leaning on me. I had the impression that other couples were walking behind us, pretend-ing the same loving abandon but trying instead to support each other, man and woman, to form a solid bulwark against an unknown danger threatening from every side.

"Did you know Aida's brother?" I asked him.

"Yes."

"He's in prison."

"I know," Claudio said quietly. And he immediately continued, with a vein of contempt in his voice. "It's cowardice, like plucking the feath-ers off a goldfinch, like jumping out of a window. It's cowardice, trust me, Alessandra: a revolution is easy—five minutes is all you need.

Afterwards, you're already a hero, and in prison all you have to do is get used to orders, to reflection, to inner peace. You need courage to keep living day after day with a father who doesn't understand you, a mother who nags you—to live, look, behind one of those windows—" he gestured towards one of the big yellow buildings—"go to school, stay quiet, go to the office, stay quiet, never ask for anything, never revolt, and face the easy life, which gradually ensnares you and sweeps you along with it."

We were walking behind our friends and we could hear them talking and laughing a short distance away. Claudio held me close and asked, "Do you care for me, Alessandra?"

"Yes, I care for you," I replied.

"Do you love me?" he asked quietly. And he pressed his rough arm against mine, wanting to make us a single entity.

I hung my head, embarrassed to back out of helping him. I wished I could say yes. Fulvia would have in my place. His person elicited such spontaneous sympathy in me, but more than anything I wanted to be sincere, and I didn't think what I felt was love. I knew how Mamma's face changed when she came home after seeing Hervey.

I didn't answer, and we walked on in silence until our friends stopped, so we could all go home together.

THAT SAME EVENING, my mother took my hand in the dark passageway near the kitchen and said in a low voice, "I'm going to speak to Papa later, to tell him we're leaving. Stay with us and don't leave me unless I ask you to."

She'd taken on a serious, hard look, as if carrying out a firm resolution. But in the past few days, she'd been acting more submissive than usual, meek, controlling those fanciful impulses that were intrinsic to her appearance. Sometimes I was afraid she'd given up on her cherished plan. But I hoped she was only trying to pretend she was a woman like other women—defeated, subdued, someone you can trust.

"Be brave," I said, grazing her cheek with a kiss.

We ate lunch. My father talked about the usual things. He wound his spaghetti around his fork with his usual fastidiousness, and I was amazed that he didn't guess what was about to happen, didn't feel the shifty atmosphere we were all moving in. But he was so cocooned in his own selfishness that nothing could have got to him.

"Ridiculous!" he would always say if you mentioned someone who was suffering emotionally. And if it was a woman he'd add, "She should go knit a sock."

Sista cleared the plates and glasses. My mother and father sat there, facing each other, separated by the white tablecloth. With one sweep of her hand, my mother brushed the breadcrumbs from the tablecloth—she seemed to want everything to be neat and uncluttered between them. When her husband moved as if to get up, she detained him with a look. "Just a moment, Ariberto. I have something to tell you."

He hovered in the room, trying to work out his wife's intentions. Reluctantly, he turned back to the table and asked suspiciously, "What's going on?"

My mother remained very calm. She folded her hands on the tablecloth, which was now free of all crumbs, and said: "In a few days I'll be leaving with Alessandra."

We had never gone on a journey. Our old-fashioned wicker and cardboard suitcases sat on top of a wardrobe.

"You're leaving?" he asked, feigning amused surprise. "And where are you going, if I may ask?"

"We're going away," my mother said calmly. "We're leaving."

There was a silence. I'd pulled my chair close to hers and we both stared at him gravely.

"We don't want to stay in this house any longer."

"What's wrong with this house? It's comfortable and the rent is reasonable. What do you have against this house?"

My mother hesitated, hoping he would understand without further explanation—just from her look—and she'd escape an unpleasant duty.

Finally she said, "We don't want to stay with you any longer."

He looked uncertain, trying to judge the seriousness of our words. We were sitting side by side, and I felt he must have seen two Eleonoras against him, equally firm, equally resolute, both expressing, with their entire being, the desire to leave him.

But after looking back and forth at us several times, he burst out laughing. He fell back in his chair with a hateful laugh. "Ha-ha," he said. "Ha-ha," and he looked at us as if we had said something really clever and funny. "Ha-ha. You don't want to stay with me, so . . ."

My mother was pale. "Please don't do that. This is a serious matter."

He kept laughing. The evening was humid and the windows were open; the wall of the house opposite seemed closer because of the heat. I was afraid that everyone in our building, in all the nearby buildings, in the street would hear my father's laugh and come knocking on our door, curious to discover the reason for his irrepressible hilarity. We— and the anxiety upsetting our lives—were the cause.

"And how will you live?" he asked suddenly. He stopped laughing and feigned a cheerful and kindly curiosity. "How will you live?"

This made him confident of his power once again: the yellow envelope the government gave him on the twenty-seventh of every month. He considered that his money gave him the right not only to treat us as landladies or servants but to laugh at us, without asking himself what lay behind our decision.

"Eh? Tell me: how are you going to live?" he insisted.

"I've always earned," my mother replied. "And I know I can earn even more."

"By giving concerts?" he suggested sarcastically.

"Yes, with concerts, too."

Papa started laughing again, and his shirt fell open on his strong, hairy chest. Our words didn't even graze his thick hide. Sure of himself, he made no effort to dissuade us from our plans. Rather, he pointed to the door, only a few steps away. All we had to do was open it to be free, and yet we were glued to the white tablecloth. He laughed.

"It's a serious matter, Ariberto," my mother repeated, trying to find a way between the pauses in his laughter. "We've made up our minds."

Then he decided that the game had gone on long enough. He stopped laughing abruptly and sat up in his chair. His tone changed.

"You two are insane." He looked harshly from her to me. "Insane," he repeated. "You need a rest cure, something for your nerves, a bromide. I've said so before, but there's something wrong with you—" he put his finger to his temple and made the gesture of tightening a screw—"here," he said, looking at us sarcastically. "Here."

"Don't do that, Ariberto!" my mother burst out. "Don't use that gesture, please!"

"Bromide," he repeated.

He got up and left the room without another word. We heard the familiar sound of the key turning in the lock.

THE DAYS THAT followed were difficult. Even our friendship with the Celantis resembled the affectionate solidarity, the intimate and sympathetic understanding that binds victims of a persecuted minority. Sometimes Mamma would come to my room in the afternoon while I was doing my homework and, for no reason, suggest I stop studying right then and go up to visit Fulvia. If I resisted, realizing that it was a pretext for her to be alone with Papa, she'd give me an imploring look: *Please, Sandi, go upstairs.*

When I showed up, the Celantis realized that Mamma had sent me so that I wouldn't witness some painful and dramatic discussion, and, right away, they gave me their loving attention. One evening I heard Lydia calling the Captain to tell him she couldn't go out because of Eleonora. I wanted to ask her to pay no attention to me, but my desire not to be alone was stronger. We'd sit on the bed, barely talking, doing nothing. waiting for the time to go by, and waiting together seemed easier. Tense and alert, we jumped at the least sound of a voice, at every noise, ready to run to the rescue. During our agonizing wait, we, too, struggled against my father with the logic of women, which men cannot understand.

One day, as soon as I came in, Lydia, somewhat agitated, announced: "She's telling him everything today."

"About what?"

"About Hervey."

I wasn't very happy about that. I feared that one loud laugh from my father could crumple, sully, and even destroy the gentle fairytale that I, too, was living through her.

"We have to speak frankly, at a certain point," said Lydia. "We can't do otherwise."

"Right," I admitted, "but not with Papa. He won't understand anything."

"On the contrary—precisely for that reason," Lydia replied. "We have to think about the law."

"What does the law have to do with it? This is all about feelings."

"Oh!" Lydia exclaimed. "The law never considers women's feelings."

"So then," I went on, "how can we make a law that's truly just when it leaves out the most important thing for us?"

"But that's how it is," Lydia said.

"And for men, Mamma?" Fulvia asked after a pause.

"It's different. With men, one never talks about feelings, only the need they have to . . . how can I put it? It's hard to explain . . ."

"You mean to go to bed with a woman?" Fulvia asked baldly.

"That's it."

There was such a revolt in me, such profound disgust that I dared to blurt out, "And instead the law concerns itself with those things?"

"Yes," Lydia replied, "for men, yes."

My cheeks flamed. "Maybe we can do without those things. It's difficult, but I believe one can." I thought about Enea and didn't look at my friends as I spoke. "But how can we do without feelings?" I asked, anguished.

Fulvia and Lydia didn't respond. A little later Lydia explained how the law worked, and the different meaning the word *faithfulness* has for men and women. She also told me that my mother had decided to admit to her husband that she was in love with Hervey, that she'd never been his lover, and that she wanted to leave precisely so she could behave honestly and spend a life with him made up of shared tastes and aspirations.

While she was speaking I began to cry. I hadn't cried for a long time, maybe years. My mother had made sure that I was a happy child. She'd taught me to be content with just a few material things and to feel rich in all the others. I honestly don't remember ever having cried as a child— only once, when I was a little older than eleven, I was afraid I was really ill. I confided in Sista because I didn't want Mamma to worry about me. And she told me I wasn't ill; all she said was that I was now a woman. Without asking for further explanation I left Sista and went to my room. I lay down on my special refuge, the little bed wedged between the wardrobes, and the knot of painful humiliation I had inside released itself in tears.

"Something should be done for women," said Fulvia. "Dario says it will happen in time."

"In time!" Lydia exclaimed. "Every woman waits for this time to come and meanwhile her life goes by, it's over."

"But Dario insists that in time something will be done. In America, women can vote and be members of Congress."

I threw myself on the bed, quietly sobbing. The crying did me good. Fulvia kept talking and I shook my head, signaling for her to stop. I hardly knew what the words "vote" and "member of Congress" meant, and I felt no desire to be one, but I didn't want this talk of doing something for women as if they were inferior, damaged beings. I wanted us to be allowed to live according to our shadowy and delicate nature, as men are allowed to live with their strength and self-confidence. *No*, I said, shaking my head, it wasn't necessary to do something for us. We, like men, simply by virtue of having been born, should also have the right to be respected for our existence.

I cried and they let me cry. Lydia patted me on the back, and that was the only comfort she could give me. I took her soft, plump hand and kissed it with grateful tenderness. Finally she said, "They must be done by now," and I went back down. It was dark.

I went to the kitchen, where Sista was ironing in the faint yellow lamplight. She looked up as I came in, and I gestured as if to say, *Where are they?*

"He went out," she replied.

"And Mamma?"

"In her room, in the dark. She'll be on the bed. She closed the door and turned the key."

I got a chair and sat by the table, where Sista was still ironing industriously. The iron, going back and forth, threw scorching heat at me. She was ironing one of my father's shirts, with its awkward long sleeves. Although she was expert with the iron, Sista couldn't master those long sleeves.

"What happened?" I asked her.

"I don't know. Your father yelled, your mother kept crying."

"Why?"

She hesitated a bit before replying, "I don't know."

"You're lying, Sista. I'm sure you couldn't resist and you went to the door to listen. What did they say?" I pushed her.

After a pause, she quietly confessed. "I couldn't hear much—your mother was speaking softly. He said, 'You'll get over it,' and she cried and said, 'That's impossible. I'll never get over it, as long as I live.' His answer was that women are—"

"What are they?"

"He said, 'They're all sluts.'"

"He said that to Mamma?"

"Yes," Sista answered, her head low as she kept ironing. "And then he said, 'You'll stay here, in this house.'"

"Anything else?"

"I don't know. He was pacing the room and I was afraid he'd catch me."

The iron went back and forth over my father's big shirt. Sista was quiet, and I no longer had the strength to question her. I stared at the shirt, eyes wide, blinded by its whiteness. I had no desire even to move, to go and comfort my mother. I looked at Sista and in her still face and inexpressive eyes, I read the ancient habit of obedience.

"What can we do, Sista?" I'd asked her one night, and her reply: "What can you do? He's her husband." "It's their business," she said another day, "stuff for people who are married and have to spend their lives together. Life is long."

I didn't want to resign myself, and yet, dismayed, I noticed that I was already abandoning my mother. I was leaving her alone, plunged deep into anguish and exhausted by crying, while I stayed there watching Sista iron. In the lamplight, the large shirt (with its round neckhole, the wrists, the shape of the shoulders) looked like a man, alive, invasive, stretched out in front of us in all the expanse of his body: self-important, self-assured. We cared for him and served him, tending to his person. I saw the black iron, like a black angry leech, slide slowly over the white shirt as if over tense, bruised skin. Sista pushed the iron under the collar, already stiff with ironing, so the fabric would stand firm there, too. Sho pushed it repeatedly, insistently, doggedly, and it was as though the black beast wanted to attach itself to the neck and suck out all the blood. Suddenly, with those harsh, stinging blows, I discovered a secret desire.

"You must teach me to iron, Sista."

Her head jerked up and she looked at me, afraid she'd been caught in her crime. She studied me, her gaunt face devoured by her staring eyes. Maybe she wished she could deny it. But after a moment she began pushing the sharp black iron into the fragile whiteness of the collar.

"Yes," she said softly. "It's something all women need to know how to do."

SO IT WAS that July 12th arrived, the eighteenth anniversary of my brother's death. For many years now, my mother and I had gone to the river by ourselves on that day. My father had grown tired of the ritual that, once the initial searing pain passed, must have seemed pointless to him, even grotesque.

"I can't go today," he said the first time, as we got ready to leave in our black dresses. "I have some important business." He offered the excuse awkwardly, as if he were covering up something terrible. But we knew very well that he never had important business. The following year he found a different excuse. After that, he never said anything.

On the morning of July 12th, my mother sent for Ottavia early. At this stage, Ottavia was coming quite frequently, though my father had never seen her. When she entered, with her lame yet determined step, the entire house fell under her power.

Even Enea was kept out of the sitting room on those days: he would sit in the kitchen with Sista, waiting for the supernatural talk to end. I imagined that all his days were spent like that, going from one kitchen to another, taking from house to house that serious, absorbed manner, which he deliberately maintained. If the visit went on for very long, Sista would offer him a piece of bread and a little cheese. He kept his gloomy expression while he ate, as if not even eating could cheer him up in that moment. He would stuff one bite in after another, silently, clasping the threadbare purse containing herbs and amulets between his knees.

At those times, he didn't dare glance at me with the slimy desire that often shone in his eyes. He was totally absorbed in the slow, greedy act of feeding himself, and his hidden animality was consumed in biting, chewing, and swallowing. His hunger and his humiliating vagabond life ended up inspiring a sort of pity in me. The passage of time had hardly changed him. His body had remained squat under his large head, and the cunning look on his face had already hardened with adult experience. He always wore black.

"I've had some manifestations," he told me on July 12th. "I saw a face appear on the wall, and one night I clearly heard a voice telling me *Write!*"

"So you, too, have chosen this as your occupation?" I asked.

"It's not an occupation," he corrected, "it's a calling."

Sista went off to spy behind the door of the living room, and he took advantage of her absence to hold my hand. The contact with his skin disturbed me deeply, and I was angry at the thought that it was a man like him who was causing that uncontrollable yearning in me. Clients would slip a small tip for him into the bag where he kept the herbs and amulets—a few lire, maybe some eggs, a piece of bread. But he wasn't mortified by his subservient situation. On the contrary, he wanted to continue accepting alms for the rest of his life, even though he was strong and healthy and could easily tackle some other trade.

"Let me go!" I pushed his hand away. "I'm leaving soon, did you know? I'm getting out of here. You and your aunt will never see me again in this house. This may be the last time we see each other," I said with a touch of spite.

Enea smiled obnoxiously. "Don't think about that. Think about me now," he said as he tried to slide his hand into the opening of my blouse.

I pushed him away with a shove. Suddenly, as if she were coming to my aid, I heard Mamma leave the living room, drawing the curtain rings back in an arpeggio.

We embraced in the darkened entrance. Her face was bright, wild.

"Today *he'll* be at the river, too," she told me.

•   •   •

WE WENT TO the river toward sunset, climbing down to the shore. The Lungotevere wasn't deserted anymore, as it had been when I was a child; beyond the Risorgimento Bridge a row of miserable tenements, green, yellow and blue, rose and stretched almost to the Milvio Bridge. Yet down on the pebbly shore everything was peaceful and intact. The tall reeds the child had pushed through to play were still there, and the grass was soft and green, starred with daisies.

My mother walked to the water's edge and leaned over the current, throwing flowers into it. She then sat by the reeds, her gaze fixed on the river. The wind blew through her hair, and her slender form seemed to sway with the reeds.

Beloved! I said to her internally, with a furious passion.

She didn't look at me, intent on the wind rustling through the sharp blades of the reedbed.

"Do you hear him?" she murmured. "It's him."

I lay back on the grass, and its coolness dampened my neck. A magical zone of peace and silence enclosed us; we couldn't hear any voices or screeching. Above me was the great arc of sky, at my side the Tiber flowed tranquil and lazy. I felt Alessandro truly present in that moment, swirling around us, boundless, in a great mantle of air: and he who was dead and we who were alive were a single soft current. The moon was sketched faintly in the sky, and I felt I could dislodge it with a flick of my finger. *Goodbye, Enea, goodbye*, I said. The current dragged me along, distancing me from the harshness of life.

"Mamma, we'll be leaving soon, won't we?" I asked with a smile.

"I don't know," she replied softly, adding, "I don't think so. Don't think about leaving, Sandi. Don't think about it anymore."

I felt uncertain, and waited for her to turn around and laugh at me, as she often did, making fun of my credulity. But this time she remained serious and still. I was afraid that she might vanish in a moment, that she'd chosen that place of sweet solitude in order to abandon me.

Frozen with terror, I sat up and cried, "Oh, Mamma, don't leave without me!"

She turned, startled by my tone. Looking at me with great tenderness, she said, "No, Sandi, don't be afraid. I could never leave without you. That's the reason I told you not to think about our departure anymore." After a pause she explained, "Papa doesn't want to let us go. He said, 'Go if you want, but you have to leave my daughter here.'"

"Me?" I exclaimed, surprised. "Why is that? We have nothing to say to each other, nothing in common."

"Yes, I know. But he says, 'The law is on my side.'"

She turned quickly to stare at the river, her face crumpling with sadness. She must have been speaking to Alessandro, staying on with him, and I suddenly felt like an outsider in their conversation because of what I carried of my father in me, which Alessandro had renounced with his death. I had some similarities to Papa—some said my hands were like his, others, my teeth—and not even my boundless love for my mother could obliterate these signs which the law allowed him to claim.

Soon my mother stood up, and we climbed the stairs and set off toward home. The Lungotevere was crowded. It was Sunday and families walked in silence, brutalized by constantly living together. They looked at passersby with interest, hoping to find some distraction in their faces. They walked slowly along the banks of the Tiber, the boundary and the pride of their neighborhood. Some young men pushed bicycles, others supported a woman's amorous abandonment. We walked past the houses where we went to rest when our bodies were tired, or to eat when the tangle of our guts asked for food; the rooms retained the odor of our skin, of our sweat, of the food we ate. On the Lungotevere Mellini you could see old apartment blocks like ours, where for years great numbers of people had been born, married, and died. They all looked alike, as if their genes had run a relay race across generations. I wanted to protest but something held me back: perhaps the sad and benevolent looks of the people going by, or the pity instilled in me by the calm pace at which they went about their obscure business.

My mother kept me close to her, as if together we were fording a dense current. Consumed with anguish, I considered myself mean and selfish: although I loved my mother, loved her desperately, I didn't have the strength to sacrifice myself to let her go. I didn't love her as I'd always believed one should love. And yet it would have taken so little: opening my hand to give flight to a butterfly.

"Mamma," I said, "leave without me." I spoke casually, as if suggesting something of no importance while people walked between us, separating us.

"No," she replied in the same manner. "It's not possible."

Silence followed. One of my classmates walked by. "Ciao," she said. I smiled and replied, "Ciao."

Then my mother took my arm so that no one could separate us, and began speaking quietly, as if to herself.

"I can't leave you," she said. "What I want to do is beautiful, and it would turn into something ugly if I did that. I tried to speak frankly with your father. I was hoping he'd understand, but he didn't."

"He can't understand."

Darkness was falling. The trees were already thick with shadows. My mother stopped and we looked over the parapet. Behind us, people kept walking by slowly.

"Let's leave, Mamma," I insisted. "Let's leave now, this instant, and not go home. Papa won't suffer, I assure you. Sista will stay with him. She'll make him his lunch and dinner, and she'll tend to his clothes. What else does he want from us? I'm sure he won't lift a finger to find us."

"I don't know. Maybe you're right. But it would be nasty, and very disloyal. I don't want to act disloyally. The whole pattern of my life would be unraveled by that, and then there would be no point to the rest, you see?"

People kept walking past us. We heard a woman's voice asking, "Gigino, are you hungry?"

"It would all become pointless," my mother resumed, "even love. And not because I'm incapable of breaking a strict rule. Oh, no! Believe me Sandi, that's not how it is—and maybe that's bad. I've already told you: it's bad. But I couldn't get used to a life that was spiritually mediocre or a mediocre love. What good is mediocre love? The street is full of it," she said. "Turn around and look behind us. Many of these people won't ask themselves a single one of my questions. They have an easy life, day after day, never questioning why they're here on this earth, or the meaning of their deeds and actions. They're the ones who wanted these inhumane laws, but they're also the first to try and get around them, with small compromises and acts of cowardice."

I stared at the dark river, saying nothing. I wanted to ask her if she really believed that others had an easy life or if a deep and exhausting, inconsolable suffering was inherent in all life. But I was fascinated by her, enchanted by the sight of her gestures as they blossomed, by the harmony of her words.

She continued, "I've often asked myself which side is right: theirs or mine? It seems to me that I was born abnormal, like people with two heads or six fingers. I've tried to adapt to their compromises. Then I was convinced that I was the one who was right. I am right. We're right. But they're stronger."

We heard them walking behind us, and some of them grazed us as they passed. They formed a strong, swollen stream that held us back as it slid by. We felt squeezed between two enemy rivers. In the Tiber, some of the reflected lights spread out, forming monstrous human faces before the current erased them. Beyond the massive wall opposite, all the lights in the city were lit and they called to us; it was like a happy island, while we sat in quarantine, unable to go ashore.

"It's very late," my mother said.

We went along Via degli Scipioni. The ancient plane trees on that street steal all the space, and their long branches, weighted with leaves and sleeping birds, embrace to block out the sky. The houses are tall and melancholy, and at night people look out of the ground-floor windows to catch the wisps of air that passes between the leaves and the mosquitoes. At some of the windows father, mother, and child sit in silence. Behind them you see dark, squalid interiors, and in their eyes is the melancholy memorialised in funerary monuments for entire families who have perished in some horrific disaster, a flood or a fire.

My mother and I felt those eyes on us, window after window. Pressed between the trees, the houses, and those looks, we felt we were walking down an endless, low stone tunnel with no light at the end. *They're stronger than we are*, I thought. And my mother thought so, too, because she quickly started running, with her beautiful, unmatched grace. She held my hand and only at crossings did she slow down, hoping to glimpse a light, some salvation. But whichever way we looked, we saw other streets, straight and inescapable, crowded with giant plane trees, gray houses, and windows.

HAVING ARRIVED AT this fairly advanced point in my confession, I fear that I haven't been completely sincere, as I set out to be. Oh, my God! Maybe it's happened; it *has* happened, I feel it, but how could I have done otherwise? For me, this is the only truth and there's no other apart from this one. I'm referring specifically to the profile I've sketched of my mother. I fear I've presented a fairy tale rather than a faithful account of her life. Maybe she wasn't always as perfect as I'm describing her, her gestures not always so ethereal, her tone of voice so harmonious. She may have said harsh things, or had unkind feelings, like all women.

But I don't remember any of that. In my memory, she has remained with her rare fairy tale of grace and innocence, with which I'd quietly like to align my own.

So it really was like that for me. I believe that the story we intend to leave behind is the secret motivation of our words and acts: you could say it's what we live for.

My mother was, for me, the finest example of womanhood. And the steeper the decline of my life, the more humiliating it was over the years, the more radiant her image became.

Our visit to the river left me troubled. I wished I could do something to repay my mother for everything she had, with her natural elegance, sacrificed for me. I was afraid that my boundless devotion wasn't enough to help her now. Sista may have feared the same, because we looked at each other, lost, and we had resumed our old habit of waiting for her at the window. Sista was growing pale and thin, like Mamma. It seemed as if she'd entrusted to Mamma the unexploited asset of her own repressed youth to spend as she liked. She saw herself living through my mother with the passionate energy she had always kept inside. When the signora went out, Sista, too, enjoyed a personal revenge, a rebellion, an escape. But immediately afterwards she'd repent of her impulse. She was restless until she saw Mamma come back into the house.

We were looking out the window and I observed her profile, as sharp as a medal. She had nice hairline, and, in her person over all, she had the plain and sober dignity of Sardinian women.

"How old are you, Sista?"

She turned around, surprised by my question.

"I don't know," she said. "You can figure it out. I was born in '99."

"Are you forty? Just a little older than Mamma?"

Without answering, Sista looked towards the end of the street at the trees on Via Cola di Rienzo. I inspected the hair on her temples: it was vigorous and rich, and suggested the image of a body still young, buried alive in black clothes and doubled over with the exhausting work of serving in a humble house like ours.

"Sista . . ." I came closer to embrace her.

"What's wrong with you?" she replied abrasively. "Be serious. Watch out. He'll be back soon. I don't understand," she murmured, shaking her head. "I don't understand what she's doing all day with that man . . ."

"I forbid you to speak of him in that way, do you understand?" I said, elbowing her hard. "He's not like other men."

Sista gave me a sidelong look full of compassion and then shook her head.

"All men are the same. They are a disgrace," she said softly, running a hand over her face, across her forehead, as if to ward off a bad feeling. "I don't see her yet," she murmured, squinting to make out my mother's cherished shape in the distance. "She's not here yet; I can't see her," she repeated, dismayed, and her arm shook on the cold marble window ledge.

As it happened, she came home after Papa did, indifferent to his reproaches. She went to bed early, without saying anything to me. It was Friday evening.

MY MOTHER WAS nervous when she got up the next day. "I couldn't sleep last night. I kept hearing Alessandro's voice calling me." She seemed disorientated and distressed.

"You shouldn't consult Ottavia anymore," I suggested gently.

"Why would you say that?" she responded sharply. "Are you against me now, too? Are you going to use the same words?"

I gave her an affectionate, chiding look. It was a sirocco day, without sun. The clouds, seen through the courtyard window, marched forward menacingly and the house seemed even darker than usual, warm and stuffy.

"The storm got under our skin. Let's calm down, Mamma." Meanwhile I was tidying, dusting, making an effort to contain my overpowering disquiet in precise actions. I'd suffered from changes in weather and climate since I was a child. My mood was subject to the wind and the sun, and even distant thunder could make me shiver, as though it were rolling up my back.

"I wish I could calm down," I said, "and stay balanced. I tried to study this morning as soon as I woke up, but I couldn't."

My mother drew me close, looking into my face as if in a mirror.

"I hope you'll forgive me," she said. "It's my fault. I got it all wrong. I should at least have saved you." She gave me a searching look before squeezing my shoulders and adding, "You must save yourself. You have a hidden strength I lack."

I looked at her, not wanting it to be true. And yet there was in me, and still is, the tenacity of my Abruzzese ancestors, the strength of those who are used to struggling alone against the snares of the soul and of nature. She could see this in me, and she almost envied it. But she didn't know that, unbeknownst to me, I, like many people of that land, also had a taste for the long-held grudge and impulsive violence, and an inability to forgive.

"I begged your father—all night—to let us leave. I begged him all night. I shouldn't talk to you about these things." She looked away. "But you need to know. I was hoping to wear down his stubbornness. I told him: 'I believe there's a moment in marriage—maybe only one—when it's necessary to be friends, the way two strangers would be.' Don't you think so?"

"There should be."

"Yes . . ." After a pause, she continued, more softly. "And yet he didn't want to understand. He just said, 'I'm going to ask to be transferred to a small town near my family in Abruzzo so your whims will pass.' He actually said 'whims.' I said, 'I won't go.' And he insisted, 'Yes, you will.' He repeated it over and over. 'You'll come, you'll come, you'll come.' And he wasn't saying it to help me; he was saying it as if he were throwing a rock. 'Your place is here!' he repeated. I looked around. Oh no, Sandi, I shouldn't be telling you all this . . ."

"Go on, Mamma. Go on."

"I looked around and saw the big black wardrobe, the black chest, furniture from his town, furniture that has intimidated me from the start. When I walked into that room, just married, I felt I'd been walled up in a tomb alive. There's a secret mismatch between them and me, a struggle that's been going on for years. You may not believe it, but I've been obsessed with that furniture, which for years has not wanted me here, has wanted to get rid of me. I've tried laughing, singing, letting down my hair as if to destroy some spell. But when I sit in front of the mirror on the dressing table to comb my hair, it reflects the large portrait of his dead sister, the one hanging beside our bed."

"Aunt Caterina?"

"Yes. It was her dressing table, and she's still its mistress. Every day, her mirror sends back an image of my face: tense, distorted, full of knots: it's a criticism, you see? A quarrel between her life and mine. There's a lot you don't know. Caterina was a strong, hard woman. Her husband left her when she was very young and went to live with a peasant woman in a nearby village. She refused to be seen as wounded or defeated by this, and she never, even for one day, admitted the truth: that is, that she'd been abandoned. Maybe because she didn't want to feel belittled, not even by herself. Though everyone knew what had happened, right after he left she explained that her husband had gone to America, where a good job was waiting for him. She pretended to receive letters, even money orders and cash, and she appeared to be proud of her husband's elevated position in America. Meanwhile, his lover went about the village, often pregnant with one of their many children. But this did nothing to discourage Caterina's proud behavior. The whole village admired her. Ariberto always holds her up to me as an example. She died young and wanted to maintain her courageous lie till the end. In her final moments, the priest told her that God would reward the strength she had shown throughout her ordeal. He believed he was comforting her, but Caterina, scowling, summoned the scant sight she had left. 'What ordeal?' she asked. She didn't even want God's compassion. She was such a strong woman. I see her in the corners of the room, her mouth twisted in a miserable grimace." Pale and frightened, she looked around. I felt her reason wavering.

"Mamma, calm down," I said. "Calm down, please!"

"I'm not that strong, Sandi. I have no strength left, none, none at all."

Her entire life lit up in her eyes in an unforgettable expression. "I love him," she confessed in a whisper, exhausted.

I looked at her then with loving compassion. What strength could my mother have at that moment?

"Get out of this place," I said. "Go to Villa Pierce. Leave with Hervey, Mamma. I'll stay."

It was the first time I'd said his name. I said it calmly. I remember how calm I was. While we talked, I polished a dark, old paperweight for which I'd always had a particular aversion. It showed a hunchback holding a thirteen. I wanted to make it clean and shiny. I wanted to find the strength to go on living there, patiently, polishing other hateful objects. To free her.

"No," she replied, "I can't do that." Her face grew even paler and she added, "I have to give him up." She pulled away from me as if she wanted to go and talk to him right there and then.

She took the raincoat hanging in the hallway and threw it over her shoulders, calling out to me.

"Sandi? Alessandra . . ."

I ran to her. We clasped each other in a desperate embrace.

"Leave!" I whispered. "Don't come back, Mamma. Leave!"

She didn't reply. She felt fragile in my embrace, staring into space, her face softly illuminated.

She seemed convinced. I was the one who pushed her out the door. "Go, go!" I urged her, and I was completely frozen inside, a solid block of loneliness and terror.

"Go!"

I watched her disappear down the storm-darkened stairs.

SHE DIDN'T COME back at lunchtime. The wind was blowing the rain sideways, and hailstones battered against the windows. We waited until it was very late. Finally I said, "She won't be coming back in this weather. She'll stay at Villa Pierce for lunch."

My father looked at me suspiciously. The previous night's scene had served only to inspire in him the cold mistrust of a guard. As soon as he came home, believing that Sista and I wouldn't notice, he opened the door of the wardrobe where my mother kept her few items of clothing. Everything was still there.

"Go up to the Celantis' and call," he said. "Make sure she's there," he added, looking at me meaningfully.

I set out as if I felt calm. I went out to the stairs, climbed a few steps, and waited there, pressed against the wall. I wanted to give my mother enough time to get away. Maybe they had already left in the big car. I tried to imagine their two profiles side by side against the landscape flying by outside the windows. I remember so well: I saw them escaping to a sunny, green countryside. My mother would never come back upstairs, never put her hand on the banister. A sharp, cold pain ran through my entire body.

I went home. "Yes, she's there. The car broke down. She'll be back at dinnertime."

My father went out that afternoon and I sat next to the window overlooking the nuns' courtyard. Sista came to sit behind me more than once, begging for some news. I didn't turn around. I pretended to rest, sprawled in the armchair; inside, I was becoming an adult.

Towards evening, Lydia came down to ask after Mamma. Fulvia was with her.

"Where is Eleonora?" she asked.

"She's not here," I said, without moving.

It was getting dark, and the darkness smelled of damp earth as it does in the autumn. It was an evening like any other. From the convent came the sound of the organ that accompanied vespers. But it was as if it were my first day living in that house, and I was facing the start of a new routine. Fulvia and Lydia were quiet, contemplating the courtyard, which was draped in leaves that shone with the rain.

Finally Lydia asked, "Where has she gone?"

"I don't know."

Mother and daughter sat with me and waited, Lydia on the edge of her chair. She wanted to talk to me, ask for a report, but she was afraid, and I was afraid, too, that she would start discussing those things. Now that it was getting dark, I no longer felt very strong.

Sista came in and sat with us.

"Sista," Lydia said.

"Signora . . ." she replied with a sob. Their lost, melancholy voices gave me goosebumps. Meanwhile, the minutes passed, and the day was drawing our suspense to a close.

"What are you waiting for?" I exploded, turning harshly on the three women. "My mother isn't coming back."

In the fading evening light I saw them stare at me in disbelief before the shock took over.

"She's not coming back," I repeated. "She went away."

Lydia quickly recovered her composure. "Did she tell you that herself?"

"No, she didn't say so, but I knew it from the way she embraced me. She didn't come home for lunch. She's never coming back."

After a moment's uncertainty, Lydia turned to Fulvia. "Go upstairs and call Villa Pierce," she ordered.

We waited for an interminable time—maybe five minutes. When Fulvia returned, she reported that my mother was not at Villa Pierce.

"Who answered?" Lydia wanted to know.

"A man's voice."

"Was it him?"

"I don't know. He was very kind."

"Then it must have been him."

"The servants at Villa Pierce are like gentlemen," I said. "They answer courteously, too."

We went back to our waiting. Lydia hazarded a few guesses. I repeated, "She's gone away," and each time I said those words, I broke out in a cold sweat.

Sista suddenly got up as if she had only just realized what was going on. She came up to me and said, "Are you saying she left with that man up at the villa?"

"Yes," I replied.

"That's impossible," she asserted confidently. "She didn't take anything with her. Her drawers are all tidy. She didn't even take her hairbrush."

Fulvia laughed at that. "He has so much money he can buy as many brushes as she wants, and also blouses and dresses and furs. Don't you know how much money the Pierces have?"

"What does it matter?" Sista argued. "It's hardly her money, and he's not her husband. The signora wouldn't wear clothes bought with someone else's money."

Sista's observation left me perplexed. Maybe we'd soon hear my mother's step on the stairs and she would miraculously appear at the door.

"She could have taken some jewelry with her," Lydia said.

And Sista, shaking her head: "It's all pawned at the Monte di Pietà."

We went back to our waiting. In the meantime darkness had fallen. My father would be home before long; we had already heard other men's steps as they returned, keys entering the locks, doors opening and closing. We moved into the kitchen, and even though we were worried about his return and about the news we would have to give him, we all hurried to prepare his supper. Lydia chose to do the salad, Fulvia peeled potatoes. Sista went to look at the stairwell.

"Do you want us to stay with you?" Lydia asked, putting an arm around my shoulders. She looked at me affectionately and I remembered when I was jealous of her. I felt comforted by her presence just then.

Fulvia, too, seemed different from when she was lying on the balcony in her dressing gown. They were women and they were with me to help in the way that only women know how to help women. Lydia offered to take me home and let me sleep in Fulvia's bed with her.

"No, thanks," I replied. "I'm fine."

Until Sista, out of breath, joined us to announce, "Here he is." The Celantis made their escape, shutting the door behind them in a hurry.

My father entered and right away came to look in the kitchen. He didn't ask any questions, but he looked around as if my mother were hiding in a corner. Yet from the mysterious look on our faces, he should have realized instantly that we were alone. I looked at him but didn't say, "Good evening," because it wasn't really going to be a good evening. I remember him saying that he was hungry and wanted to eat as soon as possible, but then we hardly touched our food. It was Saturday, and I noticed that he didn't smell of brilliantine.

We said a few meaningless things at the table. Between us was the empty spot where Sista had placed, as she did each evening, a small bottle of a medicine my mother used to take before meals, because she was anemic. I was strong, but I couldn't look at that bottle without wanting to throw my head in my arms and cry.

Sista cleared the table quickly, anxious to get rid of that empty place. I picked up a book. My father took an old card game from a chest and laid it out on the table for a game of solitaire, something he never did. And I rarely read at that time. It was as if both of us were trying to establish new habits. The voice of the radio came in through the open window: it was a song, "Me ne vogl'i'a Surriento." Ever since, when I hear that phrase, a cold shiver runs through me. "Me ne vogl'i' a Surriento." I supposed my mother was already a long way away by then, away from our city, from the landscapes I knew. I saw two headlights piercing the thick darkness below a high mountain ridge. She wouldn't write anymore, wouldn't send news of herself. I thought about how this would now be my daily life; the other had been a holiday, a gift. Even so, I didn't suffer. I was even able to hum the song to myself: "Me ne vogl'i' a Surriento."

A little later my father got up and went to close the door that opened onto the kitchen. This desire to isolate me from Sista made me suspicious. I instinctively jumped to my feet and stood next to the wall to defend myself.

"Alessandra," he said, "where has your mother gone?"

He spoke softly. I didn't know that hushed yet cutting voice of his, which was like a blade picking the lock of a chest. Surely that was how he spoke to my mother when they were closed in their room.

I didn't answer. My look was defiant.

He took a few steps towards me and asked again: "Where is she?"

He was close to me, very close. I felt the irritating heat of his body. I could see, in his vest pocket, the key to our house, where we were now condemned to live together.

I wasn't afraid. I thought my mother was far away and it was up to me to defend her, even if it meant suffering cruelly for her. So I watched him for a moment and then said, violent and precise, as if I were throwing a knife, "She's gone."

"Where did she go?"

"I don't know."

"You do know."

"I don't know," I repeated. I wanted him to believe me. That way, it would seem to him that she was farther away and untraceable.

"Where did she go?" he insisted, the question containing all his helpless fury.

"Away. She's gone away. Away."

He seized my wrist and shook me. I wished he'd hurt me, make my joints crack, harm me physically, that is, so I'd be forced to demonstrate a strength that I felt wavering at that moment. But in fact he was just holding me; perhaps he'd taken my arm to support himself.

"Where has she gone?" he repeated.

"I don't know."

In my chest, I felt the big car driving fast, leaning into curves. *Quickly!* I urged it on mentally, *quickly!* It seemed that if there was a delay we'd all be lost. *Quickly!*

"She's not coming back," I repeated furiously. "She'll never set foot in this house again."

"Who is she with?" he asked quietly.

"How should I know? She's gone away."

I felt that my face and eyes had a bold, impertinent expression. I wanted to annoy him, to make him understand that I had gone with Mamma even though the law forced me to stay.

"You know," he said. "You know everything." Then he asked brusquely, "What time is it?"

We both looked up at the big clock hanging over the credenza. It was a few minutes to ten; before long the main door would be closed, locking my mother out. It was over now; she had escaped. I took a deep breath.

All the noise ceased. The neighbors turned off the radio, the children weren't playing in the street as they always did in summer before bed. The silence had never seemed so profound: all you could hear was the dull, monotonous ticking of the clock: relentless, oppressive.

"She'll be back," my father said. "Tomorrow morning I'll have the police find her." He left the room quickly and went to his bedroom without locking the front door—perhaps fearing that in doing so he'd be destroying his last hope.

Sista and I met in the entrance hall. It felt as though I had a fever and I think I really did. I hugged her, so as not to see her sunken eyes.

"She's safe," I told her. "Tomorrow morning will be too late, right? He won't be able to bring her back. She's gone."

I imagined the borders closing like tall gates, and she was already far away, the big car racing across the fresh green countryside. On my skin and in my stomach, a raw suffering was awakening.

"She's gone," Sista repeated gloomily. "She's gone away, gone away . . ."

Just then we heard steps on the stairs. Terrified, I let go of Sista at once. The steps were ascending, closer and closer, more and more distinct. They arrived at our landing and fell silent in front of our door. I ran to open it.

Two men stood there, dressed in black. Though it was summer, they were wearing hats and they didn't take them off in greeting.

"Does Eleonora Corteggiani live here?" one of them asked in hushed tones. The other was holding my mother's purse.

I looked at them for a moment, in a daze. I said softly, "She's dead, isn't she?" My lips barely moved.

The one who had spoken nodded gravely. The other one looked around suspiciously.

I moved away from the door, swiftly crossed the hallway, and entered my parents' bedroom without knocking. Hearing the latch turn, my father must have felt sure that his wife had returned: he stood waiting beside her dressing table, stern and surly. I burst into convulsive laughter.

"What did I tell you?" I said. "She'll never come back."

Wary and uncertain, he watched me laugh.

"She's dead," I explained. "She killed herself."

I saw my father's eyes widen with inhuman terror before I fell to the floor, fainting in my laughter as if in a pool of blood.

TWO DAYS AFTER the tragedy, my uncle Rodolfo arrived. We ran into him at the door just as we were leaving with the Celantis for the funeral. The brothers embraced silently and Uncle Rodolfo immediately took my arm to support me, and he didn't let go until we returned home. I barely knew him, he had never written to me in all these years, but he was my godfather and I understood that I would soon be entrusted to him.

At the entrance, we found the porter all dressed up, with collar and tie, and some of our neighbors, the women in black. They watched us pass by, not offering a word of comfort, and followed behind us as we headed for the tram stop.

I sat between Papa and Uncle Rodolfo in the tram. Both of them were tall, with strong, square shoulders, and I felt as if I were trapped between two insurmountable gray walls. Lydia and Fulvia sat across from us. Signor Celanti had taken a seat next to Papa and every now and then patted him on the back. The two women gazed at me affectionately; I'd stayed with them since my mother's death until that moment, but now I knew I'd have to part with their affection, too, and I felt my strength ebbing. The tram, issuing from the Lungotevere, turned abruptly and lurched onto the Risorgimento Bridge. Nearby my mother had killed herself: exactly where Alessandro had drowned. It seemed as if the tram, with the thunderous weight of its wheels, must be running over her body and mangling it.

We found other tenants at the mortuary door, along with Ottavia, Enea, and the seamstress who lived across from us and made our dresses. It was still early, perhaps nine, and it looked as if the day would be beautiful. In the garden of the hospital, the oleanders emitted a fresh, bitter scent. I wasn't suffering, I recall; I really wasn't. Aida, Antonio's sister, was there, and Maddalena, who was crying, though she knew my mother only by sight. They didn't approach me, because of my father and Uncle Rodolfo, but they looked at me from a distance with grave curiosity, trying to make contact with my pain. But at that moment, as I said, I wasn't suffering.

We gathered in a group at the door of the mortuary. Signor Celanti went in and came back, followed by an old man dressed in black, and my father gave him a grateful look. Presently, a short man appeared wearing a smock and a white skullcap. "She's coming down now," he said. I realized that he meant my mother. I hadn't seen her dead. My father hadn't asked me to go and say a last goodbye, and, if he had, I think I would have refused. I wanted to preserve the image of her, animated by a sort of passionate restlessness, that I liked so much. I wanted to remember her gentle eyes and her way of walking, which was like flying. I had never seen a dead person. I was afraid I'd be frightened or disgusted, and I didn't want to be frightened or disgusted by her. So, despite everything, I had the impression that she wasn't dead, but travelling. I had lived with Lydia since the unbearable evening when my mother hadn't come home. I had found Lydia beside me the moment I recovered my senses, while my father was speaking to the police; she had made me smell vinegar. Fulvia held my hand and stroked it. Sista was on the floor praying, her clothes bunched around her. My father had come in, pale, his lips trembling.

"Signora," he said to Lydia, "they want to question you. You were her only friend. She threw herself into the river where her little boy drowned. I said they were not to question Alessandra, but they may want to see Sista. Remember, you two: she killed herself because she couldn't find peace regarding her son. Understood?" His expression was tough under his ashen complexion. Mortified, we nodded yes, yes. Papa then left with the officers to identify her. Sista took my sheets and blankets and they made me a bed on the floor in Fulvia's room.

"Here she is," said the man in the white skullcap, and behind him, on the shoulders of some rough men we didn't know, we saw a narrow wooden coffin.

That was when I began to feel an appalling pain. From the time I had come to after fainting, I had thought of my mother as a soft form fluttering through the air. I couldn't imagine her unmoving, shut up inside that box. But that macabre sight gave me the material certainty that the good part of my life was over. I felt alone amid the people all around me, and I sensed that I would never again be able to speak about the things that were so important to the two of us, things no one else seemed to know anything about.

The horse walked slowly. We followed on foot, me between my father and Uncle Rodolfo. Someone had put a large wreath of red roses on the coffin, which completely covered it. There was no name on the ribbon, but everyone knew who it was from. My father must have felt an urge to have it removed by the men in black, who were bustling about. But then he remembered that his wife was dead because she couldn't find peace after having lost her son, and so he couldn't say a thing. The air was fresh and pure, the trees bent under the gentle nudging of the wind. Gradually, with the rhythm and sound of the footsteps accompanying my mother—calm, relaxed under the wreath of roses—I seemed to discover a resigned harmony that comforted me. I felt relief in letting myself lean on Uncle Rodolfo's arm, a strong arm you could trust.

We entered a chapel of the great basilica of San Lorenzo, which I had never seen. It was a small side chapel, because people who commit suicide can't be welcomed into the bosom of the Church.

The priest came outside dressed in funeral vestments. He studied us with a mixture of compassion and suspicion, maybe because we were the relatives of a woman who had thrown herself into the river. The coffin was then covered with a black cloth and the wreath of roses placed on top of it.

I stood next to Fulvia and Lydia. Instinctively, the women had taken their places to the left and the men to the right of the coffin, as peasants do in country churches. Feeling that I was once more in the warmth of creatures like me, my sorrow overflowed, swelled in my breast, and filled me entirely.

The priest, among the clerics, recited the prayers for the dead. Indifferent to what he was doing, I stared past the coffin at the group of men, who were listening seriously, some with arms crossed. They seemed humiliated rather than sorrowful, their looks betraying dismay at the inconsiderate things women suddenly do, which they vaguely feel they have caused. I sensed that they were stunned by the violence of these sudden rebellions, since they were convinced that a child's cry, the presence of a stranger, or even a new dress was all a woman needed to console her. The porter said over and over that my mother had greeted him politely as she went out that morning: "Good morning, Giuseppe." He was amazed and told everyone. Men don't understand how women can smile and say, *Good morning, Giuseppe* right before dying. Yet something binds them so firmly to life that they try to remain part of it until the last moment, expecting salvation, perhaps, from its very energy. My mother had remembered to take her raincoat because the weather was cloudy—*Good morning, Giuseppe*—and then she had thrown herself into the river.

In the meantime, a lot of people had arrived at the chapel. I saw the Captain behind a column, pretending to be a passerby who had wandered in by chance. I instantly squeezed Lydia's arm, which she acknowledged with a slight nod. Other women from our building came in, emotional but circumspect, afraid of being intrusive. Some were crying, and all were moving their lips, putting a dramatic intensity into the prayers.

Their presence and the impulse that had moved them to demonstrate their support for my mother even though they hardly knew her inspired a desperate strength in me. So I made an effort to watch the men standing in a group on the other side of the coffin. I was overcome by rage and I wanted to chase them away so they would leave us alone. We were divided, like two armies preparing for combat, and there was already, in that coffin, one of the fallen.

My mother was buried in the municipal cemetery. The undertakers placed the wreath of roses on the grave, arranging it, smoothing it, and tucking it in as you would a sheet. My father watched, no longer mocking or threatening. His power had come to an end.

"Let's go," he finally decided. Uncle Rodolfo took my arm and Signor Celanti said that the buses are empty at that hour.

So we went home. I was very tired and wanted to lie down on my bed, see no one, and sleep. In sleep I hoped to be with my mother and speak to her. But my father begged Lydia to have me again for lunch because he needed to talk to his brother. Later, he called for me and announced that I would be leaving with my uncle Rodolfo for Abruzzo the following morning.

WE SAT OPPOSITE one another on the train, with little to say, since we hardly knew each other. We both feigned the familiarity we should have felt, being so closely related. But, as soon as he closed his eyes to sleep, I studied him carefully and when I dozed off I could feel him looking at me, racking his brains to discover what lay behind my docile appearance, the sweetness of my features. He tried to match my image with his brother's depiction of me. I opened my eyes and smiled to show that I wasn't offering any resistance to his probing.

"How old are you?" he asked suddenly.

"Seventeen," I replied. "I'll be eighteen in April."

"How far did you go in school?"

"I'll be starting my third year of high school."

Astonished, he asked, "You're still going to school?"

"Of course! what else would I do?"

"Learn to sew and mend."

"I already know how to do that," I said. "I also know how to cook."

"Oh!" he threatened, wagging his finger at me in jest. "Wait till you see the test Nonna sets . . ."

I told him I was afraid I'd fail, since I only knew how to do the basics, which seemed enough to me. I added that I liked studying, cultivating my natural inclination for literature and poetry. I also said I intended to get a degree as soon as possible so I could earn a living.

He seemed surprised by my plans. "Surely there's no need for that?" he said. "You're a pretty girl. You'll get married soon, you'll have a house and children." He smiled as he said it.

Despite the thankless task he had to perform, I felt an instinctive sympathy for him the moment I saw him. He seemed to be a straightforward man, and I felt reassured by his simple appearance. He didn't have that softness in his eyes and hands which, in a man like my father, betrayed a sly sensuality.

"Maybe Ariberto is right," he went on, lowering his voice. "If your mother had had a lot of children, she wouldn't have had time to play the piano. That's where the tragedy lay, he says."

Alarmed, I shrank back into my seat. I thought about escaping with a leap, throwing myself off the moving train. Up to then, I had obeyed meekly and accepted my departure as the obvious solution. Everything I valued in the house on Via Paolo Emilio had gone with my mother. Sista had thrown a white sheet over the piano, which took on the aspect of a ghost. The oppressive atmosphere my mother would have banished with a word or a gesture now weighed on the entire apartment. So when my father announced that I would be leaving the next day I had felt some consolation. Fulvia and Lydia sobbed when they said goodbye, and my childhood, my adolescence, everything that had, until then, been Alessandra, wept with them. The window cried, the stairway, the tap with freezing water where I washed every morning, the courtyard and the entrance, where Enea had pushed me against the wall and I had learned what a man was. Seeing Fulvia and Lydia worn down by the suffering of those days, I consoled them lovingly, insisting that it was better this way: I couldn't live with my father.

I said goodbye to him before I left. It was early and we could hardly see one another. I thought he would still be in bed as he had decided not to take me to the station. I went into his room, slowly opening the door, and found him all dressed and sitting in a chair, jacket on, tie knotted. He sat with his legs apart, back bent, one hand on the table. In the cold light coming from the window he looked like a man who had no more energy or pretense: an old man.

He turned, and, catching sight of me at the door, dressed in black, he began to cry. "Nora," he said softly, "Nora . . ." he repeated, heartbroken, looking at me and perhaps seeking her image in my face.

In all those years, I had never heard him call her by that affectionate name. And that's why, horrified, I had recoiled at their intimacy.

"I wanted to say goodbye, Papa," I said brusquely.

Yes, yes. He nodded, indicating that he, too, was ready for our parting.

From the open window came the cry of the swallows I had heard as a little girl, when I got up early and went with Sista to take communion. I tried to keep the sound in my ears, along with the air itself of my happy childhood.

On the train, I pretended to sleep, in order to create silence inside me, so I could hear their voices, high, fresh, piercing. But I couldn't, maybe because of the noise of the pistons. I could barely hear them in my imagination.

Uncle Rodolfo patted my arm to rouse me from the drowsiness in which he believed I found relief. "You're tired, aren't you?" he asked affectionately, seeing me struggle to open my eyes. Then he smiled encouragingly: "We'll be arriving in a few minutes."

NONNA WAS WAITING for us in the dining room, seated in an armchair. Aunt Violante and Aunt Sofia stood like two black wings on either side.

"Come. Come here, Alessandra," Nonna said. "Don't be afraid."

But I was afraid. Nonna was an old woman, very tall, with a big face and nose and the bearing of a large animal. The gesture she made to summon me swept up all the air in the room. She was sitting in a wide chair upholstered in white, and her shoulders were wider than the backrest. Her voice sounded like my father's, perhaps because of her accent. I walked slowly over the black and white floor tiles. With a gentle push from my uncle, I went to stand just in front of her.

"Kiss her hand," my uncle whispered in my ear. It was the large, cold hand of a statue.

When I straightened up, we looked at one another. Nonna had my father's shiny black eyes, but hers were lit with a natural dignity I had never noticed in his. She examined me, taking in my height and the width of my hips with a quick and exacting look.

"You don't look like Ariberto," she said at last.

"No," I replied, my voice lost between the high walls. "I'm like my mother."

There was a chilly silence after I said that. But it served to restore some of my strength. I looked around: the white linen curtains and white walls made the room look like the large parlor of a convent.

"It's nice here," I murmured, although I felt as if I were among the dead; or maybe because of that.

"Yes," Nonna said. "It's a comfortable house. I was born here and so were your aunts. Your father was born here, your uncle Rodolfo, and poor Aunt Caterina, who's in heaven. Your cousin Giuliano was born here—he's Violante's son," she explained, pointing to her right. "You should have been born here, too, but your mother didn't want that. She preferred a clinic in the city. And now you, too, have come."

Yes, I nodded, and I invited her to smile, but, as I later realized, Nonna never smiled. She kept looking at me, and my whole body shrank, intimidated, under my clothes.

"You're thin," she said. "Did you have some illness as a child?"

"No," I replied. "Only measles and influenza."

"Those don't count. Maybe you grew too quickly. You have no bust or hips. And yet you must be seventeen, right? We'll have to call the doctor. With a chest like that you won't be able to nurse."

I flushed, and the back of my neck felt fragile and sore. I sensed Uncle Rodolfo's presence behind me, and it was as if Nonna had torn off my bodice.

"Sit down, Alessandra," Aunt Violante said, and I was happy to follow an order, give in and show my obedience. They asked if I was hungry or thirsty, and my aunts moved away from the chair, leaving the scene they had created in order to get a *ciambella*.

They were tall, too, but even when they were moving they didn't reach beyond Nonna's large torso. A sign from her was enough to direct them from the wardrobe to the credenza. Meanwhile, Uncle Rodolfo had disappeared, nodding a brief goodbye as a sign of understanding, and I was left with those unknown women, with whom I had to feign familiarity.

"Eat," Nonna ordered. "Dip the *ciambella* in the wine."

I ate, trying to pull myself together as I did so, and in the effort I made not to stain my dress. It felt as though I were dead, like my mother, and that this was the next world, which we had tried so often to imagine.

I believe we'll live again, Mamma would say, *and we'll start over in another life just like this one. I'd like at least to be able to hold on to the memory of the days I've had.* It was exactly as she had said: whenever I mentioned my mother or our house in Rome, Nonna and my aunts pretended that I hadn't said anything at all.

"Mamma never drank wine," I noted, trying again. And again it was as if I hadn't spoken.

I lingered, taking small bites. Feeling dismayed, I wondered what I would do later and then until evening, and tomorrow. The next day appeared opaque to me, and frightening. It seemed possible to endure the rest of that evening, but no more. I couldn't even imagine enduring a week, or a month. Yet I vaguely realized that going back was also impossible. My past wasn't Rome, a city, or a house: it was my mother. And she was dead.

"You'll go up to your room now," Nonna said. "Aunt Sofia will take you. You can rest if you wish, and later I'll send someone to call you to recite the rosary with us before dinner. Remember to bring your beads."

"I don't have any," I said.

Nonna questioned me with a look. "Do you mean you left them in Rome?"

"No. I don't have any. I don't possess any."

"Did your mother never take you to church, then?"

"Oh yes, sometimes, to listen to the music."

Nonna said nothing. Sitting beside her was like sitting beside a high mountain, and I felt lost in a valley of loneliness. I wished I could make her understand how I used to pray, curled up against the window, tell her that through Ottavia we spoke with Alessandro and many other spirits in Purgatory. But she wouldn't have understood.

After a long pause, she promised me a visit from the priest the next day. "Go upstairs now," she ordered. I was getting ready to obey her when the door opened and Aunt Clarice appeared.

She was a tiny old woman, smiling, and as soft and white as a meringue, with the height of a child of ten and the wonder of childhood still on her face. Hanging from her arm was a stool appropriate for her height.

"I want to see the child," she said. "They told me in the kitchen that she had arrived.' She came towards me, curious. "I'm Clarice," she added, giggling and wagging a finger at me, as if she had surprising news. "I'm Aunt Clarice."

Nonna explained. "She's my sister."

"What lovely hair you have," Aunt Clarice said. "It's Eleonora's hair. She always washed it when she was here, and then she'd go out in the sun to dry it. Sofia was jealous," she added with childish spite, "because at the time she'd lost her hair owing to typhus. Eleonora let me keep her company on the terrace. She was good, Eleonora. She gave me money for sugared almonds. May I have a ciambella?" she asked with a faint smile when she was settled on her stool.

Once she had it, she began to eat and paid no more attention to me. Nonna waved goodbye and Aunt Sofia led me to my room. It was a very large house and in order to go from one room to another you had to cross small dark corridors; it was easy to trip on the steps. The rooms were on different levels and isolated from each other, like cells in a cloister. The doors, thick and narrow, were just big enough to let one person through. In my room there was a wardrobe, a small table, a chair, and an iron bed.

"It's raining," Aunt Sofia said. "It would be good to close the window." Meanwhile, she explained that this was the room my father had slept in as a child.

"I was meant to be born here, right?"

"Maybe," she replied with a smile. She looked at me, offering what seemed a genuine alliance. "I hope you'll settle in well. Have a little rest and sort out your things, and then come down."

As soon as I was alone, I ran to the window and threw it open again. It was raining hard: a glistening veil trembled between sky and earth. The window, painted gray, was narrow and extended down to the red floor tiles, and instead of a windowsill there was a gray railing, almost as high as my chest. The house was set solidly in the center of the village and dominated the small hovels that were visible, all jumbled together, as if propping each other up, shoulder to shoulder. In front of them, instead of streets or alleyways there were wide stone ramps, worn by the passing of peasants and their donkeys. Below the houses lay a small valley crossed by a dry stream, before me rose a hill that was partly cultivated but mostly barren and dotted with stones and yellow fields. On my right, beyond the hills I could glimpse an impressive, tall mountain, which I later learned was the Maiella.

Freed of the iron-gray clouds that were rapidly dissolving in rain, the entire landscape was soon shining like steel. A luminous fog rose in the sky, white as a sparkler; the green of the trees was vivid and clean. You could hear water running everywhere: it sounded as if the house were surrounded by swift waterfalls, but it was only the gutters. The scent of wet earth brought me the memory of days when my mother and I would go for a walk just after a downpour, protected by a rainbow.

"Mamma," I whispered. "Mamma, save me, take me away from here."

With its bare walls, my room felt like a prison cell. A cross hung over the bed. I opened the wardrobe, and two hangers swinging inside hit the wood with a sinister chime. The small table was covered in drab green cloth, frayed and smelling of mold. Living in that room would mean finding only what was necessary for survival, day after day. Before me, the Christ—nailed to the iron cross above the iron bed— showed how you had to offer yourself up to suffering and sacrifice. I was trapped, locked in, a prisoner like Antonio. *Antonio*, I whispered, *Antonio*, and I fell to my knees by the window, my face resting on the railing.

His name gave me an immediate sense of relief and peace. It actually seemed that Antonio, who was far away, and whom I'd never seen, was all that remained of my former life.

"Don't forget me," Fulvia had said, clinging to me. She had taken me to say goodbye to the balcony and the room we'd played in when I came to their house for the first time.

"My God, how many years have passed!" Lydia sighed. "I'd only just met the Captain . . ." Weakened by sadness over her friend's death, she became emotional about herself and her past. "Such a tragedy!" she exclaimed, wiping her eyes. "Ah, what suffering love is! There'll be trouble if I discover you're in love, Fulvia, and you, too, Alessandra. Trouble! You've got to be free and happy, marry a rich man . . . Love is such a torment!" she said again. We kept quiet, pretending to accept the destiny she had in mind for us. And yet, inside, we were all burning for this love that leads to tears, and even death.

"I shouldn't have encouraged her," Lydia said, her cheeks wet with tears. "I should have said, *Don't see him anymore. Think about it. You have a family!* I did the wrong thing. It's my fault . . ."

But only a few seconds later she took advantage of her husband's brief absence to come and tell me that Claudio was waiting on the stairs.

I set out unenthusiastically because I didn't love Claudio, but he had stuck around since the day we'd been out for a walk on Monte Mario, as sweet and faithful as a shadow. I never asked myself if he really loved me; I often wondered whether he merely loved the idea of looking into himself and getting to know himself, which I was the first to offer him.

"You can't," he said. "You definitely can't talk to your parents. You have to pretend you have no thoughts other than eat, study, sleep. If we tried to make them understand that sometimes we can't sleep at night because of the problems troubling us, and that those problems often suggest a break with life—suicide—as the only solution, they wouldn't know how to help other than by shouting at us, threatening us. My father would pound the table and ask, *What more do you need?* not realizing that it isn't what I don't have but what I do have, what's inside me, the good and the bad, that presents this alternative. I believe that by reproaching us—and so preventing us from revealing our worries and uncertainties to them—our parents are instinctively avoiding their duty to help us resolve them. They already know there's no solution—or at least very often they haven't yet found it for themselves. They lack sympathy. But you, Alessandra . . ." He looked at me as he would a miraculous apparition that inhabited some region of air he knew he couldn't or maybe didn't want to get to, so that he could leave me untouched in the secret that surrounded me. As soon as I went out on the stairs I saw him, wide-eyed with anxiety. I reached out a hand but stood as still as a statue, one step above him.

"You see?" I said sadly, alluding to everything that had happened in recent days.

"Ah . . . !" he replied with a sigh, earnest but powerless.

"And now I'm leaving," I finished.

"Can I write to you?" he had asked, timidly.

I had hesitated. "I don't think so. I don't think my relatives would like that."

He had then suggested he send me postcards signed Claudia. "You send me a postcard, too, sometimes," he added, his voice breaking. The staircase was dark now, and the harmony of its spiral shape made me feel a soft, limitless melancholy inside. I expected to feel agonizing pain at the thought of leaving those stairs, which had been animated by my mother's step only two days before. The sound of the water in the little courtyard fountain reminded me of the rolling wheels of the carriage that had taken her away.

At last, Claudio said, "Guess what? I passed. I got an A in Philosophy."

"Well done," I replied.

"I'm going to the university in October," he added. "Medicine. Are you pleased?"

"Yes. I don't know. I don't know anything anymore."

He stared at me, stared at everything about me, stealing it in order to preserve and contemplate me while I was gone. "I'd like you to know one thing, Alessandra: that I'll await your return for months, even years. Always." He spoke the last word almost angrily, before taking my hand and squeezing it for a moment. Then he walked off without turning around. I stood still in the dark, holding on to the cold iron bannister.

Now I was holding on to the iron railing of a window that looked out at a parched hillside and the grave majesty of the Maiella.

I looked into the glass, which acted as a mirror against the gray wooden shutter. I saw the gentle line of my body crouching on the floor, my hands, white, resting on the dull black of my dress. I was trying to understand myself, to examine myself.

But the door opened, and I recoiled towards the railing. It was Aunt Violante, thin in her long black dress.

"Oh, you're down on the floor, Alessandra?" she asked. Her voice was kind, but I didn't move. I looked at her, stunned, because her entrance had suddenly brought me back to a reality I didn't have the strength to face.

"You haven't even unpacked your suitcases," she said. "I understand. You can't really want to stay here. And yet you have to. These are difficult days, aren't they? I understand. But you'll get used to it, because in fact every day is difficult. It's lucky for you that you've come here to the country. Nonna will let you have a little time to get used to the house and the people, and then she'll put you to work. What do you know how to do, Alessandra?"

"Nothing," I replied aggressively.

All these years later, I can still see Aunt Violante's face flinch, as if she'd been struck. She said nothing. Then the tight knot of resentment in her suddenly unwound, and she said affectionately, "I hope that's not true. But I know it's not. Ariberto often wrote to me that you knew how to cook and tidy the house . . ."

"I want to study," I said, my voice hushed and resentful. "Next year I want to go to the university. My suitcase is full of books."

"If that's what you want to do, no one is going to stop you," she said, "at least I don't think so. But maybe after a little while you yourself won't want it anymore. The city is some distance from here. Sometimes it seems that it doesn't exist. And a day in the country is brief: it begins with bells, and now—can you hear?—with bells it's already over."

I jumped up and walked over to her, my hands clasped. "Oh, Aunt Violante, I'm asking you, I beg you, let me study! You mustn't stop me . . ."

"Me!?" she exclaimed, surprised. "I won't, Alessandra. But you must want it, do you understand? You, yourself. It's difficult to defend oneself. There's something so numbing in the everyday rhythm of life, and slowly, before we know it, we're caught. And there's no time, there's never time for anything. You see?" she said, hands lightly pressing my shoulders. "It's already time for the rosary."

She took a string of coarse, tobacco-colored beads from her pocket and handed it to me. The stairs were dimly lit, as were the passageways, the corridors, the pitted and uneven steps.

"Look." She stopped for a moment and pointed to a small painting in which I made out a butterfly. "I painted that myself as a young girl. I was your age, and engaged."

"Then did you stop?"

"No. I illustrated some fairy tales for Giuliano."

"And then?"

"And then I no longer had time." As she said this, she shushed me and cautiously opened a door.

NONNA WAS ALONE in the dining room, apparently sleeping. Her eyes were closed, her hands on the armrests, and she was resting upright, like some majestic horse. The armchair had been moved, and she was now sitting in front of a large cupboard of smooth, shiny black wood. It was strange to see her in that position, but I didn't dare ask anything because Aunt Violante's face, too, had again closed up and become impassive, severe.

"Did you give Alessandra the rosary?" Nonna asked without opening her eyes. Reassured, she went back to her meditation.

We took our places behind her on two chairs.

Aunt Clarice entered and came to sit beside me on her little stool. With a wink of complicity, she showed me her pocket, which was full of plums. Two servants entered and sat on the floor. Two women who happened to be in the kitchen, selling their wares, entered. At last Aunt Sofia entered, a veil over her head, and opened the cupboard.

Inside the cupboard was an altar. As Aunt Sofia began to light candles, the black and terrifying face of the Madonna of Loreto slowly emerged from the shadows. The women all knelt down and I copied them. Only Nonna remained seated, as if between her and Heaven there were a pact of equality. Her voice intoned the rosary and I responded along with the others.

Night was falling by then, and the big room was lit only by the flickering reddish flames of the candles. Bewildered, I observed these grave, taciturn people who had been strangers to me a few hours before, but who now embraced me within a mechanism so robust I sensed it could easily overwhelm a person. I tried in vain to evoke memories of my former life, Fulvia's clever expression, Lydia's tolerance. From the past I recognized only Aunt Caterina's frowning face on the open door of the black cupboard—the same face I knew from the enlargement of the photo in my parents' bedroom. Portraits of the family's dead hung side by side on the door, in matching black frames. There were stern old ladies and young girls wide-eyed with dismay. Some had heavy black braids wound around their foreheads, others sparse white hair. But what they all had in common was solid, refined faces and full breasts. In comparison, the men looked feeble and meek. It had to be those breasts that triumphed over them and intimidated them: through those, life was handed down, secure and powerful, from generation to generation. The men, bald in old age, clean-shaven and lost in their school or military uniforms, looked defeated on that grim door. I imagined my mother's portrait beside one of a fat old lady, a great-aunt who had died recently, suffocated by her own obesity. *No*, I said to myself, *no, no*. I felt my mother radiating around me like a halo, her strength joining mine. *Just try and break us*, I said to myself, challenging the relatives on their knees and Aunt Caterina, stuck to the black door.

When the rosary was over, I saw Uncle Rodolfo at the back of the room, along with Uncle Alfredo (Aunt Violante's husband) and his son Giuliano. All three were staring at me, ill at ease at having me in their house, with their furniture, their habits.

Uncle Alfredo kissed me, although he had never seen me before. Giuliano extended his hand, which was soft and moist like a priest's. We were called to the table: Nonna stood up and it was the first time I'd seen her at her full height. She was taller than my father and taller than Uncle Rodolfo. She could barely fit through the doorway, so it seemed natural to me that her glass should be larger than anyone else's, and filled with wine. She ate plentifully, demonstrating a healthy appetite despite her age. After her, the serving plate was passed to Uncle Rodolfo, Uncle Alfredo, and then to Giuliano, who helped himself with irritating greed, making sure that nothing appetizing was left. Aunt Violante chose the best for me from what was left; the rest went to her and Aunt Sofia.

There, in that vast room, furniture that seemed bulky and coarse at home in Rome revealed a nobility that was clear to me from the moment I arrived: the women's black dresses and hair appeared even blacker against the fine white linen curtains.

We ate in silence, as in a refectory, and I pretended that the look on my face was natural. But the truth was—particularly because I had so little experience of being in other people's houses—I was alert, curious, and mistrustful. I watched Uncle Alfredo, who was appraising me with furtive glances. Like my father and Uncle Rodolfo, he didn't look his age. This often struck me about the men of the south: they all had delicate pink cheeks, bright, contented eyes and very white teeth. They also seemed to take great care with their nails, keeping them rosy, while the women's soon turned yellow and cracked.

Giuliano was sitting beside me. His shirtsleeves were rolled up, and his bare arm on the table kept brushing mine. Each time it felt as if I were grazing a nettle, and the stinging irritation stayed on my skin.

"You're the same age," Aunt Violante said suddenly. "Giuliano is a little older, but you don't look at all alike, even though you're first cousins."

We turned to look at each other, and I saw everything I disliked in a man present in him. He wasn't ugly; he, too, had the nice eyes unique to men in that family. But he had a sloppy, sarcastic, sly demeanor. His hair was uncombed, his face covered in red pimples, and his hands—oh! his hands were horrible: stubby, clumsy, and still patchy with winter chilblains. They hung heavily at the end of his arms, which were scarred and scratched.

"No, they don't look alike," Nonna said.

I wanted to be polite, and overcoming my aversion, I turned to Giuliano. "What do you do?"

"What do you think I do?" he replied. "I work the fields."

"You're not studying?"

"Why should I study? I'm hardly going to be a priest."

"I'm not either." I tried to laugh. "But I study anyway."

"It's clear that you enjoy wasting time," he finished curtly.

I kept silent. Nonna's sharp, severe gaze went from Giuliano to me, sizing us up. Now, from this distance in time, I might say that she enjoyed setting us against one another, like two roosters, to see which was the stronger. I didn't react, and it seemed to me that Nonna recorded a point in my favor.

Meanwhile, the men got up without waiting for us to finish eating our fruit. Uncle Rodolfo went to the farmyard and Uncle Alfredo walked around me, looking: his gaze ran from my neck to my bosom and back, from my feet up my legs in their black stockings. I felt I had to sit still, meekly submitting to his gaze.

"Are you tired?" asked Aunt Violante, noticing how pale my face was.

"No, thank you. I'm not at all tired."

"Then we'll get to work," Nonna said. "Would you like to start on a sock, a stocking?"

"I don't know how," I confessed in a whisper.

"What do you know how to do? Hemming?" she asked again, patiently.

"Yes, I know how to hem very well."

The four of us sat in a circle and Aunt Violante opened a large white sheet between us. "There, let's do this then. We'll each take a side."

"What about me?" Aunt Clarice asked, hanging about like a child. "I get bored if I don't have anything to do. Give me some work, too."

"It's not possible, Clarice," Nonna said harshly. "Sit down in a corner and watch."

"Then I'll sing while you work."

Nonna nodded. "Good. Sing a nice hymn to the Virgin."

"I'll sit here next to Alessandra," Clarice said, and I smiled at her. Her small green eyes were clear and watery like a child's.

"Sing," I begged.

"O, Maria, our Lady of the Roses," she began.

We were bent over the immaculate white cloth. Only Nonna had the sheet raised to her level, and for that reason we felt as if we were sewing at her feet in penitence. That impression doubled my speed: I sewed quickly, contrite, absorbed in the act. The needle squeaked through the strong weave of the cloth, like a cry or a sob with every stitch. It squeaked under Aunt Violante's fingers, too, and the strong fingers of Aunt Sofia. Nonna sewed more slowly than we did, calm, with her hands of marble. My fingers were sore, like my knees when, as a girl, I'd knelt for a long time on the prayer benches at church. But I didn't slow the rhythm of my stitches, just as then I hadn't sat down to rest. Even then, the pain brought me a sort of sweet exhaustion. The faces of Aunt Violante and Aunt Sofia made me feel affectionate towards them. Again I felt embraced by the women's routine gestures: my story flowed quickly between them, a stream between secure banks. There was a fragile silence; every now and then, in the adjacent room, the men's voices were interrupted by noisy laughter.

"What are they doing?" I asked, looking up from my sewing.

"What do you think they're doing?" Nonna shrugged. "Playing cards."

.   .   .

THOSE FIRST DAYS at Nonna's house were very difficult for me. No one mentioned my mother's death. In fact, they ignored it to such an extent that I wondered whether I had imagined it so I could feel sorry for myself. The world I had always inhabited in Rome offered me no help, and I didn't adapt easily to the new order, rigorous and incomprehensible, to which I now belonged.

Besides, until that point I had been convinced that I had a rather timid nature, not at all original. I was used to living in reflected light, in the affection my mother inspired. In fact I believed that I appeared insignificant to everyone, because of my difficulty expressing what I felt.

In Abruzzo, though, they all considered me odd and capricious, and I understood very well that the surprise aroused by my ways was veined with disapproval. Nonna allowed me a long period of freedom and rest— to recover from the tiring journey, she said, and get used to things. But that freedom, which I initially exploited with great enthusiasm, became hard to endure once I realized that it had been granted for the sole purpose of studying me more closely: so that my every gesture, my every word became a confession. There were times when, remorseful, I wished I could take back some word, but my relatives had already seized it, relentlessly attributing it to my character.

Of course, in the closed rigidity of the customs there, the resignation with which I bore my mother's death and my distance from my father was no doubt judged as revealing a tough, stubborn soul. No one would have guessed how unpleasant I had found the daily company of my father. And finally no one, apart from Nonna, understood how comforting it was for me to live in contact with nature for the first time.

I would get up early in the morning to find Nonna already stationed in the middle of the vegetable garden holding a long stick with which she directed the harvesting while standing in one place. The women were bent over their full, colorful skirts, which stood out cheerfully against the green.

To someone from the city, that sort of silence was entirely new: you could hear a nightingale sketching a silver squiggle in the pellucid air with its song. And everything shone in the intense morning sun: the leaves fluttering in the wind, a short stream flowing nearby, the emerald hills, and the rocky gorge of the Maiella.

The farm wasn't large, but it was rich in vegetables and was clearly tended diligently and carefully. Just beyond it were fields and small irregular patches of woods, since the earth in that mountainous area was all terraced and stepped. Oaks and maples grew in the woods, and in autumn the maple leaves turned coral pink at first, then blood red. In that utter solitude I spoke to the trees, stooping to pluck an unknown flower, literally spellbound by the delicate design of a leaf. These lines are inadequate to convey the excitement I felt in those moments, or how immersed I became in the workings of nature. In that stupendous silence, I sometimes heard a nightingale address a compliment to me from a branch high above; or, as I sat on the grass, a splash of sunlight would fall into my lap like a fruit. I fell asleep between the roots of an old oak one afternoon, as if in a shoulder's hollow.

"Do you like the country, Alessandra?" Nonna asked when she saw me return from those walks. "Would you like to live in the country?" she repeated, bending down to pull up a weed in order to mask the interest behind her question. But a question from her was always like one asked at the Last Judgment. I said nothing, holding her gaze as she looked at me. It was a hard, determined gaze, and yet in those moments it was easy for me to understand that she loved me.

I WOULD STUDY during the first part of the afternoon—a sultry period, the silence broken only by a rooster's crow or a cowbell. A green light shone from the window, through the restless tracery of a locust tree, so gentle I sometimes had to put my head down on the table; it was difficult to concentrate at that hour. Yet in the evening my room was barely illuminated by the feeble bulb with its beaded shade, and I had to go to sleep without reading. As soon as I pondered this new habit I feared I saw in it the first sign of that surrender predicted by Aunt Violante. In any case, the few books—novels and poetry—that I had brought from Rome from my mother's meagre library would quickly be exhausted, even though I read them sparingly and often reread some chapters. Besides, I needed textbooks.

So I decided to speak to Uncle Rodolfo. He seemed to be the only person I could count on, because of the debate he had opened, on my account, with Nonna and the other women in the house. Anyway, I was flattered that he valued me enough to engage in it.

I went to visit him in his study almost every day. He would sit there for hours in case one of the peasants needed to see him. It was only nominally an office, however, and he was the first to point that out and laugh about it. In reality, Nonna never let the peasants get to him.

I liked his room. In fact, it exerted a kind of fascination over me. It resembled an old notary's office and, unlike the rest of the house, didn't have the aspect of a convent. The lamp, under its green shade, glowed with a pleasant and calming light. Tall bookshelves lined the walls, and large volumes bound in vellum stood neatly behind the glass. Uncle Rodolfo said they were Latin books and old law books belonging to my grandfather, who had done legal work in the town. Once he showed me a great dusty tome, explaining that it was our family book. He added, not without pride, that our lineage could be traced through several generations, and our forebears had been honorable and had all died good deaths. In his words I thought I could detect an allusion to my mother, and I blushed, feeling wounded. But I soon realized that in Uncle Rodolfo's spirit there was no intention to offend me. To dispel the embarrassment between us he took my arm and pointed to a framed drawing of a big leafy tree that represented our family. He then helped me find my name hidden among the youngest branches.

The sturdy tree resembled Uncle Rodolfo, and I told him so. He laughed, revealing strong white teeth. He then noted that the comparison didn't suit him, in fact, because he didn't have children.

"Why didn't you get married, Uncle Rodolfo?" I asked.

He didn't answer, but stared out the window, dazzled by the sunlight. He was, I sensed, looking back over his life at that moment and I maintained a respectful silence.

"Who can say?" he finally answered, finished with his examination and hiding behind those evasive words. With a bitter smile he said, "Some branches wither so that others can grow stronger."

His reticence was touching. The rough, determined features of his face were refined by a modesty I had always felt in him. We were alone, bound by a strong, loyal sympathy that in me became tenderness. I looked at his hunting guns hanging on the walls, his beret, the cartridge belt, two pipes, all bearing witness to his tastes as a simple and solitary man. On the worn baize desktop were a few old things he didn't have the courage to banish from his life: a watch case, a lion-shaped paperweight, and a calendar bearing the inscription "Souvenir."

My uncle unfolded a large chart showing the family lineage in geometric form. You could see pairs of siblings hanging like plates on a scale. More numerous broods took the form of a rake. Next to my father, Ariberto, my mother appeared under her maiden name, and I saw her trapped within those lines, her fair hair gathered at her neck, afraid and pale as when she sat in the boat. Uncle Rodolfo silently drew a cross beside her name and wrote a date. A little below that, my name and the date of my birth hung, alone and lost in the empty space.

TO SPEAK TO Uncle Rodolfo, I chose an afternoon when Nonna and the aunts were in the vineyard. The house was silent, the first October chill gathering in the large, austere rooms, but the study was warm and inviting. My uncle sat in his old leather armchair and I sat across from him, on the other side of the table. He listened attentively, chin in hand, focusing on my face, which was lit by the lamp. Perhaps he was surprised by my passion. It was in fact the first time I had emerged from the apathy with which I carried out my daily duties, assigned by the others. For several weeks, Nonna had been giving me various household chores, probably those she considered best suited to my nature and abilities. They were mostly supervising tasks, and I couldn't help but notice that she alone had glimpsed behind the coldness in my features and gestures a real potential for giving orders. I recall that I once had to go to the cellar to have some demijohns of wine delivered there.

"I'd like the keys, Nonna."

Struck by my request, she stopped. "The keys?" she repeated with surprise. In all these years, no one had ever dared ask her for them, and my audacity gave her pause. She looked at me, convinced she could read in my face an awareness, or, rather, a determination, that made her resolve to surrender. She slowly moved her apron aside and took a large bunch of silvery keys from her waist. I held out my hand. Once again, she hesitated for a moment, and then she said, "Here," in a voice I didn't recognize. It came from her soul, from her womb. It was the voice I imagined one would use with a lover. Bewildered, I took the keys, which shone in the shadowy light of the hall. They were cold and heavy, and I felt I had sacrificed something by accepting them, like a novice offering her head to be tonsured. I ran headlong down the cellar stairs and was panting when I returned to Nonna.

"Here," I said, handing her the keys. I felt I had won a battle.

Uncle Rodolfo listened to me earnestly, scrutinizing me. Then, with a faint smile, which initially seemed sarcastic, he took a hundred-lire note from his pocket and handed it to me.

"This is for your notebooks. If you need more money, ask me. And make me a list of books. I'll get them from Rome."

In my excitement and gratitude I jumped up, ready to throw my arms around him. But I worried that such a gesture might seem forward, and I stopped myself.

"Thank you! Oh, thank you, thank you!" I liked being bound to him by this plot devised to restore my peace and happiness.

"And listen," he continued quietly, beckoning me with a nod. "Do you have a pocket?"

I nodded, surprised, showing him the apron I was wearing.

"Come. Take this. Keep it with you at all times."

I looked at what he slipped into my hand: it was a red coral horn.

"Put it in your pocket. Don't show it to anyone. In this village we live between spells and the evil eye. Especially when you don't want to stay hidden among the branches," he added, smiling and pointing to our family tree. Seeing my name imprisoned within that foliage, I felt short of breath. Other names were crowded around mine, and I remembered my mother saying, days before her death, *Not a single person is free. No one is free. Freedom ends a few hours after birth, when we're given a name and grafted onto a family. From then on, we can no longer get away, release ourselves—in essence, be truly free. The bureau of vital statistics is our prison. We're all pressed within those books, crushed, broken—even young women, even children. They follow our path, record it, control it. Wherever you go, the men writing in those books will pursue you.*

Fascinated, I looked at the book to see my name squeezed in between Giuliano's and that of a cousin who had died a few years old. I wished I could shake off those clinging branches and make my own way; yet the foliage hid me and seemed to protect me. The families I'd known in Rome couldn't be compared to a beautiful tree in any way. But from the moment I arrived in Abruzzo I felt that I had roots like that pine that went deep into the earth and, more specifically, I realized that it had to do with my being a woman. And because of that it seemed that everyone was waiting for something from me, something that was not yet defined in my consciousness but which, with instinctive dismay, I understood myself to possess. I ran my hand over my breast, small and barely rounded, and thought of the still faces of the women who looked at me every evening from the black doors of the altar, their breasts full and triumphant. I was the branch of the tree that the sap ran through:

white, like the milk of plants. *No*, I said to myself, *no*. And I took refuge in thoughts of my mother. Remembering her inspired me with the foolish ambition of someone who has a noble title: she embellished me, she made me proud. And by now Nonna left me to it. Thanks to a certain steadiness I displayed, she pardoned that innocent obsession.. Sometimes when we were all together in the kitchen or the dining room, I began telling stories from Shakespeare, as my mother had when I was a child. Aunt Violante let go of her needle, and her pretty, regular face trembled as she followed the turns of the plot, while Aunt Sofia worked harder and pretended not to listen. Aunt Clarice clapped her hands at the end.

"You're such a good storyteller!" she exclaimed. "Is it a true story?"

"No," Nonna said tersely, anticipating my reply. "Those things never happen in real life."

I tried to protest, summoning my knowledge of history to show, for example, that the Malatesta family had in fact lived in the city of Rimini, and so it was not impossible that the tragedy was based in reality.

"No," Nonna curtly objected. "Don't insist, Alessandra. When you get married, you, too, will understand that they're fabrications, falsehoods."

"I don't want to understand that, Nonna," I protested.

"You'll understand it anyway."

Nonna's great height made it seem impossible that anyone would dare to argue with her. I called on my mother for help, but she was so fragile compared with Nonna that she provided no useful support. Besides, I had discovered that whenever I wasn't present Nonna referred to her as "that unfortunate woman," and others followed her example. Those words, used to describe the most precious person ever to walk the earth, hurt me terribly. I couldn't bear to hear them whispered in the house. So, one evening before the rosary, I decided to speak to Nonna frankly. She was sitting in the large armchair and even though I was standing, I wasn't as tall as she was.

"There's nothing offensive in those words, Alessandra," she replied after a moment of reflection. "They express only compassion and pity."

"I don't want her to be pitied." I was vehement. "She preferred death to making the compromises that other women readily accept. I don't know what all of you here think of her, or what the priests implied. My mother never did anything wrong—believe me, Nonna—she had nothing to be ashamed of."

Nonna looked at me with a mixture of astonishment and satisfaction. I caught that nearly imperceptible spark in her eyes with which she amused herself, baiting me like a rooster.

"I believe it, Alessandra" was her calm reply. "If you say it, I believe it. But even after what you've told me, and maybe even because of it, I will continue to consider her unfortunate. It's unfortunate not to know how to govern our own reactions, our own instincts. To take charge of one's own life, in other words. It's unfortunate to have such a character."

As if to raise an insurmountable barrier between us, I said coldly, "My character is exactly like hers." I saw that I had hit home, because she paled. But she collected herself immediately, gaining a sense of security from casting a watchful eye over me.

"That's not true, Alessandra. I think I know you fairly well by now, and it's not true. You're wrong to judge your mother an extraordinary woman. Extraordinary women are those who don't allow themselves to be overwhelmed—"

"Carried off by the river . . ." I interrupted, following my own thoughts.

"If you prefer that: who stay firm, you see, and don't find themselves uprooted by the current, like feeble saplings. I have no time for them!" She frowned. "Women live a life contrary to their character and their nature, their feelings and their impulses—that's why they have to be strong. Men have no need to force themselves to be strong. The lot they drew was strength; ours, weakness. But they never feel genuine urges. Or, if they do, they follow them—that's it," she added resentfully. "A man falls in war? he's a hero! Even if he wasn't conscious of his heroism. Ah!" said Nonna, striking the armrest and pulling herself up to her full, majestic height. "But how many times must a woman consciously die in her miserable daily life?" She uttered that sentence in a voice so terrible that I still hear it after all these years, and her eyes blazed in the pale light of dusk. Hearing her speak like that, I felt the same uncontrollable fear as when I arrived.

"No," I murmured, shaking my head. "No, Nonna, no, no . . ."

"Come here," she said seriously, yet she surely felt her tone was tender. "It's also wonderful being a woman. It's women who possess life, as the earth possesses flowers and fruit. Flowers have a brief life, like the clear morning light. But the evening: think how beautiful it is. The error lies in thinking that you can take everything from life. Life always asks something of us, and one must always give to life."

Outside the window lay the countryside I knew intimately by now, and the gentle, sad light of sunset instilled in me a great desire to cry. It was simply the sweetness of the moment and the pleasing outline of the mountains that made my heart break.

"Nonna," I called for help in my overwhelming loss.

"Child," she replied, resting a hand on my head.

My aunts and the women from the kitchen came in for the rosary. Setting up chairs, holy-water font and candles, they walked silently in long, dark skirts, coming and going, binding and enveloping me with their steps as if with invisible thread. I could only admire the melancholy pride of their gestures, repeated exactly day after day, which held them prisoner precisely because of the unremitting melancholy. A cold shiver ran up my spine. I wanted to flee, to free myself with a shout. But some instinct urged me to add my energy to their quiet, industrious discipline. I felt called to match my step to theirs, which was detached from enthusiasm or adventure. I knelt in a corner, throwing all my passion into prayer. But my passion was never exhausted.

•   •   •

OTHER RELATIVES OFTEN came to see us in the evening, while we were still sitting at the table. Our family was vast, since in Abruzzo even third or fourth cousins are considered close relatives. The visits became more frequent after my arrival, for everyone was intensely curious to meet me, even if it didn't show, and to see what the daughter of a reckless woman who had killed herself for love was like.

They called me by my first name right away, used the familiar "you," and asked me to get them a glass of water, an ashtray, or a chair, not observing the forms of courtesy our distant relationship might have suggested. The minute I turned away, my relatives observed me attentively, going over every detail of my modest clothing. Furthermore, they came in pairs, sometimes just men, explaining that their wives were busy with a child on account of whose illness or tantrum they hadn't been able to leave. The men of that village have remained in my memory as lively, kind-hearted, and admirable. If they came on their own, they would hazard a gift to me of fruit or a *ciambella*, taken from the credenza at home and quickly hidden in a pocket. They joked a lot and were skilled at card games and tricks. In their confident, easy conversation, they often referred to innocent chapters in their lives as bachelors. Yet when they came with their wives they barely said, "Good evening, Alessandra," and the older ones would pat me on the shoulder to assure me of the kindness with which they judged my character and the sad story of my life. Their attitude offended me, though I didn't dare show my resentment.

I had the mistaken impression that the men were of average height and their wives tall and commanding. The men would gather in groups to talk, and the women, content to be alone, would keep glancing at them attentively. Like Nonna, they hardly ever smiled, and if I sometimes let myself go in some brief cheerful impulse, I was soon met with stern questioning looks and irritated surprise. They always dressed in black, so that an air of recent bereavement hung over them: their conversation, mostly concerned with daily matters, was punctuated with sighs and comments about the harsh life of a mother or housewife.

The visits became longer after Uncle Rodolfo bought the latest-model radio, which captured the most distant stations. By this time, news was spreading even to our part of the countryside that we would soon be entering the war. It was a word I couldn't precisely define. The other war had taken place before I was born, and when my father referred to it—he had been in the Medical Corps—I thought he was showing off and exploiting a legend. I remember finding it impossible to understand how war was fought, how a soldier found the courage to coolly throw himself into the attack for reasons he often barely understood. So I began reading the newspapers, but I quickly tired of the political articles and couldn't keep it up. Anyway, the news in the dailies was never such as to cause the least apprehension.

When I walked by, the peasants would put down their pipes and ask, "You, from Rome, signorina, is it true that there's going to be a war?" I replied that I had been away from Rome for some time, but that, according to the papers, things were going well. Reassured by my words, they would go back to work. Only the women were distrustful. Every evening they listened. "What's he saying?" they would ask, even though the conversation had been crystal clear. It was their native instinct to be suspicious, and they tried to understand the true meaning behind apparently innocuous words.

Her eyes on Giuliano, Aunt Violante said quietly, "The draft cards are already arriving." The peasants would come to say goodbye to Nonna whenever a card arrived. They were young, and their eyes shone with anxious uncertainty.

"They say we're going to Africa," they all repeated. Nonna encouraged them, assuring them that it meant going on a wonderful journey. They would see new lands and come home soon, because of course the war would spare our country. They smiled, foolishly trusting: "Rome will look after us."

The men who came to listen to the radio every night smiled, too, as if they were confronting a sudden whim, the reasons for which they couldn't wholly fathom. But they imagined it to be harmless. "How can we know what they're up to in Rome?" they'd say. There was no antipathy in their tone—if anything, compassionate tolerance, as if a gentle breeze of madness were blowing in the capital. They felt they were in on a joke that would have no consequences. They were a little odd in Rome, but not evil. In Rome, I knew the people who went out to work, came back home, ate, slept, and went to work again.

"They're not happy in Rome," I said, remembering the gloomy nights when darkness fell over the courtyard.

But they just smiled, shaking their heads. "Why do they want to go to war now?" the women asked.

"Who knows!" the men replied. Then, as if making a witty joke, they added, "Every now and again they feel like doing something. Maybe this will work out for them, too."

They laughed, and they came to trust in that laugh. The women, watching them uncertainly at first, were won over in the end, settling for the convenient idea that it was men who had to deal with these obscure matters of politics and war. Gradually, I, too, let myself be won over by their trust. It was peaceful and silent everywhere; the moon illuminated the countryside and the loyal trees. It seemed the world couldn't harbor anything bad. The river Sangro rolled along cheerfully at the foot of the Maiella, already white with snow. Christmas would soon be here. I laughed: yes, surely that would work out, too, and I wasn't sure what we were alluding to. But I wanted everything around me to be peaceful, happy, and hopeful, because I was young and had many years and events ahead of me. We went to the door with our guests, where they said cordial and effusive goodbyes. Brusquely, I dismissed the thought of Antonio, which for some time had made me feel disturbingly guilty.

·   ·   ·

I WAS DISTRESSED by another thought at that time, and it concerned the living conditions of the people in the countryside and in small villages like this one. From my window, you could see the village sloping towards the valley and the stream. It was a vast pile of stones, and it seemed impossible that anyone could find shelter among them. The only trace of human life was the smoke emerging from the black chimneys.

I soon began exploring the narrow streets in front of those dwellings. But the joyful curiosity that spurs me to learn about new customs and new landscapes was suddenly quelled. The houses were all built of rough, unhewn stone, and not one had the security of a foundation on level ground. Each one supported the next, the rooftops forming small steps, and clinging to the mountainside, seeking shelter from the wind and the freezing cold of winter. The summer, though, turned the limestone red-hot and the inhabitants baked in their houses like bread on the hearthstone.

The wide valley was embraced by a chain of hills and mountains, which were tinted pink or yellow depending on the position of the sun in the sky. And in the light of the sun they looked benevolent and welcoming. But other miserable hamlets emerged on the mountainside like mushrooms, or warts, cut off by creeks and valleys, their bell towers rising from the center like a howl.

Troubled, I went to the doors of the huts and looked inside the dark, smoky spaces. A little light shone through a narrow aperture, and a geranium bloomed in a jar on the crude windowsill. The kitchens, blackened by smoke from the hearth, nevertheless maintained a nobility that I later recognized in every house and person in Abruzzo. Despite the poverty of the place and the rags the women and children wore, the only lingering smell between those walls was a good one, of black wood ready for burning. I would say that that smell was unique to the whole village, as in a large woodshed, a powerful smell that evoked snow and the hearth even in summer.

The women had worn, brown faces under black kerchiefs. They observed me, and everything about me, from my step to my gestures and my fair hair, astonished them.

"Good morning," I would say with a smile.

They never smiled. "Come in," they would reply, not wondering about my curiosity or interest. They were indifferent to everything, I noticed. They watched me compassionately, as if I, out walking with a dog, had yet to understand what a tremendous grindstone daily life was. I asked them for news about the men, whom you rarely met in the village in nice weather.

"They're laboring," they would reply, but without complaint or exaggeration, for labor is work, and in work is their bread.

I once happened to hear a woman respond with disdain, "Eh, they toil in summer, the men do. Working on the land is hard, worse than in the house. The house protects; the earth kills. In winter, though, men sleep by the fire, smoke their pipe, and rest. Us? No! Children are born in winter, too, and the polenta has to be cooked. The earth rests; a house never rests." She finished the sentence, her tone curdled and compressed with hate. After a pause she continued. "We also go and labor in the fields at harvest or sowing time. We go and work when there's a war, too. War is for men. I've had three husbands," she said calmly and without the embarrassment a woman from the city would have felt offering this detail. "The first died in Africa, the second in Spain." Her voice became more shrill. "Now I want to see where they'll send the third one to die."

I knew she was a young woman, but on her forehead and around her mouth and eyes, the lines were grooved in stone. Her skin was leathery and brown like Sista's, and, like Sista, she was ageless. She had been married a few weeks before, and yet they still called her Widow Martina. I was sitting and watching her while she kneaded dough for bread. Her rolled-up sleeves revealed the strong, muscular forearms of a young man, and her hands, opening and closing on the soft, sticky dough, betrayed an urge to violence that was released in that gesture. I suddenly remembered the fury with which Sista passed the iron over my father's shirts.

"What will you do?" I asked quietly.

"What can we do?" she returned, getting steamed up with her effort. "They're in Rome, we're here, peace to them, and we wait. We wait and we thank God it's not our job to decide on wars or send out draft cards. It's our job to work. The rest is for educated people, the ones who read the papers and books."

She seemed to be referring to me personally, so I hurried away, without looking into any of the other houses or greeting the women. For a while I felt that I was the one who would be deciding how Martina's third husband would die.

I TRIED TO talk about these things with Uncle Rodolfo. I went to his study often now. I read while he wrote, together under a circle of light from the same lamp. When I looked up from my reading, I saw only one photograph of him on the wall, from when he was at the front: bold, one foot resting on a rock, arms folded, a jaunty mustache. I thought I could attribute his boldness to the illusions he must have had, as a young man, of being fortune's darling and a favorite with the women. If he had died in the war and left only that picture behind, one would have said, "What a shame! He had his whole life ahead of him. Who knows what he could have done." He was no longer a young man. He lived in an old house in a remote village in Abruzzo, kept the peasants' accounts in a large logbook. And I knew that he was dominated by his mother, who could order him around with a wave of her hand.

As I pondered his fate, I very quickly began to fear for my own. I didn't want mine to decline like his, or to align itself with mediocrity so readily. I shuddered to think that my strength might be illusory, like Uncle Rodolfo's in that picture. Maybe I, too, would be stifled and over-whelmed, since I lacked the toughness needed to resist. Besides, I was aware that I had no experience of life. Solitude had spoiled me, and most of my knowledge was only literary. I had learned from books or from my mother, who had transformed every event into a fairy tale.

"I'll always be young," she would say. "We will always be young," she had reassured me excitedly.

Maybe Uncle Rodolfo had thought the same thing when he had that photograph taken in wartime, with his foot on the rock. Now my mother was dead and Uncle Rodolfo, writing in his logbook, had a soft wrinkle under his chin.

"Were you happy then, Uncle Rodolfo?"

Surprised, he looked up from his logbook. "When?"

"Then." I pointed to the photograph. He turned, following my gesture.

"Yes, I was. It was a wonderful time, the best time of my life." He smiled and looked into space, as if he were seeing again people, places, images; his smile made him youthful again. "It wasn't just being in my early twenties, though that's important. But we were naturally trusting at that age, and we had a respectful cordiality, a sense of solidarity with others that meant we laughed easily, happily, we weren't reserved or doubtful . . ." He was suddenly silent, as if he feared letting go and saying too much. He threw me, instead, a quick glance to measure the effect of his words.

"Now, though," I said, lowering my voice, "no one is happy, right?"

"Right—it seems no one is happy anymore." He looked down at his papers again, as if considering my question, and then he turned to look at me, trying to guess what was behind it. I didn't dare go into the cause of my discontent, but, if I thought back, I realized that it had been close, dull, and dense around me from the time I was a child. Yet no one ever had the nerve to talk about it, not even Fulvia and I when we were alone on the balcony, touching on the thorniest subjects. Uncle Rodolfo didn't want to prolong the discussion, and his look, both humble and embarrassed, made that clear.

"We can't say we're not happy, can we?"

He shook his head. "No. No one says that. I've never said it before now. And I'm sorry that you should be the first to ask me about it, because you belong to a generation at some remove from mine, so certain things in fact seem incomprehensible to you. But certain things, long ago, when I returned from the war, fit in with our confidence, our bravado, and it was natural to adopt certain behaviors at the time. Because of the risks we'd taken and the distress we'd experienced, we felt we'd earned the right to impose on others the resounding presence of our life, our strength, our laws. No, you'll never be able to understand how natural all this seemed at the time—and sound, easy, without pitfalls. We weren't much older than you are; the world seemed to have begun with us and our terrible experiences. Then . . ." He pointed to his portrait. "Then I came back here, to the country. I shut myself up in this study to discover a personal, interior life. I fell in love too. It was a long affair," he added with a shy smile. "I restricted myself, you see, to the range of my interests—family, land, house—and I lost all my confidence, pride, and what's more—you must understand this—daily life ground down my enthusiasm and sincere involvement in things that belonged to the remote past, a time now lost. Other men shut themselves up in their offices, got married, had families. People no longer spoke about certain things, or not with their earlier commitment. At the same time, those things changed, were transformed, blown out of proportion: our very silence made them grow. And now . . ." He threw his arms wide as he finished.

He looked at me, expecting absolution or a violent reaction.

I didn't really know what he was alluding to, but I realized that he meant the difficulty of achieving the ideals we had set ourselves; that is, the immense and daunting difficulty of living, which I had always sensed in the desperation accompanying my rare moments of joy. I had been very young—a child—but I already knew the melancholy faces of the women looking out into the courtyard. I saw the men go out early and come home to eat, return to the office, eat again, throw themselves into bed to sleep, tired and demeaned. I realized what a miserable machine a man's life was: "The money's all gone," the wives say; the children wait, eyes wide with hostility. "I will provide," the men respond, and once again they go out in the street, anguished, anxious. Meanwhile certain things happen and the men should think first of all about certain things, but they're no longer strong, free men, they're heads of families. What can a family do when confronted with certain things?

I felt an uncontrollable urge to carry out a dangerous mission, and, by taking a risk, deliver myself from a responsibility whose origins were unknown to me, but whose painful effects I was discovering. I was free, and as a single person I could risk everything, even my life. I'd escape at night wearing the black dress I always wore now, and arrive in Rome after a long and exhausting journey. The city had remained in my memory as a white patch of sun, with white houses, bright green trees, the sky's vivid blue. I saw myself in black, walking safely through the streets, totally absorbed in my clear duty, which was to say, *The peasants are not happy*, and to speak of mud hovels, stone houses on the mountainside, and breathtaking discontent. But I lost heart at the thought that I wouldn't be able to define that dissatisfaction, to understand its causes or limits. My ignorance made me tremble with rage. My hands shook and I looked anxiously for some revelatory sign. I wouldn't even have known where to go. I felt paralyzed simply by the question of who I might turn to. Some dark instinct told me not to: *Are you crazy? You can't do that. You have to stay quiet, quiet, quiet. We always spoke quietly about Antonio.*

DESPITE THE MISTRUST his appearance aroused in me, I would have liked to talk to Giuliano about these things. He was the only person of my age there. We might have been able to talk without our relatives' knowledge, just as I'd talked about love and how babies are made with Fulvia when the adults were out—things that seemed equally secret.

But our mutual aversion grew more evident by the day. He had noticed Nonna's fondness for me and was competing with me, even though I had no intention of fighting. Still, he was always trying to denigrate me, and his sarcasm was crude, obvious, and banal. It wasn't his boorishness that irritated me but the vulgarity of the feelings it expressed. He would circle me while I sat reading in the kitchen garden or the dining room, teasing and hoping to demolish my cocoon of well-being. My life was a calm circle; I felt its harmony, and that annoyed Giuliano. Maybe he hadn't yet had a woman, and his curiosity must have troubled him, just as my pure, honest appearance incited him against me.

"Why do you put on such airs?" he was always asking. Once he said, "You're ugly."

"It doesn't matter to me," I replied with a smile. "Really, Giuliano, I honestly don't care."

"You say that because you're full of yourself. But being pretty is the only important thing for a woman. You're too tall and you're skinny. Women should have hips and breasts, nice round cheeks. Can't you see how thin you are? No man will marry you—he'd get hurt bumping against you in bed."

He would come up to me laughing and stare, his mean, scornful eyes vibrating with stubbornly repressed desire. I'd move away, tightly holding on to a book or my sewing to cover myself. "It doesn't matter," I said calmly. "I have no intention of getting married."

"Good thing you say so, since no one would marry you for a different reason. You shouldn't give yourself such airs."

"Why not?" I took care to remain calm, but I stood up and my hands trembled.

"Because everyone knows that your mother had a lover."

"It's not true," I replied, looking furiously at him.

"Oh, yes it is. Everyone says so. Why would she have killed herself then? She killed herself out of shame."

"It's not true," I retorted forcefully. "It was because—" But I couldn't go on. It was impossible to pinpoint the tiny elements that contributed to my mother's unhappiness. More than that, it was impossible to make them comprehensible to a man like Giuliano. Defeated, I quickly ran off.

He immediately started coming after me. "She had a lover; she did. Everyone knows it . . ."

The house was deserted, and seemed to offer no escape. I didn't want to go to the kitchen lest the women hear what Giuliano kept repeating as he followed me, and some instinct warned me not to go to my room. I covered my ears. From the hall, I went out onto a small balcony where there was an old outhouse. I went inside and slid the iron latch shut, panting.

On the balcony now, just outside the flimsy door, Giuliano repeated: "She had a lover! Open up. Everyone knows it. Stop acting stuck up!"

He shook the door handle; the latch was weak and he could break it open. There was also a small window of opaque glass in the door.

"Open up," he said, "or I'll break the window."

The outhouse was hanging in mid-air because the house was perched at the top of the village, as I've mentioned. I felt I would be safe only if the floor gave way and I dropped onto the sharp stones of the street below. With some relief I imagined myself lying there, broken, arrested by an act of desperation.

Giuliano's voice repeated, "Open up, stupid. Open!" His hand shook the lock with nightmarish rhythmic insistence. "You can hear me anyway: your mother had a lover, she had a lover."

I was overcome with terror, certain that he would be able to open the door, certain that, if he did, I couldn't offer the least resistance, and in any case I didn't know exactly to what. His words had driven me in there, where I had no security or freedom of action. Through a slit looking out on the valley, I could see the beloved Abruzzo countryside, strong and gentle, which had become my dearest companion. Although it comforted me all day long, at that moment it couldn't help me.

The space was tiny, and, with a single step, Giuliano would have pushed me to the wall, forced me to hear those words whispered in my ear. I saw his face pressed against the opaque glass so he could watch me. I could make out his eyes, his big lips, and his flattened nose, a patch of white flesh.

"I can see you," he said. "I can see you perfectly." He laughed at the sight of me in that filthy place. I couldn't get away from his gaze. Backed against the gray wall, I covered my face with my hands.

"I see you. Why don't you stop being stuck-up? Your mother had a lover. It's pointless to lock yourself in the privy."

A long time went by, and I kept my eyes covered so as not to see Giuliano's angry mouth crushed against the glass. After a while I heard the dog whimpering outside the door, calling me, his claws patiently, insistently scraping the wood. The silence confirmed that I was alone. I went out cautiously and crouched down beside him on the balcony.

It was nearly evening, and I could barely see the dog's eyes in the half-light. I made out the sad slant of his mouth, the forlorn crease in every dog's muzzle. He let his head fall in my lap. Reassured by my presence, he was soon asleep and breathing heavily. The warmth of his body under the smooth fur spread to my legs, comforting after my humiliating imprisonment. I leaned my head against the wall and, looking up, saw a few bright white stars emerging against the dark cloak of the sky. It was a lovely, peaceful evening. I caressed the dog. A little later, I heard Aunt Violante calling me from the house.

"Alessandra! Alessandra . . ."

I didn't answer. I hoped they'd forget me out there in the dark, not only that evening but forever.

I SLEPT LITTLE that night, and the following day the event with the rooster took place. It was one of the things everyone cited as proof of my brutality. When asked, then and now, why I behaved like that, I replied,

"I don't know." Everyone thought I was being reticent, yet it was the truth.

There were a lot of hens in the chicken coop and one gorgeous rooster. Everyone in the village talked about that rooster, because of the richness of his feathers, their golden-green color, the boldness of his crest. He had come in a cage from the north, and the servants regarded him just as they would a special guest.

He was never the first to come running when the corn was scattered on the ground. The hens rushed over happily, shaking their ample hips like busy housewives. They pecked avidly, deftly, but governed by a respectful solidarity. The rooster came later. He was tall, much taller than all the hens, and his step was stately, solemn. Walking, he lifted his feet adorned by feathered spurs He would lean over the hens and, aiming at their necks, suddenly peck at them, cruelly and with great mastery. He would peck at them one after another, rapidly, as if delivering thrusts from a dagger. Often, a drop of blood would stain the hens' soft white plumage. They would flee, leaving him alone with the remaining feed. And then the rooster, revealing a sudden greed, would quickly devour the fat yellow kernels of corn, his beak pecking precisely. He was splendid. His feathers trembled with the force of his gluttony, his wattle lit up with the vivid color of blood, and his crest appeared even more brazen and pompous. His neck, swelling with the sense of well-being that comes from feeling sated, attracted me. It was light and beautiful, with luxuriant feathers.

I called him, enticing him with a handful of corn. Trusting my voice and my person, he came closer, stepping warily and solemnly; for a brief moment the one eye beneath his upright crest stared at me, assessing me as he did the hens. I was kneeling on the ground and I sensed that he might hurt me, suddenly peck at me—not out of viciousness but because of the guaranteed right he was permitted to assert. We looked at each other: his eye was as hard as stone. Suddenly I grabbed his neck, my fingers digging into his feathers; and with deep disgust I held his soft, bright body between my knees.

My hands are long and thin. Looking at them, you would think they were weak: delicate, feminine hands. You would think it, I said. But they've always been extremely strong, with a taste for subduing things, snapping sticks and branches.

Under the soft ruffles of the rooster's gaudy feathers, his neck proved to be fragile, though swollen with food. I imagined it white, blue, and violet. I squeezed. His body thrashed between my knees, wings flapping, provoking an irritating horror in me. But the irritation made me redouble my grip. I squeezed within the secret warmth of his feathers until the rooster was still. He rolled on the ground and from there stared at me, looking dreadful with his hard, stony eye.

It was late morning, almost midday. The farmyard was sunny, but the rooster's lovely feathers slowly faded, as if color were leaving them along with life. I was still kneeling and my black dress was dusty. I quickly washed my hands at the fountain, entered the cold, dark stairway, went up to my room, and threw myself on the bed, eyes closed, exhausted.

ALTHOUGH NO ONE had seen me, I immediately confessed to having killed the rooster. The maids looked at me with respect because I had dared to perform such a bold act. There was a long discussion about who would pluck him. No one wanted this task, as if it would mean perpetuating the crime. At last, a sturdy, dark woman called Adele said, "I'll do it," and she set to work with some zeal. The feathers flew around her and her curly head shook with every yank.

"All feathers, measly body."

Nonna came up to my room to interrogate me. Her visit had been announced, so I was expecting her, calmly, as I had expected the headmaster after I had injured Magini at school. All the same, when I heard her step on the stairs, I was overcome by an uncontrollable anxiety. I felt I wouldn't know how to account for my act, which in all honesty I couldn't explain even to myself. Once more, as when I was a child, I wished I could believe that a supernatural being had possessed me—my brother Alessandro—to whom I could attribute every shameful or cruel action. But I could no longer find refuge in that easy way out. I felt wholly responsible, though unable to prove my absolute innocence.

"Why did you do it?" Nonna asked. She sat across from me, her tall knees supporting a hand-warmer. The black dress draped over her legs looked like a pedestal on which her torso rested solemnly.

"I don't know," I replied, and she didn't believe me. I persisted in searching myself, hoping I would suddenly understand the mysterious motive behind my deed. But I simply felt empty and tired. "I don't know."

"That's not possible. Did you want to eat him?"

I shook my head, smiling.

"Giuliano might have done it out of spite. But not you. You knew I cared a lot about that rooster. So why?"

"I don't know, Nonna."

She seemed disappointed, offended. "I thought," she said regretfully, "that you would never resort to lying. I've forgiven you. I don't want you to be afraid of me. I've forgiven you. So now, tell me."

"I don't know," I repeated, shaking my head. "I don't know."

I felt a deep, savage desperation. I honestly didn't know why I had done something that I considered horrible but which had also given me a deep satisfaction. I thought about the confidence with which Adele had pulled out the feathers, the rooster's thin body, his limp, frail neck.

"You did a good job killing him," Adele had said, and everyone had looked at my hands.

"I want you to trust me, Alessandra," Nonna said. "I have a lot of faith in you, a great deal of faith. Since you arrived I've felt stronger, though at first I was afraid for you—you said you were like Eleonora. But it's not true. You're not like your mother." After a pause, she added, "You're like me."

I watched her, enthralled by her formidable appearance. Maybe this similarity, which wasn't yet clear to me, would soon manifest itself, irrepressible, like the impulse that had driven me to kill the rooster. I leaned towards Nonna. I felt animated by a new power that would exaggerate my features and my height.

"You might not realize it right away," she went on. "I didn't know myself to be as I am, either. But slowly, slowly I acquired strength. Day by day, I should say. You spend your time reading, which isn't good. Books make you weak, make you suffer, enslave you. One doesn't need to suffer. One needs to eliminate suffering from one's life if one wants to be strong. The only thing that's worth the suffering is bringing children into the world. With each child I brought into the world, I felt myself living once more."

I gazed at her, fascinated by this majestic goddess to whom it seemed natural to offer a sacrifice of human blood or live babies.

"I've noticed that you like the countryside, and you like walking around the farm. I know you well by now. Listen," she confided in a quiet voice, "the farm is yours. Look at it," she said, gesturing towards the valley and the hillside. "Look how beautiful it is, how tidy. The square vineyard, fields of grain rising in terraces all the way up to the olive trees."

For the first time, her voice was tender and emotional, the voice of a woman and not of a great mountain.

"The property stretches along the riverbank and the river bathes it, nourishes the earth like a mother her child. Grass grows thick and the ears of corn grow plumper each year. Before long, in spring, the orchard blossoms, and then the fruit comes in: rich, ripe, and firm. The cellar is full of perfumed fruit; it's astounding."

She took my hand and continued. "Giuliano won't have anything but that little bit from his mother. Only a little, a pittance. He's like his father. I've told him so many times, 'Study. Find a job in the city.' I was waiting for a girl. You—I thought you were lost. When I found out that your mother was dead, I said to Rodolfo, 'Go and get her. Bring her here.' I couldn't sleep the night before you arrived."

We looked out the window at the countryside together, and Nonna's eyes were alight with excitement. Slowly, she moved her black apron aside, and against the black of her dress the shiny bunch of silvery keys appeared. The evening light settled on the steel and sent out incandescent reflections. Nonna passed her large hand over the keys, gripped them in a long, lingering caress.

"I remember the day when you asked me for the keys. It was as if I were already dead and you had taken my place. Your step was sure as you went down into the cellar. Your light hair stood out in the dark. Sofia and Violante are afraid of the dark, but you're not. You're like me."

Trembling, she put a hand on my arm, then my shoulder; her face wore the determined, impatient expression of the diviner who has found water. Motionless, I waited for her to draw me near or put her arms around me.

"You must stop reading books," she murmured. "Leave them to the men . . . I used to read, too, before I got married, and I played the harmonium. When your grandfather died I had it taken to the attic and locked it up there.

"I was still young, just over thirty, with five children to raise, the house, the farm. So I had to be very strong. Fortunately I realized that, and I became strong. Very strong." She sat up straight as she spoke. Maybe she had begun growing at that time. From that time, her hands had become large, her bearing noble. "The harmonium is bad for you, like reading books. You don't need to read books: you'll be in charge."

Tempted by Nonna's words, I looked at the valley and the hill opposite, trying to imagine them mine. I was expecting a strong reaction—an eager, satisfied thrill. I tried to imagine the land belonging to me like the flesh on my shoulders and breasts, the river flowing in my veins. But I felt, instead, that I belonged to the earth. One couldn't be master of the earth; it was contrary to nature. Again, and more than ever, I discovered my distaste for ownership.

Everyone called Nonna "the Mistress." It was natural; she was entitled to the name by some inherent right, not only by her property. In that place, I realized, it was property that established one's social position: a field was tantamount to a noble title. Nonna wore a queen's crown on her head, though her property was modest. Yet her every word and gesture revealed a powerful sense of ownership. Sometimes when the weather wasn't cold or foggy she would sit in the middle of the field. A maid would bring her a chair—I think it was an ordinary chair, but it seemed taller than the others. She would sit and sniff the air, the wind, slowly turning her large white head. The chair was covered by her skirt, and it looked as if the ground itself were rising up to support her on that throne. So it seemed right that the earth belonged to her, and the fruit trees, right up to the high plateau with the olive trees. She commanded them from afar as an orchestra conductor does the instruments furthest away. Under her gaze the trees quivered and gave up their fruit; willingly the olives squeezed into the press, offering her their thick, yellow juice. "Wonderful," she declared, licking the oil from her fingertip.

Sometimes I sat next to a cherry tree with delicate, transparent foliage. "Get them to give it to you, Signorina," Adele suggested to me one day. Aunt Sofia had the almonds, Aunt Violante a walnut wood. During the harvest, when the fruit was knocked down with sticks, the two of them were vigilant around their trees, quickly calculating the fruit in terms of money. But I found myself blushing at Adele's words. It was as if she were trying to persuade me to buy a slave. Besides, those trees belonged to Nonna and were planted on her orders. She had watched them grow, cared for them, pruned them. It was said that one night a few years ago snow fell and then froze. The branches creaked and groaned under the weight. Nonna came down to the orchard with her long stick and, by herself, began to free the trees of ice, which fell and broke with the sound of glass. The next morning, she brushed aside the family's anxious, affectionate protests.

"It was cold like the nights Rodolfo didn't come home and I waited at the door. The night Caterina died, too, and I kept watch over her." I had never kept watch over the trees as if they were children, and therefore they weren't mine.

However, since I was treated with greater deference I realized that Nonna must have spoken to some of them about her intention to leave me the farm. I had never inspired much fondness except among the simple folk. The others seemed to wonder who I really was and what I wanted. Then they began to realize that I was the likely heir to the farm, the house, and the hillside. And so when I walked by there was the mistrustful silence that surrounds a master's presence. A child only a few years old got up from the step where she was sitting and fixed me with large, frightened eyes. I was unhappy; I felt a sudden chill in my limbs, an ominous warning. Above all, I had the feeling that from then on I would be alone and unable to communicate with anyone.

"Why did you get up?" I asked the little girl, shaking her by the arm. She didn't answer, and continued to look at me in bewilderment.

"Why?" I insisted. "Why?" I shook her harder, but she didn't fight back. I let her down on the step with a thump. The girl didn't cry. She seemed to expect my gesture, or some other cruel, inexplicable gesture.

I would be mistress of the pig. Behind the house was a foul sty. The hog would come out and stare at Nonna, who weighed him up visually. They both stared, taking the measure of each other, and from under all his quivering fat the pig had a sharp, wicked look. "Not yet," Nonna decided.

The maples in the wood were red when the pig was killed. A lacerating human cry rose from the farm, a pitiful lament. We were gathered around Nonna in the dining room, sewing, and my hands shook. Disturbed by that terrible cry, I would have liked to stop working, plug up my ears, and go away. But I looked at Nonna's calm face and kept on sewing. We finally heard an even sharper scream, a gurgling.

"It's done," Nonna said, dropping the white cloth onto her lap.

The pig was carried off on a stretcher made of branches, like a loyal adversary, now defeated. Over the farmyard hung the hot, sweet smell of blood.

It hung thick in the kitchen while the pig's flesh was prepared for the winter. All the women were there, united in a rare euphoria. A few of them sat at the table, while others went from the table to the large kitchen sink, white aprons stained with blood.

Seeing me at the door, Nonna invited me: "Come, Alessandra."

"Come," they all said, animated by childlike glee. "Come, come!"

We were well into autumn, and the days were short. A warm light from the lamp over the table lit the soft red of the ground meat ready for sausages or cotechino, the dark red hunk of lean meat for salting. I went forward timidly; I seemed to be walking on living flesh. Nonna was checking the guts against the light: black and blue, transparent, they swelled and dangled disgustingly. Then, judging them to be intact, she handed them to her daughters and the maids for stuffing and tying. The women cheerfully pressed the meat into the long intestines and tied the string.

The walls reflected the meat's brilliant red; in the shadowy corners reddish spots seemed to thicken. The bright, vermilion blood in a vast container mirrored the lamp. Aunt Sofia moved the container and the liquid shook, flowed over the edge, and gushed onto the floor.

"It's good luck!" the women exclaimed. They all wanted to dip their fingertips in it. With the blood Adele painted two red spots on her cheeks.

"The pig is dead!" she hummed and with the blood drew a cross on the huge snout sitting in the sink.

"The pig is dead," Aunt Clarice echoed, clapping her hands.

They worked fervidly, revealing surprising skill and inciting one another to go faster. Violently, they thrust the meat into the stubby trotter and then pushed it, nails and all, into a neighbor's face to startle her. They laughed. I saw their hands glistening with red blood, dull with thickened, dark blood. The cloying, nauseating smell of blood stuck in my throat.

Nonna, standing, plunged the knife into the cold, sinewy meat.

I would be mistress of the pig.

"No!" With a loud cry, I turned and fled, groping my way along the hall, my eyes blinded by moving red spots of blood. "No! No!" The portraits of my Abruzzese ancestors accompanied me from wall to wall, their faces dark, still, and severe. I read in them the deep satisfaction of having been mistress of the pig.

"No," I whispered. "No." That wasn't my story. My story was in the box where Mamma had jealously preserved the veils of Juliet and Desdemona.

A FEW DAYS later, Aunt Clarice came to my room. "Listen, Alessandra." And she climbed on the chair, letting her small, black-shod feet dangle in the air. "Is it true that Eleonora is dead?"

I looked at her uncertainly for a moment. I felt I would have to make up a lie, as one does with children.

"If she's dead," Clarice continued without waiting for my answer, "I'm very happy. Because then I'll see her, too, in paradise. Lots of people are already waiting for me there: Mamma, Papa, Cesira, and then many aunts, cousins, nieces and nephews, and my grandmother. She loved me so much when I was little. They'll throw a big party when they see me. I can't wait for that moment. Who knows what will happen? I'd like to arrive and surprise them all sitting in a circle, saying, 'Clarice is certainly late!'"

Sitting beside her, I stroked her smooth, shiny white hair. "Would you really be happy?"

"Of course," she replied, as if offended, shrugging her shoulders with a cat's delicacy and grace. "I don't want to stay here a minute more. I'm old now, and I'm bored. I do nothing all day. Winter goes by quickly since I go to bed at sunset and sleep; in summer, though, the days never end. I'm bored. I'd like to go to paradise and hear the music."

Her skin smelled like rice powder and sugared almonds.

"What music do you like, Aunt Clarice?" I tried to get her to talk.

"All kinds of music. When I hear it, I feel I'm in church, and I'm well. Eleonora played the harmonium when she came here; you were only just born. We once went to the attic together and she played a piece—I remember it still—called 'A Waltz Dream.' She played softly so Nonna wouldn't hear, as if there were something wrong. I don't understand what can be so bad about music, but I never understand anything. In the kitchen the maids laugh at me when they talk about dirty things, the things men do. I don't understand, and I'm glad I don't. I don't like men."

"You never liked them? Not even when you were young?"

"Oh, no! They really used to frighten me. Nowadays I don't pay attention to them. And then, look," she lowered her voice, "men don't understand a thing, I can tell you that. Who is it who keeps the house going, who washes, irons, cooks? Who knows how to make desserts? Women. The women do everything. Men drink, get drunk, argue about politics and don't conclude anything. When they're home, you have to say 'Yes, yes,' the whole time and then do the opposite. Do you think a man would know how to play 'A Waltz Dream'?"

"I don't know," I whispered.

"Certainly not! I assure you, he wouldn't. Giuliano shoots birds and kills them. What skill is there in that? Alfredo takes peasant girls into the woodshed and they come out red and ruffled like hens. What idiots. Uncle Rodolfo makes fun of me, you know, for wanting to go to paradise early. Really! He thinks it's nicer to stand around watching him play cards and drink wine."

Her expression turned sulky. "But don't you worry . . ." she added thoughtfully. "As soon as I get there, I'll tell Eleonora to let you come soon. Are you happy?"

Seated at her feet, I looked up at her but didn't reply. The light falling from her hair clothed her in white, as if by some miracle a dove had flown into my room.

"You're not answering," she said. "I understand: you wouldn't like to die, either. It must be because you don't want to leave the men. They've already enchanted you. Why else would a woman not wish to die? There's the wonderful scent of lilies up there, as there is in church for Corpus Domini. The saints carry white flowers and Saint Cecilia plays music. Eleonora plays 'A Waltz Dream.' And here? Here it's all work, having children, nursing those children, working in the fields, working in the house, working all day long. And always being afraid of the men because they're ill-tempered or because they have a lover and spend money on her. Always trembling, crying—always crying because of these troublesome men. Why shouldn't women wish to die, unless they've fallen under their spell?"

With a small leap, she got out of her chair and took my hand. "Come," she said. "We'll go and ask Nonna if she'll take us to the attic to play the harmonium."

Nonna said yes. She took the key from a storage room and, calling her daughters, preceded us up the dark stairs.

She climbed slowly. We held back out of respect, and because we were all wearing black we appeared to form a procession.

The attic was actually bright, and full of old, disused furniture piled up in corners. The dusty flight of old beams ended at a low window, which opened onto the sweet hills and the sky, fading with the approach of evening.

"Here we are." Nonna closed the door.

There were cobwebs everywhere, so tidy and clean that they had by this time taken on the settled character of decoration. Dust veiled objects so that they lost their precise outlines and took on the fantastical aspect of a dream.

Aunt Violante looked around. "We haven't come up here for a long time."

"It's so beautiful!" exclaimed Aunt Clarice. "When we were young, Nonna and I often came to the attic to open the trunks. We spent the afternoon looking, trying on, touching. All the brides' white dresses are here—our mother's, Nonna's, and lots of great-aunts'. We'd put them on chairs, upright, with their arms out. The silk still speaks, it goes *shu, shu.* It got dark; the dresses seemed like ghosts. Shall we open the trunks tonight?" she suggested in her little voice.

"No," Nonna said firmly. "That's enough now. We're too old. I don't want to get emotional. Alessandra will see all this one day. We're here to be peaceful and play a lovely hymn."

The harmonium was big. In its presence, even Nonna's gestures grew smaller. In fact, I'd say that when she sat down in front of it she seemed, for the first time, to be dominated. She pressed a key that had "angelic voice" written on it, unfolded a sheet of music, and began to play.

It was a hymn to the Virgin, which my aunts sang with pious devotion. Aunt Clarice climbed on a stool so she could more easily read the words.

I was discovering, through their habit of singing together, a deep affinity between the women in my family. Nonna led us and we followed intently, none of us letting her own voice project, so that the singing would be uniform and pleasing to all. Aunt Violante's sorrowful face seemed to cast off its weight, and Aunt Sofia's severe face opened up to the sweetness of the tune.

The attic united us in a quiet sense of well-being, and I suddenly understood how simple it was for a woman to enter a religious community and become part of it—and what enchantment I might have found in one. I was overcome by an intense longing for that solitary, passionate life, expressed in the ardor with which I gave myself to the singing.

I IMAGINED A tiny cell with neat bricks and a window like the one I used to write at. The shadow of the iron bars formed a large cross on the floor, and obeying that cross seemed to provide the ultimate well-being. I imagined the exhausting solitude of other women like me outside the walls; and I felt that this other solitude was a balm for all the problems women face.

On the way home from my walks, I would see the village: rough, gray, and forbidding like the ones patron saints hold in the palm of their hands. It was a gloomy heap of stones; the stones formed houses—and those houses allowed no escape, no reprieve. I could see our house, high above the others, with its narrow windows. I would go in from the light outdoors, and yielding to the dark felt like bending to the yoke. I often had trouble sleeping at night. In the winter, you could hear the Sangro flowing like a distant drum roll. And the house spoke in the silence. It was a very old house. Nonna maintained that it was two hundred years old. Every morning for two hundred years, women had knelt to uncover the embers in the ashes and blow on the coals, and the fire had begun to splutter in the darkness of the sleeping house. They invariably spent every hour of their lives in that house: there, they grew from children to women. They knew a man in the marital bed, gave birth to children, grew old, and finally men shouldered their coffin and carried them away, hard shoes pounding the cobblestone streets. In the fearful silence of the night, I heard restless dead women walking up and down the halls and stairs, keys jangling at their sides. Nonna said she had heard Aunt Caterina laughing one night years after her death, when her husband's lover betrayed him. She said, too, that she often heard Ortensia Boni, a young wife who had come from the Veneto and died in childbirth, walking through the house. I heard Ortensia's light step when the wind rose, and I heard Aunt Caterina laughing in the creaking of a window.

"You'll get married here," they all kept saying. Nonna spoke of an advantageous marriage. So that room would become my nuptial chamber, and that was the ceiling I'd see with a man at my side; there I'd give birth.

"These are comfortable beds," Nonna said, "iron beds. You can hold on to them." All that was left was to take the crucifix off the wall and place it on my chest when I died.

I wanted to rebel against that sordid destiny. I felt I had it in me somehow to carry the message my mother had entrusted to me. I imagined myself in a laboratory, dressed in white, surrounded by test tubes and stills. No! It was always the human element that attracted me. Then I pictured myself wearing a toga in court. Behind me sat a humble middle-aged woman, hands on her knees. I was speaking, exhausting myself. *Save her!* I was saying. *She's innocent!* I repeated. *Gentlemen of the jury, she's innocent. All women are innocent.* But I could never be a lawyer; my shyness would prevent me. And yet I felt it was my duty to do something for women—I had to, at the cost of negating or sacrificing myself. A voice inside me ordered: *Become a saint!* I was irresistibly attracted by the warmth of a community of women. I longed to be locked in a humble cell with a coarse pallet, like Chiara of Assisi. The gaunt face of St. Francis appeared to me behind a grate. "God," I whispered, arms at my sides, "Lord God, take me!"

But I was not a believer. When I considered becoming a nun, I was really thinking of exalting myself. I persisted in trying to make myself better. Every day, I hoped to be more transparent, purer, an extraordinary being, a wonderful woman. I could be a saint without praying, without taking vows. *Yes*, my mother urged in her sweet voice, *yes! Become a saint.* Gradually, the pale face of St. Francis was replaced by the thin face of Antonio behind prison bars, his eyes bright with fever. *Alessandra*, he said, *Alessandra! Yes*, I whispered, exhausted. *A saint for love.*

IN FACT IT was in Abruzzo, when I looked wild, with uncombed hair, my body chastened in black dresses, that I became aware of my physical appeal.

I saw my reflection in the river and the trees, and in the attractions of the country I found confirmation of my personal attractions. The season rendered me more beautiful as it adorned and embellished the bushes and flower beds. My hands blossomed like meadow saffron against the dull black of my dress. *How pretty I am!* I thought, admiring my hands against the light. I was burning, like the soil in the meadow, like the sand in the river, and the throbbing of my blood fashioned an image in which I seemed suddenly to have become a woman.

It had happened a few days before. I was coming down the outside staircase that led to the farmyard holding a pitcher of fresh water from the fountain. It was that still, empty time during the siesta. The corner of the house threw a blue shadow over the staircase, and I was descending slowly to stay cool. The farmyard, the kitchen garden, and the fields lay under the blinding glare of the sun.

I heard a hoarse, angry wheeze, which was immediately answered by another. I stopped and the water sloshed in the pitcher.

Two men were threshing corn in the farmyard, naked to the waist, their chests and shoulders shiny with sweat. Both gripped long flails, and as one brought his down to strip the corncobs, the other raised his with a vigorous upswing of arm and shoulder, twirling it in the air. One rose up, the other bent down, two levers on the same machine. They had adopted the same monotonous, mesmerizing rhythm, and it was in bringing down the flail that they let out that raucous and desperate cry, that wheeze.

I stood still against the wall, enthralled by their regular, rhythmic movement. I couldn't take my eyes off the two men. In the sun their chests shone, the shiny lacquer of sweat was a mirror. The shade of the staircase was on fire, scalding; the cicadas buzzed, and the blood in my temples pulsed to the bold rhythm of those male arms in motion. The men hadn't seen me; I was breathing quietly so they wouldn't notice me. I stood there, fascinated, unable to take my eyes from that rhythm. I flinched with every crack of the flail, and in the cool shade my body was covered with sweat like theirs under the sun's assault. They never tired. It seemed to me that my hidden presence spurred them on. I didn't want them to stop; I wanted them to keep going forever, and I felt that I would be the one to faint there on the stairs. When it seemed I couldn't last a moment longer, I put my lips to the pitcher and drank thirstily, the cold water trickling from my lips to the neckline of my dress. *You're back, Alessandro*, I whispered. *Get out of here!*

NEVER AGAIN, FROM that moment until the day I met Francesco, did I believe myself to be pretty. And in fact even in Abruzzo, while other girls my age were sought out and courted, everyone considered me to be odd, ageless and sexless.

Only Uncle Alfredo seemed to find me attractive when he looked at me. But I always saw a vein of condescending sarcasm in his eyes. It was as if he were aware of some crime I had committed and so he had me in his power while also allowing me freedom. *What a good actor you are*, I read in his eyes. He smoked quietly, watching me as I cleared the table, sewed, attended to the housework. *I know you for who you are*, his look said. I was tempted to turn abruptly and confront him. *So, come on, speak! What do you want? Let's show our hands.* I couldn't maintain a calm demeanor with Uncle Alfredo looking at me. His presence muddied everything. It was as if he were scolding me for deceiving my relatives, masquerading as an honest girl. *But I am*, I wanted to tell him. Yet I kept quiet and played along.

By this time, Uncle Alfredo had obviously tired of the company of his wife and sister-in-law. He preferred to come down to the kitchen in the evening and sip a glass of wine, standing and joking with the maids.

It had been apparent for some time that he was interested in me, baiting me with mean wisecracks. Aunt Violante let him do it, treating him as if he were a child delighted by some new fancy. Yet she would keep an eye on him to see how far he would go. *No*, she signaled, shaking her head one evening when he invited me to go up the hill with him to watch the lunar eclipse. Aunt Sofia did the same once when she heard him ask me for a little wine, and I never asked why.

He was the only one who spoke about my mother. "She was pretty," he said. "She went to bathe in the river because she suffered from the heat. She was pretty." Meanwhile, he would look at me and under his gaze my clothes became veils, my appearance shameful and mediocre. I couldn't bear the thought that he had looked at my mother like that, too. I closed my eyes, trying to forget that we were both women, and many things bound us together, including the squalid and repugnant experiences that women conceal from one another. *Come here*, Uncle Alfredo seemed to be saying. *Come here. I know you're thinking about certain things . . .*

I despised him; he was a coward. His cockiness, paraded within the tame family circle, revealed the thread of natural cowardice.

"Turn off the radio," he would say, pale with anger if we listened to foreign stations. "Turn it off. I don't want to get into trouble." It seemed that it was precisely his cowardice that pushed him towards me, counting on all the little acts of cowardice that are in every human being and that were also in me, the ones I fought against.

Nonna never listened to him when he spoke. Once she called me over to her and said, "Lock your door at night." Aunt Violante was there and Aunt Sofia heard her, too. They didn't ask why. I wanted to ask, hoping they would say, *There are thieves in the country, chicken thieves, and they might scare you.* But no one said anything.

That night when I turned the key in the lock, my hands shook with shame.

I DEVOTED MYSELF to my studies with a passion. I would sit for hours at my small table, until my eyes were tired and red, my back aching. I told myself that I had to build character and broaden my knowledge, whatever the cost. I was always asking Uncle Rodolfo for new books and money to buy notebooks. I wrote to Rome often, and stayed in contact with my friends and classmates. I told them about my studies and my reading, determined to keep within the circle of my favorite interests.

Fulvia's letters often mentioned the idea my father was harboring of moving to a new house. At first I thought the memory of my mother in the dark rooms on Via Paolo Emilio troubled him. Maybe he still heard her playing the piano or begging him to let her go. Sista looked for her everywhere, Fulvia wrote. She sat in the kitchen, in the dark, calling out, "Signora . . ." One evening she went to the Celantis' house, pale and confused. "I heard the Signora going upstairs, to your house," she said.

But I no longer suffered from the loss of my mother. I was sure she had confidently entrusted her memory to my care and my life as a woman. In fact, the reason for her death and its manner left me with a serious responsibility. I couldn't disappoint myself without disappointing her.

I was certain that if I had spoken about these things with Aunt Violante she would have understood me. Maybe so that we would speak about them, she often came up to my room and kept me company while I studied. She would read the titles of my books and then look at me with dismay.

"I don't think it's good to know too many things," she would say. "I have this idea that the more things one knows, the more difficult it is to live."

Aunt Violante was very beautiful despite her sad face, the face of a woman in mourning. She often told me that as a girl she used to paint her long, almond-shaped nails. Towards evening, we would open the window and look at the trees in bloom, the green fields. I began to understand that there's a window in the life of every woman. At the first sign of spring, in April, Aunt Violante said quietly and resentfully, "Now we're going to miss the spring, too."

I turned to her and her dismay infected me: everywhere I looked—in the inviting blue sky, the soft abandon of the earth—I discerned a subtle threat to my peace.

"Aunt Violante," I said quietly, "I'm at a very difficult age." I wished she would reassure me as perhaps Mamma would have done. Instead she replied seriously.

"I know. But you're so strong. You wouldn't be able to recognize the girl I was in you. When I was young, it seemed to me . . . No, it's ridiculous."

"Tell me!"

"It seemed to me that I was made of glass. Every tiny thing wounded me, made me cry. It might be the rain, or one of my mother's expressions. You couldn't talk to her; she was very intimidating. We all had to live laced up in our corsets. You're lucky the corset was abolished. At the time, my only pastime was to press flowers between the pages of books. Sometimes I'd copy them in watercolors. It was arduous living with Sofia, who had a harsh, arrogant character and was always reprimanding me. She was unforgiving."

"Aunt Sofia?" I asked, amazed.

"Yes. She's changed now, she's greatly changed. A lot of things have happened in twenty years. Poor Sofia has changed."

There was an embarrassing pause before she resumed: "Yes, yours is a restless age, but a brief one. After it comes a very difficult age. Every day, one hopes it will be over. Instead, it's never-ending, this unbearable middle age. Luckily for you, you're strong. I'm very religious, and I have Giuliano. When Giuliano gets married, I'll have grandchildren. I think constantly about the birth of Giuliano's children. I'll be very busy then—children cry at night, and I like getting up at night to rock babies. It's not right, though, for someone to rock them every night, bring them up, keep them well, educate them—and then war comes. They're saying that war is on its way. It seems impossible to me. There are too many children in Italy to truly have a war. Do you think I'll be able to hide Giuliano? I'm afraid I'm going to have to suffer through that experience, too. And then, finally, I'll become old. Old."

As she repeated the word, a wonderful peace emanated from her; every muscle in her face relaxed and her skin was like a polished stone.

"Ah!" she said, with a deep sigh of relief. "I, too, will have the right to my old age. I hope to get fat. As it happens, I don't think it's too far away. I'm already forty-two."

"You don't look it," I observed.

"That doesn't matter. I'm already very advanced. I have the right to get old," she repeated with a hint of resentment. "Sofia is much younger than I am."

From up there we could make out Aunt Sofia moving across the wide expanse of the farmyard. She was giving orders to some workers. Serious, precise, she was wrapped up in her task, accepting it totally, yet without conviction. For the first time, I noticed that she was slender, with rounded hips and graceful gestures. She must have been about thirty-nine, my mother's age at her concert, Lydia's age when she went out in her black hat to see the Captain.

"She's young," I whispered.

"Yes," said Aunt Violante. And she added after a pause, "She'll grow old, too." She stared at her with angry intensity. Then she called out, "Sofia! Sofia!" for the pleasure of seeing her turn, making her obey.

Aunt Sofia immediately bowed her head again and set to work once more.

"She's changed a lot, poor Sofia," Aunt Violante commented. Adele had once hinted at a grudge between the sisters, and about Aunt Violante she had said, "She's jealous." I suddenly remembered Uncle Alfredo's tone of voice when he called "Sofia," and the docility with which she served him. She would glance at her sister first, as if to get her consent. *No*, they had both firmly advised me, and in their eyes was the same knowing expression.

"She'll grow old, too, poor Sofia," Aunt Violante said, relaxing into the chair, as if abandoning her struggle. "We'll all get/grow old. Thank goodness."

FRIENDS AND RELATIVES visited almost every night to listen to the radio because war was said to be coming. We sat around it, waiting for the usual imperious voice to begin speaking. By now, it spoke of how impatient we all were to take part in the war. Although I lived in a

narrow circle, I strongly doubted it was true, since none of us felt
hatred for those we would have to attack, nor real friendship for those
with whom we would be fighting. In fact, we were indifferent to all of
them, and I felt that we were to blame for that indifference.

Sometimes it didn't seem possible that something new was actually
about to happen. Each day was the same as all the others, and as long
as you kept the radio off you could ignore everything, enjoy nature and
daily life. I thought back to my childhood, and remembered what my
mother had told me about war and the horror Hervey had felt for it ever
since he was a boy. She had also explained what a conscientious objec-
tor was. Anyway, all this seemed to pertain to Hervey, Mamma, and
their extraordinary world, which had always been forbidden to me
and my peers.

In his letters, Claudio often referred to the possibility of war. I was
amazed that even he, so thoughtful and reflective, could accept this
disaster as he would a meteorological phenomenon like rainfall.

"I wish I could see you before I leave," he wrote. Nor was he worried about me or what might happen to me. Maybe he thought we were
both responsible for the catastrophe, and that we should atone for it
together. In fact, his behavior convinced me that my responsibility was
equal to his, and the responsibility of all women was equal to that of
all men.

I began to regret never having taken an interest in politics and
being obliged by my own ignorance to rely on what others said. Until
that point, although it was easy for me to take an interest in most subjects, political matters had bored me. The moment I noticed my own
curiosity, I quickly realized, with some confusion, that it was something
to keep secret, like the presence of Alessandro. So I would have liked to
ignore political issues, content to share the conclusions offered by the
voice on the radio. But I couldn't help finding the voice off-putting, since
both its tone and its words were different from those I had learned to
love throughout my life. My reaction was instinctive, and following it,

I tried at least to imagine the distress I might feel seeing my country invaded by foreign armies, by troops speaking another language. I realize that this may sound like heresy, real sacrilege, but I recall that the speculation left me completely indifferent. I rebelled only at the thought of the chaos the soldiers would bring to the small village I lived in. It bothered me to imagine the noise they would make walking across the farmyard, and I knew I would do almost anything to prevent an act of violence, whether against them or us. I tried to become fonder of the name "Italy." I said it over and over to myself, with affection, until I began to feel moved by the memory of things I'd read in school. And then, spurred by emotion, I went outside. *This is Italy*, I thought as I looked at the white ribbons of road our people walked on: women carrying jugs on their heads, peasants with bundles of straw, barefoot children. *Our people*, I thought, and I felt a surge of affection for them, a tenderness evoked not so much because they were poor people busy working as because they were people busy living. I struggled to imagine what I would have felt if the farmers hoeing were foreigners rather than Italians. I felt no revulsion, no hostility, but, rather, a desire to speak all languages and get along with all peoples.

In the morning, I often saw squadrons of planes in the sky over the mountains: shiny, metallic, buzzing. The buzzing pierced my ears like a drill; that buzzing, yes, was unbearable because of the clear determination it expressed. The planes crossed the azure skies quickly, decisively, and, as they passed, the birds, of course, fled. The sun was reflected with an evil glare on their open wings, and the peace of the countryside was tarnished. In the enclosed valley, the din of the engines demanded an echo from the sleepy mountainsides. The earth shook, the trees trembled, the water in the river rippled with a shudder. As the planes cut across the sun's rays, they threw a cold shadow over the ground as clouds do before a storm. One after another those shadows passed overhead, causing me to shiver. The hum wiped every picture from my mind, every kind word from my ears.

You could see the colors of the Italian flag painted in a circle on the wings of the planes, and I hated them. The big tricolored circles passed menacingly over me, replacing the sun's warmth with cold shadow. I was afraid. I had never known fear before then, and it filled me with shame and disgust.

ONE EVENING, ALONG with the others, a young man appeared, dressed in black, and I knew right away that Nonna had chosen him as my husband.

"Get up, Giuliano," she said, so the young man could sit next to me. When he sat down she had a good look at him; she then ran her eyes over me, making sure she considered me objectively, and her face took on a satisfied expression.

"Would you like another piece of fruit?" Uncle Rodolfo said to me. "A little wine?" I realized that he was trying to break the ice, that he wanted me to think this was an evening like any other, and that I was still the same for him—a young girl it was his duty to protect. I looked into his eyes in a gentle gesture of gratitude. I cast my mind back to the story he had told me about his long love affair. She was a married woman, Adele had told me. They met at night: she would cautiously slip out of the house and wait for him at the bottom of the garden, covering her face with a sheer scarf. Looking at him that evening, I found it easy to understand how someone could wait eagerly for him every night. She would surely have thrown herself into his arms immediately, against his broad chest. I wished I had been in the place of that Emilia who had loved him so much. Emilia: a fine name. *I'm in love with him*, I thought with a quiver of horror. He was my father's brother, and thirty years older than me. Yet I felt that he was the only one I could confide in. I would have been happy to go and meet him, like Emilia, and offer myself as a gift. I instantly recalled his way of looking at me when I entered his studio. "How beautifully you walk, Alessandra!" he had said to me one day. I had blushed and laughed to change the conversation, and he had followed along.

We looked into each other's eyes across the white space of the table-cloth. We were alone, in religious solitude. It was then clear to me that he loved me. For an instant I loved him, too, desperately. It was one of the most intense moments of love in my life. Our kinship drew me irresistibly through some ancient affinity inciting a dangerous, fascinating bond. He had my father's beautiful hands, but his were strong and noble. With one of them he pointed to my neighbor and said, "Do you know Paolo? He rarely visits because he lives in Guardiagrele."

He was a good-looking young man, if not very tall. He soon turned his attention to me and I noticed what a nice smile he had.

"You're studying, yes?" he asked. He then asked if I liked the countryside.

Giuliano replied on my behalf. "She likes it, sure. She likes getting up late and going for walks with the dog, sitting under a tree to read. Coming back home to find lunch ready and sleeping in the fields. Picking branches of blossoms and ruining the almond grove. Putting flowers in vases, wildflowers, daisies. She also likes strangling chickens and splitting wood with her hands, like charcoal burners. Raw pork disgusts her, but she'll eat with relish if it's roasted. I think she likes the country," he concluded with a harsh laugh.

Nonna sent him from the table with a look.

"Why, Nonna?" I smiled, hoping to dissuade her. I turned to my neighbor and said, "It's true."

We laughed together, and a good feeling spread through the room.

Paolo came back often, because there was a strong, lively sympathy between us right away. I hadn't frequented any people of my age other than Giuliano for a long time. Paolo was intelligent and open. All I had to do to cheer up was look at his face and his tousled hair. I laughed a lot when he was there, and I had fun.

I don't remember what we talked about. He didn't share my inter-ests. I think mostly he told me about his life in the country, but his presence brought a healthy youthful flavor to my day. As soon as he arrived, I would go toward him—passing between the black shadows of my aunts—and my eyes lit up with happiness. I watched the clock, saddened when he went away. We were never left alone, and the constant vigilance annoyed me, because there was nothing about our relationship that offered grounds for suspicion.

He looked at me, smiling, a little surprised by my carefree manner. I felt that at first he had been ready to think ill of me, but he was soon disarmed by my frankness. Compared with my peers, I had always seemed almost too reserved, but here my habit of revealing my personal tastes and expressing opinions really seemed bold. The women carried their every passion hidden like a guilty secret, and dared show only what they felt about God or their children. So much so that sometimes, spilling all the weight of their other passions into them, they sometimes went overboard and prayed dramatically, shamelessly. They hugged their children so hard that their fragile bodies seemed suffocated in the maternal embrace. Paolo said I was different from the other girls.

"You never sew," he explained. "You're not preparing your trousseau. Here, where we live, girls start preparing their trousseaux from the time they're children. They work patiently. When you go to visit them, their legs are always covered by the large white sheet they're working on."

"Do you like those girls?" I asked him.

He replied, "Yes."

An offended silence fell between us. I felt like crying. I didn't study for several days and I learned to knit, moving my long hands effortfully. I was trying to conform to a model of woman that held no surprises. But I couldn't. Paolo won't come back, I predicted.

But he kept coming back. "Talking to you is like going on an excursion in the mountains. At every turn in the path you discover a new landscape. I can talk about different things, with you, from what I usually discuss with girls." A little later he interrupted himself, sorry he'd let down his guard, and asked if I liked children.

No one in the house talked to me about him, and I sensed danger in that silence. Whenever he arrived, Aunt Sofia would call me from under the window. "Alessandra, Paolo's here."

I often wanted to burst out, "Tell me about him! Come on, let's talk about him." My relatives' silence held me captive. I felt something establishing itself, taking form, and I intended to gauge just how far they would dare to push this barbaric dominance over my person. It was a contest between Nonna and me. And more than that: between me and a humiliating tradition. I knew that no young girl in Abruzzo sees a young man very often unless he is her fiancé; otherwise no one would marry her, and she would have no choice but to find a husband in the city. Besides, I wanted to protest against the fairly widespread habit, among farmers, of making the engaged couple marry as soon as the question was asked and the dowry fixed. After the wedding ceremony she goes back to her parents, and the husband, too, takes up his life again with his family. Sometimes it's years before they can set up house and live together, since the wedding takes place when they are barely out of adolescence. And in this way, if he becomes weary and abandons her, her reputation isn't compromised. You sometimes saw a young girl in the fields accompanied by a young man with his arm around her shoulders. "That's her husband," I was told. They held each other's hands lovingly, kissed in the shade of a tree, the wife pressed against the trunk in an embrace. "He's her husband," they reassured me.

They had to part at sunset, in the melancholy time before evening, and return to their own homes. The stars came out, the crickets polished the heady summer air and honed the courage they needed to separate. The women would accompany their husbands for a short distance—as long as possible— as if to detain them. Standing still, they watched the men go off, waving until the shadow of night swallowed them up.

"Why can't they stay together?" I would ask.

"He doesn't have the money to buy a bed or raise children."

I pictured the young girls mercilessly pinning the blame on the men. The men would promise *Soon, I'll do it soon, I'll find the money—maybe even steal it*. Adele said, "If they don't have a bed, there's always the cool grass in the fields."

At night now, it was really difficult to sit still and study. It was as if all my curiosity had been exhausted by my direct contact with nature, and the mystery that governs the universe had already been revealed by the rotation of the sun. The truth of every religion, and of poetry and music, was in the air. The scent of cut grass wrapped around my head. Paolo would announce his presence with a faint whistle.

I would close my books and run downstairs into the dining room; my black skirt swirled around me in the rush. I smiled. In a few days I would be turning eighteen. I seemed to have a good role as the heroine.

Since Paolo had started coming to see me life had become easier, the house brighter, my relatives prone to an unexpected tenderness. One day Nonna wanted me to accompany her to a room on the ground floor, which no one entered apart from her; at one time it had been used as a chapel.

"Come in," Nonna said, pushing me, hands on my shoulders, and shutting the door behind us.

It was a large, dimly lit room, the walls painted violet, and full of dark, imposing wardrobes, some with noble shapes like the kind you might see in a sacristy. I felt as if I'd descended into a cellar that had not seen air or light for years. Wardrobes and walls, black and violet, all became confused in the oppressive darkness.

"Here we are," Nonna said, with a flicker of satisfaction. Her eyes shone with joy at having caught me in a trap. The heavy door wouldn't have let even the most desperate cry escape, and the window was protected by a grate. I started to say something.

"Ssh!" Nonna ordered, her gestures commanding my attention.

She pushed aside her apron and the shadows started at the keys' magical gleam. She felt for them, fondled them, chose one, and, detaching the bunch from her waist, put the long shiny key into the lock of a black wardrobe. She inserted the key into the lock delicately—as if afraid that the wardrobe would rise up at the violence and knock her down, killing her. Finally she opened the doors, and the room's darkness was dispelled by the white linens arranged on the shelves.

One by one, Nonna opened the other wardrobes, anxiously seeking admiration in my expression. The room was clothed in glowing white. "Look," she said. "Look." She took my arm to bring me closer to one of the large open wardrobes. "Touch them," she urged. She herself guided my hand, sliding it over the cool sheets. "Touch," she insisted.

"There are so many of them," she said. "Do you know how many?" She hesitated, weighing my capacity to keep a secret, before saying, "There are more than two hundred. Two hundred and sixteen. Some are new and untouched. No one has ever unfolded them—maybe you will, or one of your daughters. Better your daughter's daughter," she added, as if in a dream. "This one—" and she slid her hand over one of the embroidered linens—"this one is your bridal sheet. It has an initial A. It was part of my mother's dowry. Her name was Antonietta. Look: A."

The initial was framed by leafy branches. At the top was a pansy that looked like a girl with a flower on her head. "These," she said, "are the children's sheets."

She held me close. We stood still with that linen smelling of lavender, and I was almost as tall as she was. She caressed my forehead, collecting all my thoughts in her large hand. It seemed that I was no longer dressed in black, no longer wearing black shoes, that my hair was not tightly braided. Every girl's dream came to me gently: I was dressed as a bride, and everyone was smiling at me. *She's so beautiful!* they said as I walked by. Then I lay down on the embroidered linen sheets, and Paolo laughed with me. We were young together.

"I feel peaceful," Nonna continued. "My tomb is ready, and it looks towards this house." From the cemetery, spreading across the green hillside, it dominated the village from on high, as if from paradise. "I'll see you. You'll have to get up early and always be first. The house sleeps, the men sleep. They're lazy, and expect to have coffee brought to them in bed. At that hour, you are really in charge. You walk through the rooms, along the hallways, go to the pantry, the cellar; opening and closing with your keys. Always wear them at your waist. When you go to bed, put them under your pillow. I couldn't sleep unless I felt the keys under my pillow. The day I die, you'll know where to find them."

From that evening on, she kept me with her more often. She wanted me to understand her with a brief nod or look, and in fact I understood. And it was that very affinity which alarmed me.

By this time I really had to study in secret. If I heard her step on the stairs, I would put my books away. I turned to Uncle Rodolfo once more and begged him to intercede with Nonna so that she would let me go to Sulmona for my exams. While they argued about it I sat in his study, as if waiting to be pardoned. But when he came back from their conversation he opened his arms in resignation: Nonna had said no.

I went to the window so he couldn't see my eyes, which were brimming with tears. Trembling uncontrollably, I looked at the green valley, blocked by the Maiella as if by a hulking, insurmountable mass.

"I'll continue to do everything I can." Behind me, Uncle Rodolfo muttered an apology.

"I'm sorry I took your money for books," I said, not turning around. "I'll give it back."

I hurt him, and I wanted to hurt him. He and Nonna had another argument. They spoke for a long time in the sitting room with the door closed. I discovered later that he had spoken not only about me but also about my mother, and about the Emilia he had loved so much. Eventually Nonna came to an agreement with her son. "You say she'll be finished after this high-school diploma?" Pausing, she appeared to have calculated the time, the days. At last she decided.

"All right. Go."

Aunt Sofia took me to Sulmona. We looked rather grim, dressed in black, and everyone stared. I recall Sulmona as very dusty, and I was always thirsty. The girls waiting with me for their turn to be examined were wearing flowered dresses and had done their hair and put on lipstick. One of them asked me if I was a novice.

I said no but felt I was lying. I was trapped in the discomfort I always feel when I'm with a lot of people—I have a sense of boundless love for everyone around me but am unable to express it.

The exams didn't seem difficult. I tried to help my peers, especially the girls, with the written ones. They accepted, but then looked at me suspiciously, wondering what I was after. None of them guessed the truth. I wished at least one exam would go badly so they might stop looking at me like that, might feel sorry for me and comfort me. But the exams kept going well instead. I felt uncomfortable as I left the hall, and I thought it was because I was so tall.

ON THE LAST day, when I went to find out my results, Uncle Rodolfo accompanied me. The novelty of finding myself alone in the streets of Sulmona with him took my breath away. We weren't walking close together, and we didn't look at one another. When our eyes met, we immediately turned away, as if they were burning. He showed me the city and its buildings. I talked about Paolo and even told him about Claudio and the letters I received, but neither one nor the other seemed to truly exist. It was as if I were inventing them on the spot.

I got high marks. As I read them out, some of my peers observed me, and I laughed as if it were all a gift, free credit that I didn't deserve. Uncle Rodolfo took my arm and everyone said goodbye as we left.

It was bright and sunny outside and the stones sparkled. I felt an inexpressible joy, I laughed at nothing, and felt that my presence was causing an unusual stir everywhere. Uncle Rodolfo looked at me as I laughed, as I walked and moved, and so I laughed, walked, and moved more happily. We drank a vermouth, and, since I wasn't used to it, that small amount of alcohol heightened my exhilaration.

"I'm old," I said. "In a few months I'll be going to the university." Veins, limbs, hair—nothing disguised my youth. "Old!" I repeated. The radio announced a broadcast for five that afternoon. I predicted that all our relatives would come to the house to hear it, and, perhaps because of the vermouth, began to laugh at them as never before.

"I don't want to see them! I really don't!"

So Uncle Rodolfo suggested we have lunch in Sulmona and take the six-o'clock train back.

I need to make room for this memory among all the others: it's so important. In the years that were to follow, when I was living with Francesco and even now, this memory often crosses my mind the way a train crosses the dark countryside with all its lights on, before it disappears.

Uncle Rodolfo led me by the arm, and, just as I had since the first day, at my mother's funeral, I willingly trusted in him. He chose a small trattoria with a lacy pergola of wisteria leaves: we looked pale under that green roof, but it was the healthy, snow-white pallor of babies. The hostess approached us with a smile of affection and complicity. I didn't feel awkward, even though it was the first time I had eaten out with a man. The woman observed us, wondering perhaps if I was the lover or the daughter of the man I was with. But her opinion didn't interest me; I allowed Uncle Rodolfo to take the responsibility, just as I leaned on him when we walked together arm in arm.

The sun shone through the moving patterns of leaves, and the table-cloth looked like water in motion. I took a piece of bread and when I tried to break it I noticed that my hands, usually so strong, were limp and weak.

"You break it," I said. "I can't."

It seemed impossible that a man of forty-six could still be so young. I hadn't been this happy for a long time—since my mother and I had stolen flowers from the railings. I laughed, and he watched me laugh. I was voracious, and he enjoyed seeing me eat. He ordered unusual, exquisite foods for me and was annoyed not to find them. He apologized and I let him. Slowly, he poured wine in my glass from a dusty bottle. Then he stopped, tentative: "Will this be too much for you?"

I still remember, after all these years, the tenderness in his look when he asked. He showed such awareness of a woman's fragility combined with such keen concern for my health and happiness that I wanted to test my power again, just a little.

"I don't think so," and I took a long drink before saying, "I'd like to smoke."

He rummaged in his pockets, embarrassed not to be offering me fine cigarettes. I started smoking inexpertly, blowing the smoke a long way away. *Maybe it will be bad for me*, I thought, pervaded by faint dizziness. But I felt calm because he was there, and he would take my arm, lead me out, see to everything. I could give in to weakness and malaise. I would come to in a bed softened by white curtains and I would see bright flowers in the room. He would be kneeling beside the bed, devoted and happy. Yes! I could have fainted if I had wanted to. Never again would I have such relief from the relentlessness of daily life.

"Emilia wasn't afraid when she came to meet you, was she?"

"Who told you that?" he asked me, dumbfounded.

"Are you upset that I know?"

"No, not you. In fact, I've been on the verge of telling you many times. But then I thought that these things aren't suitable for your age. But you're much older than your years; I can speak to you as I would to a mature woman. And this maturity of yours touches me and makes me worry about you."

He took my hand and covered it with his. My hand stayed there, sheltered and protected. Even today, if I close my eyes I can still remember that moment. I see once more the green summer light, and my hand is the innocent hand of a child.

"Emilia died, didn't she?"

"Many years ago. You were just born. She died in Cesena, where he had been transferred. He was transferred quickly." He went quiet for a moment before continuing with bitter irony: "Maybe Nonna didn't tell you."

"She wasn't the one who talked to me about it."

"Ah, I see. That's it. After all, Nonna did play a part in this story at the time. Since then we haven't been the same. Or at least I'm not the same anymore. Nonna can't change. And Emilia is dead."

"Was she pretty?" I asked quietly.

He took a photo from his wallet. She wasn't pretty to me. Her face was round, and she had a white veil over her chest, heavy blond curls on her forehead. She looked old.

"She was twenty-four here. She left the following year. Your hair is blond like hers."

"It's my mother's hair."

"Right. I barely remember Eleonora."

"She was an extraordinary woman."

"Like you?" he hinted with a smile.

"Oh, no!" I replied sincerely. And I began to speak about her with enthusiasm. My mother appeared instantly, as if summoned by my words, and she looked around, astonished. She was green on the waxen white of her hands; her face was a tender leaf. When I spoke of her step, she approached softly, quickly, and the day was proud of her. Uncle Rodolfo watched her, fascinated.

I was happy. There was a bouquet of wildflowers on the table, with a few sprigs of lemon verbena. "I'll take them with me." I said an affectionate goodbye to the fat lady who was smiling at us.

"We'll be back," I said.

Uncle Rodolfo looked at me before repeating, with emotion, "We'll be back."

We went out into the dusty street. There's so much dust in Sulmona. He took my arm and we began walking. He should have taken me away that day. Everything would have been different. I was a weak woman, and women lean on tall, strong men like him. I can't forgive him for not having done so. My thoughts rage against him, and I wish he would read these pages. *So why didn't you do it?* I pummel his chest. *Why didn't you take me away?*

He said instead, "Shall we go and listen to the radio?"

And I smiled. "Yes, let's go."

We walked in silence, our joy expressed in our lively, bold gait. I was smiling. I still believed I was leaning on him, and yet with every step I was moving away from that happy day, from the legend of my mother. I was becoming Alessandra, wholly Alessandra, and every step was leading me inexorably towards Francesco, towards Tomaso, towards my solitary life.

The radio said that war had broken out.

WHEN I OPENED the window the next day, I thought everything would be different. So I was surprised to see that the sun was shining, the meadows were green, the sky empty, the peasants working in the fields. I hoped I had just had a bad dream, but what I had experienced the previous day was still so vivid in me that this cheerful hope soon vanished. Worried, I looked around, questioning the faces of all the people crossing the farmyard. Their faces were serene, lacking in malice. It made me think our parents had exaggerated the descriptions of the other war: I imagined there hadn't been a single calm, sunny day, that the sky had always been dark, the air lacerated by terrifying roars, echoing with cries and groans. Instead, you could hear the familiar voices of the hens, the lost bleating of the sheep. I smiled, thinking that being at war wasn't so terrible after all.

In the following weeks, quite a few young men left, but they left feeling calm, all of them convinced that they would soon be home. Those who stayed worked grudgingly. They sat outside their houses smoking and waiting for their draft cards. Paolo was away in Guardiagrele. When he came back, he said only, "Have you heard?" But he, too, smoked a lot, and when we were together we were no longer lighthearted. I couldn't understand why, since nothing had changed—nothing. Claudio wrote that life in the city, too, went on as before, except that he was spending a lot on newspapers.

Yet an oppressive anxiety was in the air, in the eyes of the women, the pallor of their faces, their spasmodic movements when they dressed or caressed their children, the somber prayers slipping out of the churches. A veil of fear and uncertainty wreathed the days; a hateful veil hung between me and poetry, as Giuliano had predicted. I raged desperately against that veil, surely created by my imagination. I tried to react, by refusing to accept the war. It was easy, I told myself: nothing was upsetting the normal course of my days. I read, I made plans for study and research. I wrote long letters to Claudio, without referring to these events. I bought a new dress; I walked through the house singing to dispel the oppression closing in on me. I no longer listened to the radio. I didn't want to know anything. I responded absent-mindedly when anyone reported the news to me. This made me seem still colder and more selfish. Even Uncle Rodolfo looked at me in surprise, and I enjoyed keeping up this behavior. I would walk through the village making it clear that I didn't want to linger with anyone. I wore a black kerchief on my head and kept Giuseppone, the dog, on a leash. But the voice on the radio followed me everywhere. There was always someone in the house sitting next to it, nervously moving the dial. Even when I was in my room, I imagined a hand hovering anxiously over the switch. In the village the sound of the radio spilled from open windows into the streets. It was waiting for me at the table in the café, at the pharmacy and the grocer's. I didn't want to listen to the words; I didn't listen to them. But the insolent tone of the voice got through to me, muddling my thoughts and inciting revolt. "That's enough!" I murmured with restrained anger. "Enough! Enough!"

Nonna never spoke about the war. Like me, she wouldn't bend to the hateful arrogance of what was happening. But she'd turned paler, a large cadaver. *Why?* I wanted to protest. *Nothing's happening. Turn off the radio. All you have to do is turn it off.* But at night, when the radio was silent, I felt the urge to go through the dark house into the empty sitting room, flick the switch, and feverishly move the dial until I found that voice. By this time it had become part of the very air I breathed: when it fell silent, I couldn't breathe.

I waited for Paolo's visits with increasing impatience, although they didn't bring me the same joy. I hoped that he would actually have the power to turn me back into the person I had been until then. One evening we were unexpectedly left alone. Paolo had dined with us, and no one had switched on the radio. It seemed as though everyone wanted to seek refuge in an artificial calm. Aunt Sofia had been the last to leave the room, carrying the big white tablecloth in a heap over her arm. She went to shake it in the farmyard; the hens would peck at the crumbs in the morning. She didn't come back. At first, Paolo was disconcerted by the unusual freedom we had been granted. He looked around, trying to understand what it meant. Finally, he asked me to go outside with him. There was a beautiful moon.

We took the trail that led halfway up the slope to a little path of white poplars. White leaves moved like butterflies on the poplars and crickets stirred in the grass, shy silver bells that couldn't drown out the angry croaking of the frogs.

"Paolo," I said. He took my arm.

I was unhappy. There was always a thick veil between my thoughts and my happiness, between that stroll and a happy one. I tried to laugh, to say something pleasant and light, but everything sounded fake, seasoned with foolish, reckless flirtatiousness. Since my mother's death, words no longer created around me the fascinating and poetic world in which I had learned to feel alive, and I knew that only when I could speak that language with a man would I know love and happiness.

"What's wrong?" Paolo said.

We were sitting on a low wall, and my foot touched the fresh dewy grass.

"You're so different from other girls," he said. "Why aren't you happy now?"

"Are you happy?" I asked.

"I am, yes."

I looked at him warily. I was afraid that he was hiding the melancholy of that moment and the dangerous times we were living through, and would treat me like a child. But his face was sincere. So I understood that only men have strength and security—none of them ever had my mother's bewildered face, the sorrowful face of Aunt Violante, or Lydia's pitiful face whenever the Captain was away. I was gripped by a sudden desire to claim that strength of theirs. I wanted to steal it, take it with me, get rid of the thick veil that stood between me and carefree happiness.

"I want to be happy, too," I told him.

Paolo moved closer to me. His face was in front of mine and his bright, dark eyes clouded over. How beautiful a man's features were! The strong nose, the wide forehead. Paolo's skin was tanned and a pleasing odor came from his open shirt, the odor of skin that's been out in the sun for a long time. I closed my eyes, confused.

That was my first kiss. Actually, I didn't think it was the first: Claudio had kissed me a few times, but they had been short, sharp, timid kisses. Paolo's lips pressed hard against mine, hurting me, and I opened my mouth to avoid them. Then he gave me a long kiss, forcing me to open my teeth, and he held me there, astonished.

We broke apart and I wanted to run. I was restrained by the fear that he wasn't normal, that he would run after me and make me submit to some brutal urge, taking advantage of the deserted place. He began kissing me again, and I let him, horrified, but also curious to feel that earth-shattering sensation again. I wanted to wipe my mouth, but worried that Paolo would be offended, as if I didn't want to drink from his glass.

"Why?" he asked me when he saw that I was sad. "You mustn't be upset. I love you, and we're engaged." As he said those words he held me, stroking my shoulders, not asking himself if I welcomed his bizarre way of kissing.

"No," I said.

"What do you mean, no?" he asked distractedly, going back to kissing me.

"No," I said again, wiping my lips. "We're not engaged."

"Yes, of course we are," Paolo insisted, anxious to get back to our interrupted kiss. "We're getting married soon, before I can be called up."

"No." I jumped down from the wall. "We're not engaged. I'm not in love with you."

He sat still. His hair was mussed, his white shirt was wrinkled, his trousers didn't fall right, and his bare skin showed over his rolled down sock. He stared at me, his amazement so genuine that I was suddenly furious at myself, at my difficulty in being happy. That's when I encountered for the first time that lost, childish look I was to see so often in Francesco's eyes. Oh! all it took was a man looking at me like that for me to feel that I was a despicable creature gripped by some sort of madness. I felt regretful, and I wished Paolo would forget what I had said, forget me, actually; I wanted to apologize. *Dear Paolo*, I said to myself, *darling!* And moved by the way he was disappointing me, I stroked his forehead to console him. *Dear Paolo, come on! Do something to relieve this weight bearing down on us.* I felt that all we needed was to come up with a loving word, one of those my mother used to magically conjure up happiness. I felt so alone that not even the mountains, the trees, or the stars in the sky were enough to keep me company. No villages were visible in the mountains now. The countryside was deserted. We were alone on the earth, he and I, man and woman, condemned to live together for ever.

"You don't want to?" he asked sulkily, fixing his hair. He spoke curtly, no longer the friend I liked to laugh with.

"No," I said.

"Why did you let me believe you were happy, that you cared for me?"

"As a matter of fact, I was happy." And I looked into his eyes so he would understand my absolute sincerity.

"Well? Why don't you want to marry me?"

"Look . . . Maybe it's difficult for you to understand me, but I'm waiting for it to be beautiful to be alone with a man on the earth, not distressing and horrible. I'm waiting . . ." I almost said, *I'm waiting for Hervey.* But I made a quick decision to keep those words back. He wouldn't have understood them; no man would have. So my gaze caressed him, as a mother's would, straightened his hair. *Dear Paolo!* I said inside, *dear Paolo.* It seemed to me that he was on the riverbank, on solid land, and I on a flimsy sailing ship, moving farther away.

FOR SEVERAL DAYS I went to wait for him in the evening at the outer edge of the farm. Only Paolo, by returning, could have comforted me and reassured me that I was like other women. I peered at the path between the oaks, the one he usually took. All I saw was grass, trees, and sky. Not even the arrogant voice of the radio reached that far.

I would reappear in the farmyard with the first shadows, carrying in my black dress the melancholy of waiting in vain. No one was surprised by Paolo's absence, so I understood that they knew everything. But I wondered just how much they knew. I was afraid that if they looked at my face they would reproach me for being acquainted with that violent way of kissing. I was overcome by an uncontrollable restlessness that drove me to hide, believing I was hateful and annoying. From my high window, I could see them all intent on their work. I noticed that their gestures were slow and relentless; the rhythm of a gesture became a rule for life. I was no longer studying, I wasn't looking after the house: I was skirting the edges of the rule to be industrious. Fragile, caught between two powerful mechanisms, I was reduced to listening to the radio for hours and hours.

Next to the radio I found Uncle Alfredo. Sometimes, I spontaneously went to sit by him. He always looked at me ironically, the way he looked at all women. But I was afraid he knew about Paolo's kiss, my conversations with Fulvia, and Enea's hand grazing my breast. Once, he said, "It's true. You look a lot like your mother."

At those apparently harmless words, I wanted to cover my face and burst into tears. I was troubled by regret for having damaged her memory. I couldn't bear to see my image reflected in the window anymore: I saw sin in me, in this tall, thin, blond person who was an obvious anomaly there. It was no longer enough to hide my books, my diaries and letters. Giuliano's hostile look, Uncle Alfredo's ironic gaze, and my aunts' sorrowful eyes stung me. They made me feel possessed, incited me to open the window and hide myself in death.

"Nonna," I said one evening, "I can't go on."

She sat white and majestic as I'd seen her for the first time, the day I arrived. I spoke quietly, not daring to look up at her. It was difficult to admit that I was defeated.

"I know," she replied calmly. Her shoulders rose above the back of the chair, and her head was framed against the sky in the window, higher than the mountains. From up there she surely saw everything, which made it pointless to speak. I huddled at her feet, took her hand. I felt like I was in church.

She asked the question I'd dreaded. "Why did you behave like that with Paolo? You seemed happy."

"I was happy," I replied. "I waited for him anxiously. I've waited for him anxiously for all this time. Oh! I liked seeing him come to the house, and going to meet him . . ."

She interrupted. "You liked going for walks with him alone in the evening?"

"Yes, I think I did like it."

"So why don't you want to marry him? You like getting kissed by a man, but you don't want him as your husband?"

I hesitated before replying. In the face of Nonna's implacable severity it was difficult to convey certain subtle reactions.

"Yes, I like him," I said, determined to speak frankly. "But I believe love is something else."

"It's not something else. You're mistaken. All men are alike. They say the same things and do the same things. They're men. Paolo is an honest and courteous young man. He would have respected you. You could have had a child soon. When you're expecting a child, you're very grateful to men. Then you feel truly alive. Your body swells and you're suffused with a bountiful sense of well-being. You're hungry, thirsty, sleepy, and all your instincts are refreshed. You have the assurance that you're healthy and fertile, like the earth when the grain sprouts. You hold no grudges towards men; they're your children, too. In fact, you're permeated with a tender maternal compassion at the sight of them getting worked up over actions and problems so pointless, pathetic, compared with the triumph of your life."

"I don't hold a grudge against men. It's just that I'd like to have the confidence and strength they have, and can rely on, at any moment."

"It's not strength," she replied, clapping her great hand on the armrest. "It's lack of compassion, and yet only those who feel pity are strong. Do you understand? Remember that. I'm afraid you've got it all wrong, imagining them as the master and entrusting them with your happiness. You've got it wrong. The house is ours, the children are ours—we are the ones who carry them and nourish them—and therefore life is ours. Even the pleasure they give you is a sorry thing you have to keep secret; they'll use that secret to keep you subjugated and humiliated. It's only when you're expecting a child that you finally become secure. Then the tie that binds us to men is no longer base and despicable but splendid! We're the ones who benefit, who feel proud of it. You become fat and beautiful and your breasts swell with milk. You alone are needed to feed your child; he asks for nothing else. Even the pain of bringing the child into the world is a sort of grotesque pleasure. If you are really a woman, you should have the desire to experience it. Ariberto's birth was very difficult. I called to him, 'Son, why do you want to hurt me so much! Have pity! Go slowly.' At such times, men stand outside the door, frightened and ashamed, and they have no peace. You are the one with the strength to face—all by yourself—the terrible moment in which life is handed down."

Nonna's words fell on me from on high, boulders rolling over my weak person, the dreams I held dear. *No,* I thought, spinning around in the dark, *no, I don't want to possess that terrible strength. I don't want to!*

Crushed by the awareness of my misery, I said, "Nonna, forgive me. I thought I'd become strong, like you. Let me leave. I can't take it."

"I know," she said, her voice pained and muted. "I told you to forget the books, forget the music. One must be tough, and get rid of all that—get rid of it!" She said, as my mother had, "I wanted you to be happy."

I shivered, clasping her knees. I felt the river running swiftly below me, around me, and I clung to a trunk on the bank, to a rock. "I'm frightened—help me!" I whispered, exhausted.

From the house of the neighboring farmer came the voice of the radio. It entered the room and came right up to us; we inhaled it. The mild summer evening was filled with threat. In the voice of the radio we heard the droning of the airplanes, the furious plunging of the airplanes, the flaming spiral of the airplanes—three airplanes, six fallen airplanes.

"I'm afraid," I confessed. "Nonna, I'm afraid."

"We're all afraid," she said. "In fact, it seems now that this fear will never leave us. I'll have to be afraid for only a short time yet; I'm old. But I can't forget your face when you came back from Sulmona the evening war was declared. You understood that no one would be able to escape that fear. In any case, what we're living through is your time, and it's right that you should interpret it better than I can. I still had some hope, then, of being able to save you. I thought about making a shelter in the pantry—it's a strong stone cave. All that night I pondered absurd and fantastic ideas. lining a room with steel, even though I wouldn't have had the money to do it. I thought about this room for you . . . for Paolo," she said quietly. "I wanted to hide the linens for you, the sacks of grain. To make something like Noah's Ark. *I'll be stronger than war*, I thought. But it isn't possible. The war breaks in anyway.

Your father wrote that Sista is afraid and wants to go back to her village in Sardinia. He can't be on his own, with no woman to take care of the house, to iron, cook, and mend. I tore up the letter and didn't even show it to you. At first I thought I'd send Adele."

"It's better if I go."

After a pause, she nodded. "Yes. It's better."

We stayed close to one another in the silence. The radio went quiet, and we heard the voices of the crickets, the whimpering of a dog. *Goodbye*, I said silently, *goodbye, goodbye.*

My aunts came in and I jumped to my feet in an effort to collect myself. But the discreet silence we had always maintained was broken. We knew one another intimately, as only women can know other women, even when they think they have never confided in one another.

"Alessandra is leaving," Nonna said. They showed not the least surprise. It was decided that I would leave in two days' time, on Monday. On Monday morning, Uncle Rodolfo put on his boots for going into the country.

"I'm sorry. I would have liked to take you to the station. The farmer will take you in the buggy. I have a lot to do, so I can't." He took my hand.

I looked at him. *Why don't you kiss me?* I asked with my eyes, *why don't you kiss me like Paolo?* Once again, I was surprised to think that a man of forty-six is still very young and attractive. *Kiss me*, I urged, *take me in your arms and kiss me!* I begged him to do that and free me of everything life held for me, of all the things I had to do. We both knew what my departure meant. I myself had to set off, leave, alone for the first time. Nonna had given me money for my ticket and she had also solemnly given me a little more as a gift. I would never return to that house, so I looked around to say goodbye to the peaceful life that had spurned me. Behind Uncle Rodolfo I saw his rifles hanging, his pipes, his photo taken on the Carso, and my name on the great family tree—free and alone on the outer branch, in the empty space.

"Do you understand?" Uncle Rodolfo said. "I can't go with you. We'll say goodbye here."

They were all at the door when I climbed into the buggy with the farmer: Nonna in the middle, Aunt Violante on the left, Aunt Sofia on the right, and the servants behind, as in a photograph. Giuliano sat on the ground, brushing his shoes with a crop. There was a moment of quiet, then Aunt Clarice burst into tears.

"Why is Alessandra leaving?" she sobbed. "Is it my fault? What have I done? Did I do something wrong?"

Then, lowering her head, Nonna gave an order and I moved as if to resist and hang on. But the farmer whipped the horse and the clatter of the wheels on the cobblestones soon drowned out the shrill sound of Aunt Clarice's crying.

WHAT STRUCK ME most on my return was the darkness that concealed the city, because of the blackout. In fact, as the train entered the station in Rome, it seemed to bend down in order to slide into a grim and forbidding tunnel. I barely recognized my father in the darkness; he had come with Sista to collect the baskets. During the long separation, our correspondence had been sporadic and cold, so it seemed pointless to feign a rapturous reunion. He was quick to see to the baskets.

"Do you have your ration book?" he asked in a whisper, and when I said I did he drew a sigh of relief. "I've been worried about that all day."

My father had left the old house in Via Paolo Emilio and had taken up residence in a very small apartment in the new buildings along the Tiber River in the Flaminio district. This intensified my impression of having arrived in an unfamiliar city. I walked silently through the maze of tall white buildings, following my father and Sista as if they were strangers. I didn't even look around, because I was carrying a heavy wicker basket that scratched my wrist. I was shocked by the elevator, which was modern: the doors closed by themselves. Just as when I had arrived in Abruzzo, I was surprised by the feeling that I might be dead and living in the next world. Maybe you could die more than once, each time giving up someone or something.

The three rooms were suffocated by the old black furniture. My father had replaced the double bed with a smaller iron one. Every trace of my mother's presence had disappeared: clothes, photographs, even the piano had been sold.

"I threw out whatever I didn't need," my father went on to say. He showed me the bathroom, the built-in wardrobes, and the kitchen, asking with some satisfaction, "Do you like it?" I said yes, but actually I hadn't put that question to myself, and all I asked for was a corner to sleep in, since it seemed—even more so than when I had arrived at Nonna's—that I had committed a serious sin, for which I had to be forgiven.

The lamps gave off a dim, yellowy light. At the time, my father was beginning to experience the first problems with his sight. He threw open the window: the darkness was impenetrable. A black river separated me from the neighborhood where I had lived with my mother.

In the morning I realized that the apartment looked down over the bridge and the reedbed, so that it was, for us, like living at the cemetery. But my father certainly hadn't noticed that, nor did he feel discomfort.

"We're very close to the Vatican as the crow flies," he said. "I don't think we need to worry about bombs."

Sista wandered around the blue-and-white stove looking lost. She called me *Signorina* and addressed me formally. I accepted this without protest because it seemed to me that we were all changed, and the old ways were no longer valid. We had nothing to say to one another, and when I had exhausted all the news about Nonna's health and how things were going in the country, there was nothing to talk about. I remained in an attitude of servile gratitude. I was happy to have my own room, a window. I wanted to find a way to repay him, so when my father said, "You'll need to cook and see to the house," I accepted enthusiastically. I said I would go and register at the university the following day and actively look for work: he could count on me.

He smiled, reassured. "You'll see," he said. "If you help me when Sista's no longer around, we'll be able to live reasonably well. Right now we also have an allowance for the air raids. A man who comes up from the country brings us a little meat. And it's nice in this building. I've discovered a widower on the first floor and I play cards with him sometimes." After a brief pause, he met my eyes. "Nobody here knows anything. Do you understand?"

The tone of his voice clearly indicated that life with my mother had been a fairy tale. She and I should have regretted making it up.

I WENT TO see Fulvia a couple of days later. As I approached the street I had lived on for so many years, my legs weakened along with the energy of my steps. I recognized the places, the shop windows, the salespeople sitting behind their counters, but it was as if I had never seen them in reality and had only been told all about them. The swallows came up to me with a loud cry of greeting: I recognized them. They were still my family. Rapidly they swooped down to the street, spreading heartrending desperation everywhere. I heard them screeching inside me.

Cautiously, nervously, I proceeded up the stairs. I stopped in front of what had once been our apartment. I expected the door to burst open and to see Mamma coming towards me with her ineffably graceful steps. *Oh Sandi,* she would say, *you've come back* . . . But it said "Ridolfi" on the door, and I kept going.

When Fulvia came to the door, she barely recognized me. Then she yelled "Alessandra!" gathering me in a frantic embrace.

She was so worked up she no longer knew where to sit down with me. She was tempted to open the door to the Japanese salon that we never entered, but I stopped her just in time. We sat on her bed, in the room plastered with new photographs, showing her in a bathing suit. I had never seen her like that, nor did I know about her new hairstyle or the dress she had on. I was on the verge of tears.

"Sandi, I'm happy you've come back! I have so many things to tell you—how will we manage? We'll have to spend whole days and nights talking. Won't you stay and sleep here tonight? I'm sorry Mamma isn't home," she added. "She went—"

"To the Captain?"

Fulvia paused before picking up again, serious: "No, the Captain was transferred a short time after your mother died. It was a drama! This one . . . this one is a contractor. He has a Fiat 1500."

"Ah, I see. So many things!"

"Oh, so many . . ."

"And Dario?" I asked with a smile.

"He's there," and she pointed with her chin to the building opposite ours. We went to the window and looked at the narrow, dusty street—a sad corridor. The facade across the way was blue in the twilight. Dario wasn't sitting at his table studying, as I had always thought of him while I was away. His open window revealed a frayed white curtain, a drab interior. The open green fields, the splendor of the mountains in Abruzzo flashed through my mind, luminous and dazzling like landscapes in dreams. But my life was here. I had returned, sweetly and lovingly.

"How is he?" I nodded towards Dario's window.

"Good," she replied. "He's affectionate. Sometimes, though, he's so difficult, incomprehensible, and he disappears. But maybe since you've come from somewhere else, you won't understand. This is a difficult period for them. Dario was drafted, but he was exempted because of his sight. Luckily, it's over now, but I had some agonizing days."

"Because he left?"

"Yes, but more than that—can you believe it?—I thought I was pregnant."

With a jolt, I moved away from the window to hide my face in shadow. I could feel myself blushing violently, all the while unable to take my eyes off Fulvia's face and body. I thought I had misunderstood—maybe Fulvia and Dario were secretly married?—but, more than that, I was upset that I had been excluded from this confidence, betrayed, even, since during the past months I had continued to think of Fulvia as she had always been.

"Right." She looked away. "Right, you don't know anything. It happened in the fall, on October 13th."

I kept staring at her. Silent, wide-eyed, I listened to the words slip out easily while she crushed a cigarette on the windowsill. She had taken up smoking.

"I wanted to write to you about it," she went on, "but some things you don't want to write, they have to be discussed, and then I was worried that your correspondence might be read by others. Do you remember? I didn't write to you for weeks at the time."

I nodded.

"You kept begging me. You were worried, and I was stacking up your letters. I couldn't go back to writing as I had before, even if nothing had actually changed. And then I told you, *sorry, some important things have been going on* . . . Remember?"

I nodded again.

"That's what it was."

Meanwhile, I was feeling an increasingly bitter resentment because of that silence. Throughout the long months, I had continued to write to someone who no longer existed, and to have been misled grieved me. I couldn't even think about judging Fulvia's conduct; I judged only her failure to be open with me. Besides, from the time we were very young, we had sworn that as soon as one of us got married we would tell the other every detail of our first night of making love. But now I guessed that she wasn't going to tell me anything. If I reminded her of our pact, she might laugh and treat me like a child. I thought about Dario's tall figure when he waited for us at the corner of the square, his lazy, supple walk, and it seemed to me that he was responsible for Fulvia's betrayal.

She came over and drew me to the windowsill. In the growing darkness we could still see Dario's window and his deserted desk. Also visible was the white of a bed at the far end of the room, a jacket draped over the back of the chair. These signs of a man's daily life appeared mysterious to us, incomprehensible.

"It happened here," she said, "one night when Mamma was out at the theater."

I wanted to turn and look. Maybe I wouldn't have noticed anything as I entered, I was so used to seeing her still in my memory. But something definitely must have changed. Impossible that it had happened among the old trunks in the room where Fulvia introduced herself to me when we were children. "I'm Gloria Swanson," she had said, piling her hair over eyes painted with charcoal.

Here, I thought. *Right here.* "Tell me," I whispered.

Fulvia began to talk, staring at the window across from her with loving resentment. She said she had resisted him all summer.

"But my resistance was just stubbornness, purely formal. In my dreams, I'd already given in a long time ago, and I had to fight with myself more than with him. He realized that, and he watched me struggle, not even pleading his own case. He knew I was his best ally, and he left me alone in that terrible battle. We saw each other every day, twice a day, and there was always some resentment between us that left me feeling at a disadvantage, because I didn't know how far I could count on my intentions. I was afraid I was digging in mostly because of social conventions. I would have been glad to give in if he had promised to marry me. He didn't talk to me, sometimes didn't even hold me. 'Sorry,' he'd say if he gave in and kissed me or his arm brushed against me. I was irritated by his occasional sarcastic smile, a vaguely pitying smile that I wasn't used to in him. That smile was the only trap he set for me. In all other respects, he became docile, sweet, and always ready to come running when I called. Faced with his generous tenderness, I felt like an unworthy, scheming creature, overcome by a sordid and persistent greed. More than anything, I felt like an actor in a play: solely out of respect for a comforting tradition, I was pretending to be shocked by a sin I was ready to commit. When I was certain that my fear of sin was something I'd made up, and that I was actually eager to commit the sin, well . . ."

"Well?"

"I told him, 'Mamma is going to the theater tonight. Come up for a moment—just for a moment, all right?' Even then I was lying. I wanted him to insist, for it to be him forcing me, making me—"

"What about him?"

"'All right,' he said."

"And when he came up?"

Fulvia was silent for a moment, and then she whispered, "He was trembling."

After she said this we both looked at his window, our gaze lingering on it with tenderness. I thought back to the day when Lydia had said to me, "Come and meet my daughter." I had approached the world Fulvia represented for me timidly, with the sense that a new period was beginning and that our meeting would be a serious test: my games and confidences revealed my whole character, and it was dangerous to entrust them to someone else. And so I trembled. Dario trembled, too. He had taken a risk by going into that room. And I hoped that it would be Fulvia's and my games that endured; that he would leave defeated and humiliated.

Fulvia continued. "We saw each other a lot. Every time Mamma went out in the evening."

The words *saw each other* had assumed a new meaning for her, and I blushed to think that I was her accomplice in their hidden significance.

"Nothing happened for months. I began to be frightened just when Dario was called up, and while he was going through the medical screening. I couldn't believe it was true. It seemed unfair that something we'd done so casually, as kids, could have the same consequences as a church wedding with the consent of one's parents, the priest, and everyone else. It felt impossible precisely because we were used to seeing each other here, in this room. It seemed like one of so many things we did, so many conversations we hid from my mother and yours. Do you understand?"

"Of course."

"I was protesting just as much against Dario's departure. That was as unfair as the unknown creature imposing its presence on me. We didn't want the baby any more than we wanted the war. I didn't discuss my worries with Dario. It seemed like such a depressing, mortifying thing, something a woman resorts to when a man is about to leave her.

And he wasn't open about it, either. He said, 'I'll come back soon, you'll see. What can they do in the war with a nearsighted man like me?' We laughed and went to the country. I'd stretch out on the grass and lean against his knees while he stroked my hair. We got into the habit of talking politics as if we were both men. Yes—reading the papers and discussing politics was our love talk. On the way home, I'd read his name under the letter C, tracing it with my finger on the draft posters fixed to the walls: CLERICI DARIO. Those lists had been put up on every street we walked down. CLERICI DARIO was singled out everywhere, followed and watched. He couldn't escape. The posters knocked the breath out of me. I couldn't think of anything besides that terrible worry, the inescapable presence nesting in me like a hideous hydra, squeezing, strangling—and the war. Dario would say goodbye to me at the door. 'Bye, Fulvia.' Sometimes I'd say casually, 'Come on up later.' And he'd say, 'Oh, O.K.' One day he said, 'I have to present myself tomorrow.' Oh, Alessandra! You can't understand, you don't understand."

It was the first time she'd said that.

"At the time," she went on, "I very often thought of killing myself. I thought of throwing myself into the Tiber. I'd look at the water and think how easy it would be to end it all there, like going to sleep under a soft blanket. I thought about your mother, too. It was as if she were calling me, as if she were saying 'Come, Fulvina! It's nice under here.' I saw myself leaping down from a wall, saw my body plunge in and disappear. But I stayed there, stuck to the wall, and not because I was afraid. You know I'm not a coward. I felt that I belonged to the earth and to my anguish, that I had to savor it, bit by bit. I didn't feel I could escape the law of pain, when I'd spontaneously obeyed the natural law of lovers. Do you understand?"

"I do."

"Then Dario was rejected, and I was reassured. What a relief. That was a horrible period . . . Now we're calm and we've started arguing again."

We stopped talking, and she put a hand on my shoulder.

"You're still wearing mourning?' she asked, touching my black dress. "Buy yourself a bright dress. Cut your hair. You should try to—"

"No," I replied curtly. But then I hugged her, afraid I'd offended her. I started talking about my journey and my return, but it was hard to resume the conversation when she was so changed, and the room so different, too. Meekly, I tried to adapt to it. I told her I hoped to see Lydia and I'd stay a little longer, even though it was late.

"Mamma won't be back for supper," she said, somewhat awkwardly. "She's out to dinner tonight." She paused before adding, "She's going to the theater."

"Ah," I said, and we fell silent. We loved each other—with a difficult, profound love.

"Then I'll go now. I'll call you tomorrow."

I went slowly down the stairs in the pale shadows. And I saw my mother descend quickly in her blue dress, off to meet Hervey.

It was quite difficult at first to get used to living in the house on the Tiber. My room was small, and the furniture had been arranged there carelessly, according to the utilitarian criterion of my father and Sista. Trunks were piled up in a corner, along with suitcases covered with a frayed, rust-colored percale. The sleepiness of the furniture— which, coming from the vast austerity of the house in Abruzzo, had already looked out of place in the apartment on Via Paolo Emilio— contrasted with the bright hallway, the modern kitchen, the tidy bathroom. I couldn't find a welcoming corner. My room opened onto a small stucco balcony, like a bathtub. The people you glimpsed in the courtyard didn't have the tolerant features of the residents of the old building.

"Don't stand there looking out," Sista said, shaking her head; more than once, people had lowered their green blinds to protect themselves from her good-natured curiosity. Gazing into the courtyard, she let her eyes run over the white walls, the lowered blinds, and then, with a sigh, she said that the war had changed the mood of the people. My father made Sista, then me stand in line for hours to buy a certain type of fruit or vegetable he had never shown any interest in during peacetime. I indulged him willingly, and he was pleased with my newfound docility. He didn't realize that it was more dangerous than rebellion. To tell the truth, he no longer provoked rebellion in me, only apathy and irritation.

I soon realized that it was going to be more difficult to endure living with him than I had imagined. He was constantly suspicious of me, carefully hiding the money so I lacked even what I needed to buy stockings or take the tram. He was happy only when he saw me busy with household chores.

"Anything good?" he would ask. If he came home with a package of prosciutto or anchovies, he would put it on the table between us and insist on offering me some so that there wouldn't be any left for Sista. "Wouldn't dream of it," he would say. "Prosciutto for the maid in these times!" The rift between us grew deeper every day. I stayed in my room for long periods, as if I were living in a boarding house. My father went down to see the neighbors on the second floor and never asked me to go with him.

Everyone in the new building watched me pass by, curious about my clothes. I always wore a fairly long black dress, even though the period of mourning had passed. I wore heavy black shoes I had bought in Abruzzo and my hair in a bun on my neck. When I went down the stairs quickly in my dress, the girls turned to look at me. They were all well groomed and made up; they exchanged teasing comments behind my back and then laughed.

"Signorina, why don't you wear your mother's dresses?" Sista asked me a few days before leaving our house, sure that I would never use them as long as she was there. The dresses were all kept in a chest. "He wanted to sell them," she explained. We had adopted the habit of never naming my father. There weren't many dresses—gray, beige, black. I chose a black one. I also took the raincoat, which had been found on the riverbank. In the trunk there was also a long bundle of crackly tissue paper.

"What's this?" I asked Sista.

"The blue concert dress," she replied.

There was a long silence. Once more I heard the decisive, resonant tone of the piano. I listened to my mother playing and smiled at her, all the while stroking the white tissue paper, which whimpered and rasped.

"Have you heard anything about him?" I asked tentatively.

"No," Sista replied. "Nothing. Except . . . Well: I used to go to the cemetery quite often with flowers. But the vases always had fresh flowers in them, the wildflowers that the Signora liked. The custodian told me that it was always a tall, handsome man who brought them: 'Her husband,' he said."

We clasped hands over the crackling tissue. I couldn't get the bold, fiery theme from *Rustle of Spring* out of my head, with its notes ringing like laughter.

"We shouldn't keep going to the cemetery, Sista."

"No. Signora Lydia said that if he ran into someone there he might not go back. Best to leave them alone, Signora Lydia said."

"Yes," I repeated. "Best to leave them alone."

"That's why I prefer to go. It's not because of the war—I told him that, because I couldn't explain a lot of things. One way or another, we have to die. They say you don't even have time to feel anything in the bombings. I'm going because I can't take it anymore. It was already difficult waiting for you to come back."

I accompanied her to the train at dawn one morning.

"I'm scared of being seasick," she said to mask her apprehension.

I knew there was nothing waiting for her in Sardinia. Her parents were dead. She was going to work as a maid for one of her brothers, and she didn't want to stay with me. She couldn't bear to watch me walk. "It upsets me," she had said to Lydia. "It's like I'm watching the Signora." The day was turning foggy. The station was still dark, and we waited quietly for the departure time as we used to wait for my mother, lost in the twilight with our fear.

"The Signora . . ." Sista spoke as the train began moving. "I stole all the photographs."

So I was left alone. I took up the habit of studying in the kitchen. The saucepan boiled on the stove, and the gurgling of the water, the purple flame kept me company. My father was pleased because it saved on lighting. I was never so alone as during that period.

A short time after my arrival, Claudio left to go to the officers' training school in Milan, and his departure was almost a relief, a liberation. During that period he had done nothing but wait for the moment he could see me, and if I lingered over my studying or went to see Fulvia, I felt I was committing an act of cruelty. If I let him come with me, he was happy to bask in the sweet glow of my proximity, and when he looked at me he became almost handsome; every noble sentiment was reflected in him. I thought he should die at those moments; he had nothing more to learn from life.

"I'm leaving tomorrow," he said one evening. "Within twenty-four hours."

He seemed calm. He was so full of suffering that he had no room for despair. "If you're not tired, I'd like to suggest that we go back to that avenue, on Monte Mario, where I first realized I was in love with you." I said yes. I sensed that he wanted to take inspiration from his initial romantic obedience in order to find the strength to accept the new obedience that awaited him. Up there, we had spoken of Antonio, and Claudio was uncomprehending and scornful, accusing him of cowardice. He said that protest was more cowardly than accepting all life's sad requests.

I leaned on his arm, and he devotedly supported me with everything in him. Yet I felt I was suffering the same injustice that he was by leaving. I could no longer ignore the war if it was reaching even my childhood friends, my closest friend.

My peers never spoke about the probability of leaving, or else they joked and made light of it. But, like the young peasants in Abruzzo, they no longer put any enthusiasm into living. They got up late, stayed in bed for hours reading and smoking while their mothers and sisters served them solicitiously, acknowledging their right to idleness and inertia. They felt they belonged to the war now, and were waiting for it to call them. The more they hated the draft, the more unavoidable they felt their duty to wait. Maybe it was this awareness that made them surly from the time they were boys. Not even Claudio's great love for me was enough to suggest that he revolt. Women protested because war wasn't their destiny. Nonna thought about building a shelter, Aunt Violante about hiding Giuliano in the woods. And I suffered by being unconnected to the harsh and mysterious relationship between Claudio and the order he had received, between Claudio and the possibility that he might die.

He begged me now, as he had on the eve of my departure for Abruzzo, to write to him. A few days before, I had received the last of his letters, signed *Claudia*—a childish subterfuge.

"Address the letters to Infantry Officer Cadet Claudio Lori," he advised me now, fearing that I might forget something and the letter would be late reaching him, or lost. Officer Cadet Lori no longer had anything in common with the youth I had met for the first time on Fulvia's balcony. Already, he seemed to smell of leather, like all soldiers. I imagined him jerking to attention, speaking with the inhuman voice the uniform requires in order to respond: "Yessir!," in order to command: "You must leave immediately and show up punctually on the African front where, in sixteen days, at zero zero twenty-eight hours, you must die."

"Don't leave!" I begged angrily.

Moved by my words, he explained at length that tomorrow was the final deadline for arriving at the infantry training school in Milan, and, knowing me ignorant of all things army, he smiled and added that he

would be one of those with the golden rifles on his cap. Yet this jokey
explanation was an expression of his regret that I wouldn't see him in
his military uniform. He hoped his appearance might give him an
advantage and pleasantly surprise me—into love, perhaps. He couldn't
know that from childhood I had had an aversion to little boys who played
war games. There had been one in the courtyard who wore a *bersagliere*'s
cap all day long. Whenever I looked at him, he would strut and then,
irked at not having aroused my envy or admiration, he would point his
index finger at me and pretend to shoulder a rifle: "Bang bang!" He was
a frail, weak child, and he often appeared on the balcony wrapped in a
shawl, with a *bersagliere's* cap on his head. My mother said maybe he
felt well and strong only when he was wearing that cap and so we should
humor him.

"See?" she mused. "War isn't proof of strength, it's proof of weakness,
proof of fear," she added. "Only fear and weakness can incite men to kill
other men who have done no harm."

The real danger of war, in fact, seemed to lie precisely in the fear
and inertia that, like a dense fog, gradually and inexorably overtook us,
robbing us of our faith in the future. The elderly could at least sustain
themselves on the past and their memories. In fact, they scrambled to
safeguard them as jealously as they protected their material goods.
Some buried money and jewelry without realizing that by doing so they
were depriving themselves of their right to enjoy it. As for the young,
who had only the future: there was nothing left for them.

Remembering the photo of Uncle Rodolfo I had seen in Abruzzo, I
looked at Claudio and tried unsuccessfully to imagine him in that
cocksure attitude, arms folded, foot resting on a boulder. And yet they
were facing the same experience, at the same age. Uncle Rodolfo had
often spoken to me of that time, his jaunty tone suggesting that partici-
pation in the war was an expression of adventurous and exuberant
virility. And when Uncle Rodolfo in the dim light of his study told me
about the troops' departure—their joyful, confident marching, their

songs, the flowers women threw from the windows, the flags snapping in the wind—I felt I could hear in the room the sound of military fanfares slowly approaching, and my eyes lit up.

Now, however, one heard the sound of muffled, disorderly footsteps rising from the streets at night. A small group of young men passed by, looking shabby in their summer shirts. Carrying bundles or suitcases, they walked silently behind a man in uniform. Hearing that melancholy shuffle, people sighed and turned over in their beds. Their windows remained tactfully closed. At night, the recruits left the city, at night they boarded ships, at night the ships left the black waters of the port. Bundled into their rough uniforms and crowded into the hold, they didn't even have hate to sustain them, nor did instinctive masculine arrogance—which had seen them play at war when they were children—count for anything now, because they knew they couldn't weigh their value as men against that of other men. Conscious of the frailty of human heroics in the face of the harsh impact of machines and bombs, they knew that what awaited them was the cowardly act of a man who runs to hide in a hole and trembles, shaken by the explosions of the bombs; trembles, ashamed of his own powerlessness. Every night I heard that melancholy shuffling. Fulvia heard it, too, since both of us lived close to a barracks. The old people slept; we couldn't. For those were the steps of our childhood friends, steps we'd heard in the school playground, steps that had accompanied ours on romantic strolls—until they moved off and fell silent. At dawn, the passage of the recruits was marked by orange rinds and cigarette butts.

And so it seemed that nothing was happening. Rome was a peaceful city. Enemy pilots glimpsed it from above—white, innocent, pressed around the large cupola of St. Peter's, seemingly intent on prayer—so they moved off quickly and respectfully. But you could no longer hear the friendly murmur of the fountains in the squares: Piazza Navona was silent, the Four Rivers frozen in fear. Instead of the beloved voice of the water, you heard the arrogant voice of the radio. When I was in bed at night, it found its way into my room through flimsy walls. If I slept it filtered into my dreams, with the shrill scream of the sirens. I would wake up drenched in sweat, my eyes wide in the dark. Fulvia said, "These are our best years. This is what we were waiting for: love, our youth. I had so wanted to turn eighteen, to have an evening gown in swirling pink chiffon."

Arm in arm, Claudio and I walked back up the wide boulevard in silence. "It's getting dark," he said anxiously. "I can't see your face anymore. When will I see you again?" It was a deserted spot. We leaned against a tree to speak. But the radio found us instantly from the one house nearby. It sounded deceptively like birds' warbling, and then the unrelenting voice began to speak. Claudio seemed not to notice it as he strained through the darkness to see my face once more. Already he belonged to that voice; it was as if the voice were looking at me lovingly, enticing me. "Give me a kiss," he begged. *A kiss before dying*, I thought, and the way he risked death through passive obedience was absolutely loathsome to me. I turned my face away from his gently insistent lips.

"Oh," Fulvia said, "our mothers were so lucky that they could even kill themselves for love."

THERE FOLLOWED A dark period, one of struggle, hostility, and discouragement. I enrolled in the faculty of letters, and although my father wasn't happy about it, he didn't oppose it.

"You just need to find a job."

I didn't know where to look. We didn't have any connections. I talked to Fulvia about it, and Dario, and I read the job ads in the paper.

I began teaching myself shorthand with the help of a textbook. I would fall asleep over my notebook in the kitchen and wake up cold, late at night.

I wasn't used to the heavy burden of housework in addition to my studies, and so I was very tired. I got up at daybreak and went to bed late. I hadn't thought that doing the dishes or sweeping up would be so arduous, nor did my father, because he was always observing that the house wasn't very clean and we didn't eat well.

In the afternoon I went out to look for work. When people asked what I could do, I was quiet before suggesting, "I can do anything . . ." They asked if I had relatives at the front, and they would make a note of my address, saying they would write to me. But no one wrote.

I even applied in a perfume shop, where they were seeking "a good-looking girl." A young blond woman, elegantly dressed, came up to me and with icy courtesy asked what I wanted, meanwhile scanning my black dress and raincoat. I said I had come about the job. She asked me to wait, and I was glad to stay inside for a short time amid the bottles all lined up, the bright jars, the sweet scent of face powder. She came right back to say that the job was already taken. I said "Thank you," admiring her all the while and smiling because she was very beautiful. A few days later, when I had my photo taken for the tram pass, I looked at it and realized I would have done better not to respond to the ad.

"Any news?" my father asked relentlessly every evening as soon as he got home. I would hear him coming up the stairs—the elevator had stopped running because there was no electricity. With each stair his dull, heavy step drew nearer and, with it, my admission of defeat. I trembled while he disdainfully read out the titles of the books I was studying and thumbed my lecture notes. One evening he said, "Women who really intend to earn either study to be midwives or learn to work as seamstresses."

I was so alone that fear sometimes got the better of me. No one came to our house, the telephone never rang. Overwhelmed by a bout of depression, I didn't even have the energy to leave the house or cross the bridge.

"I can't," I told Fulvia. "I have to do the mending and ironing." I said it with childish resentment, as if I were being punished. Sometimes, though, I would leave everything and go to Via Paolo Emilio, where the cold wind blew. The presence of Lydia and Fulvia conveyed an immediate feeling of well-being. They were always excited about some-thing that inspired them. They would be busy measuring fabric for a dress that absolutely had to be ready the next day, cutting and basting it. Or they would fill me in on a raffle launched in aid of a tenant. Fulvia, combing her hair, asked if I had found a job.

"Such a shame!" she sighed, putting on mascara.

Lydia was talking on the phone to the contractor, hiding behind a curtain so we wouldn't hear what she was saying. Fulvia did the same when she spoke to Dario, and then they would come out and recount everything.

It was good to be surrounded by that feminine warmth, with under-wear tossed here and there, haphazardly, curlers, dresses. I relaxed on the big bed the way my mother used to.

"Get some rest," said Lydia, offering me the hot water bottle.

One day Fulvia phoned me. "Come here right away!" she said.

"Has something bad happened?"

"No, something good. Come!" Not waiting for me to say yes, she said, "Ciao!" and hung up.

I arrived out of breath, having scaled the stairs two at a time. As soon as I went in, I asked, "What is it?," taking off my raincoat.

"Guess," Lydia replied.

"I'll tell her," Fulvia cut her off.

"What's it to do with you? I'll tell her!"

After a pause that only served to ring the news with tension, Lydia announced, "He's found you a job!"

"He" was her contractor. It was a modest position for the time being, in the administrative offices of his business, but one had to look to the future, they said, and maybe before long I would be able to replace a secretary who was getting married and moving away.

"I hope you won't show up in that dress," Fulvia said. We sat on the bed and praised my benefactor's kindheartedness at length.

Lydia said modestly, "Believe me, he's a really fine person."

I knew he was an engineer and his name was Mantovani. Lydia begged me to be discreet, though not to protect her, she explained. By this time, Signor Celanti had set up house by himself in Milan. But the engineer was in a delicate situation, and, in addition, his wife had heart trouble. "I wouldn't want to have that on my conscience." Lydia sighed, fluttering her lashes.

Mantovani was a good-natured, no-nonsense man in his sixties from Turin. Following the interview, Lydia called me straightaway and in a tone of flattering condescension told me I had made a good impression on him. "He says you're a refined person."

I thought it was due to my mother's old skirt suit, which I had decided to wear, and I breathed a sigh of relief. I had been fairly discouraged after the bad outcome at the perfume shop.

I had felt indifferent at the time, but later I started to think about it, especially because I often walked by the place, which had a large window on the Corso and was one of the most famous perfume shops in Rome. There were always elegant customers inside, and the saleswomen would have been their equals if they hadn't tried so hard to be refined, and come across instead as contrived and fake. The window reflected my sour face, my thin figure in the long raincoat, and, behind me, the gray asphalt of the street, people swiftly passing by, locked in their own thoughts, girls going home from work and girls, like me, who couldn't find work and whose fathers would ask, "Any news?," to hear them say no, while they peeled the potatoes and burned their fingers. I stared at the women sitting in the shop, puzzling over what color lipstick to choose. An uncontrolled resentment rose in my soul. I wanted to throw a rock at the window and break it, and I tried to justify that resentment by attributing it to a protest against society's injustices. And yet it was just envy, jealousy. I thought those women were probably stupid and mediocre, with shallow interests. But these thoughts, which I threw at them violently, as insults, did nothing to undermine the power of their beauty. At such moments I felt that I would give up even the memory of my mother in order to look like one of them.

I moved away from the window, dispirited. I imagined how happy a man would be to meet them for a date: the joy my presence had always elicited in Claudio's eyes was dimming, disappearing. I got long letters from him, but he didn't write very well: he went on about his course and military life. My days were a dark tunnel. "Nothing new," I would reply to my father. Peeling potatoes, washing clothes, looking at my reflection in the dirty dishwater—all this, it seemed, wasn't enough in return for my small bedroom, the little food I ate. "You can't go on like this, without doing anything," he would say.

He cheered up when he learned I had been hired by Mantovani's firm. Then again it was easy to discern, behind his apparent satisfaction, his annoyance at no longer being able to humiliate me every evening when he came home. At the end of the first day, he asked, "So?" and then said, "Thank goodness," with a compassionate smile for the firm of Mantovani for making do with such an employee.

I let him attack me and didn't even try to defend myself. I kept walking down that endless, dark tunnel, and that was how I spent that sad phase of my life, which lasted for more than two years. The work itself didn't rouse my interest, nor did I find the company of my colleagues very pleasant. Almost all of them attempted, like my father, to work as little as possible, considering the fact that they had consented to sit between those walls from eight till two enough to justify their salaries: as soon as they heard the bell at two, they would hurry into the street, eyes full of revenge. I didn't love my work, but I preferred doing sums or typing to chatting with my rather unappealing colleagues, who, with the aid of a primus stove, managed the complex preparation of cups of bad tea, only because the administrative director had advised us to save on electricity. They would hide the primus stove, exchanging bland witticisms and telling political and even dirty jokes. The constant tapping of my typewriter annoyed them. I was often still bent over the large general ledger, struggling with unruly, hostile numbers, when it was time to leave. They had the mentality of schoolchildren and took a dislike to me as if I were top of the class.

The accountant would hover around me suspiciously and then go over my sums. As with my father, I detected a slight vein of irritation when he said, "Well done!" I noted, however, that he behaved the same way towards the best of my female colleagues. There was always a slight element of suspicion in men towards the work of women. They were always expecting us to make mistakes and wanted a chance to pardon our errors. The accountant walked down the corridor while the cashier was balancing the books. The cashier would hear him going back and forth just beyond the door, and his monotonous step wore on her nerves. The numbers got all jumbled up and rolled down the columns of the ledger. The accountant thought that pacing the corridor another twenty times might be enough to get her to stop and call for help: *It doesn't add up, sir.* Three or four of us, all women, would run over to her: she was agitated, putting her hands to her forehead. She was a middle-aged woman with three children. We helped her, and I would even break down and make some coffee on the hateful primus stove.

"Calm down," we'd say. "Take it easy and calm down." We were all standing behind her when he opened the door, at the end of his quota of laps.

"Well, *signora*?" he would ask.

We were pale. "Balanced, sir."

No, there wasn't much justice for the poor girls who worked with me. Maybe they weren't always agreeable or pleasing to look at—some were messy and left the polish on their nails till it cracked, while others pretended to be blond, though their parts betrayed black roots. Sometimes they were nervous because, like many of my fellow students at the university, they hadn't decided between a serious career and the desire to find a husband, and this indecision manifested itself in one way or another.

"You are always so punctual," the men would say. "Sign in for me, *signorina*." And, content with the men's appreciation, the women never said no. That's what their mothers had done and their grandmothers; so that's what they did, too.

They would get up at daybreak and hardly wash, since no one wants to wash with cold water in winter. But they would heat water for the men, and tidy up their room. After making breakfast for their father or brothers or taking a younger sister to school, they would hurry to crowd onto a tram. Sometimes they had to run so as not to miss it, and all women look ridiculous when they run, but they weren't worried about that, only about being late. They would arrive breathless, getting there sometimes just in time to sign in. If the door strictly shut out latecomers, they would stand before it in disbelief, attempting to joke yet trembling inside, since their student's insecurity remained intact. When the door opened up again, the porter would say, "Go to the accountant," in a caretaker's gruff voice. They would go to the accountant, some with a string bag on their arm and in it the lunch shopping, already done.

"Don't forget," the accountant would say, "there are already too many women in these offices." I always arrived with wet stockings. I had only one pair, and they never got dry during the few hours when I slept. During exams I slept for barely two or three hours a night. I would study in the kitchen, since it was less cold; the warmth from the soup lingered there for some time. My father would go to bed and snore. The steady rhythm of his peaceful sleeping filled me with an uncontrollable desire to sleep. All the windows in the courtyard were dark, and I breathed in the neighbors' sleep like thick, soporific smoke. The words got jumbled up before me, dancing between the lines, entering into the fleeting dreams I had when my eyes closed without my noticing. Sometimes I had exhausting nightmares: the professor was questioning me and I couldn't answer because the office porter was kissing me on the lips; meanwhile the main door was closing and I could no longer clock in, and the professor threw me out of the university. I would wake with a start and open my eyes: only a few minutes had passed on the big kitchen clock. My father's monotonous snoring wore away at the calm of the night. I'd go to the kitchen sink, wash my face, and go back to studying.

My father never asked if I was tired. In saying this, I don't mean to imply that he treated me badly—he pretended to believe that my chief interests were the kitchen, the market, and the house. He never asked if I liked my work; all he cared about was alerting me to pay raises and benefits for employees at my level.

"Well? How did it go?" he asked when I came home from my exams, furrowing his brow and feigning excessive concern. I passed them easily, with mediocre marks. He cheered up and brought home a bottle of wine that evening, even though he knew I didn't drink. Once a week he invited me to go out with him, and it was worth accepting: he would take me for a gelato, as he had when I was a child. I think he congratulated himself on those occasions for having always been a wonderful father, in spite of great sacrifices. In the morning, when it was still dark, I took him a jug of hot water for shaving; sometimes I had to hold the mirror up for him since he didn't see very well. If my face looked tired, he would ask, "So what have you been doing?" Claudio's letters made him suspicious, and I think he read them in secret, because I would find my drawers in disarray, and the instinctive suspicion he felt towards women had only grown with my refusal to marry Paolo. In his view, that refusal was so devoid of common sense as to suggest that I was harboring some crafty plan—which is why he sniffed around my day, hoping to find out something about it. Already he was irritated by the fact that I would soon graduate, while he had only a high school diploma.

"It's not worth getting a degree these days—everybody gets one," he said offhandedly, implying that he scorned them. The fact is that he only liked women who complied with the traditional model, or those with whom one found pleasure or distraction. Once when I had the flu, Lydia came to visit me. I noticed that in speaking to her my father used chivalrous, suggestive phrases, slightly indecent, like Uncle Alfredo's glances. Although Lydia had never liked my father, I saw that she was pleased with his old-fashioned compliments. She spoke in a flirtatious voice and pushed her coat aside, suddenly feeling the heat, and laughing greedily, her breasts, now heavy, rising with her laugh.

"Your generation was different from today's," she told him. "You knew how to treat women. And then," she added, sighing, "southerners . . ." The Captain was a southerner.

Because of the blackout, my father decided to accompany her home. She waved him off, but at heart she was flattered by his gallantry.

We were alone while Papa put on his overcoat. "I'm worried about Fulvia," she whispered to me. "You should get her to speak to Dario, to take the initiative. You're both over twenty now. You, too, poor girl . . ."

They said good night, and I was alone in the apartment. Outside the door, I heard Lydia laughing, pretending to be afraid of the dark in the stairwell. My father lit her way with the flashlight. I realized from the sound of her laugh that night that she was no longer a young woman.

THE LAST LETTER from Claudio arrived when Dario had already learned from Claudio's family that he had been taken prisoner. Fulvia and Dario came to bring me the news, calling me from beneath my window. I barely heard them since a military column was passing by on the Lungotevere. They often went by these days, and they made a lot of noise.

"Come down," Fulvia signaled with a wave. She didn't want to come up because she didn't want to run into my father. I went down and we met amid the dust and noise.

"Terrible news," Dario began, "Claudio—"

"It's O.K.," Fulvia interrupted when she saw me go pale. "It's O.K.. He's been taken prisoner."

In the letter I received a few days later, Claudio was demoralized but calm: it was precisely through that painful calm that one could detect the hint of a new obedience, a new humiliation. "Maybe this is the last letter I'll write to you." On Monte Mario, he had said, "It's the last time I'll see you." Claudio was twenty-two, and already there had been many "last" things for him.

Every evening the radio broadcast the names of some of the prisoners to reassure their families. The cold, the dark, the poverty, and the fear shut people up within their walls, as others were locked behind bars, and the radio, until now the relentless voice of war that kept them apart, was now the only voice that brought them together.

The radio broadcast only a few names at a time—ten, twelve—with a silent pause between one name and the next. It was a new sort of silence—alarming and terrible—and in it you seemed to hear the slow breathing of the sea; it was a pause that portrayed the desolate earth of Africa in the black void of a dangerous night. In that emptiness, a man's fragile name appeared and resonated for a second, only to be instantly erased by another long pause. The apartment seemed populated by all those faceless names, crouching in corners like the spirits after Ottavia's visits.

Claudio's name had not yet been uttered. Every night after the last name, we felt the return of that emptiness measured by long pauses.

"Maybe tomorrow," I thought aloud.

"Why are you upset if you don't want to marry him?" my father wondered. I didn't have the strength to be offended at those moments.

"Try to understand, Papa," I said. "He's my best friend." On those evenings, not even my father dared to speak bluntly. The names intimidated him, filled him with melancholy respect.

"When I was young," he retorted, "girls didn't have male friends."

I knew that was true, and I felt a kindhearted pity for him and the coarseness he had always found in his relationships with women. He studied me all the while, wavering between curiosity and suspicion.

I often felt inspected like that, by my colleagues and at the university. I went to classes in the afternoons only; in the morning I went to the office, where I now held the position of secretary. I had a new skirt suit: a gray jacket with a pleated skirt. Fulvia scolded me because I chose dated styles and wore dresses that were too long. I had had my hair cut, but it was too fine and hung lank beside my face. Fulvia shook her head, but Lydia said, "I like it. It's her style, and it was Eleonora's style, too. She also looked as if she were wearing the clothes of someone who'd died years before."

These words, uttered casually, resonated profoundly with me. I begged Fulvia to let me try on one of her dresses. "No, you're right," she herself acknowledged. "Never mind." I went back to wearing my high-necked blouse and long skirt, but I kept looking at Fulvia's dress, a red-and-white floral print. I was enchanted by that dress and wished I were plump and smiling, a young girl with wavy hair and soft lips. I thought I could see in her clothes and features the chance to join in and enjoy life. Fulvia closed the wardrobe. "No," she said. "You can't dress like this."

We saw each other less often now that her life revolved around Dario's mood and schedule.

So I often went out with some students on Sundays. They were from the country, mostly, and lived in furnished rooms on the edge of the city; they brushed up against it, its houses, its customs without managing to become part of it. I felt good when I was with them, and I shared their uncertainty. Since we had no money, we'd go and sit in the gardens at the Villa Borghese or take walks along the Appian Way. We'd visit museums in the morning. Some of the young men would take me home on the tram, hoping to carry my books. They all thought I was repeating a year, and were surprised to learn that I wasn't yet twenty-one. They trusted me to the extent that one of them once asked to borrow a small sum of money. It was a silly sum, and I had it in my purse.

"Forgive me," he said. "I'd never have dared ask it of another woman." As we parted, he jumped on a moving tram and threw me a kiss. I walked back home because I had no more money. As I walked, I felt I was on my way to meet Uncle Rodolfo. *You're tired*, he said. *I don't want you to be so tired.* He stopped a carriage and took me to dinner in a brightly lit trattoria with lovely music, and bought me a beautiful flower to pin on my dress.

I called him, but he didn't come, and I didn't know how to get out of that dark tunnel on my own. I'd sometimes let a classmate walk with me through the darkness; I'd let him kiss me, too, on Viale di Valle Giulia when he took me home. Once I let someone kiss me in a shelter

during an air raid. But they were sour kisses and tasted of cheap cigarettes; I felt like a man putting up with a kiss from another man.

"Don't call me!" I said, making a huge effort to use the familiar *tu*.
"My father doesn't like it." And when I got home to my father I was
relieved and grateful for the excuse he had unwittingly provided.

"It's late," he said, without reproach. He had been losing his sharp-
tongued confidence ever since his eye disease had forced him to stay
home. He managed to hide his infirmity for some time. Unbeknownst
to me, he had been to the eye doctor. He always wore dark glasses. Once
I held out a cup of coffee and he didn't see it.

"Papa," I said to get his attention. He blushed, and extended his
hand uncertainly.

"I can't see well anymore," he murmured. Not much later, he had
to tell me where he kept our money.

In a short time he had become a sad man, though the illness
improved his character. He didn't turn bitter, as so often happens in
such cases, nor did he want to attempt an operation, for it offered little
hope. "Maybe later, when I can't see at all," he said. "I can still see," he
assured me. "I see everything through a white veil." And then: "I can
still see shadows."

My presence brought him no comfort: I didn't love him, and when I
thought about my first memories I had to remember that he had never
loved me, either, as he had loved my brother. When I was born he had
apparently paced the corridors of the ward nervously as he waited. "A
girl?!" he had exclaimed. Irritated, he put on his hat and went to sit in
the café. My mother cried and told me later that I, too, had cried mourn-
fully, as if intuiting how unwelcome I was.

He often talked about this episode when I was a child. Maybe, as
with all adults, it didn't occur to him that it might be painful for me to
hear. He would laugh as he told the story, patting my cheek afterwards.
But his gesture depressed me hugely, for I detected in it both tolerance
and forgiveness.

By now he had had to ask to be excused from the office. At the end of each month, I handed him my earnings together with his, not to foster the impression that he was still the head of the household but to show him that I earned much more than he did—he could still make out the banknotes extremely well. And he did notice it. He would say, "Women are paid well these days." And then he would recover himself right away, adding that it was because of the war. "Isn't that it?" he would ask. I didn't answer. "Maybe you expect a woman to earn as much as a man? You'll see," he sneered. "You'll see when the war comes to an end."

"We'll see."

He was exasperated by my calmness. I took care to be more and more obedient and accommodating, to anticipate his wishes. I neglected myself and found satisfaction in my difficult tasks. My office work, my studies, the apartment, and the assistance I lavished on my father overwhelmed my sturdy yet slight physique. I was exhausted when I went to bed at night. He was becoming weaker and weaker. He even asked me, "Are you tired, Alessandra?"

"No, I'm not," I would reply, to continue the battle that we had been waging since my childhood and from which I was emerging the victor.

THE SIGNS OF his defeat became clear one evening. We were still sitting at the table after dinner. "Would you like me to read you the paper?" I asked.

"No," he replied. "I don't want to know how things are going anymore."

Overcome with exhaustion, I couldn't make up my mind to exert the effort to get up, undress, and brush my teeth, and yet the idea of bed held an indescribable sweetness. I had started putting an empty spumante bottle, refilled with hot water, between the sheets. It was the only sign of affection to greet me at the end of the day.

"Look," my father said.

His unusual tone worried me. He had used it when he said, "Nora . . ." the morning I left for Abruzzo. So I guessed that now he was about to speak of her. We hadn't mentioned my mother since, and that silent commitment was one of the fixed points that made living together bearable.

"Did you meet him?" he asked quietly.

I took a breath, and an imperceptible smile tugged at my face and lips.

"Yes, of course. I saw him often."

I thought I could detect a clear invitation in his silence: so even though, like him, I had barely seen Hervey on the day of the concert, I began to talk about him, describing his character, his voice, his mannerisms. These images pricked like pins in my father's darkened eyes. Yet as soon as I stopped talking he would ask more questions, at first timidly, then becoming more and more precise. Reassured, I gave short answers so that he would have to ask me more about the tiny details.

That's how we got into the habit of talking about my mother and Hervey. Every evening now, when our neighbor didn't come up to keep my father company, I would go to his room and sit across from him, pitiless in the dark. The silence became crowded with images. Eventually, he'd ask, "So?"

And I would start telling him stories. Every evening I would embellish the magical figure of Hervey with new attractions. Remembering my mother's conversations, and relying on my romantic fantasies, I reconstructed the story of their meetings, their conversations, even their looks. He never asked himself how I had come to know all that, but he listened, his face unmoving as stone. I understood from his questions that he hadn't thought about anything else during those years, even when he seemed to be thinking only about rations or money or provisions. He was irritated that my mother had not committed adultery, since fighting a love that was purely spiritual was beyond him.

"It wasn't necessary for them to be lovers," I told him through his melancholy darkness. "They were much more than that." I knew I was hurting him with those words.

"Do you think your mother hated me?" he once asked.

"Hated you!?" I exclaimed, indignant at his hope of having perhaps stirred such a sentiment. "No, no," I continued, conciliatory. "She felt only pity."

"So," he went on, "is that why she didn't leave? Out of pity?"

"No." I was determined to cut the last tie that he believed still held her to him. "She stayed so as not to leave me."

As soon as I said those words, I noticed that his stony face showed relief. The ice in it passed into me and ran down my back. All at once, I began to fear that I was responsible for my mother's death. Yes, I, and my love, had bound her, imprisoned her. I myself had pushed her into the river; my weight had dragged her to the bottom and filled her mouth with water. By now my father was convinced that the fault was mine, but he said nothing. He wanted to trap me in some disgusting complicity.

I went out and walked across the public gardens, stopping to watch the children. Some were beautiful, and all of them seemed to have open and innocent expressions. The mothers sat on benches and watched them, knitting with blue and pink wool. I sat down on a bench, too, and motioned for the children to come over.

"Come here," I insisted until they approached, overpowered by the threat in my eyes. I felt their arms; they were soft, smooth, and pudgy. *Yes*, I thought, and Nonna's words came back to me: *They're sweet, children are. Sweet, soft, innocent.* We looked at each other and I smiled, caressing their soft skin and seeing my reflection in the watery blue of those blameless eyes. Gradually, however, I saw an unforgiving power surface in their innocent, bewildered gaze, one that drew strength precisely from that simple innocence, that defenseless fragility. Their safety in fact resided in the soft skin that no one would have the courage to hurt, in the security enjoyed by the weak, who need protecting. Their mothers quickly unraveled blue yarn, pink yarn, unaware of the chance their children would have to bind, suffocate, and kill with the treacherous softness of their pudgy hands. I had killed my mother merely by existing.

I ran to Via Paolo Emilio, crushed by remorse. It was Lydia in fact who delivered me from my nightmare.

"What do you have to do with it?" she asked harshly in order to bring me to my senses. "You don't know what happened between them, those nights. Your mother begged him, groveled on her knees. 'You can't leave,' your father replied. 'You couldn't go even if you left Alessandra. I'll have you reported at the borders—a husband can do that—and I'll have the police surprise you. Try it,' he'd say."

"No," I said to my father. "I don't think she ever loved you, not even when she agreed to marry you. It wasn't love."

My father didn't answer, and his silence was an acknowledgment of his guilt. On one evening only, his face suddenly grew animated. "Shut up!" he said. "Be quiet, you snake!"

I got up and left him alone. He could no longer be on his own. Perhaps, in the darkness behind his eyes, memories assailed or frightened him. I went on convincing him that my mother wasn't in the cemetery but under his window, in the green water of the river; I told him that she often came into the house, that I heard her walking around with her light step.

"Here she is," I would announce. "Can't you see her?" But he couldn't.

After a short time he called me back, his voice begging, whining. "Alessandra, come here. Forgive me."

I took him his soup, his wine. Politely, I spread the tablecloth in front of him, thinking of the innocent hands of those children.

IT WAS OCTOBER when a fellow student studying architecture offered to take me to an opening at the Borghese Gallery. I liked studying the history of art, and I often sought out a young professor standing in for someone who was ill. His name was Lascari, and I thought I would do my thesis with him when the time was right.

In the meantime, I went to museums, and, since I had little free time, I sometimes spent lunchtimes there, eating my sandwich guiltily behind a newspaper. The galleries were deserted then, and it seemed as if the statues were waiting for me. I would show up at the door of a room and smile, whispering, "Here I am." It may seem immodest of me, but whenever I found myself alone in nature or before a work of art, I felt that it had been impatiently awaiting my arrival in order to reveal its secret splendor. Lascari had surprised me once when I stepped into a gallery, unconsciously imitating my mother's gait.

"What are you doing here?" he asked with mock severity.

Blushing, I hid my sandwich behind my back. I wanted to ask him for some advice on methods of study, but I didn't have the courage. He was the only one who treated me jokingly, like a child. I could never find the right words when I was with him, and I even used imprecise verbs and the wrong adjectives. I was sure he found me lacking in intelligence, and so I worried that he wouldn't want to take me on.

Lascari was also at the opening. At first when I saw him I fled, afraid that he would question me as usual with ironic kindness, asking what I was doing with all the adults. I felt even shyer that day because of the exhilaration I had felt walking across the park to get to the Borghese Gallery. It had been raining, and then suddenly the sky, cloud free, had revealed its most dashing blue. Iridescent pearls quivered on the boxwood hedges, and a robin chirped, fluttering amid the acacia branches. Fresh drops rapidly fell from the branches, stinging my face in jest.

"Sorry," I said to the student, who was waiting for me at the door. "I'm late, but I was walking slowly."

His unpleasant appearance bothered me, his purple hands and his untidy hair, but if I had been alone I wouldn't have been brave enough to go in and mingle with the crowd. He knew a lot of people and kept stopping to say hello, introducing me by my surname alone. I blushed awkwardly and said nothing. I didn't understand anything and I felt bored and lost. Suddenly I saw Lascari go by again, and I made a sudden involuntary movement.

"Bye," I said to the student. He held me back. "Where are you off to? Wait—"

"No, I can't."

He grabbed at my sleeve. "Wait—"

"I said I can't; I have to go speak to Lascari."

He restrained me and I wriggled free, irritated by his arrogance. I felt an increasingly violent anger. Lascari was already on the stairs, with a friend, and I was terrified that I might miss him. But I freed myself, crossed the room, and started down the stairs quickly, quickly, and even more quickly—lightly, as if I were flying. It was a spiral staircase, like the one on Via Paolo Emilio. My long, pleated skirt opened up in a circle, and I was hit by a sweet sort of dizziness in the gray spiral of the stairs.

They were at the door. "Professor!" I called out. I stopped, red-faced and panting.

They both turned around. "Oh, Alessandra," said Lascari. He came back and introduced his friend to me. I smiled, still breathless from running. It was Francesco.

FROM THAT MOMENT forward, I remember everything, every detail of what became my life, and I will recount it all—bluntly and with ruthless sincerity. Perhaps only here does the story begin to have real importance in terms of the purpose for which it was written. But I couldn't keep silent about everything that led to our meeting: Francesco was in me from the first moment, from birth, when my father was irritated because I was a girl. It was Francesco who kept me company while I sat at the window threading daisies. That's why I recognized him when I saw him walk by, why I flew down the stairs, forcing him to turn around.

Even now, Francesco sits beside me and talks. He says: *Alessandra, you were so beautiful at that moment! Breathless, holding your hand to your heart. Lascari said something silly to you, remember? He said you seemed to have walked out of a nineteenth-century painting. I was ashamed of the inane things men say to young women and I didn't want to talk like that. It didn't seem right for you, which is why I learned to speak to you from then on through my silence. You were so beautiful, and I had never seen all the grace of the world in one person. You fell in between us and we started walking. Lascari walked easily beside you, but I couldn't adjust my heavy masculine tread to your graceful step. From that moment on, I found myself clumsy and awkward, and it's always been like that; that's why I acted out of sorts. Ah, you were so beautiful, Alessandra!*

In fact he left us abruptly, and I watched him walk down the avenue by himself. Lascari explained with a smile that Minelli had a closed and suspicious character. He had known him for years, since high school. I remained serious, silent as he spoke.

Francesco called the next day. "Forgive me," he said. "Lascari gave me your number. It seems I was boorish."

"Oh, no . . ." I was confused.

"I'm sure it's true. I had a lot to do."

"Oh . . ." I didn't know what else to say.

"I'd like to see you," he added, "to make amends. I'll be at Lascari's lecture tomorrow morning."

I said yes, fine. I remember that immediately I wanted to call him back and say I couldn't, since I was at work in the morning, but he had disappeared, and I didn't know where he lived or who he was. He was nowhere to be found in the entire city. Yet maybe for that reason the entire city brought him back to memory. I sat by the telephone, my hand still on the receiver. My father felt my heavy silence.

"What's the matter?" he asked, irritated.

After a moment I answered. "I have to be at the university tomorrow morning." And hearing the words "tomorrow morning" again, I felt that I would have to wait forever, and didn't know how to while away the time. I turned back to the phone: it was hard, black and silent. I said, *Not tomorrow morning—right now*. My thoughts ran wild around the city. I got the telephone book and anxiously skimmed it; Minelli was a common surname and I didn't yet know that his name was Francesco.

I knew your name was Alessandra, though, he tells me as I interrupt my writing to listen to him. *I was glad I'd never known a woman with your name, because other women weren't like you. I repeated it over and over that evening, so that the next day I'd be familiar with at least something about you. I said it in different accents. I was alone in my office and should have been preparing a class. But instead I sat in my armchair, head against the backrest, and said* Alessandra *naturally, as if calling you from one room to another,* Alessandra *with sarcasm,* Alessandra *in a bad mood, in anger. Yet it seemed that your name was protesting, so I began to say* Alessandra *with tenderness, as if in prayer. I was smoking and the room was thick with a perfumed haze.* Alessandra, *I said with love. I found it easy to say your name like that. I wanted to hear you say it, watch your lips curl around it. That's why I asked your name right away the next morning. You were surprised, a little disappointed.*

His question chilled me. We walked together in silence for a moment. I thought he was so lacking in curiosity about me that he hadn't even asked my name when he called Lascari.

I felt humiliated by having prepared for a role that no one was asking me to play; there was silence, and in that cold silence I felt confused and depressed.

A student went by and said, "Good morning, Professor."

I tried to pull myself together. "You teach?"

Francesco nodded. "Philosophy of law. I have tenure." His voice sounded serious, almost sulky, as if he regretted giving information about himself. It was hard to tell if he was pleased to be with me or was peevishly yielding to an obligation that he couldn't avoid. I don't remember what we said to each other at first, because we were speaking the language people use to make conversation when they have nothing in common, relying on whatever comes to mind. For a moment I considered objecting to such trite subjects, but then I realized that we were using them as a barrier against other things we didn't want to talk about. We abandoned ourselves completely to the wonderful novelty of walking together, without asking ourselves where we were going. I had always walked by myself, or maybe leaning on Uncle Rodolfo, or letting Claudio lean on me. But that day I discovered for the first time the harmony of walking in step, and it led us along streets I didn't recognize, pavements unrolling before us, with trees for company. I wasn't particularly happy, and in fact I was so gripped by emotion that I couldn't be happy, but the idea of interrupting our walk alarmed me, as if I suddenly had to stop breathing.

"And what's your name?" I asked abruptly.

We were walking but not looking at each other, and he replied hesitantly, as if reluctant to surrender.

"Francesco," he said quietly.

I blushed as if I had heard an intimate confession. I held his name suspended lightly between my fingers as a fragile thing, something just born. I was thinking *Francesco*, he was thinking *Alessandra*, and the awareness of his name living in me, of mine having settled in him, made us feel happily agitated. Trailing after our names, we emerged from our secret selves to meet each other, we spoke of ourselves indulgently, as if speaking of an eccentric friend of whom one is very fond, despite his or her imperfections.

All at once I realized that we had arrived at the river; if we simply turned to the right, we would be at my house after a few steps.

"Oh!" I exclaimed, with such profound regret on my face that he instantly asked,

"Where do you live?"

"There—" and I gestured vaguely as if pointing at an enemy lying in wait. "When I was a child I lived in Prati, across the river."

"I've always lived in an old house in Piazza del Ponte Sant'Angelo."

"The river ran between us."

We laughed, and as I felt the words leading me into a sense of confused fear, Francesco asked how old I was. He explained, "I was on the other side of the river eleven years before you."

The wind was blowing my hair and I had to hold it back. "I'm sorry I didn't know. My mother always forbade me to cross the bridge."

He laughed, thinking I was joking. "And now?"

The Lungotevere was very windy and our words blew away as soon as they were uttered.

"My mother is dead now. I live with my father."

"You must regret having arrived so late," he said, and I blushed.

We turned our backs to the wind and my hair swept against my cheeks. As if in obedience to some troublesome duty, Francesco said, "I must see you again."

"When?" we asked each other. We both wanted to say, "Tonight." But we said, "Tomorrow."

I HAVE TO collect my thoughts, run after them, pin them down. Because when I go back over that period of my life, that sweet period when I met Francesco, they quickly become agitated, stirred up, surging and swelling as if driven by a violent wind. At the time, I raced around delightedly, eager to express the wonderful impetuosity and excitement I felt. There was a vibrant spring to my step; when I went downstairs, our neighbors barely caught sight of my black dress as it flew past them. When Mantovani called me in, at work, I would open the door to his office with a joyful momentum that left me blushing. As I typed, the carriage moved along with a flurry of keys; the sound was a hailstorm in summer. My colleagues, amazed, looked into my office and I'd say, "Good morning!" with a gay and triumphant smile.

I opened the windows, ran the water in the bath, beat the eggs, and scrubbed the clothes, all at that light running pace. Everyone turned around and stopped, astonished.

The fact is that all day long I was running towards my date with Francesco, and as I raced I easily carried out my daily tasks. I stopped only when I got close to him. As soon as he came towards me, I felt the moment had come to stop. After a few seconds of silence, during which all we felt was our nerves relaxing, our breath lengthening and becoming regular, we began to speak to one another, talking hurriedly and anxiously, even interrupting one another, and apologizing with our smiles.

"What does he say to you?" Fulvia asked.

"Nothing," I replied, my face alight. "He doesn't say anything." In fact, we were both eager to speak only of ourselves, coming out of a dark past, and heading towards each other to introduce ourselves. And everything that I had until then guarded jealously I was now burning to share with Francesco. Through these stories, I started to know myself at last, and at the same time I got to know him. It was a wonderful feeling.

I spoke to Fulvia about that happy eagerness and she listened, her hands joined as if in prayer. "I told him about you," I said. She smiled, grateful to have been admitted, however briefly, into our enchanted conversations. "I told him about this room and the games we played when we were little."

"And he hasn't said anything to you yet?"

Five or six days had passed since our first meeting. "No, nothing."

"He must be very much in love if he's not even speaking," she considered.

Once, finally, I had the impression that we were meeting as lovers. It was raining, so we had decided to meet in a café, and I arrived during a cold downpour, which playfully stung my face. I was wearing my mother's long raincoat with the hood up. I spotted Francesco as soon as

I entered, sitting at a small table with a cup of coffee. Intimidated, I crossed the shabby, bare room to where he was sitting, a tall, thin man, slightly bald. I felt I didn't recognize him apart from his outward appearance—gray suit, tie, coat folded on a chair. He stood up and, constrained by the table in that cramped space, he bowed a proper greeting, as a man greets a woman with whom he has a date. There was another couple sitting in the opposite corner; the man was in uniform. They held hands while they looked at each other. Seeing myself in them, I suddenly blushed.

Francesco followed my gaze. "Forgive me—I thought of meeting you here because it's near your house. I didn't want you to get too wet. Shall we go?"

"No, why?" I replied, but the rain was making my shoulders cold, as well as my back. I didn't want to take off my raincoat, to get comfortable in that dreary place. I was reminded of the time I had surprised Lydia in the *latteria* with the Captain.

The waiter brought the coffee in small glass cups. I drank it with no enthusiasm, considering it a ritual to consume something on a date like ours. All that time, Francesco was watching my hands with loving attention. I was watching him, too, because as we walked together I had only got to know his hard profile, his prominent jawline.

That day, though, he sat right across from me. Slowly we moved closer to one another, like the other couple. I felt his hard knees, saw his rugged face, his high forehead, and I knew, from the small red scratch on his throat, that he had cut himself shaving that morning. He looked into my eyes, at my lips, and I didn't shrink from his gaze. Instead I offered myself, unsmiling, my expression intense. And in our urge to deepen our acquaintance, I believed I recognized the anguished presence of love.

"Yes," I replied to Fulvia in the evening. "You may be right. Perhaps he is in love with me."

She was curious. "Tell me! Tell me more," she begged. "What's Francesco like?" She called him by name, as I had never dared to. From a distance, it was easy to feel I knew him, and I started talking about him, describing him. He seemed less timid, and he let us look at him, an unknown body that we hadn't allowed ourselves to imagine in any detail until now. I hesitated.

"No, maybe he's not handsome," I said. "I don't know—he's tall." I added, "Much taller than I am. And also . . . No, it's pointless. You wouldn't understand."

"Tell me."

"Well, his neck reminds me of a horse's neck. But you won't understand. It's silly."

"But I do. You said the same thing about Hervey the day after the concert. It made a big impression on me. I looked at your mother and thought of a horse's neck. I was young, you know. But to hear you speak, it sounds like her story is continuing."

We were lying on the bed in her old room, where she now saw Dario. Fulvia went on in dismay, "I'm continuing my mother's story."

FRANCESCO WAS WAITING for me in Piazza San Pietro. I was the one who had chosen the place for our date, unconsciously hoping to find the streets that had been dear to my mother and Hervey. We started walking between the old palaces of the Curia.

We gradually walked farther from the built-up area and climbed the Janiculum on a lovely country road, the same one I had taken so many years before to go to the concert at Villa Pierce. It was I who had provided the opportunity for that memory; nevertheless, it caught me off guard so that I became emotional.

"My mother loved this road very much."

I had never spoken about her with Francesco, or with anyone else who hadn't known her. When I returned from Abruzzo I had kept firmly to the version suggested by my father. In the conversations with Francesco I had only hinted at something that had shaken me profoundly and perhaps changed the course of my life.

"My mother was so happy whenever she walked here," I said, and gently prodding my nervous reticence, I began to talk about her, her tastes, the extraordinary way she walked. I talked, too, about Nonna Editta.

"My mother read Shakespeare to me, aloud but in secret, since my father didn't want her to. I was seven. I would repeat those lines in bed at night, and that's how I learned to pray."

He listened to me not with Claudio's humble, unassuming attention or Paolo's wondering amusement but with an interest my words had never elicited before. And the intimacy these confidences established between us seemed not temporary or casual but generated by distant roots, as if we had known everything about one another for a long time. Galvanized by the story, I turned to see Francesco looking at me with such new emotion in his face that I stopped and blushed.

"You're so like your mother!" he exclaimed affectionately.

"Me?" I stopped, confused.

"Yes, I think so. When you talk about her, you're sketching your own portrait."

I lowered my head, uneasy. His presence made me feel not just relaxed and happy but unsettled and dismayed. Maybe my mother, too, had been not only happy when she walked along this street. Maybe she, too, had been afraid.

Feeling lost, I turned to look at Francesco: we had stopped in the blinding red light of the sunset, and in that light he looked flushed with deep disquiet. I seemed to find in the smooth planes of his face everything that until now I had loved only in myself and in nature; I was driven towards him irresistibly, as I was towards trees, bodies of water, and my own reflected image. All that was most secret and hidden in us now passed easily from one to the other in a look. Oh! reliving that moment and those which followed, the light during our encounters, the splendor of the landscape, the softness of the air, and the living presence of Francesco, I feel my strength waver. A sweet languor suffuses me, my eyes fill with tears, and my words become jumbled, trembling on the sheet of paper.

"My mother killed herself for love," I whispered.

IT WAS GETTING dark when I got home. I had begged Francesco not to accompany me, making excuses. But the truth was that I wanted to be alone for a few moments. There were a lot of people on the neighborhood streets at that hour. In the thick darkness of the blackout, you could see them go by quickly, in and out of shops for the last purchases before dinner. I was walking in a dream, my face burning, and I got some relief from a gust of wind that lifted my hair. People's arms brushed mine, they bumped into me, but I didn't turn around. Francesco's face was before my eyes. I called to him and he answered. We spoke a language no one else could understand.

From that instant, my love for him was not separate from me but a guest whom I welcomed with intensely joyful gratitude, and who, to put it briefly, filled every bit of me, body and soul. I like to linger over this point. Since then, and even now, despite the painful and terrible things that happened between us, my eyes have always been full of his face, and everything else has appeared through it, transparent: countryside, fields, houses, city streets . . . I could see even the trees only behind his face, as if painted over a curtain. Tomaso's face, too, his lovable laugh, I saw through the face of the one I caressed from that evening on—not only with romantic thoughts but with all the good and bad ones that have been in me since birth.

I climbed the stairs lightly and went into the house. I ran straight to my bedroom window and looked out. "Tomorrow," I said softly, repeating the terms of our date: "Tomorrow at five."

My father called and I ran to him. He sat calmly in the room barely lit by the moon's icy glimmer. "You're late, Alessandra," he said. "I want to eat." His voice no longer betrayed spite or irritation, and the misery of his condition seemed to lend him solemnity, ennobling his features.

In his dark suit, he blended into the dark chair. His white hair and the smooth marble of his skin made him resemble a statue, like Nonna.

I took a small chair and sat at his knees. He glanced towards the window even though he could barely see anything now. Everything about him, shape and thought, seemed to close around the name Nora, which he was intent on repeating and guarding. "Nora," he had learned to say one day, as I was now learning to say "Francesco." I owed my birth, and knowledge of the same feeling, to the feeling he had had for my mother. The grudge I had held for so many years suddenly dissipated, humbling me in an act of genuine contrition. I remembered how I had dreamed of abandoning him, the cruel joy with which I had bullied him every evening in order to hurt him.

I was overflowing with love, intoxicated with kindness, and it seemed as though my generous impulses ought to be aimed at my father, more than anyone, and settle on him. I stared at him with tender gratitude, remembering his old habit of taking me to get a gelato when I was a child. Even now he would sometimes say, with humiliating contradiction, "Come with me, I'll take you to get a gelato." But what moved me most was remembering his monotonous days, totally governed by his office schedule, and the despondency that that pace of life had generated in him. His naïve narrow-mindedness, his self-important banality— in other words, everything that had irritated me or enraged me suddenly elicited deep emotion. Because it was also to all this that I owed my appointment today in San Pietro.

My thoughts were red-hot: surely he could feel their heat. He turned towards me slightly. "What's the matter, Alessandra?"

I didn't respond right away, not wanting to lie. There was no room left in me for a single lie, a single deception. I listened anxiously to the confirmation of what was upsetting me, and, having heard it, I felt light as a feather when I confessed: "I'm in love."

I expected him to spread his arms and smile so that I could finally take refuge in him, put my head on his shoulder, cry, perhaps, and open up. Instead he flinched—I put it down to surprise—and asked, "Who?"

"His name is Francesco."

As soon as I had said his name I shuddered. I felt I had committed a serious indiscretion, and I feared that in his house, in the study he always occupied at that hour, Francesco had abruptly raised his head at the sound of his name. I thought I saw an expression of astonishment and mockery on his face. I had been unable to resist the temptation of saying his name within the walls of my house; I was, like all women, incapable of keeping a secret.

"You don't even know his surname?" my father asked, offended. And somehow I realized I had made a mistake in speaking about it. "What's his name? What does he do?"

Intimidated, I answered quietly. "Oh yes, I do know. His name is Minelli, Francesco Minelli. He's a university professor."

"A professor?" he repeated, his tone vaguely contemptuous. "The worst category of state employees: they're penniless, but arrogant and pretentious. Where did you meet him? And why hasn't he come to speak to me?"

I stood up, hesitant to reply. Every word of his cast out a little of the ineffable enchantment that had suffused me until then. "Why?" I asked timidly, trying to bring him back to the affectionate picture I'd drawn of Francesco. "Why should he come to speak with you, Papa?"

"Because that's what honest men do when they want to marry a girl."

"But he doesn't want to marry me. I never said that."

"Oh, no? Fine. So what does he want to do, then—amuse himself?"

Horrified, I fell silent. From his first question, I wanted to ask him to keep quiet, not to ruin the joy I had been allowed to feel for the first time.

"He doesn't want to marry you! Just have fun. I believe it. And you actually come and tell me that."

I was trying to understand the meaning of the words "have fun" as applied to us, Francesco and me. Those apparently innocent words made me blush uncontrollably. I worried lest Francesco should hear our conversation and retreat in disgust and disappointment, his lips curling in a sneer.

"What do you have to say?"

"Nothing, Papa. I'm going to prepare dinner.'

The house was silent, dark, and depressing. I wanted to hide in that darkness, to disappear. I felt so alone that not even the thought of Francesco could keep me company. I would no longer dare go to him, carrying my father's humiliating words. On the stove, the water hissed in the pot. Before long I would have to put in the pasta and heat the sauce. I couldn't avoid it that evening, either. And after that the ironing was waiting. I couldn't even throw myself on the bed and cry. My mother took me in her arms. *Oh,* she said, *I didn't want you to be a girl, either.*

The phone rang in the silence. I waited a moment, surprised that someone should be calling just then. And then I ran.

"It's Francesco." He hadn't called again, after the first time. His voice was warm and controlled, his face was before me in the black emptiness of the receiver.

"Oh thank you! Thank you."

"For what?"

"For calling me."

"Of course. Am I bothering you?"

"What do you mean? On the contrary . . ."

"Forgive me. I couldn't wait until tomorrow. I wanted to tell you something."

"What?"

There was silence, sweet silence, welcome darkness.

"Well, it's not important anymore. I wanted to talk to you about today, but—"

"I understand."

"You do?"

"Yes," I said quietly. "I wanted to speak to you, too."

There was another silence. We didn't have the rhythm of our gait to help us: our words were stripped down to their meaning.

"It's a long time till tomorrow."

"Oh, yes!" I confessed in a whisper.

"But things are already better now."

"Much better."

"Forgive me. Good night, Alessandra."

"Good night, Francesco." It was the first time I had used his name. We kept silent for a moment, bound by the telephone cord; I heard his breathing through the receiver. Then he hung up, I hung up. Slowly— so as not to suffer from the click putting an end to our conversation.

My father said nothing. We ate, and on the other side of the table he felt my strength and determination.

A FEW DAYS later, on November 11th, we met at the Borghese Gallery. Inviting me to go back to the place where we had first met, Francesco's voice had remained suspended in an anxious question. Looking at him seriously, I had said yes.

I looked anxiously for Francesco from room to room, not greeting the paintings as I went by, the statues I loved; in fact I shunned their mysterious immobility. I walked swiftly, with my mother's gait, and stopped only when I saw Francesco standing in front of a picture. He was looking at it, but he saw nothing as he heard my step coming closer. That's what he told me later.

"Here I am," I said without smiling. We had the pained, troubled faces of those whose unwitting happiness has given way to the bewilderment of love.

We walked side by side, admiring the paintings. You could see spaces on the walls where works had been removed because of the war. We stopped in front of them, afraid, gazing at the weave of the burlap, the tangle of cheap thread. I thought I might be abandoned, desolate, like those walls. Francesco took my arm and I clung to him, to protect us. "No," he said, "I'm exempt from the military because of my university teaching."

I groaned inwardly, suddenly fearful. I called on Nonna for help, thinking of the shelter she had wanted to build for me in the rock. Francesco stood opposite, looking at me. "We could see each other earlier tomorrow."

"Yes, at three," I replied. We wanted to be sure of seeing each other tomorrow, the day after tomorrow, in an uninterrupted string of days, so we could find the calm we needed to regard one another forever. It may not be easy to understand that the extraordinary memory of November 11th is of me leaning against the wall and him standing opposite, the two of us looking at each other. When he looked at me, I was conscious of myself for the first time: my eyes, my mouth, the smooth expanse of my forehead. And I finally understood why they had been drawn on my face.

I don't recall exactly how he told me that he loved me. He spoke in a brusque, confused way. Maybe he didn't say anything, and I said everything silently as I looked at him. But for years on the eleventh of every month I expected to feel beautiful as I did that day. Of course it's immodest to say this, but I believed I was more beautiful than my mother on the day of her concert, more than Nonna Editta on her gala nights. I had her romantic face under the feathered hat, Ophelia's hair, Desdemona's cape.

WE SAW EACH other every evening. A stubborn ruthlessness energized me throughout the rest of the day: I was coldly determined to set the time of our date apart from every other hour of my life. I no longer felt inside the blessed happiness of the first moments but an impassioned tenacity with which I dedicated myself entirely to love. It seemed to me that this was the only way to help the improvement of myself that I had been waiting for since adolescence. In fact, I had become more intelligent and faster: at the office, the promptness with which I carried out my tasks and the sense of responsibility I had acquired earned me the men's respect. At home, I performed my chores expertly in order to arrive at my date on time, leaving behind bright rooms, fresh, tidy linens. I liked carrying within me the neatness of a mopped kitchen, pages beautifully typed, methodically pursued studies. Around that time, I took an exam and got top marks, with distinction.

By now, we had got into the habit of meeting in secluded places where we could kiss. With the fear of air raids, the city was ever darker; while this caution reminded us of the dangerous presence of war, Francesco and I took advantage of it. Although we couldn't admit it, every morning we looked at the weather to find out whether we would be able to hide in the shade of the gardens at Villa Borghese. We desired each other ardently, and, if bashful at first, I soon abandoned myself to that desire, which gave me no respite: seeing Francesco move even when we were sitting and talking in a café renewed the turmoil I had felt in Abruzzo watching the two peasants threshing corncobs in the farmyard. Every movement of his hands aroused in me the same sensation, and I had to stop myself from looking at him when he moved, in his detached way, so as not to tremble, as I had then. The first time we kissed, I felt a sharp contempt for myself. I didn't think we needed to resort to those methods to prove the fire of our emotions. Besides, I was held back by a vague sense of shame; at such times I felt as though my eyes were losing the sweet clarity with which I usually looked at Francesco. My face would change, and I was afraid that he would be surprised to discover someone else in me, someone entirely different from the person he knew, and he would reproach me for having tricked him. I thought about the time Enea had found me alone in the house and came over to kiss me. His face was distorted, vicious, and, by accepting the same expression on my own face, I felt I had become complicit with him. It was as if at many years' distance I were calling him back and opening the door. In the dark shadows of the oaks, Francesco looked at my face and I hid it with my hand. He pushed my hand aside, wanting to know me even with the look I had fought against ever since I was a child. *Get out of here, Alessandro!* I said inside, and I set as a model for myself my mother's perpetually chaste face. Yet when Francesco kissed me I saw him animated by the same passion that drove him to explore my intentions, my past, my thoughts. It was in fact easy to move from the most candid of confessions to the most transporting of kisses. Sometimes it was the actual stories I told about my mother that pushed me to the edge of this sweet abyss.

I told Francesco the story of my mother and Hervey. I can't judge whether my version of their story was faithful to the truth, because every time I told it to my father I embellished it with so many inaccuracies that by this time I wouldn't have been able to distinguish them. We had started going to sit and look at the Lungotevere in the evenings, near the place where my mother had let herself be carried off by the water. I told him about Alessandro, about the anniversaries of his death, about my mother throwing daisies into the river.

"I don't want to meet your father," he told me, his brow furrowed. He looked at the water, the trees. "Being here is all I need to feel that I'm at your house, with your family."

Oh, he really was an extraordinary man, Francesco, and reflected as it was in his life, mine seemed extraordinary, too. He now navigated the story of my childhood and the story of my mother with affectionate intimacy.

He rarely spoke about his own mother. He said she was very thin, like him, and always wore a choker of white ribbon around her neck. When I called and she answered, coldly, I felt that I was coming up against that choker. No, she certainly couldn't compete with someone like my mother, who had killed herself for love. Along that stretch of the Lungotevere, above the reedbed, the trees were green and slender. In spring they bloomed with pink down, which smelled like powder and sugared almonds. It seemed to me that we kissed there with greater abandon; while Francesco was kissing me, I could hear the river rushing by. We wandered around Prati now as if in a church.

•   •   •

FRANCESCO OFTEN EXPRESSED curiosity to meet Fulvia, but I was hesitant to introduce them. To me it seemed that they had met some time ago, through my conversations, and were already bound by everyday intimacy. They would have had to back up, pretend not to know one another. It would have been awkward to put on an act in front of me. I could predict that, and so I delayed. Francesco insisted, thinking that Fulvia was the only person who knew about our meetings, since I'd said nothing about the wretched conversation with my father, and having an unknown witness bothered him.

"But after all," he asked, "what does Fulvia think of me?"

"Oh, she really likes you . . ."

He shot back, "Why should she like me? She doesn't know me at all."

I explained that we often spoke about him, and an innocent male vanity encouraged him to measure himself against the person I had portrayed. Yet I knew that his introverted nature would spur him to do anything he could to belittle himself. I didn't dare ask him to be friendly or polite. I recalled my first impression of him, in an effort to predict the impression he would make on my friend.

At last I arranged the encounter. We agreed to meet in the street.

"Fulvia is always late," I observed, hoping she wouldn't come. Francesco was feeling insecure. Maybe he, too, wished she wouldn't come. We were walking back and forth at some distance from one another, and in asking a friend to be part of our secret I seemed to be less in love. Francesco was wearing a brown suit I didn't like very much. I didn't really want Fulvia to meet him in that suit.

"If she doesn't come soon, we'll leave," I said. But just then I saw her in the distance. "There she is!" I announced. Her clothes were showy, as if she were going to a party, and she wore a pair of dangling gold earrings that were conspicuous against her brown hair.

Francesco said, "Is that her? I imagined her differently."

It was very difficult for Fulvia. We went to sit in a café and the conversation dragged. She and Francesco examined each other unsparingly.

I tried to help them, highlighting first one and then the other, but I felt that Francesco was stronger, since he had my love to sustain him. Fulvia couldn't view him separated from that sentiment, and she therefore supposed he had virtues greater than those revealed in his insipid conversation. She, on the other hand, sat alone across from him. Conscious of being on her own, she tried to compensate for it with excessive liveliness. I recall being cowardly: in order to distinguish myself from her, I retreated into my strictest reserve. I pulled away, my silence accentuating my slenderness, which made her beautiful figure seem too voluptuous.

We couldn't get past our reciprocal discomfort, and the more we tried, the more entangled we became. There wasn't a moment of relief. Fulvia served the tea, smiling, and poured the milk.

"No sugar, right?" she said to Francesco. I felt myself blushing.

"How do you know?" he asked, amazed.

Fulvia, disconcerted, looked at me.

"From me," I said. "I don't remember how it came up . . . You have a good memory," I said coldly. I let her drown. *Forgive me*, I begged silently.

We finally said goodbye at the door. Fulvia went to meet Dario, who had started working in an office. She pretended regret that he couldn't meet Francesco.

"It's a pity," I said. Francesco and I began walking, and it took some time before we managed to feel alone again.

"Poor Fulvia," I sighed. He said nothing. I was afraid that he didn't love me anymore. All I needed was one of his silences to feel that fear, to shift my worried and bewildered thoughts to him.

"What are you thinking?" I asked.

"She's nice," he said, but he was holding back.

"And?"

"I don't know. Meeting her, I wouldn't have thought she was your friend."

"You have to get to know her," I admitted.

"Did your mother like her?"

"Oh, well, she barely knew her," I said disloyally. I was irritated with him for making me lie. I wouldn't have been so harsh about one of his friends. I would have begged him to tell me what Francesco was like as a child. He didn't ask anything. He hadn't seen in Fulvia the balcony, the courtyard, and hadn't understood how important her existence had been at certain points in my life. He judged her for what she was, and not what she represented for me. We had slept in each other's arms the night my mother died. Most of all, I accused Francesco of not understanding that it was precisely because of everything Fulvia and I had been for one another that she couldn't act spontaneously or feel confident. Meeting him and admitting him into our affection had so intimidated her that she needed that bright dress, those gold earrings. I squeezed Francesco's arm, hoping for a friendly word for Fulvia.

"She knew I never take sugar in my tea," he observed sarcastically. "You tell her everything, then? Everything?"

I didn't answer. His nature, although it was frank and pleasant, seemed to withhold some areas, making them difficult for me to penetrate. It was difficult, for example, to know what he did during the day. He was always evasive, always shifty. He never spoke to me about his work, apart from brief ironic references that were perhaps meant to imply excessive modesty. He always brought the conversation back to us, and I willingly agreed to follow him.

Nevertheless, I felt every evening as I left him that he had kept something back, something really important about himself. If I hadn't known where he lived, who his parents were, and what his profession was, I would have doubted that I knew his true identity. There were times when I suspected he had a wife somewhere in the world, and so I often said that marriage wasn't important for me, only love. I also banished another worry that often assailed me: that is, that he had a lover and didn't dare leave her. This fear arose from the fact that he sometimes arrived late for our dates, or put them off at the last minute. One evening at the Villa Borghese, I saw him turn suddenly, as if he feared he was being followed. His mood was changeable, and his face would suddenly cloud over for no reason. It wasn't to do with me, of that I was certain. On the contrary, in those moments he held me close to him.

We were walking together one evening, Francesco holding me close in the angry way that was the first sign of his restlessness. He seemed to want to defy an adverse wind that was trying to separate us, a storm. I didn't ask anything but moved closer to show him that I, too, wanted to fight the battle, even though I didn't know the adversary. We sat down on an isolated bench and lit a cigarette. I asked him, "Is something troubling you, Francesco?" I tapped the ash from my cigarette, feigning nonchalance, but I regretted having solicited an intimacy to which I had not yet been admitted despite his love for me.

Francesco studied me first, annoyed that his feelings should have been so obvious. Then, averting his gaze, he said, "Yes, very much," and took my hand, folding it lovingly into his. "It's nothing to do with you," he began again, his tone warm and reassuring. "Our love doesn't come into it," he explained quietly, with his usual restraint in uttering certain words. "Or at least, it doesn't come into it any more than the rest—the rest of our life."

"What do you mean?" I pleaded, and ice ran under my skin: a sudden fear.

"Not today," he said. "Don't ask. I don't want to think about it. I assure you: it's something that doesn't directly concern you and me."

"All right." I agreed and didn't press him. He looked at me tenderly, appreciating my discretion not because he saw in it that naïve feminine docility, which, on the contrary, irritated him very much, but simply because it was proof of our mutual trust. I said goodbye as I did every night. I smiled and he, too, attempted a smile. He clasped me to him in the dark entrance hall.

"Bye," he said, and left abruptly.

I waited for him to get home and called. He wasn't there. I called later: he hadn't come back for dinner. I was sure that that embrace had been a goodbye. I looked out the window, hoping that by chance he might go by and at least I would see him one last time. In the dark you could make out the grassy shore, the reedbed. *Help me!* I said to my mother, *help me!* and I hurled my call into the river's black water. The Tiber, flowing in front of my house, went past Francesco's house, too. *Help me!* I sobbed, entrusting it with my desperate message.

I even called during the night, but as soon as I heard the bell and imagined it ringing through the silence of the rooms, I hung up, disheartened.

Maybe Francesco would understand and call me. I waited in the dark by the phone, in my nightgown, afraid of waking my father. Francesco didn't call. I was sure he was with another woman. "It doesn't matter", I whispered. "Call me anyway."

I succeeded in speaking to him the following morning, after a sleepless night. He was always laconic on the phone. "What is it?" he asked.

"Nothing. So will we see each other at six?"

"Of course, that's fine."

We met in a small café. I was happy to see him, to rediscover the color of his skin, the features of his face, his slightly threadbare blue shirt, and yet I was overcome by uncontrollable anxiety. I wanted to behave as I'd planned; that is, to say nothing, to content myself with seeing him. I knew it would be wrong to reveal how curious I was, how painfully jealous, but his presence cancelled every one of my intentions. I was upset. I felt that the other customers were watching me suspiciously.

"Let's go. We can't talk here," I said presently.

"Yes, it would be better," he approved.

His agreement frightened me. So there was something. It wasn't just a worry or a ridiculous speculation. There was something, and he was getting ready to confess. Maybe he wanted to leave me, didn't love me anymore. Once again, I hoped it was something to do with money, a gambling debt. I was ready to accept whatever he might confess.

We took a few more steps in silence before he said, "I'm being watched by the police."

I flinched, terrified and relieved all at once. "Why?" I asked quietly, clinging to him. "What have you done?"

"Nothing," he replied with a cynical smile. "I'm an anti-fascist."

I remember that with the word I felt a violent blow to my chest. It was a word that terrified me, although I didn't know what it meant. I really could not have specified what it was to be an anti-fascist. I had never seen an anti-fascist. From time to time I read in the paper that one of them had hatched a plot, set off a bomb, or been shot in the back. Anti-fascists were outlaws, suspicious individuals, banished: Francesco belonged to that species and I had been walking with him for months without knowing it. My heart was pounding, and I felt vaguely nauseated, as if he had suddenly revealed he was suffering from some shameful disease.

All these thoughts rushed through my mind in a second. But after a silence I said only, "Oh."

"Does it upset you?" Francesco asked, his tone contemptuous.

"No. Why should it upset me?"

I was afraid of him. I feared that he might mistreat me, beat me, pull a bomb out of his pocket. I felt I had fallen into a trap, and unconsciously I responded with cunning, pretending to take the news without surprise or disapproval. But I wouldn't have dared repeat the word *anti-fascist*, just as I wouldn't have dared to say aloud some of the words written on walls that I had looked up in the dictionary as a child. I had believed I knew everything about him; instead he was suddenly becoming mysterious and incomprehensible, like Antonio. I hadn't thought about Antonio for a long time. To show how open-minded I was I said, "My friend's brother was arrested with the communists."

"When?" He stopped abruptly.

"A long time ago, in '36, I think."

"Ah, old news. They're making a lot of arrests even now. I was warned by the police a few days ago."

I couldn't overcome my uneasiness, a childish desire to cry. People walked by and I didn't dare look up, disheartened to be on the arm of a man tainted by a secret flaw. I was suddenly struck by an uncomfortable thought: maybe I had always had a preference for a suspect or guilty man. That's why I had left Abruzzo, why I had refused to marry Paolo, and everyone had always mistrusted me: my father, for example, when he tapped his forehead and made a gesture as if he were turning a screw; Uncle Alfredo when he looked at me as if to say, *Take off your clothes*. I hung my head.

"What's wrong?" Francesco asked. "Maybe you'd have preferred me to be a fascist?" he added with bitter sarcasm.

"No, no," I replied, suddenly frightened. "Or, I mean, I don't know. I never asked myself that question. It's more that I didn't think anti-fascists were people like you."

"Ah," he said, mildly amused. "And what did you think they were like?"

"Well, for a start, ordinary people . . ."

"What does 'ordinary' mean?"

"People of a different class from yours, terrorists . . ."

"And according to you, a professor couldn't be a terrorist? Couldn't kill, if necessary?" He seemed irritated.

"Well of course," I said, surprised to see his face looking so pleasant and lovable. The same face as the day before. "I don't know," I whispered. "I don't know anything."

"Look, there's the truth. You don't know anything." He spoke harshly, and, mortified, I said nothing. I was afraid he would abandon me, judging me a cowardly little thing. It was worse than if he had had a lover. It was over. He no longer loved me.

"It's precisely because too many people know nothing that I'm an anti-fascist."

He said that in the tone he used when he spoke to me every day, and it was sweet to recognize him in it. So I contented myself, almost reassured myself, and didn't ask for further explanations. We were on a lonely street behind Castel Sant'Angelo, one of my beloved streets in Prati. I was crushed between Francesco's arm and the memory of Antonio. "They're not happy," Aida said. I couldn't find the strength to be happy as before, either. Maybe it was worse than if he'd left me. We were no longer happy, and he never had been.

I leaned against the wall in the dark and began to cry.

Francesco came up beside me and took my shoulders. It was the first time he had dared to embrace me in the street. He pulled his hat just over his eyes. *An anti-fascist*, I thought, *I'm being embraced by an anti-fascist.*

"Do you mind very much?" he asked, looking at me lovingly.

I shook my head no.

"Do you love me?"

I nodded yes.

"Why are you crying?" I shrugged my shoulders while he went on. "Don't cry. I love you so much. Forgive me—I should have told you right away, but there are things you don't talk about with someone you don't know. And later I was afraid of losing you. I worried that you might leave me. You won't leave me, right? Say you won't leave me?"

I shook my head joylessly: no, no. People walking by observed us with curiosity. "Tell me you love me," he insisted. "Are you mine? Tell me. Smile. Don't worry. I don't believe they'll arrest me. But if it does happen you have to believe it's only for a short time. They'll lose the war . . ." I looked around, though Francesco was speaking quietly. "They'll go. And then we can finally be happy . . . We'll get married then, we'll work together, and then you, too, will be truly happy . . . I'm sure you've never been truly happy."

His eyes were euphoric beneath the dark brim of his hat. I felt I was encountering his real face for the first time, as I had seen Paolo for the first time when he sat on the wall after kissing me.

"Think about it. Have you ever been happy?" he went on.

And, as I looked back—at my poor neighborhood, at the big apartment blocks where the days unwind in a dreary, relentless rhythm—my
entire past life seemed truly painful and bleak after the brief fairy tale
I had lived with my mother. I had never truly been happy. I hoped my
restlessness would finally subside and wear itself out in him, in our love.
But instead we had to keep going, walking together through a dark,
sordid tunnel.

"It's true," I said, looking at him intensely. "I've never been happy."

Instead of consoling me, he smiled radiantly, as if realizing only in
that moment that I loved him. He kissed me for a long time on the mouth.
And while he was kissing me I was thinking that he wasn't the same as
he had been the day before but a man I didn't know at all. Humiliated,
I returned his kiss with neither joy nor pleasure, and on his lips the salty
taste of my tears blended with the cold flavor of smoke.

THIS MAY SEEM excessive, but on my way home that night I felt as
though someone were following me up the stairs. From the moment Francesco made that terrible confession, I had the feeling that we were under
an ice-cold spotlight. Entering the apartment, I was gripped by an uncontrollable anxiety. The radio was on, and the arrogant voice circulating
through the house seemed to be looking for me, pointing at me sternly.
I peered at the telephone, the door, afraid that everyone knew, that a
neighbor had warned my father and he wasn't saying anything in order
to keep me at his mercy. Lascari had to know it, too. In fact, he seemed
annoyed to learn how intimate my friendship with Francesco had become.

Feeling acutely guilty, I served my father submissively that evening,
suspicious of him and of his blindness, too. I feared that he was faking
it, so he could watch me, that he would suddenly reveal himself and,
point-blank, accuse me of seeing Francesco, as if I were a member of
some cult. If he had said something against him, I would have replied
boldly, *Yes, I'm an anti-fascist, too, have been for years—since Antonio
was arrested.*

I was amazed at that odd coincidence. Maybe, I thought, I'm a weak woman and I instinctively seek out strong men. Still, puzzled, I asked myself if they really were stronger—or maybe weaker, as Claudio maintained. Everything was against Francesco. He had talked to me about the difficulties he had with his students, because of rumors about him, and there was even some possibility that he might be dismissed from his teaching job. Until that day I had believed Francesco to be confident, even haughty, but now I understood the reason for his austere solitude. Pity for that solitude had propelled me towards Antonio at the time, and now it made me stay with Francesco, yearning to comfort him.

I tried to picture him in his house, which I'd never seen. I admired him, I comforted him—as if he were an unsettling, romantic character in my charge. I couldn't guess what he did, and so I couldn't follow him in the double life he was leading. I imagined that at night he went out disguised, like a nineteenth-century conspirator. I saw him again with his hat pulled down, as when he'd held me in his arms on that street in Prati. And I felt that I would follow him wherever he went, maybe stationed near a door to watch for the arrival of the police. I was inextricably bound to him through some complicity, though I didn't even know what it was. I was ashamed to ask: *But what do anti-fascists do?*

That was one of the nights when we heard the warning siren. There was one on the roof of the house next door that howled into my window. We kept still at the first alarm, but every time it went off again my father became paler. I myself was afraid, because that sound seemed to be calling me to account for my innermost thoughts. Every scream of the siren pushed me from behind, obliging me to flee, to hide. "Shall we go down?" I suggested.

We were leaving the house when Francesco called to advise me to stay calm, but the confident tone of his voice almost made me think he had some mysterious connection to the planes that I didn't dare imagine. So his encouragement, rather than reassuring me, was worrying.

.   .   .

I COULDN'T SLEEP that night. My clothes still bore the odor of mold from the cellar-turned-shelter. We hadn't been bombed. But since the news of the war was less and less reassuring and there were now daily bombings in other cities, we could no longer hope to be safe, not even in Rome. We sat in the shelter on wooden benches, my father's arm in mine. Next to the women sat sleepy children, trying to enjoy the nocturnal adventure and staring at my father's eyes with a mixture of fear and curiosity. The men went back and forth between the outer door and the shelter, providing scraps of information meant to soothe us.

"They're not coming," they said. "They don't dare come to Rome." They always spoke allusively. "They're not here," they would announce as they came back into the shelter. Or "They're not shooting." Just as Aida had once said, "They're not happy."

They seemed to be talking about Francesco's friends, and were therefore implicitly referring to him and me. A woman who was trembling asked me how I could be so brave. The sleepy children watched me, trying to appear innocent and defenseless so Francesco wouldn't hurt them. I saw other women, clothes crumpled, clasping their children to them with lost, fearful faces. The men reassured them with obvious lies, not looking them in the eyes or holding them by the arm, like Francesco when he asked, "You're not leaving me, right? Tell me you won't leave me!" I could put up with anything now, even war. I leaned my head against the rough, moldy-smelling wall of the shelter. All I had to do to find myself with Francesco was close my eyes. *We'll get married then*, he had said. We'll go down into the shelter together, I thought, and if the shelter is rocked by bombs we'll tell each other, *Be brave! I love you*. Francesco had wanted to tell me just that when he called. When the siren stopped, everyone started giggling nervously.

"They don't have the courage to come to Rome," they said. And they seemed to be giving me defiant looks. My own expression was tough. I was already Francesco's accomplice and he had said, "There's no doubt about it: we'll lose the war. Then we'll be happy."

Still, I found it hard to get warm between the cold sheets. I kept seeing the children's questioning eyes, the fat women trembling. *Why are you doing this, Francesco?* I asked, and I heard the hum of the airplanes. The children tried to laugh, but suddenly turned pale and stopped talking. *Are you sure it will save them? And are you sure they want to be saved?* I wondered whether he had the right to upset their lives and the lives of women who perhaps asked only to be like my mother. He was upsetting my life, too, but I accepted it. I accepted his conditions, any misfortune. I would go to prison every day and take him his lunch. I would wait in line with the other women, as Aida had, with hot broth in a mess tin. I hoped he would tell me that for him I was always more important than everything else, even his corrosive discontent. Instead, he said we had never been happy. I wished I could call him and beg, *Talk to me! Tell me that you were happy at the Borghese Gallery.* But I couldn't do that: his mother was sleeping, and surely he was, too. I thought he might even be arrested at night. The neighbors had looked so weak, dragged from their slumber when the siren surprised them. I saw him walking sleepily between the white statues on the bridge at Castel Sant'Angelo, flanked by two police officers in civilian clothes. They were taking him away from me. "Francesco . . ." I whispered, exhausted by love and fear.

MY DATES WITH Francesco were troubled and anguished. Just as at first we had contrived to have several free days ahead, now our main goal was to establish what we would do if Francesco should be arrested. He worried that, because I saw him daily, I would end up as a suspect.

"Forgive me," he would say, kissing my hands. "I can't go without seeing you."

Those were moments when I still found joy in our love. I wished that I would be arrested, taken to prison, tortured, and I would never utter his name. "I'm not afraid," I would tell him. On the contrary, that oppressive fear ended up enhancing the flavor of our encounters. Every evening left us heartbroken, fearing we wouldn't see each other the following day. And as soon as we separated we would turn back and say goodbye one more time, our words confused and disconnected, until he abruptly broke away from me and darkness swallowed up his beloved shadow.

By this time, I lived my days in a state of nervous tension. Yet everything seemed as it had been before. It made me feel breathless and alarmed. I would have preferred it if in some way the danger would expose itself, so I could fight it more easily.

"Go on," I would say to Francesco. "Tell me how it went."

"They called me in, together with a friend. He was detained while I was only cautioned."

"And then what?"

"Then—nothing. If I carry on and they find out, they'll arrest me."

"What will you do?"

He looked at me tenderly, took my hand and kissed me for a long time without replying.

"You'll carry on, right?" I insisted.

"What else can I do but carry on? I wouldn't be myself. I'd have to change my life's plan, my thoughts. You wouldn't recognize me. You might not even love me anymore."

"What else can I do but carry on?" I said in turn to Fulvia. I had resisted the temptation to speak to her for several days, but then I found it impossible to lie to her or alter my tone of voice on the phone.

"What's wrong?" she was always asking. Faced with my obstinate silence, she came to the conclusion that Francesco no longer loved me, and that suspicion made up my mind. We shut ourselves in the room where we used to play and I told her. Fulvia put a hand on my knee and listened to me seriously. Finally, she asked timidly if I intended to go on seeing Francesco.

"How could I not?" I asked, looking around at the room I knew so well, the old furniture. "Do you remember the day when Aida announced that Antonio had been arrested? Maddalena tore her doll's eyes out." I had the feeling that I was carrying on from that time. Then Fulvia asked about Francesco's activities, but I didn't know anything: he talked to me about meetings, speeches made to students, printed pamphlets . . .

"Like Antonio!" she exclaimed.

"Right." And I observed that nothing had changed over many years.

"They're not happy," I repeated. Their discontent got to us and oppressed us. I wanted to protest, to shout. "How can someone adjust to not being happy? It would be better to be taken to prison, better to throw oneself in the river . . ."

As soon as I uttered those words an icy terror gripped me. Aunt Violante's melancholy words came back to me, and Nonna's proud ones, which, in advising me to adapt quickly to the idea of resignation, expressed the same amount of bitter experience. Nonna and Aunt Violante had spoken to me harshly. Both of them loved me, which was why they didn't want me to get used to being happy. When I was a child, my mother, too, had sometimes pulled me away from the window where I was lingering in the company of my dreams. Nonna had locked her harmonium in the attic.

I struggled free of these thoughts, taking refuge in memories of Francesco. Together we had to fight in order to defend the circle of love we lived in. I would never adapt to being unhappy with him, or reduced to all the dirty little things that made the room where Fulvia and I had played so messy.

"We're getting married," I told Fulvia.

Francesco and I often talked about it, and by freely alluding to our future we seemed to be testing our confidence in it, its unassailability. So once more, and very slowly, our relationship prevailed. Each day was seasoned with danger, and the wearying work at home and in the office that I had borne easily before now weighed on me as a cruel imposition. I no longer studied and I neglected the house. My father's blindness seemed revealing of the blindness in which he had lived his whole life. I accused him of never having struggled, of having slept peacefully, trusting in the State and the prospect of his pension.

Francesco had lent me some books, which I kept among the linens. I read them at night and then hid them; but the house, the walls, and the furniture seemed to betray their presence. By now, I, too, was guilty because of that reading, which was enough to establish proof of my complicity with Francesco. I was in a hurry to marry him in order to deepen that complicity. He looked at me admiringly, his eyes lit with tender gratitude: I admired my reflection in him. Oh, those were beautiful days!

"I want us to get married as soon as we can," Francesco said. "I'll go and talk to your father."

I opened the door to Francesco timidly. Until now, I had presented myself to him only through my own myth-making. I had spoken to him about the Abruzzese furniture that had oppressed our house and my childhood, about the nightmare their presence symbolized. I was afraid that when he saw that furniture he would find it normal and inoffensive, might think my imagination had got the better of me. But I had told the truth. In fact, when he entered he immediately noticed, with some appreciation, a large wardrobe that a neighbor said might be valuable: it was the black wardrobe that had loomed over my childhood bed. I had always thought Cola lived in it because it creaked at night.

Francesco looked around, perhaps considering that we were a family of modest means. His house, as I saw later, was different. His father had been a magistrate: there were books everywhere in glass-fronted cases, even in the entrance hall, whereas our hallway held the scales Papa used to weigh the flour that came from the country.

I had told my father the day before. Rather than welcoming the news with joy, he had hesitated with cold disapproval, almost aversion: in this way, Francesco fell short of the figure he had liked to imagine, in spite of my efforts. We embraced one another all the same. He had wanted to shave that morning, and wear a dark suit; he had asked me which tie I was handing him. I had bought some flowers, and, with a view to offering Francesco coffee, I took some pretty cups that we never used from the credenza.

I left them together. When I came back with the coffee they had got to the main point of the meeting: Francesco had provided information about his family and himself, and said that we intended to marry within a month. He knew I had no dowry at all apart from the trousseau Nonna would send from Abruzzo and a piece of land when she died. When I entered the room, my father was talking about that piece of land, and it sounded as if he were negotiating the sale of an animal. Easily, between men, they had dispatched that brutal duty, which seemed to embarrass them in my presence. I no longer felt any love for Francesco, only a desire to rebel and run. In fact, he had made no objections and said instead that such details didn't interest him. My father added that I was a tolerable housekeeper and earned a good salary at work. Francesco laughed. I hated them. I served their coffee resentfully. Francesco said as he left, "He's a good man." I closed the door behind him as if he were a stranger.

I was hoping at least to find happiness in the approach of our marriage, but I felt trapped on an unstoppable treadmill. From the day Francesco had come to speak to my father right up until our wedding, we were busy running around, sorting out problems apparently related to our love but that were nothing but distractions. Since I was used to solitude and secret meetings, I found myself disoriented. I felt we were committing a serious error by welcoming so many people and so many things into our jealous intimacy. I revealed my fear to Francesco. He smiled, convinced I was joking, and kissed me: when he did, I no longer believed we were making a mistake.

We were poor, so our preparations were few. Our apartment, however, was in an elegant building in Parioli, which intimidated me at first. Actually, what really intimidated me was the porter, who respectfully greeted "the professor" and then, glancing at me, showed his disapproval of the professor's choice.

His judgment pained me, and I worried that Francesco didn't like me. He was very busy at the time, and he didn't look at me as much. And when he didn't look at me I no longer felt pretty. I bought some clothes, but, since Fulvia had helped me, Francesco worried that they were eccentric or loud. Fulvia and Francesco were getting to know each other better and did everything they could to become friends, but they never reached the point of using the familiar *tu*.

Meanwhile the fear, which at first only seemed to grow distant, slowly disappeared completely. It was impossible to think that anything could happen to two people honestly bent on preparing for their wedding. Throughout those days, Francesco couldn't deny that he was happy. Sometimes I thought he had even exaggerated imagining that he was in danger, and the thought made him all the dearer to me, increasing my desire to be with him and protect him. And, from the time we saw our new home, the fear of having lost our cherished solitude also disappeared. Only a few weeks, and then our lives would be as they had been at the Palatine and at Villa Borghese.

I had expected the days before the wedding to be idyllic. It was spring: the city, the river, and the color of the sky had changed, and I wanted to enjoy it all with my beloved. Every day I promised myself a romantic walk the next day, but the next day we didn't have time. One evening we went back to Villa Borghese; the trees were gauzy with new leaves, and the sun was now setting late, the days growing longer: we couldn't find any shade. We kissed each other hurriedly, afraid of being seen; I had hoped we might spend a pleasant evening, as when we first met: in fact I imagined it should be even lovelier now that we no longer harbored fear or a sense of guilt. But we couldn't recover the same passion: I found that those stolen kisses no longer satisfied us, eager as we were for the complete freedom ahead of us.

"You know," I said to Francesco, "I'd like to go back to Villa Borghese—often—to kiss. Even later," I specified. "I don't want us to lose this sweet habit." The spring evening around us was tenderly inviting. "We'll always go to the Janiculum, to the Palatine, always . . ." Suddenly I clutched his arm. "Francesco, I'm afraid. None of these couples walking past us are married."

"But yes, of course they are."

"No," I insisted, dismayed. "No, I'm sure of it. Let's ask them."

He laughed affectionately. Lately I had rarely seen him laugh: a sudden apprehension pushed me towards him.

"I'm afraid," I repeated. "Married people never come to Villa Borghese. They come with their children on Sundays. No, Francesco, right? Promise me that it won't be like that? We'll still take walks together, won't we?"

"Yes," he assured me, looking at me with sweet gravity. "Yes, I promise."

He said it just like that, so I had to believe him. We went home slowly, arm in arm. I told him about Via Paolo Emilio, the dreariness of married life, the arduous and melancholy existence I had seen all those women leading. For the first few years, the young wives waited impatiently for Sunday, hoping to find in their husbands the ardent and devoted lover of before; later, they didn't expect that, either, but learned to make a nice cake for Sunday. I rummaged anxiously through my memories, searching for at least one couple who had been saved.

"None of them," I said, frightened. "Oh, my God, none. If they go out together, they go to the movies. Fulvia and I used to see them yawning in the intermissions."

"How could that happen to us?" Francesco asked. He began talking about my imagination and my character, and I calmed down: I so loved hearing him talk about me. In the fragrant evening I felt light and happy again. We smiled, happy as we left the villa, not knowing that it was for the last time.

DURING THAT PERIOD, Francesco introduced me to some of this friends who, like him, were unhappy. He was satisfied that I liked his friends and he noticed instantly that they liked me. On those occasions, I made pleasant conversation and always said intelligent things; I was no longer Alessandra, I was Alessandra impersonating the woman Francesco loved: I liked it that he loved a singular woman. Alberto and

Tomaso were drawn to me and they listened with curiosity. Alberto was forty and a philosopher. He didn't teach anymore; he wrote books he was forbidden to publish; the manuscripts circulated among his friends. Tomaso was a journalist; he wasn't happy, but it seemed that he was. It was his trade, he said; but I understood it to be his character. Tomaso was twenty-seven, and he jokingly called Francesco "the boss."

At first they both hesitated to hand over their friend Francesco, especially Alberto. Later, they themselves offered him to me, looking at me with sympathy. I felt that Francesco loved me very much when the two of us left, alone and arm in arm. We were tall and we walked well together; but our step had become too confident.

THE MEETING WITH his mother wasn't so easy. I would have liked to arrive accompanied by Francesco, but on the phone he said, "We'll wait for you," and I didn't dare reply.

It was a truly beautiful afternoon, with the sunny sky reflected in the gray waters of the river. Intoxicated by the new season, I arrived a little dazed, my hair disheveled, a dreamy expression on my face. This had often happened to my mother as well: being distracted just when she wanted to make the best impression. I was instantly intimidated by the spacious entrance with antique furniture and red curtains: I couldn't help comparing it with my entrance, which was dominated by the scales.

More than anything, I missed having Francesco's help; for the first time he wasn't mine alone, but also the son of an older woman with a white ribbon around her neck. I had a bizarre sensation: I didn't dare look about, ashamed to see the things that surrounded him and which roused in me a profound melancholy. His mother observed me: she wasn't happy about our marriage, since I was poor and had to work. However, she didn't show her opposition and was even courteous: only in passing did she ask me if I was a good typist, and Francesco hurried to clarify that I acted as secretary to the director. It was true, but he said it because he was ashamed of me. And yet he had always shown that he thought highly of me for the work I did, and he had informed Alberto and Tomaso about it himself, adding that I also found time to take courses at the university. His mother said she regretted not being able to help her son so that I would be able to leave my job.

"Why, Signora?" I replied. "It wouldn't be fair. Even if Francesco were very rich, I would still like to work, to contribute to our expenses. It's an unpleasant feeling to be a burden on a man's work. After all, my mother also worked: she traveled every day to give piano lessons."

There was a frosty silence and I realized I had made a mistake. A maid came in carrying a tea tray with some beautiful teacups on it. *They, too, have brought out their best teacups*, I thought. But it wasn't enough to make me ashamed of my mother.

With feigned nonchalance I helped the maid serve the tea. Francesco watched me with satisfaction, and even his mother seemed to appreciate my gesture, which was actually easy and obvious. Any girl would have been able to do it, but not everyone could have done my job at the office. The conversation turned to our preparations, and I started feeling confident. I looked at the photos in their frames. Signora Minelli did not approve of our choice of apartment, despite the difficulty of finding one at the time. It was too small, she said.

"You need to think about the future. You're getting married, you know, to have children . . ."

"Oh no, Signora Minelli," I interrupted, hoping to reassure her. "That's not why we're getting married. We're marrying so we can be together forever."

Once again, my words established an embarrassing silence between us. Francesco put an arm around my shoulders.

His mother gave a tart smile and poured herself another cup of tea. She glanced at Francesco before saying, "She is very charming, in her naïveté."

I wanted to fight back and explain that I wasn't naïve and never had been. But Francesco squeezed my arm, signaling me to be quiet.

To dispel the embarrassment, he spoke about other things, and I felt I had fallen into a trap. They talked about the relatives and friends they would have to invite to our wedding, asking themselves if they had to invite Signora Spazzavento to such an intimate wedding, bearing in mind the possible reactions. I admitted that I didn't have any relatives in Rome; I didn't imagine, as it turned out later, that Aunt Sofia would come from Abruzzo to attend the wedding. I said I had only one friend, who lived in Via Paolo Emilio. So it was decided to invite Signora Spazzavento. I listened, lost in melancholy. It seemed that the ceremony and preparations would have nothing to do with the conversations Francesco and I had at Villa Borghese or on the Janiculum.

"And where will you go afterwards, for a short honeymoon?" Signora Minelli asked as we were heading for the door. Francesco kept his arm in mine, so I felt stronger.

"Forgive me, Signora," I said politely, blushing. "That's our secret."

When we got to the street Francesco seemed unhappy with my reply. I tried to explain that I hadn't wanted to reveal the place where we had decided to spend our first days alone in order to somehow rediscover our furtive, secret times. He drew me towards him in the shade of the plane trees on the Lungotevere.

"But yes, of course," he said. "I like it, this whim of yours."

I hastened to explain that it wasn't a whim. "Fulvia understands," I told him. "She understands it very well."

"Well of course." He nodded, hoping that I would stop being contentious, because he wanted to kiss me.

As it happened, from the moment we fixed the wedding date, he'd started grabbing me suddenly around the waist and kissing me, conscious of his rights. And gradually, as his confidence grew, I became more confused. For some time I'd thought of nothing but the first night we would spend together. I couldn't distract myself from the sweet, unbearable expectation. The thought of that night in all its details occupied my mind even while I was answering the phone at the office, while I was typing or taking letters in shorthand dictated by Mantovani. It even unsettled me to measure the blue dressing gown I had ordered. Blue, in remembrance of my mother's dress. I went to sleep imagining Francesco untying the knot on that dressing gown. It was like a film playing out endlessly in my imagination, and it wasn't so much desire that attracted me as the religious meaning of the rite we would perform in joining together. I lost myself in imagining the words Francesco would say, as when I was in church and an uninterrupted flow of words of love filled me; I pictured his gestures and lowered my eyelids. I imagined entering our room, gracefully presenting myself to him. The room, different from all the others I knew, was vast, elegant, with loosely hanging draperies; I walked across a soft carpet. The light was subdued and tall flowers in a corner—tuberoses—gave off their perfume. I had never seen such a room; I imagined the rooms at Villa Pierce were like that.

We were alone one day in our new apartment: the delivery men had gone, having brought our shiny bedroom furniture, a gift from Signora Minelli. The door had closed with a thud, and we found ourselves facing each another, Francesco and I, across the large bed. The impeccable new furniture looked as if it were still in the shop window: the mattress was intrusively, shamelessly white.

Francesco pushed me to lie down across the mattress as he kissed me, and he lay down next to me. His face wore a different expression when he was lying down: it was a new face. I caressed it to gain confidence. I had never lain down with him: he was kissing me, and I couldn't see his face anymore. From the courtyard came the voices of children playing.

"We're alone. Shall we?" Francesco whispered as he started unbuttoning my blouse. I disentangled myself from him and jumped up. He followed, telling me not to be afraid.

"I'm not!" I told him. "But do you want to do it here? Here?" I looked at the cold room, the white mattress, the electric cord hanging from the ceiling. "Here?" I repeated, all the while thinking of myself in the blue dressing gown. *No, of course it won't happen the first night,* I had thought. *It will be so difficult already, staying in the hotel alone with him.*

He tidied his hair. "Sorry. I love you so much. Let's go."

WE WERE MARRIED in Sant'Onofrio, a romantic little church at the foot of the Janiculum. I chose it in memory of our first walk together, and because my mother often spoke of it. In the evening, she would leave Villa Pierce with Hervey; they walked slowly, and would then go into the church to rest for a bit. When we came across it for the first time, we had the impression of having entered a place that was doubly sacred.

"They must be here, too," I said, casting a wondering glance at the pews.

The night before our wedding, Francesco left me at the door to my building, just as he used to. Aunt Sofia had arrived, and she was sleeping on the cot, so it had become impossible to find a moment of solitude, of freedom. We had become like two business partners, anxious to conclude an advantageous deal: we called each other briefly, at set times, and spent hours in the gray corridors of the registrar's office. I found Fulvia waiting for me at home with Aunt Sofia. They were admiring the sheets Nonna had sent from Abruzzo. My father looked at them with his hand. One very beautiful sheet was spread out between them.

"What are you doing?" I asked. "Leave those things alone!" And then I apologized. "I'm really nervous." But I went on to say, "Fold them all up again," and went to shut myself in my room with Fulvia.

Fulvia was really kind that evening. It was a terrible evening, the most difficult I had ever faced, even worse than when the officers came with my mother's purse.

When the door was closed, Fulvia looked at me tenderly. "Sandi," she said. I paced the room before hugging her and resting my head on her shoulder. Timidly, she said, "I brought you a present." It was an expensive present and I imagined she had had Mantovani's help.

"Thank you," I said, beginning to cry.

Fulvia caressed me. She had never been nor would she ever again be so sweet. "Cheer up!" she said, and then, "You love him a lot, right?"

"Yes, that's just it," I replied.

We looked at my open suitcase, ready for the next day's departure. You could see my blue dressing gown folded up. I had never had a silk dressing gown and Fulvia knew that. We were sitting on a trunk and the room was very untidy: shoes tossed around, torn letters, faded cotton bedspread.

"So many years . . ." Fulvia said. There was a deep bond between us, between me and those trunks and the old sewing machine that had once punctured my finger as a child. I thought I would have to abandon everything that had come with me to that point.

"I'm scared." I stood up suddenly and looked straight at Fulvia. "I'm afraid I won't be happy, you know?" I added, agitated and frightened. "At this moment, I don't love him anymore. I can't even remember what his face looks like."

Fulvia turned on me a look so compassionate it almost unnerved me. "Calm down," she said. "This is how it is today, and it will be worse tomorrow."

"Worse?!"

"Yes, maybe." Meanwhile she was putting my slippers back on the blue dressing gown. "And then it will pass, and you'll be very happy."

DURING THE CEREMONY I thought about Fulvia's words, expecting the joy to return, but it never did: I wasn't at all emotional. It felt as though I were attending an Easter or Christmas service. The church looked very beautiful: Fulvia had thoughtfully decorated it with flowers. She and Lydia wept, moved to see me at the altar. Their eyes were red and they blew their noses loudly. Signora Minelli turned around to look at them and Francesco also turned, not even moving his arms, which were crossed over his dark suit. They were condemning them, of course, not realizing that the women were thinking about Dario, Mantovani, and the Captain, and feeling emotional at the thoughts all women have when another woman gets married.

I wore a short white dress that afterwards I wore all summer long, and in my hair I had a small piece of white lace that had belonged to Nonna Editta; when I mentioned the lace, Francesco at first seemed to approve of my romantic intentions. But a little later he said, "Won't it look theatrical?" I was mortified: I didn't understand what he thought about the theater or, above all, about me. Yet in the morning as I walked to the altar with my father, Francesco whispered to me for the first time, "You look very beautiful," as he awkwardly held out a bouquet of gardenias.

In the end, the only thing that moved me during the entire ceremony were those gardenias and the birdsong coming from the peace of the distant square, weaving between the notes of the organ. I took them with me on the train. As I was leaving the house, I turned around: "The gardenias!" Everyone kissed me, and Aunt Sofia said, "I like your husband," looking from him to me as if comparing us. My father was moving to Abruzzo and would travel with her a few days later. He wanted to say goodbye to me alone in his room.

"So, Alessandra?" he said. "It's over."

He took my hand and once more I felt the dry warmth of his skin. On his finger he still wore the gold ring in the shape of a snake: I saw his hand once more reaching for my mother's, and I thought of Francesco waiting outside the door. "Are you happy?"

"Yes," I said, but it wasn't true. I was just in a hurry.

"That's good. I thought it would be difficult for you to be happy . . . Yes. You know very well what I mean." It was the first time in twenty-two years that my father and I had talked together. Just as Aunt Sofia had, he said, "I like your husband," instilling in me a vague sense of fear. "I hope you'll come to Abruzzo soon. I'd like Francesco to meet your grandmother."

"Of course. Or you'll come here; you could stay with us."

"No, thank you," he replied decisively. And he said again, "It's over."

Francesco was calling for me, and we left the house cheerfully, in a rush.

"Goodbye!" said Fulvia, looking down from the landing.

"Goodbye!" I waved my hand in the empty stairwell. A few doors opened as we went by. The porter smiled in sympathy and so did the few neighbors gathered at the entrance. A girl on the third floor threw us a geranium plucked from her windowsill.

OUR MISTAKE WAS in having anticipated the journey too eagerly. We had spent weeks and months imagining it, but it was over so quickly, gesture after gesture, minute after minute.

We had decided against Capri and Naples because of the bombings, and had instead chosen Florence. I was glad that it was a city near a beautiful river. When we got there, Francesco became irritated with the bellhop, and I heard him raise his voice for the first time; he was right, and I was infected with his irritation. On top of that, there was an argument as soon as we entered the hotel because they hadn't reserved us a room with a window on the Arno. I had expressed the wish; Francesco had written to the management days before, and he was right to be angry. He argued with the doorman and the manager, not realizing how embarrassing it was for me to witness the dispute. He kept saying, "I wrote clearly: a room with a view on the Arno." The others protested. I was alone with our bags, holding the gardenias. In the end we got the room, and as soon as the door closed we went to look out the window.

"Ah!" he exclaimed in a tone of revenge, yet still too irritated to enjoy the view of the river.

Yes, our mistake lay precisely in having expected too much from that day. Maybe we should have waited for the day to go by. In fact, we didn't even eat dinner: I myself said, "I'm not hungry," because all I wanted was for the ill-humor and the cold uneasiness to lift. I was waiting to feel happy: I forced myself to be so, smiling and trying to concentrate on the sweet novelty of being alone with Francesco. *Help me*, I said to him silently. *Help me, talk to me.* I needed to hear him talk about me, about himself, about our love, in order to turn all my attention again to the two of us. I couldn't stop thinking that he was feeling as I did, smiling and kissing me only because he had a clear duty to do so at that moment. It would have been better if we had gone for a walk along the Arno, trusting in the harmony of our steps. But we stayed in our room, pretending that we couldn't resist giving in to desire. I couldn't get the bellhop's arrogant face out of my head, the manager's rude words from my ears. At the sight of my blue dressing gown in a heap on the floor, I thought of Fulvia. The previous guests had squashed two mosquitoes on the white wall.

AFTERWARDS, FRANCESCO FELL asleep. The silence was heavy, and the small alarm clock Fulvia had given me as a present ticked away, measuring the interminable passage of time. The sheet left Francesco's bare shoulders exposed, and I looked coldly at his skin, which I did not know. He had seven moles on his shoulders, arranged in such a way that they reminded me of the Big Dipper. His neck was smooth, tender, and inviting. I called him: *Help me*, I said in my thoughts. *Wake up, talk to me, take me in your arms.* My answer was the even rhythm of his breathing, and it deepened the silence, making my loneliness all the more anguished.

It had all been different from what I had imagined: I had imagined that Francesco would kiss my hands, barely looking at me, and, little by little, with loving words, would coax me to accept his bolder moves. And yet he hadn't spoken at all: maybe he thought that at certain moments actions, too, can be love. But no: he was eleven years older than me, yet I was a woman and knew that looks and words say more about love than gestures, which also serve to express feelings that are in fact different. Usually so tender, he seemed to have suddenly become severe, all rushed moves: no matter which way I turned I collided with his arms. I pushed him away from me so I could look into his eyes, to feel myself alive and loved in them; but then his arms were around me again and I couldn't see his face anymore. *Francesco, my love*, I whispered silently, *look at me*. I felt that my whole body was pleading with him, along with that secret voice he had so often shown he could hear.

If I'm honest, I have to confess that intimacy with a man didn't amaze me; nor did it elicit in me the revolt and surprise of my first kiss with Paolo. I hadn't expected that kiss or its unsettling novelty: since I wasn't in love with him, I hadn't made an effort to fantasize about it. But, because I loved Francesco, I had imagined his every move and already accepted it as love. What did amaze me was that he didn't look at me tenderly afterwards, didn't call me his queen and kneel before me. We lay beside each other for a little while. He took a cigarette from the nightstand; my blood was running cold, yet he smoked calmly, staring at the white ceiling, the old curtains. *Uncle Rodolfo*, I said silently, *Uncle Rodolfo, come here, help me*. I saw his eyes again, the day we had lunch together in Sulmona.

Francesco and I talked as we smoked in an effort to feign nonchalance: he went over some of the day's details, suggested itineraries for the next day, even recalled his argument with the manager, displaying a male satisfaction with the successful outcome.

The gardenias beside the bed gave off a sharp scent. Whenever I smell their perfume, I return to that night. As I looked at them, I reproached myself for being unfair and ignorant, for forgetting everything expressed by their presence. I pictured Francesco going into the shop and pointing to the gardenias: I was flattered that he had chosen those flowers with me in mind: smooth, soft, scented.

"Francesco," I said, "your flowers spoke to me throughout the day. Even now they're speaking, and they're a great comfort. I wanted to thank you. Thoughtful acts of love like this are very important to me."

At first he was silent. But then he said, "Look, I must tell you the truth. It was Fulvia. I confess: I wouldn't have thought of it. Maybe it's something lacking in me, or maybe a man never thinks of these things. Fulvia called me. She asked tactfully if I had already got you some flowers. I said no, I didn't know—I didn't know which flowers to choose, which you'd like most. I was stuck. And she very politely offered to help me. She told me that she'd take care of everything and she gave me the florist's address. All I had to do was go and pick them up. She was really thoughtful. You know, I didn't like her, but after this gesture I realized how fond she is of you. She was so insistent that I say nothing about it! But I wanted to tell you, because you know her even better, and because now I understand why you're her friend. We'll send her a postcard tomorrow," he added.

It was Fulvia. Yet she'd smiled encouragingly when I showed her the gardenias, saying, "Look what a sweet idea Francesco had."

"Oh!" she exclaimed brightly. When we came back from the ceremony she embraced me, dismayed. "You're leaving . . . you're leaving . . ." she murmured. Then, "Goodbye!" She smiled through her tears and leaned into the stairwell. She remained at my house to pack my father's suitcase and put away the glasses we had used to drink spumante.

"Yes," I agreed, "a beautiful postcard with a view of the Arno."

Surprised by my voice, Francesco asked, "What's wrong, Sandra?"

"Nothing. Why should anything be wrong?" I felt nothing, in fact, but bitterness.

I stayed awake for a long time. Every now and then, Francesco would shift his arm, and I moved farther away. When the gray dawn brightened the sky behind closed shutters, I fell asleep, consumed by melancholy. It was Francesco's arms, again, that woke me in the dark, with just the sunlight filtering in. I was no longer his enemy, as I had been before my brief sleep. He kept his arms around me and we talked, looking into space. We talked about things and plans, no longer about ourselves, about knowing each other, seeking each other out. So many people had entered our closed circle: Signora Spazzavento sent a lovely gift and she told my mother-in-law that I was charming, if too thin. Francesco said that I should put on some weight and suggested that he himself would see to it that I followed a cure. Embarrassed, I pulled the covers up to my shoulders.

Francesco got up then and opened the window, announcing that it was a beautiful day and that we could go for a walk. So he said, "Excuse me, dear," and smoothing his hair nonchalantly, he left me in bed and went into the bathroom. I heard the bathwater running, the scrubbing of a toothbrush.

He's brushing his teeth, I thought. *I don't know what he's like when he's brushing his teeth.* It was as if the wall were made of glass, and each of us could see what the other was doing, though we were both cleverly pretending to be alone. I heard him get into the bath, making a lot of noise, and start soaping himself vigorously. *He can't possibly do that every morning—he's making a show to hide his embarrassment. Yes, he's overdoing it because I'm here listening.* He scrubbed energetically, giving himself quick slaps on the back, singing. He was so timid in his swaggering that I suddenly felt overwhelmingly tender toward him. If I hadn't been so confused myself, I would have liked to help him get over the initial awkwardness of our daily intimacy.

I lit another cigarette. There was no ashtray by the bed, and the bed, so disheveled, made me feel acutely uncomfortable. I closed my eyes so that I could go back to sleep and avoid a difficult day, but mine was not the only odor on the sheets now: as I moved around, I smelled the lavender of Francesco's brilliantine. It had been his scent from the day we met, and I smelled it whenever he came close, whenever he kissed me: the very scent of our love affair. Yet in that instant I was so disturbed to find it in my bed that it seemed completely unfamiliar. The smell aroused painful, guilty memories. It belonged to the untidiness of my body, of my hair. It was tied to the splashing that was coming from the bathroom, to the masculine voice singing so confidently, to the gray coat hanging on the coat hook under a black hat; and it was no longer the gray coat Francesco wore as he came to meet me on our dates. It was that of a man who had taken off his clothes to go to bed with a woman. I felt alone, spoiled, crumpled, even though it was the first awakening after my wedding. I never imagined it would be necessary to carry out the usual actions that morning, too. I thought everything would magically take care of itself.

"Francesco!" I called, feeling lost.

He appeared a few seconds later, in a striped dressing gown, not particularly new, with a towel around his neck that he was using to rub his cheeks, which in places were still dripping with soap. "Sorry, dear one," he said gently. "What is it?" He went on drying his face.

I had called him impulsively, crying out. I liked that he was wearing an old dressing gown, surely the same one he had worn when he came to answer my phone calls; the pocket was a little misshapen by the weight of his cigarettes. If he had worn a new dressing gown I would have insulted him, I think. *Hypocrite, liar,* I would have said. I hoped he hadn't noticed the pretentiousness of my blue dressing gown of artificial silk. I considered not wearing it and putting my coat on over my nightgown, as I had done in Abruzzo. Nevertheless, his old dressing gown, his slippers with the heel folded in provoked in me an irrepressible urge to cry. Because it seemed simple enough to graft onto each other two ephemeral lives, meticulously prepared for a pleasant, quick encounter: if the bed had been neat, if the bleak hotel had been transformed into a luxuriously furnished room, if everything around us had been indicative of comfort, of unconcern with daily worries, and if we ourselves had appeared to conform to our aesthetic ideals, then my state of mind might have been happy and carefree. *Francesco,* I would have said in the intonation I knew so well, which made men turn, surprised and touched as when they hear carillon music, *Francesco, please order our breakfast.* I would be very hungry, with the capricious hunger of the rich. But it was difficult to intertwine our lives as two poor people, used to struggling on their own and deeply in love. I begged him: *Hide that blue dressing gown of mine! Hide it now, Francesco. Let's not pretend we're others. We must accept ourselves like this, in the disorder of this bed, with my disheveled hair, your old slippers. Come here,* I would call him desperately. *Let's face this difficult morning together.*

Instead he said, "Sorry, my love. I'll be out of the bathroom in a moment."

He went on drying his face and his thin hair stood up at his temples.

I turned and started crying, burying my face in the pillow so as to sink into last night's scent, the scent of masculine sleep, which I was encountering for the first time. And in the bitter depths of that desperation was my vast love for Francesco, which I wanted to free from the servitude of the bed and the sheets. I wished we were united in some angelic, mystical way, innocent, freed of the laws common to all creatures.

"Francesco," I whispered. "Francesco . . ." An image of the Pierces' garden came back to me, the tall cedars of Lebanon inhabited by horses, of Emilia, who covered her face with a gauzy scarf to meet her beloved. And me, lying there between those sheets, still unwashed.

"No, what is it?" he insisted, holding me tight. "Have I done something to hurt you? Tell me, please. Surely I have. When?" he asked anxiously. "Yesterday evening? Last night? This morning? You must tell me. When? You have to tell me everything. Everything."

"No," I replied between sobs, "really, you haven't done anything."

"That's impossible," he pressed me. "Sweetheart, forgive me. What have I done? Sandra, tell me . . ."

Later, we went out. There was always a thick veil between me and happiness. *I'm the one who has ruined everything,* I told myself. *It's my fault.*

YES, HE TELLS me now, and his voice trembles as he becomes argumentative; it's only when we speak of that night that he seems to want to defend himself. Maybe because in remembering it I, too, fail to write calmly, to master my pain and fury.

Yes, he says. *It was your fault. And you were the first to suffer because of it, I'll admit. Oh, Alessandra, you didn't know how difficult it was to face those hours, which I'd already experienced in my imagination for months. It's difficult to live up to one's fantasy, to dare to perform actions that aren't heavy or contentious in your mind but in fact assume their crudest aspect when you engage in them. If I didn't love you—you have to believe me, I insist that you do—everything would have been very simple. With another woman, I could have acted coldly and gone beyond her expectation of me. But it was you, Alessandra, and I love you. When I saw you come in wearing the blue dressing gown, emotion wrung me so hard that I felt pitched back to the dizzying turmoil I felt when I was little more than eight years old, and I saw a little girl I was in love with looking out the window. I never managed to speak to her when we met: I looked at her adoringly, but she called me "mute," or "stupid," and laughed at me. Oh, you were so lovely and you moved with such grace, and the acts we had to perform in order to fulfill our unavoidable obligation—they all seemed vulgar before your enchanting person. After all, I really didn't desire you that night; I said, "Let's go to dinner," and I only wanted to watch you moving in that beautiful color you were wearing, kiss your hands—then leave, perhaps, humiliated by being a man. But the thought of my sweet, cruel obligation and rough, male disregard drove me to overcome my fears. I wanted you to understand all that, but I realized you couldn't, because I was the first man you'd known. And the error arose precisely from the great love I felt for you, which kept me so respectful towards you. What happened that night should have happened right away, as soon as we felt we were in love; and it should have happened unexpectedly, ahead of our fantasy. Then, when I saw you coming in that blue dressing gown, I could have mastered the part of me which went ahead without me. It was a terrible mistake, and it encouraged me to go through with my terrible obligation as soon as I could, in order to avoid disappointing you. That's when I first felt resentful towards your mother, who wasn't brave enough to confront the actuality of love, its ordinariness and its possible breakdown, its end. She wouldn't have done us so much harm if she'd been Hervey's lover: you would have spoken to me about it in some other way, and you yourself would have been different. I raged against her in my thoughts, accusing her of cowardice, hypocrisy, practically insulting her. Oh, Alessandra, it was an argument I'd nearly started with her, revealing to you how men really are. I loved you so much, and inside I was saying "darling," I said "my queen," but it seemed impossible for me to dare to be so familiar with you. I was so worn out by those bitter struggles and worries that—afterwards—I fell asleep immediately. I didn't want to witness your thoughts, I didn't want to know if you were suffering. That was my only fault. Oh, Alessandra, it wasn't easy to talk to you then: you were a timid girl on your wedding night. You're a woman today and today you can understand. Forgive me.*

I THOUGHT I had forgiven him immediately. As soon as we went outside, I matched his familiar stride once again. It seemed as if I could forget everything, even the gardenias. In the afternoon I was bold enough to put one in the buttonhole of my black dress. I didn't know that our anguished night would haunt me from then on, subtly penetrating my blood and every fiber of my being, like a bad seed. And yet at the time it was so well concealed that it allowed me to be happy. I was so happy that I sent Fulvia two postcards with silly, excitable messages. Leisure and the chance to give ourselves wholly to love effectively helped us. We went to the Uffizi together and Francesco stopped in front of a painting.

"Now leave the room," he said with a smile, "and then come to our date, like that day at the Borghese Gallery."

I came back in, and there was such a dramatic and disoriented expression on my face that Francesco laughed. "Try again," he urged.

I went back in as myself, in caricature. We laughed, we kissed. And we surprised two German tourists, who also laughed; we were so happy that we were cheered by the Germans laughing. We went to trattorias where small orchestras played and had our photograph taken on the Viale dei Colli, following all the usual honeymoon suggestions with childish delight. We went to bed late in one another's arms.

· · ·

WE RETURNED TO Rome the day before my leave was over: we didn't have a cent left and had to carry our own bags at the station. It was very amusing, and Francesco admired my good nature; maybe he didn't remember that I was used to being poor. I said I would collect my salary a few days in advance, and Francesco laughed, saying that it had always been his dream to be a kept man. We went to dinner that night at his mother's house and I advised Francesco not to tell her we were out of money; I didn't want her to think that he had spent too much on me. There was the Florentine straw hat that he had touchingly insisted on buying for me; it framed my face really well, in fact, and I regretted that I couldn't wear it, since no one wore hats anymore. The straw hat was large, and so at the station, because of the suitcases, I was forced to put it on my head. It provoked much childish glee because everyone looked at me. The porter in Parioli saw us coming on foot, carrying our suitcases and with that hat. It was unfortunate, because he immediately formed a bad impression of us as new tenants.

The house was charming, an attic: a red-tiled terrace extended outside our bedroom. I thought I would be able to read and study there peacefully. But in the beginning I never found time to study because we didn't yet have everything we needed, and we had to adapt in make-shift ways. I didn't ask Francesco for anything, fearing that he would call on his mother for help: she might have reprimanded him for marrying a poor girl, who earned very little, besides. I decided to neglect my studies at first, and do a bit of extra work in the afternoons. The cost of living was constantly increasing, and it wasn't easy for the poor to get provisions. It was worse for those who, like us, had to keep up appearances.

I didn't have any help: the building in the Parioli district was even more impenetrable than the one on the Lungotevere Flaminio: the court-yards were closed and highly polished; not even the maids looked out on them. I didn't know the neighbors' names because there weren't many nameplates by the doors: no one seemed to use the stairs or linger on the landings. In that house you were born without joy, died without drama, and observed good manners. The doorman barely greeted us, because we didn't have a maid, and I must confess that I was ashamed to go past him with my shopping bag.

To break free of that harsh prison, I often went down to Prati, happy to feel myself among nice, friendly people once more, and I would go back to our house on Via Paolo Emilio. There was a lot of dust in the entrance: I wondered if it had always been that dirty; it didn't seem possible. The woman at the door immediately asked about my health, about my husband, and enjoyed calling me Signora. Francesco's political difficulties put a halt to his professional activities, and, with the effervescence of our first days extinguished, we faced very grim living conditions. We not only jumped every time the doorbell rang; Francesco was increasingly cautious on the phone and in meeting his friends. We often went hungry, even though we both protested that we had eaten enough. It was no longer possible for Francesco to take on jobs that, alongside his small university salary, would have allowed us to live with only minor complaints. I could no longer study, and the house hadn't yet assumed the welcoming look I hoped for. The only things in the study were Francesco's desk and a few bookcases from his mother's house. It was very unfortunate to have dining chairs but no armchair; at first I hadn't considered the problems it would cause between us. In the study, still cold and empty, it was impossible to sit on the chairs and talk; it felt as if we were in a dentist's waiting room. It was easier when friends came, and we'd sit around the little table; but, imagining Francesco wanted to be alone with them, I would feign sleepiness and go to bed. Yet if it was just the two of us sitting in the chairs, it was impossible to initiate the interesting conversations on religion, art, or our spiritual plans, which were our favorite topics during our engagement once we had stopped talking about our love or our future married life.

After dinner, we would go and sit on the bed, but we were tired, and Francesco would soon say, "Shall we continue talking in bed?" We were so tired that we immediately fell asleep. I made a courageous effort to ensure that our life remained faithful to what we had imagined, but there were two things I couldn't fight: the discomfort brought about by our lack of armchairs, and Francesco's surprise at our lack of money. He was in the habit of handing over everything he earned, which was very little. But from that moment, and for the rest of the month, he seemed to think that in my hands the money became inexhaustible. "Is it gone?" he would ask, astonished: in his surprise, I thought I detected an accusation that I had squandered it. Blushing, I would hurry to explain how I had spent it: I wanted to get a pencil, add up some sums. "No," he said gallantly, "you don't have to account to me for anything. You can spend the money as you wish, do what you want with it." But those sentences threw me into an angry rage, which I nevertheless managed to overcome. I insisted on doing the accounts, but he balked at it, so I remained silently accused of squandering the money on myself. One day I prepared a list of expenses and got him to read it with surprise: there were no expenses other than household ones, already pared to the minimum, really only the essentials. After he looked at it, he gave it back to me, repeating, "But of course, sweetheart, it's pointless to justify yourself. I've already told you that you can do what you like with the money."

I put off my exam preparations until the spring, and I was glad to give Italian lessons to a young high-school student. She was a rich girl and full of herself; she made me wait and called me Signorina, claiming that all teachers were spinsters. She had a bad habit of snacking during the lesson, and her books were stained with chocolate and milky coffee. At that hour, I would be feeling terribly hungry: I waited, minute by minute, for the snack to arrive and I appeased my hunger by watching my student eat. Sometimes she would offer me a slice of buttered toast or a piece of cake; Francesco and I filled up on salads of tomatoes and beans. Every day, whether to demonstrate contempt or indifference, I told myself firmly to refuse. But I never could.

I thought about my mother more often now that I was giving those lessons, and, climbing the stairs in my student's villa, I wondered whether my mother managed even in those moments to retain the inimitable grace of her step. Guessing that she did, I felt dispirited. When my student was busy, the servant had me wait in the entrance; he was a giant of a man and his height increased my uneasiness. The family members greeted me with a quick nod as they passed through.

I couldn't give up the teaching, but one evening as I was leaving I bought two jasmine plants to console myself. I put them on the terrace, where they looked very pretty, and their scent perfumed the room. Francesco was late coming home, and whenever he was late I was consumed by the same terror I had felt waiting for my mother. But as soon as I heard him coming up the stairs I sat on a cushion on the terrace, so cheerful with the flowers. I had gathered my hair in a topknot and stuck a sprig of jasmine through it. Francesco looked for me everywhere, but I didn't answer. He called, "Alessandra!" with a touch of dismay in his voice. He found me and we embraced instantly, happy and reassured. After dinner he sat on the cushion with me and we looked at the stars from the terrace. Later, from our bed, too, the stars appeared in the window. Early the next morning, I hurried to Lydia to borrow money for groceries; I said goodbye quickly and, afraid I would be late for work, descended the stairs rapidly, with my mother's airy step. Francesco and I got into the habit of staying at home in the evening; thanks to the terrace, we didn't suffer from the heat. We would lie down on the bed, and at times like that I wasn't tired or poor: I was in love. Francesco's arms now no longer hurt when he hugged me. They were very long, and I was glad I was thin: his arms wrapped around me like bindweed, finding their natural place around my shoulders and at the indentation of my waist. When he wasn't holding me, I felt that my body was unprotected.

AT THE BEGINNING of fall, Francesco was obliged to take on a small private afternoon job with one of Alberto's relatives. He often didn't come home to dinner, so that he could meet with a group of friends who, like him, were unhappy; when he was late I always feared he had been arrested. I would call Tomaso for news. Tomaso, who had always been so clever, confessed that he was also having difficulties at work. By this time, Francesco could no longer write, and there were signs of growing coldness everywhere: he went reluctantly to the university, where everyone avoided him but no one had the courage to criticize him openly. They turned their heads when he went by or barely said hello, timid as children who have been told not to do so by their parents. Even Lascari avoided him, claiming that he was very busy.

It was a sad situation, made worse by our poverty, which was becoming unbearable. We had a debt with the grocer opposite, and I would leave the house quickly, pretending to be distracted for fear that he would confront me in front of the porter. I couldn't stand his attitude; at that time, porters were all in the service of the police, and we assumed that he knew about Francesco's political position. Francesco had advised me to be careful but polite. For some time in fact, the porter had seemed eager to stop and talk to me: he hinted at the substantial tips he received from the other tenants, the clothes the woman on the third floor gave his wife: lovely, gorgeous, just like new. Above all, he tried to find out who was visiting Francesco. I would make a vague reply and take refuge in our apartment.

I always came home tired and worn out. Every day I walked long distances to save money, and, treading the gray asphalt between gray houses, I thought back to the beautiful walks I had taken in Abruzzo. Since I'd been married, Nonna wrote to me frequently: in her plain, concise style, she asked about my life and studies; I would reply that everything was going well. In every letter she asked if I had something new to tell her: in other words, if I was expecting a baby.

I would find her letters when I came home tense from the office, with a bag of groceries. I had to cook and tidy up in a hurry in order to arrive on time at my student's. In the evening I would start worrying again about what was still left undone: the ironing, or mending the few linens we had. I thought of Nonna sitting in the garden, contented in the peace and well-being of the country. If I had answered her with a *yes*, she would have sent me the sheets meant for her great-grandchildren, some baby's smocks, a sack of polenta. I would be forced to stop working and Francesco would have to provide for everything himself, since having his child would assure me the right to be supported forever. I would never again come to him without the baby: he would always be with us, he would sleep with us, and I would hold him by the hand between us during our walks. Every day I would announce to Francesco truthfully that the baby needed shoes or vitamins and that he would have to find the money somehow: he would simply need to work harder, give up his beloved studies for the time being. Anyway, if he really had to give them up forever, because of increased expenses and my lack of income, he could find happiness in the thought that our child, in twenty years' time, might dedicate himself to the interests he himself had had to give up. Nonna could add another branch to the tree onto which she had grafted her own robust and secure life.

"I don't think we'll have children right now," I wrote. "I'm too poor, or maybe I'm not poor enough. More than anything I'm too in love. I want to be alone with Francesco; I would never be able to give up love; otherwise, I would have married Paolo and stayed with you."

Nonna remained silent for some days before replying, "Dear Alessandra, you are very bold. I don't dislike bold people. But, in my view, depriving oneself of children is not only a serious sin; it's also a serious risk. I hope you will succeed in being happy alone with your husband. If you don't, you won't even be able to blame your defeat on the sacrifices you made for your children."

Those words from Nonna hit me hard. They often came back to me during the day, harsh and relentless, just like her. *I hope you will succeed.* Spurred by this challenge, I worked with greater precision and determination, trying to establish some pleasant breaks in our day. Considering the life we led, it was difficult, yet I always managed to be clean and tidy, and I kept myself calm, smiling, and harmonious. I ironed and freshened my clothes, and the only thing that troubled me was not being able to buy myself a pair of nice stockings: mine were always mended, so I was forever hiding my legs, even though I knew they weren't bad. I rejected the idea that poverty could be stronger than our love, and I tried to convince myself that everything was connected to the fact that Francesco was unhappy: they had begun investigating him at the university and we were anxious about the outcome.

"They'll lose the war," he told me once. "Then we'll be free, and we'll be happy." It's painful to reach the point where you hope your own country will lose the war, but it was my firm desire. We never went to the shelter during the air raids: we went out onto the terrace in the cold and held each other tight, hoping the bombs would fall, and kill us or liberate us at last.

Alberto and Tomaso came to see us more often, and now we, too, were always talking politics, like Fulvia and Dario, letting our house resound with the arrogant voice on the radio. It was as if it used that tone to admonish and threaten us, but at night we would close the door, sit on the floor, and press our ears to the speaker, listening to forbidden stations. We waited; Francesco turned the dial in the silence. Finally we would hear a dull knock: insistent, wary. We felt as if we were in prison and someone outside were knocking on the wall to give us courage. I remembered what my mother had told me about Hervey, that when he was a child and had a fever he imagined knocking on the hull of a submarine. *No one's answering!* he yelled, tossing and turning, *no one's answering anymore!* I thought that within a short time we, too, would be unable to respond.

We sat on the floor in the cold until late. I had to leave early for work in the morning and Francesco would hug me: "You look tired." He never looked at me, and, if he did for a moment, that was all he could find to say. Yes, I was very tired and of course you could see it in my face, but he shouldn't have said so, because those words took away a great part of my strength. After all, he knew I had to continue to be tired. So I was also afraid of being ugly.

Only now, since I've been here, does he look at me. He's sitting in one of the two large leather armchairs that I so wanted to have, and which one day I succeeded in getting into the house, solid and trusty in their width and weight. Francesco sits in his chair, and every time I raise my eyes, I see him looking at me intently, with loving devotion.

I DREAMED OF having them face each other, precisely so that Francesco would look at me. I was convinced now that most of our unhappiness had to do with our not having those armchairs.

Fulvia said, "Yes, you need armchairs." She offered to vouch for me in a shop where you could pay in installments. I decided to ask Mantovani for an advance on my Christmas bonus.

"Things are going poorly?" he asked, looking up from his papers.

"Yes . . . sort of. But it's because I'd like to buy two armchairs. We don't have anywhere to sit at home."

He made a gesture of disbelief.

"Well, yes, naturally we have some chairs," I said, blushing, "but it's not the same. My husband studies until late in the evening; you can't study very well sitting on an uncomfortable chair. Besides, he's always tired, and—"

"Aren't you tired, Signora Minelli?" Mantovani asked, leaning back in his swivel chair and looking at me.

"Naturally, yes, I'm tired, too. But I'm often in the kitchen doing chores."

"And your studies?"

"I'm a little—how can I say it?—stalled at the moment. I have to give lessons in the afternoon, so . . ."

There was a silence while he looked at me. Mantovani was always very good to me: I marveled that he was so good because he was rich, and the rich are often absent-minded.

"I really believe that you, too, have a right to your armchair, Signora Minelli."

He called the accountant and gave orders that I should be advanced a small sum. "Today," he said.

"How should I mark this advance?" the accountant asked.

Mantovani thought about it for a moment and then said, "Overtime bonus. Bonus . . . for the purpose of resting."

The sum was a bit more than I needed to buy the armchairs. I didn't dare look at the accountant, because I was embarrassed. I stared at Mantovani, seeing him only dimly through the foolish, uncontrollable tears that were filling my eyes.

"Oh, thank you," I said as soon as we were alone. "Maybe I shouldn't have . . ."

"But you should," he said firmly. Then he changed his tone, adding, "I come from a poor family, but my father, who was a construction foreman, had an armchair. I remember it well: it was covered in red percale. Who knows what happened to that armchair . . . There were eight of us children and my mother worked hard. She worked harder at home than my father did at the construction site. She chopped wood, fetched water, and still never dared to sit in that armchair. Mi father never gave it up to her. When I became a man and thought back on his behavior, I felt resentful towards him. And by the time I was able to buy an armchair for my mother she was dead. That's how I remember her, sitting on a chair in the kitchen until late, working for all eight of us children." He lost himself in another pause and then concluded, "Ah, yes, I'm thoroughly convinced that you, Signora Minelli, have a right to your own armchair."

I bowed my head slightly and left; I was too emotional to speak, but of course he understood: he who understood everything about women and armchairs.

Unfortunately, the day Francesco saw them for the first time there was a complication that more or less ruined the surprise. It was his birthday, but, since he knew that I had no money, he wasn't expecting

a present from me. Under my instructions, the armchairs were delivered in the morning, when he wasn't there: I was free because his
birthday fell on a public holiday. I had been working since that morning
to polish and tidy his study; I had bought flowers, and since my mother-
in-law had expressed a desire to give her son a gift, I had dared to ask
her for the rug from his old room as a bachelor. She was happy to give
it to me and I spread it out between the two armchairs. Furnished this
way, the study looked really welcoming. I sat in an armchair and
imagined Francesco sitting across from me, looking at me as he had
when we were at the Borghese Gallery.

But when I heard the key turn in the lock, I also heard another
man's voice along with Francesco's: he had come home with Tomaso,
whom he had invited to lunch. It was a coincidence, of course, but he
hadn't considered that I might have preferred to have lunch alone
with him on his birthday. They came in and I blushed, as if caught in
the act.

Francesco stopped. "What's this?" he asked.

"Splendid!" Tomaso exclaimed, sitting in one of the new armchairs
to try it out.

"It's my gift," I said.

"But where did you get the money?"

"I got a bonus."

He, too, sat in an armchair, bouncing on it to test it. "It's really
comfortable," he said. He looked at Tomaso. "What am I always telling
you? Get married."

"Thank you." And then he got up and came to me. "You did well."
He took my chin and kissed me. Tomaso coughed at our display.

"The rug is from your mother," I said, and I went to the kitchen
to make lunch. I had prepared two cups of fruit salad, which I now had to
divide into three. Much later, I told Tomaso: "As I was dividing them, for
the first time, I felt troubled."

·   ·   ·

YES, BIRTHDAYS AND saints' days are difficult dates in a marriage. Unfortunately, I have an extraordinary memory of those dates from childhood. My mother was poor, and I can't think how she managed to buy me a gift sometimes. The gifts were never useful: new shoes, gloves, or a scarf. For my twelfth birthday, I remember she gave me a goldfinch. She came to wake me, smiling cheerfully.

"What do I have here?" she asked, showing me her beautiful hands clasped together. I was pale, my heart in turmoil. She opened her hands and the little bird flew into the room, alighting on the wardrobe.

Yes, the question of celebrations is really important for a man and a woman. During our marriage Francesco often forgot our special dates, and when he did remember I always imagined, mindful of the gardenias, that he had received a timely call from Fulvia. In fact, Francesco's presents always made me profoundly melancholy: they were the gifts of someone who couldn't afford to spend money on something whimsical or foolish. He once gave me a pair of stockings, showing that he had noticed my real need for them: he had seen the mending, the large runs sewn up, and, worse, hadn't talked to me about it. It was an unexpected humiliation, and, to keep from bursting into tears, I took refuge in harsh sarcasm.

"Why did you spend all that money?" I asked. "It's my birthday and I would have preferred a few flowers and a card saying you regret I arrived so late."

"So late?" he repeated, baffled. But he quickly pulled himself together. "Oh yes, my love, forgive me. I understand. It's true, it would have been a lovely idea. You always have good ideas." He looked regretfully at the beautiful stockings lying on the bed, the long shape of the feet.

His mortified look went right through me. "No," I protested immediately, putting my arms around him. "No, it was just a joke. These stockings are really beautiful. It was a joke. I'm sorry. Have you forgiven me? Let's be happy now." Despite that intention, however, I inadvertently reproached Francesco again a little while later. "Why don't you write love letters to me anymore?" I asked.

He looked pained and perplexed. "It's true," he replied. "Maybe because I can talk to you now whenever I want to."

"But you never talk to me about love . . ."

"I never talk about love? You must be patient, Alessandra. I'm really nervous right now. A lot of important things are happening, and it's difficult to think about anything else. Maybe you can't understand, because you're a woman."

"We always used to talk about you and me," I observed, feigning indifference, yet my skin was hurting, "not about men and women. Remember? We promised never to do that."

He nodded. "I know. But it may be impossible. I understood a moment ago when you mentioned the card you wished you'd received for your birthday today. You're always expecting something from me that you'd do in my place. You, a woman."

"But I'm suffering!" I burst out, abandoning all self-control.

"I know," he said. "I understand. But that's just how I am."

I found his sincerity shocking—he didn't react or object. All he did was to set my nature as a romantic and sensitive woman against his as a firm and decisive man with no mercy.

"Then why did you act like someone else at the Borghese Gallery and the Janiculum?" I asked. "Why did you trick me?"

"Oh, Alessandra, why do you say that? I've always been the same, I promise you. I've never acted differently. Forgive me, but sometimes I'm afraid you've taken me for someone I'm not. Nothing has changed about me: on the contrary, I appreciate you even more now. The only thing that's different is that we never have time—"

"We used to find it—"

"You're right. I don't really know how we did it. And then every day I'm more unhappy with what's going on. It always seems like we're getting there, but in fact we never do. It's demoralizing not to be able to work or express your opinions . . ."

"I haven't been able to study anymore, either."

"I know, and I really regret that. But at least you express yourself through love. I'm afraid it's always like that between men and women. Every couple thinks they'll be the exception, that they can escape . . ."

"No!" I shouted. "Please, don't say that! Be quiet!"

"You see, darling?" he began calmly after a pause. "Even that is a strength in women: always wanting to ignore the truth."

"So you think that I should give in? That I should give up?"

"No, that's not it, darling, but we have a different way of feeling. There's the matter of the glass."

"What glass?" I asked in amazement.

"Oh, it's simple: when I see a partially filled glass, I see it as half full; you always see it half empty."

I laughed, but inside I froze. He seemed to have defined our characters with the words *opposite, incompatible.* So it was pointless to reveal to him another reason for my suffering: his habit of saying "I love you" rather than "I adore you." He would have insisted it was the same thing; yet I had Fulvia, Lydia, Nonna—many people who loved me but only him to adore me.

I said nothing more; he changed the subject, convinced he had dispelled our bad mood with humor. Maybe he hadn't appreciated the gravity of what we had said to each other. But I did when, a little later, I found myself alone again behind the wall made by his shoulders.

It was still cold in the bedroom: the terrace where we spent our lovely summer evenings now let the frost besiege us. As I lay awake, I was tormented by a nightmare. In the apartment above ours, the one next to it, the modern white buildings rising up beside ours—in all the buildings in Rome, all the buildings in the world, I saw women awake in the dark, behind the unscalable walls of men's shoulders. We spoke different languages, but we were all trying in vain to make them hear the same words: nothing could get through the unassailable defense of those shoulders. We had to resign ourselves to being alone behind the wall; and to holding one another together, supporting one another, forming a cluster of suffering and expectancy. It was the only comfort we were allowed, besides work, giving birth, and crying, and that was our real relief: crying, alone, sitting in blue kitchens that become dark and sad at sunset; in gray kitchens where the children play on the floor and cry, too, their voices woeful and already grownup. Some of us, like Nonna, were satisfied to be the mistress of large wardrobes full of linens, dark and solemn as coffins; others, without realizing it, were reduced to forgetting themselves in a succession of rich, trivial, and pointless days. But all of them, whether occasionally or always, slept in the cold behind a wall. All of them. I heard them moaning, begging, but not being heard: because a woman's voice is only frail breath, whereas the wall is stone, cement, and bricks.

FRANCESCO WAS ALWAYS more affectionate with me for a few days after a little squabble. During the first year, this persuaded me to let go of my fears and increase my determination to guard against the lazy snare of habit. So I worked at being perpetually serene and smiling, believing that our early happiness could be reborn in an atmosphere of calm more easily than in one of bitter argument or mutual accusation. My nerves were healing: it was as if a beautiful, tranquil sea were spreading through me. Tedious days followed, revolving around our monotonous work schedules. We saw each other only at lunch, and my hands were then full of plates, pans, and glasses. In the evening we stayed home, but Francesco couldn't see me because he was always hiding behind his newspaper. We would read till late and then turn out the lights and go to bed, performing the same gestures, already tempted by sleep. Lying in bed together no longer excited us—it was only relief for our aching legs and our hips, heavy with fatigue, as when I was alone. All the same, from the depths of that tiredness, I knew immediately if

Francesco didn't want to sleep. He would move closer to me and ask, "What are you reading?" He would take the book from my hands, barely glance at it, and put it on the bedspread. That, with not a single word of love, was the preamble. Then came the same movements in the same silent order. It was tacitly understood that if I held on to my book Francesco would go back to his reading or turn over and go to sleep.

Those sordid embraces made me feel bitter and humiliated: I couldn't help comparing them to the lovely evenings when we went up to Villa Borghese, always talking, eager to get to know each other. It seemed that only in order to know each other better and love each other more did we give in to kisses and caresses. I wanted to resume our cherished, interrupted conversation and talk about myself and my memories, but by this time Francesco knew them all. Besides, when I tried to revive our conversations on the same subjects—speaking in the same tone of voice, using the same descriptions—Francesco looked at me suspiciously, as if I were acting. We could no longer delude ourselves about our future life. By now we knew: we were living it.

And I knew that this life would not be enough to make us happy. We had grown up, and we had grown as humans, too. Even the innocent happiness of our days in Florence would have failed to satisfy us now. I had grown out of the habit of marriage, and it would make me feel as though I were wearing a tight dress. After all, during our engagement we hadn't intended marriage to be an aim or goal. We just thought that we would be stronger as two, and, well, that we would help each other fulfill our inmost goals and improve each other. So now, as I noticed the progressive decline in our life together, I thought I was to blame—that I had deteriorated so much personally that I didn't deserve Francesco's attention. I would then spiritedly reaffirm my proud intentions, fight against the defects of my character, and blaze victorious. I couldn't buy books, but Tomaso always borrowed them for me from his father's library—he was a scholar of theosophy. Tomaso had a ready intelligence, quick and expressive. I liked talking to him.

He looked at me when I spoke, with the surprise natural to large, clear eyes. But the growing interest these conversations aroused in me brought painful disappointment rather than comfort; I wanted it to be Francesco attending to my problems and my reading. He was also much more intelligent than Tomaso. But, because of a sudden modesty established between us after our wedding, Francesco and I never talked about things close to my heart. When I offered to do something for him, he would ask me to type what he had written, and I had done it diligently and enthusiastically for a while. Or he suggested I replace the lining of one of his jackets. Perhaps it was at his suggestion that his mother invited me to visit when I had time, to knit garments for the soldiers.

Signora Minelli invited several friends to her house in the afternoon for this purpose. While they knitted, they discussed recipes for desserts with no eggs or sugar, tea as a substitute for coffee. I went to these gatherings two or three times, but I didn't have a single recipe to offer. The ladies looked at me dumbfounded, never dropping a stitch but raising their eyebrows, judging me to be lazy, idle, I suppose, even though none of them worked and they all had maids. They forced me to confess: "No, I don't know how to make dessert." They gave my mother-in-law furtive glances of understanding and commiseration. Besides, my work was poor: my knitting needles weren't clicking rapidly, like theirs, with the rhythm of gossipy conversation. Because of the dismissive way they spoke about other women, I imagined that all those ladies were perfect, and I found myself feeling somewhat envious. Our house lacked almost all the utensils they mentioned. I never had my hair done, and when I washed it I dried it in the sun on the terrace. I didn't frequent the well-known stores; I did my shopping in our neighborhood. And when I told them that Francesco and I never went to the movies, the women stared at me, incredulous, suspicious even, worried that I had dared to make fun of them.

At such moments, my mother-in-law turned to me and stroked my hair. Maybe she, too, regretted that I didn't know how to make dessert and that, in the end, I wasn't like her friends' daughters and daughters-in-law. But Francesco told her how we had paid for the armchairs with my bonus. Once, he had been ill with a high fever; we feared it was typhus, but it was only poisoning from the terrible cigarettes he smoked. I called my mother-in-law immediately and, opening the door to her, I begged, "Help me. I'm scared!" I watched her move about the bedroom confidently: I had no experience tending the sick, and I had always been in good health. I sat by the bed, looking at Francesco, and the flannels I put on his forehead were like kisses, fervent prayers begging him to get well. I stayed by his bed for hours, unmoving, watching over him with doglike faithfulness. I noticed his mother observing me. During those hours, she took off the white ribbon around her neck so as to be more comfortable, and her old skin sagged.

"No, Alessandra doesn't know how to make desserts because my son doesn't like them. He didn't eat them when he was a boy, either." She paused and her choker moved as if to let her swallow something. "Anyway, she hasn't much time," she explained. "She works as a secretary in an office. She earns a salary, and that's how she helps her husband."

The women went on looking at me with cold hostility. There was no point in condemning them; they had grown up in a society in which women who worked were considered to be different from other women.

One evening, Francesco came to pick me up. He smiled tenderly when he saw me: maybe because of my way of dressing, which had remained somewhat old-fashioned, or the meek expression I always had, I looked like a waif the others might be welcoming out of pity.

On the way home, Francesco was still smiling at the thought of me with his mother's friends. Since he had started living with me he had changed a little: for example, he no longer cared what Signora Spazzavento said.

"You know," I said, "when I'm with them I have the same painful feeling I had with my classmates at school. I was tall, taller than everyone else: the tallest barely came up to my shoulders. So they looked at me as if I'd been planted in the class as a ploy. It was also the case that I had the highest grades, which made me even more embarrassed. Now, at least, the socks I knit are really ugly."

Francesco laughed, but I suddenly turned serious. "Look," I resumed. "I don't know how to make socks. I can't get used to soothing the evil produced by violence, as others do. I'd like to work actively so that we don't resort to violence at all. Do you understand, Francesco?"

We were walking slowly along the paved and winding boulevard at the time called Viale dei Martiri Fascisti: here and there were stretches of uncultivated land heaped with trash and detritus.

"So," I said, "I'd like to work with you."

Francesco didn't reply right away. I saw his thin profile against a sky already bright with the promise of spring. I blushed, as if feminine reserve had failed me, and I had been the first to declare my love. But I had spoken impetuously, as when I'd said to my mother, "Don't leave without me!"

"I don't know exactly what I could do," I insisted. "But you would know. The other night, Tomaso said I could be useful."

"Who said that?"

"Tomaso."

"Tomaso isn't married," he replied harshly.

"What does that have to do with it?"

"Tomaso doesn't understand anything."

"Why do you say that? When you go out and you don't tell me where you're going, I know you'll be with your friends. I stay home, tied to my chores, very often in the kitchen. But I feel we have a bond of solidarity, so tight it almost hurts. I stir the soup, and every circle I trace in the pot is driven by a will so exact, a feeling of connection to you so deep, that it makes me believe that my peaceful act of housekeeping can miraculously produce the same effect as your risk, your struggle. It's like that when I line up in the morning for groceries before going to work, while you're asleep. In the winter, it's still dark and very cold; the women all complain, they're not happy; with each step forward in that line, I picture you sleeping. It seems to me that you can sleep only on condition that I don't abandon my post, even though my hands are so numb with cold they feel like they're falling off. But this no longer seems to be enough. I've become so strong inside, so powerful . . ." As I said this, I drew a finger over my brow to hide my timidity. "I know I could help you."

We walked a little further in silence. Francesco took my arm and squeezed it hard, let it go and again held it and squeezed it. We were a single person with only one step; we were encircled by a gentle marching tempo that urged us on. Moved, I thought: *We're married.*

"No," he said. "It's impossible."

"Why?" I asked, disappointed.

"Because these aren't things for women."

"But there are a lot of women who work with you. And actually Tomaso told me—"

"Ask him why he doesn't let Casimira work."

"Who is Casimira?"

"A girl," he replied evasively. But he insisted: "Ask him why."

"Maybe Tomaso doesn't believe this Casimira is brave enough, or ready, or—"

"Exactly. I think about you what he thinks about Casimira."

I said nothing for a moment before asking fearfully, haltingly, "You mean, I'm not—"

There was a pause. At last Francesco confessed quietly but firmly: "Yes."

We went home without speaking. We were no longer a single person, but two different people: one had courage and the other didn't.

YES, FRANCESCO NOW tells me, *and I was the one who lacked courage. You didn't know that a few days earlier Marisa had been arrested. She was Alberto's girlfriend; I wasn't brave enough to suffer as Alberto suffered. You didn't know her because she was pregnant and didn't want to be seen. She was very apprehensive about you: she was separated from her husband. She was a singularly courageous woman, Marisa; almost as courageous as you are. She always wanted to carry the most compromising material, claiming that her pregnancy would protect her, and in fact it was unlikely that suspicion would fall on her. She didn't live with Alberto but in a furnished room in the apartment of a seamstress. From the time she and Alberto started working together, they were very careful. They never left letters in the room or anything that might give away their friendship, and they met away from the porter's gaze. She was a really intelligent woman, Marisa, almost as intelligent as you are. Yet it was her condition that gave her away: she fainted while she was walking down the Corso. She was taken to the hospital nearby, and someone opened her purse, which was full of printed material. It was a nurse who called the police—another woman. As soon as Alberto found out, he hid with a different friend and from hour to hour we expected that Marisa, in her condition, and exhausted, would talk. Alberto waited impatiently to learn that they were coming for him; it would have been a relief. But the days went by, and our apprehension grew. Alberto wanted to go and turn himself in, but we persuaded him that it would be pointless, if not actually damaging, now that she, too, was guilty—and we didn't know what arguments she had used in her defense. By showing up, Alberto would surely harm her. "It's my fault," he kept saying. "I was the one who let her work with us. Maybe she'll talk tomorrow: if she does, they'll let her go." But she didn't talk, because she was brave, and you, too, would have been brave. That's why I wasn't.*

COLD AND UNPLEASANT weeks followed. Francesco rarely spoke to me and he stayed out late. I made a show of not wanting to know where he had been. One Sunday I made a cake: when I set it on the table, he questioned me with a look.

"It's your mother's friends' famous recipe."

It was terrible and we barely touched it. Because we ate in the study, the cake sat there in the silence for the entire evening.

By that time we had a fair number of friends and they often came to see us. At first I didn't like them disturbing our solitude, and then I started inviting them, dreading our dull evenings. Tomaso was one of the most regular, and sometimes Denise came, too, an older woman who wore a beret and knew all the comrades living in Paris. Her demeanor was masculine, and she greeted me with a nod, the way the Germans do. She would talk all night and never say a word to me. Occasionally she seemed suddenly to remember me and her manners. Then she would smile kindly and ask if I had children, forgetting that she had asked me that before. "They'll come," she would reassure me maternally, and, turning to the men, she resumed the conversation that interested her. She was always talking about when freedom would come. But for me, she thought, the only thing that mattered was having babies.

The presence of that woman irritated me. "She's not wrong though," Lydia sighed. "You ought to have a baby."

"I think so, too. But later, when I'm thirty, say, and not so eager to live for Francesco and for us."

"No, it's better now," Lydia insisted. "When you're thirty, you'll be even more eager to live, still more at forty. Children bind a man to you; they keep him. When there's a child, a man always comes home, even if he's betraying you."

"He comes back because of the child?"

"Of course. But that way he can't abandon you, either."

"Oh, how terrible!" I said, hiding my face. "What a disgrace!" Imagining Francesco with another woman made me hot with jealousy. I pictured him with his comrade, her lusterless hair poking out from under her beret. *I can't leave Alessandra*, he was telling her. *I can't leave her because of the baby*. He looked at her tenderly while I waited at home, haggard, holding a baby.

I wanted him to leave me as he would a man, a friend. Maybe—afterwards—it would be a good time to run swiftly down the stairs: I saw myself walking towards the river, the wind ballooning my raincoat. Francesco no longer loved to hear me talk about my mother. He once said that she had been of an age when one must learn to renounce things. He also said that, all in all, my father must be a good man.

"But she couldn't settle for a good man!" I replied scornfully.

"Then why did she marry him?"

"She didn't know him, maybe, or maybe she thought she was stronger."

"We always think we're stronger."

Another time, he said, "Nonsense," and "At any rate, she did you a lot of harm."

"Me?! My mother harmed me?"

"Yes, and I don't think that twit was worth it."

When he said that I moved away from him, horrified. *Twit* was a word I had only read in books and to me it had the grating sound made by a knife scraping on a plate. I couldn't bear to hear Francesco calling Hervey a *twit*, belittling my mother's romantic past. I knew now that he condemned her: he had told his mother that mine had drowned by accident.

"What an extraordinary woman," Tomaso had murmured, admiring photographs of her.

There was a time when Francesco and I were always in agreement, exhibiting the same taste and opinions. Yet now, in discussions with others, we were always on opposite sides. Very often I shared Tomaso's opinion, maybe because he was only a few years older than I was. But what really pained me was noticing that, while Francesco's friends listened to me readily, agreeing that my ideas were admirably clear and that I had a solid grounding in political problems, too, he himself never seemed to consider anything I said. I excused him, thinking that he only ever saw me busy with domestic chores, and maybe he supposed, like my father, that they constituted my chief interests.

One evening, during these discussions Francesco spoke to me rather rudely. I stopped talking and Tomaso came to my defense. I looked at him gratefully: he looked back at me, as if apologizing to me for what Francesco had said. Tomaso had a lovely bright, open face and shiny, wavy brown hair, like that of my childhood friends. The memory flooded me with waves of warm tenderness. *Thank you*, I said again with my eyes. When we said goodbye, we clasped hands for a long time.

THE MOST MISLEADING virtue of marriage is the ease with which one forgets, in the morning, everything that happened the night before. Encouraged by the clear color of the sun's first rays and the energy and rhythm of everyday gestures, I was always the first to turn back towards Francesco.

We had been married for more than a year. Days followed days; months quickly swallowed months; the seasons turned. I always said, *Now I'm working, and later I'll be happy; now I'm washing dishes, and later I'll be happy; now I'm standing in line, and later I'll be happy.* Francesco had learned to kiss me on the cheeks, with a light peck; he never kissed me on the mouth anymore. And yet there had been a time when we didn't know how else to kiss. Later he kissed me on the mouth only when he approached me at night. Finally we got into the habit of reading, and he didn't really kiss me at all. He no longer told me what he felt on account of his love for me; maybe he thought it would be superfluous to talk about it now. Yet love lies precisely in the need to express it constantly, and in the desire to hear it constantly expressed. I no longer knew what was inside him, and I couldn't allow him all that liberty simply because I knew he was hungry, thirsty, tired, had very little money or political problems.

He never used my name when he drew close to me at night. I said his passionately, though. "Oh, it's you, Francesco . . ." I would say, wanting to be sure, every moment, that it was really he, the most beloved being in the world, who was giving me that pleasure. For both of us, those brief nightly encounters soon became a secret, prohibited zone where we were permitted to wander only furtively, although we each had the other's permission. In the morning Francesco never spoke of what had happened, as if he wanted to forget a weakness, an unseemly surrender.

Tomaso called often, his voice cheerful and youthful. "Don't stay home all the time, Alessandra. Do you want to go out? I'll come with you. Let's go all the way to Prati. I'd like to see the house where you used to live. In Prati there's always a nice smell of honeysuckle in the evenings. Come on, let's go! Shall I tell Francesco?"

I said I was very busy, even though his invitations made me long to return to my old neighborhood. But I wanted to go there with Francesco. I hoped that he, too, would notice the spring. I spoke to Tomaso briefly, then went back to the kitchen thinking myself a hypocrite. I didn't want Francesco to notice the spring; I wanted him to notice me.

I put down the plate I was holding and dropped into a chair. I was alone in the house, just as when I was a child, but the excitement that stirred me was no longer focused on the trees and the sky visible from my window. It spilled over into me, into my physical life. The blood ran beneath my skin with the vibrant, steady rhythm of youth. I stood up and went to lie on the bed in the dark, cool bedroom. My lips were burning with a great thirst.

It was so long since someone had kissed me on the mouth. It didn't even seem possible that it was a natural way of kissing, or that I had tried it. I closed my eyes, imagining a mouth settling on mine with the angry tenacity of kisses won after a long wait or a fight. I resisted, doubtful, as before diving into a river, and then I lost myself, I was submerged. I tried to remember every detail of how a kiss happened, every detail of the moment when I was overcome and my teeth parted. But the precise sensation escaped me. *What's it like?* I asked myself, bewildered. *I can't remember what it's like.*

I got up, brushed my hair, changed my dress, and carefully powdered my face. I didn't put on lipstick because I felt as if all my blood were concentrated in my lips. And then I waited, dreamily, idly, not bothering to set the table or cook the food: surely we wouldn't think about eating.

Francesco came home and I was waiting for him at the door, my white dress a fresh gardenia in the darkness of the hallway.

"Oh, my darling," he said, "I'm happy to be home." He went to the bathroom, and the fresh water running in the sink revived my furious thirst.

"What is it?" he asked.

"Nothing, my love," I replied. I was waiting for him to turn around, see my anticipation, welcome it like a gift.

"Is lunch ready?"

"No, it's not ready."

"I'm hungry." He headed for his study and I followed him.

"Nothing is ready, my love," I said. "We'll eat later, afterwards. We'll eat at four."

"Why?" he asked. "What's going on? What happened? If you're tired, I can help you," he offered politely.

I gave him an intense look. And my life was concentrated in my bare lips. *What is a kiss like?* I implored him silently. *I can't remember anymore, Francesco. It's terrible: help me! I don't want to lose that memory.* I was thirsty and I felt I might fall down, exhausted by that thirst.

"No," I replied. "Thanks. I was joking. It'll be ready in a few minutes."

I crossed the room unhurriedly, went back to the kitchen, and made a cheese frittata that Francesco liked a lot. My thirst slowly left me, fell away in contempt. In place of that sweet thirst, a solitary, wearying cry settled in me, like the whining of a dog.

AND THE NEXT day I forgot. It was an exhausting alternation of hopeful mornings and desperate evenings. The nights were dark interludes.

One Sunday started out with an act of unplanned laziness, since we had forgotten to reset the clock after the time change. We were worried at first—Francesco was supposed to have left for an appointment some time earlier—and then childishly gleeful. It was as if we had decided not to attend to anything important and enjoy our day off. Through half-closed shutters, the sun prodded us awake. "Stay, Francesco," I said tenderly. "Stay."

"You stay," Francesco said while I held him by his pajama sleeve. "Stay. I have to go out now. You know what we'll do? Let's meet in the center and come home together slowly, enjoying the sun."

"Piazza di Spagna?" I suggested enthusiastically.

"If you like." Before he left, he threw open the window and the sun splashed over the bed at my feet. "Ciao, Sandra," he said.

"Ciao," I said, and I smiled at him coquettishly. I felt as if I'd been in bed for a long time, because of an illness, and that that day I had to get up and start my convalescence.

In fact, when I went out of the building that day everything celebrated me. The air was mild—neither too cool nor too warm—and my clothes felt so right it was as if I weren't wearing any. Colorful laundry hung at the windows and the large mimosa in the garden opposite was in flower. Oranges blazed in their baskets; bottles of red wine in shop windows were giant rubies. The tram ran with a cheerful jingling, and a boy at the rear window waved his hand gaily, surely believing he was on a fine train. There were a lot of people walking in the street, and all of them looked at me intently; I was on my own but walking quickly, showing that I had a clear purpose, or, rather—it was obvious—a date. Everyone must have known that I had a date with a man, and that was why I was looking so confident.

I turned onto Via Veneto as if onto a stage. My step commanded the sidewalk: there was a playful boldness in my eyes; the earth and the beauty of the season bowed before me. I was proud, a queen with a whip in my hand. Men looked at me with a persistence that would ordinarily have bothered me. That day, however, I hinted at an invitation as I walked rapidly towards my date. In window after window I saw my reflection, and found myself irresistibly attractive, recognizing a quality I didn't believe I had: a provocative manner of the sort that instantly stimulates a man's desire rather than his admiration. Maybe it was due to my joyful breath, swelling my breast under the jacket. I was pleased to be wearing that old gray jacket again, faithful and safe, well cut, like a friend you can count on. Francesco really liked it. In fact, I suddenly remembered that I had been wearing it the day we first met. The memory startled me, I had a moment of bewilderment. I wished I could go into a shop, call Francesco, and say, *I'm coming to meet you dressed as I was the day we met. I'm on my way. Wait for me, Francesco!* But, uncertain where he was just then, I was gripped by an irrational anxiety. *Is he still alive?* I wondered. I pictured him lying on the ground, pale, with a lot people around, as happens after a car accident. I pushed through the crowd. *I'm his wife,* I said, *let me through!* My anguish was so intense that I moaned and cried. *Francesco!* I shouted inside, *Francesco, wait! We have to experience this happy day!*

I entered Piazza di Spagna from Via Propaganda Fide, an aristocratic street that had always intimidated me.

I stopped at the corner of the piazza because some peach branches were crowding the sidewalk. "No," a woman was saying to the florist, "they're too expensive." The blossoms had the scent of the apricot pits I'd enjoyed crushing on the windowsill as a child: a bitter, forbidden scent.

"I'll take them," I said, and I was pleased with the tone of my voice. ("What a voice you've got, Alessandra," Tomaso had once said to me. "I don't always catch exactly what you mean when you speak. Forgive me—maybe it's rude, but I sometimes want to close my eyes the way I do at concerts; I want to listen to the music.") I paid with my last fifty lire and carelessly pocketed the change.

Francesco was already there, next to the palms. I remembered what he used to say when we were engaged: "You're like a palm tree: tall, slender, with your hair ruffled on top of your head." I was really flattered by the comparison. Maybe he had chosen that place on purpose. I couldn't stop smiling, proud of myself and of his love for me. I took my time walking towards him; I liked making him wait. He hadn't seen me yet and thought he was alone. I saw him pacing impatiently.

"Francesco . . ." I whispered fervently.

"Oh, my love!" he exclaimed. "What a wasted morning. I arrived late, and they had already left. That damned time change." He turned and said, "What beautiful flowers!" Then, caught up in his worries: "I need to try and call Alberto."

"Shall we walk?" My voice invited him to recognize me in the splendor of the morning.

"No, no, it's too late. He might call and not find me."

He moved a peach branch out of the way and took my arm. We began to walk. On the tram, he sat next to the window holding the flowers, which were quite cumbersome.

"FRANCESCO . . ." I SAID later, to rouse him gently from his sleep.

I was still waiting patiently for my cheerful day off. Alberto called. "All is well," he said. "My aunt will arrive in a few days," which meant that in a few days the Allies would land in Sicily. Every night on the radio we heard them, knocking at the door of our prison. They were coming towards us, the almond, orange, and bergamot trees bending at their passage. I was happy, even though I felt those trees bending inside me.

"Are you happy?" I asked Francesco. But he was still closed within the rigid walls of his thoughts. After lunch he had lain down on the bed, picked up a book, and fallen asleep. I waited submissively, like a child who has been promised something: my great calm threatened to crumble and take me down with it. I focused on the book Francesco had placed on the nightstand; it sat there, splayed open so he wouldn't lose his place. He would leave it like that before he turned to me in the evenings, eager to go back to his reading after those brief interludes. It was a pact between him and his book, from which he begged forgiveness for this momentary neglect. Sometimes I feigned sleep: there was an ongoing struggle between my wounded pride and that hateful book, with its rigid spine.

I called again, "Francesco." He woke up and I gave him a long kiss, a desperate invitation.

AFTERWARDS, I LAY on the bed with my arm over my eyes to protect myself from the sun coming through the window—or maybe because I felt acutely ashamed, like those women who are violated and then abandoned in the country, their clothes rumpled and torn. And the shame of that violation seemed exacerbated by the fact that I was the one who had asked for it, and, however fleetingly, enjoyed it.

Carefree voices rose from the street to the darkness of that room, penetrated by rays of white light. Francesco wanted to go back to sleep; it was only my silence that kept him awake. In that silence he discerned an accusation and, with some difficulty, managed to reassure himself, even though he was convinced of his innocence. I felt it was precisely his fear of me that prevented him from uttering a single word, and yet I understood that, if he had, it would have been the wrong one.

Finally I said, "I want to talk to you, Francesco."

He didn't reply, didn't show the slightest curiosity. Maybe he knew what I was about to say. His naked body lay on the sheet: it was a youthful, confident body, revealing the presence of hidden strength in the muscles of his shoulders, neck, and hips.

"This can't go on. Do you understand?"

"What have I done?" he asked calmly, after a moment.

"Nothing. You haven't done anything, but I have to talk to you. Sorry, be patient."

"I'm listening."

His tone was conciliatory, but rather than soothing me it stirred up my bad mood. I would have preferred him to admit that he didn't love me anymore; the fact that he had acted like that despite loving me was the chief cause of my resentment.

"I have to talk to you. One day you'll have to remember that I said all this to you. You won't be able to reproach me for keeping quiet. I need to tell you everything frankly. I'm not irritated and I'm not nervous." I took his hand, which was lying on the sheet. "It's precisely because I love you that I have to talk to you."

He saw that I wasn't angry and I felt that this increased his apprehension. His eyes lit up with pain and tenderness. Francesco really was beautiful at that moment.

"I want to talk to you honestly. I want to tell you things one never says to men because they respond in sharp, cutting ways. Please don't react like that. Let me speak."

My tone was so unusual that Francesco turned to look at me in astonishment. It was the tone in which I spoke to Fulvia, Claudio, Tomaso, in which I'd spoken to Francesco when we first fell in love.

"I'm betraying you," I told him. "I betray you countless times every day in my imagination. It's not important," I added, "that I betray you with your own image. Because that image does what you never do, says what you never say, and so it isn't you: it's someone else. You can't measure up to this imaginary person as you might a man different from you—a stranger. If I were betraying you with someone else, I would at least feel remorse or regret: as it is, I feel only resentment."

The room was enveloped in gray shadows: tangles of light, like stars, shone on the shutters, and sounds reached us slowly, muffled, with the rhythm of the waves of the sea.

"You wanted to sleep," I went on. "You always sleep afterwards, while I stay awake thinking. We haven't talked for such a long time.

You don't know who I am anymore, what is in me, the value I give to every act or word of love."

He said something, mentioned the desire he had had for me a short while before.

"Quiet," I suggested, taking his hand. "Don't talk about these things. What do they have to do with love? It's not love if you want to cry afterwards. I knew what love was from the time I was a child. I thought about it day and night, by the window or in my little bed between the wardrobes. I know. I know it all, and I know it very well. All women know what love is, even if they sometimes pretend to forget, to adapt, not to think about it. Love shouldn't be confused with a commonplace act that offers pleasure, that satisfies or satiates like drinking or sleeping. You yourself should keep me from it: you shouldn't let me debase myself; you shouldn't allow us to debase ourselves together."

"Why?" he asked earnestly. "It was wonderful."

"No, it wasn't wonderful. Your desire was aroused by the languor that precedes sleep and not by love for me. Love is something else. You didn't even kiss me on the mouth," I said, covering my face. "Love is a continual questioning, kissing, embracing, looking at each other, wanting to reflect each other whatever the cost, a continual fear of losing each other just when one might seem to be most attached. 'Do you love me, Alessandra?,' always doubting, 'Do you love me, Francesco?' Don't tell me that you're sure of my love, because I'll confess then that often while you're taking me, I don't love you. And you don't know it: you're obtuse, imprisoned in your body, pursuing a precise goal of your own; you don't love me, or you wouldn't leave me by myself. It's terrible to be alone in those moments. It's not enough that you care for me. Affection is enough to justify my living and working with you, eating with you; it doesn't justify my lying here on the bed with you, naked."

"Alessandra!" he chided gently.

"Don't scold me. Don't be a husband, a relative. If you scold me I won't continue talking to you, and you really need to know. Only love justifies my being here with you in this way. And this isn't love. Do you understand? It's not in these acts. Listen: we don't have an easy life. We have no money, both of us work, and sometimes I'm tired. Life hasn't been easy for me since I was a child, but I never noticed because I had a legacy of unlimited love, which always kept me from feeling poor or tired. As a child, I sat by the window and waited; I was calm, quiet and good. I waited. Women are capable of any strength or sacrifice while they're waiting. But they don't want to cry afterwards; they don't want to feel like crying, with their hands over their faces. They can't—do you understand? It's a punishment: they can't do without love. That's why I betray you. I betray you every day. And with that dreamy image of you I walk, we read together, we talk, we make such intimate confessions to each other that we both know everything about the other, the angel and the devil we carry within. We have long, happy, young nights: dawn's light comes through the windows while he's still holding me in his arms, whispering sweetly in my ear. Don't laugh, please. It would really end everything if I thought you wanted to laugh while I was saying this . . ."

"I'm not laughing," he said. He took my hand, and his body no longer looked so muscular but weak and tired.

"Someday I might even betray you with someone else." The figure of Tomaso crossed my mind; I rapidly rejected it, feeling antipathy and revulsion. "Maybe it wouldn't be that important. I'd continue to live with you, openly and affectionately. I'd always be the same: honest." I could speak to him frankly because up to that point he hadn't meant more to me than I did to myself. "I'm sure it wouldn't be very important. But I wanted to talk to you so you'd understand, so you'd know that women do everything possible to resist love. Love, though, is always stronger than they are."

"Yes, I understand," he said.

He drew me close: we held each other, naked, in a sad and desperate embrace.

•   •   •

AND THE NEXT day I forgot. Yet if Francesco was late coming home I was afraid it was because my openness, instead of bringing us together, had created an immense gulf between us. I waited restlessly by the windowsill. Sometimes, to avoid being anxious for a few more minutes, I would go to meet him at the tram stop. When I saw him, a lovely warmth immediately surged through my veins. My love withstood every shock, unwavering. This made me feel angry and, above all, afraid. It seemed terrible to me that my love survived despite my unhappiness.

Lydia suggested that I see a palm reader: she gave me several addresses but told me that, of all of them, she really trusted Adele, who had predicted that the captain would leave her, and in fact she had advised her to cast the evil eye on him. "I didn't do it," Lydia confessed, shaking her head. "It seemed impossible. . . ."

I myself wanted to find Ottavia again: my mother came to visit me every night and looked at me, pained at being unable to communicate.

At home one evening we talked for a long time about spiritualism: Francesco refused to give credit to such phenomena and in fact shrugged his shoulders, whereas Tomaso maintained that he had had intriguing experiences.

"Look, Alessandra," Francesco said once we were alone. "I want to ask you to stop thinking about these things: they agitate you and they're not good for you. Don't listen to Tomaso . . ."

"Are you jealous of Tomaso?" I asked with a mischievous smile.

"No, why should I be?"

"Because he's courting me."

"Ah, I know. He spends all evening looking at you."

"So?"

"So what should I do? Forbid it? I've known Tomaso for too many years. I know he does it to pass the time, or maybe even out of politeness. You're the only married woman . . ."

"I get it. So you think that no one could be seriously interested in me?"

"Well, no, and I'm living proof, it would seem. But it's much easier to court a married woman. Do you really want me to worry about Tomaso?"

"Why not?"

"In the first place, I know you. And then," he added after a short pause, "forgive me my vanity: because I think I'm worth more than Tomaso."

"Well, that's true, but—"

"But I don't like these conversations. Tomaso is joking. I know him well."

I knew that Tomaso wasn't joking, however. Sometimes I tried to get Francesco to realize it, but he always reacted the same way. It annoyed me that he considered me foolish enough to delude myself about my admirer's intentions. One evening he called him a twit.

The following day I went out with Tomaso for the first time without Francesco's knowledge, but it was only because I wanted to see Ottavia, and Francesco didn't want me to. We were as happy as children and laughed at the thought of what Francesco would say if he found out about our escapade. Tomaso imitated his voice, the tone in which he would have reprimanded us. I laughed, touched at the thought of how well Tomaso really knew Francesco. He watched me laugh.

"Francesco is so extraordinary," I said, and then we were embarrassed for a moment.

Ottavia was no longer there: she had been evacuated to her village. We stood at her door in an old street near Piazza Navona, disappointed. We looked around, thwarted, and, not knowing how to occupy our time, we went to sit in a café. It was a small place, frequented by couples. Smiling, I said to Tomaso that I was compromising myself for him, and he, smiling back at me, said that, alas, it wasn't true. I had a fleeting sense of shame in front of the waiter, who was curt with us, and I hid the hand with my wedding ring. I confessed it to Tomaso, and he jokingly made a show of being offended. "Why? Couldn't I be your husband?" We laughed. We laughed often, but in a forced, awkward way. That's how we started talking about marriage and, above all, relationships between men and women: in other words, about love. Each of us had much to say, and we interrupted each other as we talked, our sentences overlapping. Meanwhile, the café was emptying. I was startled when we looked at the clock.

"Oh!" I said, confused. "It's so late already."

Tomaso gazed at me, his light eyes smiling good-naturedly. "You're so beautiful, Alessandra," he said. We walked part of the way in silence and then separated. I said, smiling: "We can even confess to Francesco that we went to see Ottavia; anyway, we didn't find her . . ."

He interrupted. "No, please, Alessandra. Of course we could, but I like having a secret with you. Even an innocent one like this."

I felt I could grant him that, and that was how the delightful day ended. I hadn't spent a day like that for a long time, I thought as I went sadly up the stairs. Someone was playing the accordion beneath our windows. Looking down from the terrace, I saw that it was a group of workmen. *What a sweet, pleasant tune.* I could have stayed there for hours listening to the accordion.

I told Francesco I had been to see Fulvia. Then I felt insecure, and I waited for him to turn around and scold me harshly: *Why are you lying to me?* I blushed, even though I had done nothing wrong. But Francesco was sitting on the floor listening to the radio; because the volume was turned down, it seemed that someone was whispering in his ear.

"I went to see Fulvia," I repeated, hoping he would notice the lie. He nodded, showing he had heard, and signaled for me to sit beside him.

I saw less of Fulvia. We had been to see the palm reader one morning, the one her mother had recommended; she lived in a lonely street near the Colosseum. I had had to ask for several hours off from work, making some excuse I no longer remember: the subterfuge exhilarated me and, above all, the freedom, which I wasn't used to enjoying in the morning. We laughed going up the dusty gray stairs: Adele lived in the attic. In the entrance we immediately saw a number of women, all waiting patiently. They sat along the walls and looked at the glass door: through it you could see Adele's shadow.

It was a very humble house: on the walls, besides several oleographs, hung numerous images of the most revered saints. The entrance was dark and barely illuminated by two minuscule lamps which burned before an image of Sant'Antonio. The reddish glow seemed to ignite flames in the eyes of the waiting women. They were modest women, for the most part; one held a baby and, every now and again, she said, "Behave," even though he wasn't moving. There were a few flashy women with bleached hair, acting huffy, pretending to be there out of some onerous duty. And then there was Fulvia, who had come to find out if Dario would marry her, and me. I was no longer the child who sat at the window, the girl who flew down the stairs to meet Francesco. I was one of the many who no longer had faith in themselves and were reduced to asking for help from a fortune teller. Maybe I looked as lost as the woman beside me, letting her purse dangle from her knees. Like the rest of them, I had no shame about revealing my defeat to other women. I looked from one to another, and their misery aroused both compassion and revolt in me.

"There are too many people," I said to Fulvia, and dragged her away.

I had invited her to have lunch with me. Francesco had been away for several days; he had gone with some comrades to a meeting in Milan. I was in the habit of accompanying him to the station, and we would smile till the last minute. But when the train started moving, sliding slowly along the tracks, it was as if my blood were draining from my veins. My smile faded, and the fear that was now woven into our lives returned to grip me. Each time, it seemed risky to separate, as if, through some carelessness of our own, we might never see each other again. I went home, and our building felt like a big empty box. The door groaned upon opening. I closed it, and a sinister thud echoed throughout the deserted apartment. The first night was terrible; I couldn't fall asleep. Then, slowly, peace wrapped itself around me like a smooth white bandage; solitude called to me, tempting and flattering. I could do anything I wanted with my afternoons, but none of my ideas seemed equal to the unlimited freedom I had at my disposal, and I ended up staying home, sewing by the window.

Fulvia took over. "Francesco isn't there?" she asked. "Then I'm coming. I have so much to tell you! We can never talk when the men are around."

It was true. We went for weeks without seeing each other, saying, "There's no point." If Francesco was with us, I paid little attention to Fulvia, and that little was superficial. It didn't surprise her. She knew that was the role every woman has to play, and she also knew that I was sincere in playing it; the role a woman plays with a man at her side is very different from the one played by a woman who is alone.

We often ended up locking ourselves in the bathroom to talk. I didn't approve of such stratagems, but I was too weak not to rely on them.

We were the first to find this approach depressing. And yet when Fulvia arrived we were immediately anxious to be on our own: our initial exchanges were banal and I realize that, no matter what Francesco said, we barely answered him. We needed to talk about things that were vital to us and leave Francesco alone, as he was even when we were with him. In fact, when I smiled and asked Fulvia, "Do you want to comb your hair?" or "Would you like to take off your coat?," all three of us were happy. Francesco would pick up his paper and we would go off down the hall, letting our uninteresting words echo in the space behind us. As I turned the key in the lock, Fulvia dropped her bold, lively manner.

"Well?" she would ask attentively.

I'd sit on the edge of the bath. "I'm desperate."

"If you only knew . . ." she would respond with a sigh, referring to herself. Our faces were tense; we looked lost. Every so often we'd stop talking, put an ear to the door, and then start up again, our voices low.

"Can you imagine: yesterday I set the table with flowers because it was the 11th, and the 11th—"

"Yes, I know."

"Well. He smiles, says, 'What are we celebrating today?' I wanted to burst into tears, but I say, 'Guess.' I was wearing the same dress I wore that day, my hair was soft and loose, the way I had it then. 'Guess,' I said again with a smile. He didn't remember any of it. I had to tell him everything."

"And then what did he do?"

"That evening he brought me a bottle of perfume."

"It's strange," Fulvia said, "how men think they can fix anything by spending money . . ." Meanwhile we'd watch the door, putting a finger to our lips, and talking out loud about unrelated things. I didn't like to acknowledge that despite loving Francesco so much—or rather precisely because of it—I was forced to demean myself like that.

SO WE WERE having lunch alone, and the relaxed yet animated atmosphere that women establish when they're by themselves spread through the house. I went back and forth to the kitchen, casually serving Fulvia at the table. I didn't have to keep myself in check, and it was indescribably restful: when I was with Francesco, I was constantly afraid that an action or word of mine would be enough for him to think ill of me. A woman always understands the pain of another woman's life. She knows how easy it is to make a mistake when she's tired: women are always very tired. Fulvia looked affectionately at the house that I tidied, swept, and dusted every day, and her gaze was a sweet caress on my shoulders.

We ate on a folding table in the study.

"It's nice in here," Fulvia said. The sun pressed against the half-closed shutters, trying to violate the dim light; the air, already hot, and a stubbornly rising desperation made me feel as though I couldn't breathe.

"I don't feel like eating," I said. "And also—sorry—nothing's very good. I don't dare keep food in the house because of Francesco, not even a grain of rice or a little oil. They aren't brave enough to make a targeted arrest; he's too well known. But they'd gladly do it on the pretext of some small crime like stockpiling. That's how they work."

I realized that my desperation was also coming from the fear that something might happen to Francesco while he was alone in an unknown city. Even though I had heard from him only the day before, I was suddenly convinced that he had been arrested, in Milan or during his journey. I pictured him getting off the train between guards, imagined the pain I would feel hearing the news. I felt it in my throat: a suffocation, a torment. Yet I knew that not even then would I have been able to die to escape it. It would be only more pain to endure. I drew a hand across my forehead to erase the nightmare, or—better yet—my love.

"Come," I said when Fulvia had finished eating. "Let's go to my room and lie on the bed and talk." It was nice in the bedroom.

"Excuse me," she said, "I'm going to take off my clothes. It'll be cooler and I won't wrinkle my dress." She stretched out on the bed in a short black slip that revealed her shapely legs and her breasts swelling under the lace. I went on talking, not really keeping track of what I was saying. I pretended to look in her eyes, but I was looking instead at her rounded, white breasts. *A woman's breasts are so lovely!* I thought.

"Why don't you get undressed, too?" she invited. "It's a relief."

I hesitated. I was tidying the room and I couldn't decide to take off my dress, because I was ashamed of how skinny I was. I resolved to go on a cure to increase the size of my breasts.

"You're so pretty!" she exclaimed when I had undressed. "You're like a reed," she added in a slightly ironic tone. "I've never seen a reed. It's a word you see written, but it suits you. I like the sound of it. Reed. A word half woman and half man. What is it, anyway—a reed?"

"It's a plant that grows near the water," I explained with a smile. "Or at least I think so. A very pliable plant."

"Ah!" she said, already distracted. "Come here. Lie down and rest. When two women are alone together, they always end up lying on the bed chatting. Remember your mother and mine?"

"Yes," I answered wistfully.

"They always talked about Hervey. I grew up with such a strong desire to know him . . . But maybe it's better like that. Do you know, whenever Dario hurts me, I always think of Hervey to get even. But if I'd known him I would have found him just like other men."

"I don't think so," I observed, a harsh reprimand in my tone.

"Yes. Yes, maybe worse. In fact I'll admit that once, last year—I never told you—I heard some talk about the Pierces. I was with a group of people who often go to concerts. They were talking about his mother and about him, too. You know what they said about Hervey?"

"About Hervey?" I repeated, pale. "Tell me."

"They were saying that he's crazy, a maniac, that he suffers from obsessions. Actually, I seemed to understand—"

"What?"

"I don't know. Maybe it's only my impression, but anyway . . ."

She fell silent, tongue-tied, and she looked at me, hoping I'd guess what she wanted to say.

"Tell me," I begged. "Go on."

"So they were saying that he's not normal. No . . . how can I put this? That he doesn't like women."

"Nonsense!" I exclaimed. "How is that possible?"

"Of course," she admitted right away. "It's not possible."

We remained silent, smoking. *There's never anything about him that hurts me*, my mother would say. *I talk and he answers as if I myself were answering*. It was hot; despite the closed shutters, the air was turning muggy and unbearable. I was quite sleepy, and only my wish to keep talking about those things kept me awake. It was unbelievable that a man never made the wrong move or said the wrong thing.

"Or maybe . . ." I whispered, considering a bleak theory, not daring to turn my eyes to meet Fulvia's.

"Right," she replied.

We fell silent. A sweet melancholy spread through us, along with a need to be comforted. Meanwhile, we smoked and resorted to casual conversation to relieve the weight of our silence.

"Here's the ashtray."

"Thanks."

"Sorry."

"Don't tell Francesco, if he talks about—" I begged her.

"Oh, come on! You see I hadn't even told you. I didn't remember it myself. I don't know now how—"

"Well, yes, of course . . ."

"Maybe because we were talking about your mother, about when we were girls. Whenever I look back on that time, I want to return to it. Why did we become adults, get involved with men, all those things?" She smiled and added, "I don't think I've ever told you that I was in love with you when I was a child."

"With me?" I repeated, confused. My heart was beating wildly.

"Yes. That's why I treated you badly. Then I'd start to cry."

"Oh," I said with a quick, hesitant laugh.

"I liked your name, your elegant ways, your dress buttoned all the way to the neck . . . everything that made you so different from me. So I acted rude and outrageous in order to offend you. I ignored you and went for walks with Aida and Maddalena to make you jealous, to hurt you."

"Certainly I was jealous," I replied in a faint voice. I was staring ahead into empty space. But in my memory I was contemplating Fulvia's face as a child, as well as her loose, black hair on Francesco's pillow, her beautiful soft body, the sweet incline of her breasts. *Oh, I thought, a woman is such a wonderful thing. Why doesn't anyone know how to see her or love her completely?*

"When it comes down to it," she said playfully, "it's too bad we're both women. We could have got married. Would you have married me?"

"Of course," I answered. "I'd have taken you to Venice for our honeymoon."

She laughed softly, and so did I. But an awkward emotion wafted around us. It seemed to me that this hadn't happened by chance. A clear-eyed strength was born in me, along with the fiendish determination to keep Fulvia in that room and never let her leave. We would stay locked in the house, surrounded by the order and disorder of women as by a precious ring. Thoughts and desires appeared to run freely between her and me, with easy understanding. I wanted her to remove her slip and show me her breasts. *We're both women*, I'd say, *there's nothing wrong with it, is there?* She had mother-of-pearl skin. Silently, I took up a bitter argument with Francesco. I wanted to show him that I understood the religious attention owed to a woman; I would know what words to say, what fairy tales to invent. I felt consumed by angry resentment when I remembered that he never uttered my name during the moments that should have been our sweetest but were bitter instead, and cruel.

"Yes, it would have been lovely to get married. But just as we are: two women. Ah!" I let out a sigh of regret, giving vent to all my frustration at not being supported or understood.

Fulvia took my hand to console me. She so wanted me to feel at peace that *surely*, I dared to think, *if I asked her to do something for me—show me her breasts—she would do it.*

I lingered for a moment, squeezing her soft, plump hand: a refuge for my strong hand.

The doorbell rang and I jumped as if caught in the act. I decided not to answer.

"I'm not answering," I said. The bell rang again, insistently. "Wait!" and I leaped up from the bed. "It might be a telegram from Francesco."

I put on my dressing gown and came back carrying a silk dress. "It looks like it came out well at the dyer. What do you think?"

"Yes," she said, sitting up on the bed. "Looks like it."

"She was fair," I said. "Eighty lire." I looked for the money in my purse and went back to the door.

When I came back to the room, Fulvia was standing, buttoning her blouse. There was an awkward moment, and she seemed to be in a bad mood. So I went up to her. "Come back tonight," I whispered. "I never go to the cinema. Let's go together and then you can come and sleep here. We'll be alone. It's cool in the evening—this window looks onto the terrace. It's lovely; you can smell the jasmine."

She looked at me uncertainly. I took her wrist between my fingers. "Come. Did you hear me?"

"Yes," she replied quietly, and we said no more.

I WAS RIGHT on time, but Fulvia wasn't there. The men watched me walking outside the cinema, waiting, alone, the street lamps casting white light over me. I was annoyed, worried that Fulvia would back out of our agreement. When she finally arrived, she wanted to apologize for being late, but I didn't let her, since the last feature was about to start.

I had bought the most expensive tickets: Fulvia seemed unsurprised and behaved as if we were meeting for the first time. We didn't talk about Francesco or Dario—we were like two new acquaintances who don't yet have much to talk about. She avoided looking at me and yet, feeling my gaze so often seeking her in the dark, she checked her posture, keeping her shoulders straight and elegant, and smoothed her hair. I was tense with fear that something might stop us from going home together: I even worried that she had forgotten my invitation. So I said, "If the sirens sound tonight, there's a safe shelter at my house." Fulvia didn't answer, and I felt reassured: she would come.

We exchanged views on the movie, which was completely uninteresting to us and not very good. Our comments were rather silly, and I realized that we were trying to recapture our childhood intimacy. We went back to the same language and, most of all, regained the impression we had then of doing something wrong whenever we were left by ourselves. We would go to the movies with Sista and, in the dark, while the film was dealing openly with problems we hardly dared to mention, we felt that we were other people. To hide her embarrassment, Fulvia always made comments out loud. She once burst out laughing while the actors were kissing for a long time. I had come to understand the key to her former coarseness, and to the sudden indifference that now shielded her.

"Fulvia, here, I bought you some chocolates."

The theater wasn't far from my house. I pointed out the street as if she didn't know it. It was a moonlit evening and the new neighborhood was white; it felt as though we were in an unknown city in Algeria or Morocco.

"It's lovely here," Fulvia said. I made some enthusiastic reply so she wouldn't hear the passersby talking about how inviting that clear, bright sky was to airplanes.

We groped our way up the dark stairs, and I led Fulvia by the hand. The sudden darkness made her hesitate, and her steps became heavy with resistance. Galvanized, I had to pull her somewhat so she would follow me. This, too, was a winding staircase: interminable, enveloping, unreal. Our breath was echoing and my hand trembling as I slowly opened the door. "Shhhh!" I said.

I continued to lead Fulvia through the dark house. The moon came through the open windows like icy water, and the room was fragrant with jasmine. I felt the scent leading me to Francesco. I drove away the reminder.

"Look!" I said to Fulvia. "Look how beautiful it is up here."

"Oh . . ." She sounded surprised. From the terrace you could see the new buildings in Parioli, the lonely, flat, mournful countryside: the river, running low between its banks, was a strip of shadow. But the big buildings, the broad plain, the trees, and the hills—they all got lost in the endless expanse of sky. It appeared, in fact, that only the sky was alive: with moonlight, the imperceptible motion of the clouds, the brightly shining stars. Up there on the ninth-floor balcony, it was as if Fulvia and I were destined to be the first to see that enchanting, treacherous element.

"It's terrifying . . ." she said.

"No," I encouraged her, "they're not coming. We have to go back to trusting the sky."

I went in and hurriedly chose a nightgown for Fulvia from among my few items of lingerie; I decided to offer her my best, the one I had bought for my wedding. I closed the shutters and, turning around in the dark, I unintentionally bumped against her; she jumped and uttered a hushed cry.

"Wait," I said.

I went to the bathroom and came back in my nightgown. I was decisive in my gestures, but that brusque decisiveness and the sharp tone of my voice gave away the extent of my discomfort. The room was still dark. When I turned on the light I saw Fulvia standing there. She hadn't dared to move an inch, and she was so bewildered that I felt a desire to console her, to talk to her for a long time and welcome her into my sheltering arms.

Instead, without looking at her, I asked abruptly, "Would you prefer to change in the bathroom?"

"No, thanks," she answered modestly. "I'll do it here." She turned and pulled her blouse inside out, saying that she had a lot to do the next morning. At last she let her flowered skirt fall and stood in her slip, which revealed her plump knees, all pink in the heat. Her slip was worn. She guessed what I was thinking and, with a nod to her underwear and mine, she said, "There's a shop in Prati that sells on installment, without points."

She hesitated, with a faint smile, at once fearful and evasive, and then she took off her slip, so she was naked as she unfolded the nightgown.

Her pale body caught the dim light of the lamp, a large milky blur that hurt the eyes. She couldn't undo the ribbon that kept her from getting her head through the neck hole of the nightgown: her whole body was moving, scrambling to cover up. Her legs tightened and her arms flailed nervously in the white silk concealing her head. I could easily look at her body without her eyes forbidding me. It was young beneath her radiant, lily-white skin, but, because she was quite shapely, it somehow seemed tired already—a body stronger and more rounded, yet I recognized it to be like mine in every crevice, and, because of that resemblance, I was overcome with heartrending pity for the suffering inflicted on every woman's body: from the shocking insult of adolescence to the abuse of the wedding night, from the distortion of the belly to the laceration of childbirth and the exhaustion of nursing a child right up to the humiliations of old age, when youth forsakes it. I stared at Fulvia's body with such intense sympathy that I wondered if she noticed, since she was thrashing around in the tight nightgown. I felt that she was about to rip it apart just to escape my scrutiny. At last, with an angry cry she said, "Help me!"

I went over and loosened the ribbon, and she sighed with relief as she stuck her head through the neck hole. She looked around, as if fearing that during those few brief seconds something had changed in the room. Reassured, she turned to the mirror.

We saw each other, both dressed in white, like angels: behind us, the white expanse of the bed. Even though we were very different without lipstick and with our hair done simply, we seemed like two young sisters who share a bedroom and await their future and their dreams together.

I tied the tie at her waist.

"This nightgown is so pretty!" Fulvia exclaimed, holding it out gracefully. And, turning her gaze on her dreamy image in the mirror, she moved beyond the confines of the bedroom to meet someone to whom she would offer herself.

I, too, leaned in towards my lovestruck face as I contemplated my image. Without moving, we penetrated the mirror's polished pane and, barefoot, we went off lightly to meet Hervey.

"Help me," I said to Fulvia as I collapsed onto the bed, sobbing.

"Help me," she responded. *Dario! Francesco!* we said. We slept in each other's arms all night.

SOMETIMES I FELT that only in old age would I find comfort. Then maybe I would be able to reach the lucid calm I aspired to. I intended to age quickly—soon—but it was difficult, since I was very young, and youth carries the urgent need to attribute everything to love. *Maybe*, I said to myself, *a purely spiritual arrangement would be very helpful to me*. And with this hope I thought a lot about Tomaso. I had met him one evening and we had taken a long walk together. As soon as I got home, I told Francesco about our meeting. I didn't tell him, however, that we had talked about my mother the whole time. Tomaso had wanted to know more—every detail. He had even asked if I had a photograph of Hervey. Every time I saw Tomaso, I would linger by the parapet of the terrace on my return, lost in thought. Then I would run impetuously to Francesco and cling to him.

With that embrace, I spoke to him. Silently I confessed, my head buried against his chest. But he couldn't hear my voice then, either. By this time, I was afraid that if he did hear it, he would scold me like a relative: he would ask me not to see Tomaso anymore, not bothering to think about why I was so happy when I did see him. His writing, and the struggle he was involved in with his friends, kept him company—this, too, was a way of speaking, of expressing himself. It wasn't fair that I could never speak.

But I wouldn't want this story to make Francesco appear to be different from the person he really was. He was good, and, more than that, he was the most intelligent man I had ever met. But I was a girl like so many others, and that's why I'm going on about myself: to make myself known. Everyone knows who Francesco was.

I liked him a lot. He wasn't handsome, as I've said, but he had a natural elegance that in men is expressed as reserve and moderation. I have often observed how everyone at some point appears ugly or unpleasant: but I always liked Francesco. Sometimes when we were at other people's houses we became separated, yet I still felt bound to him by an invisible thread. He held the end of that thread without even looking at me. *I love you*, I would tell him, and it was as if I were choosing him over everyone else all over again. *Do you understand? Turn around, darling. I love you.* But he never heard what I was saying to myself. *He's a hateful man*, I thought, *selfish, cold*, and I felt that invisible thread squeezing my wrists. *Leave me!* I said to him. *I want to breathe.* But despite my resentment I felt indissolubly bound to him. He was my husband, and those unvoiced difficulties and burning disappointments were ours. I gave him the right to be my enemy.

I loved him, and I don't mean to accuse him. I simply want to talk about what he was to me, since everyone is aware of his value as a writer, what he meant to his students, and his friends know what he was like as a friend, his mother how he was as a son. But I am the only one who knows him as a husband. He never imagined that I was the same woman he had once loved and desired, or that I had the same personality and the same needs I'd had then. Francesco was very intelligent, and yet he seemed to think that everything in me had changed solely because I had become his wife. He said to me, "Everything must begin, afterwards." If he had said "Everything must end," I might not have married him, because I knew I wasn't strong enough to give up everything. I had remained the same—and in addition I washed the plates he ate on, shone the shoes he walked in, copied his manuscripts and then hid them in the kitchen cupboard, stood in line. I would have preferred eating bread and oil to washing dishes and standing in line. It isn't true that these things are women's work: women do them when they need to, and, above all, to be helpful and pleasing to men, as they do many other things for men if they love them—even the horrible, cruel things I did. And men believe they are compensating for all that by guaranteeing they will support them. But they rarely do so, in truth: sure, there are women who sleep till noon and when they leave the house go to the hairdresser, the dressmaker, or the theater, while men work day after day to give them leisure and comfort, flashy furs and jewels—and they are content with that. I didn't know any women like that and I never met them because they passed by quickly in their cars. Instead, I knew the women who worked with me, the women who lived in Via Paolo Emilio, those who stood in line in the cold, a baby in their arms, the ones who sat next to me on the tram when I went to the office or to give lessons. Almost all of them did the work of maids at home; but we don't say "I'm supporting you" to a maid because she gives us reliable service in exchange for money and food, a place to sleep. Yet a wife does the same work as a maid and a kept woman; she nurses her babies and looks after them, sews their clothes and mends her husband's, not even earning a maid's salary. Despite this, her husband can tell her, "I'm supporting you."

All of that I did willingly, and often, when I was making the bed, I would put my cheek against Francesco's pillow; when I turned the cuffs on his shirts I felt as if I were holding his wrists between my fingers; and if, standing in line to buy the zucchini he liked so much, I wasn't in time to get any, I felt anger and envy towards those women who could cook zucchini for their husbands. I typed his manuscripts, worried when he didn't come home, encouraged him to work with the comrades, and I dressed for him, styled my hair for him—did everything for him. I would do the lowliest things for him, as I have done, so long as he noticed that I was still the same woman who flew down the stairs at the Borghese Gallery, so long as he would look at me, amazed, as if I were a marvelous creature. Because women do all that and give life to children, too, asking nothing in return except a few words of love.

I put off hope of hearing those words from one Sunday to the next. This might seem ridiculous to someone who has never worked and doesn't know the merciless grind of the hours or the blind rotation of the machinery of the week. I loved Sunday, though; the sun seemed more dazzling and the sky clearer, and I believe they actually were. I never went to church, but I liked hearing all the bells: I liked seeing girls' bold expressions and their new clothes; looking from the window at maids who smoothed their hair with oil and then went out, disoriented and overwhelmed by their freedom.

I waited for Sunday inside me, too: I postponed it from morning till lunchtime. Then, in the afternoon, Francesco worked and I read or did some sewing beside him. *It's barely six*, I would think, *there's still time*. He would look up and say affectionately, "You look tired." It would be eight, eight-thirty; and I would give up and ask, "Are you hungry?"

"Yes, thanks," he would reply, stretching a little.

I'd go to the kitchen. *It's over*, I thought. *Today, too, it's over.* My throat was dry, parched, and stiff; my skin shuddered with tears. But the next day I would forget. If it was raining, I looked forward to the next day of sunshine; if I was working, to a day off; I even reached the point of trusting in the power of something new to wear. *Today*, I would say; *maybe tomorrow*; but it was useless. I didn't feel younger or prettier, and I was only twenty-one. As I walked down the street I felt that I alone among all those women had no eyes, no footsteps, no hands.

ON SUNDAYS FRANCESCO always brought pastries home for me. Our street was a dead end, quite narrow and flanked by the new apartment buildings studded with small balconies where people liked to appear on weekends when the sun was out. The bright white package from the pastry shop stood out sharply against Francesco's dark suit, and it was the first thing the neighbors noticed when he came down the street. They would look out for him, surely thinking that such affectionate thoughtfulness contrasted with the seeming austerity of a professor who should be worried, since his political position was neither welcome nor clear.

"Sandra, I brought you something sweet," he would say.

"Oh, thank you." I said, smiling, "thank you," as if each time were a surprise.

I remembered that when we first got together Francesco and I would go and sit in cafés to talk with greater intimacy and calm. We carefully avoided the secluded cafés so dear to couples because we didn't want our relationship to be confused with theirs in any way; we considered ours to be entirely different from all the others. We became regulars at the cafés frequented by elderly men who spent their entire afternoons there. We often ended up in a café on Via Nazionale, sitting next to a group of government pensioners quietly talking politics; they changed the subject whenever anyone approached.

As soon as we sat down, Francesco and I would start talking in a rush, eager to fit into the little time we had everything we wanted to say to one another. The waiter would approach and we would turn away, annoyed, putting off the tedious obligation of ordering. As soon as the waiter moved off, we smiled again happily, as if we had heroically won our solitude. But he left a plate of pastries on the table: cannoli, *sospiri*, little boats filled with cherries. Their presence was an insult, an affront even, because it gave the impression we were meeting there to satisfy hunger, or because of the pastry shop's reputation.

We often saw a few taciturn couples around us. The man would be reading a newspaper, the woman greedily consuming a cup of gelato topped with candied fruit. When the gelato was finished and the paper read, they would entertain themselves by observing the other regulars, only rarely exchanging a word or a nod. "Husband and wife," we would say, laughing. The husband would check the bill and the wife, too, would look at it with a frown, but I turned my head while Francesco hurried to put a few grimy banknotes on the tray, embarrassed, and we went off arm in arm.

Now, though, a year after our wedding, we rarely went out together. When we happened to do so, it was always for some precise reason. We never went back to Villa Borghese to kiss, or to a café to talk.

"Why do we need to?" he said one day. "We can talk at home now." But at home, instead, Francesco read and wrote, and I cooked, made the bed, ironed; we could never talk. So many times I would have liked to suggest going to a café to talk the way we used to, when I was free of household chores and would show up not even knowing whether he had enough money in his pockets to pay the bill. But now I was afraid that even if we returned to the café we wouldn't have anything to say to one another: he would open a newspaper and perhaps I would envy him that paper.

Finally, the thing we most feared took place. Francesco came home one evening and said that the university had finished its investigation into his affairs. I looked at him, pale, my eyes questioning. After a brief pause he said quietly, "From now on, I can't teach."

We embraced in silence. It was something so serious that we couldn't even find the strength to talk about it in the following days. It was difficult for both of us to sleep at night.

"Good night, sweetheart," he'd say. I would reply, "Good night, my love," and the darkness fell over us, thick and oppressive. I sensed invisible, threatening presences in the dark around us, I'd hear a car stop at the front door, and my heart would start pounding. Francesco lay unmoving; I thought he was asleep. The night was interminable, the alarm clock marking each minute that separated us from the day when Francesco would stop being unhappy. *I'm here, darling: go to sleep*, I said silently, and it seemed as if he were sleeping cocooned in my blood and my limbs. I wanted to hide him, defend him from the invisible eyes watching him, the invisible fingers warning him, the arrogant voice on the radio.

In our vast bed, we didn't touch; and yet it was as if we were holding hands: I felt bound to Francesco by an indestructible solidarity and a fierce desire to defend us. We bore the same name, and it wasn't enough to inhabit the same house: we wanted to share the bed, the sheets, sleep. "Francesco," I whispered, calling him close.

He was awake; he turned. We sought each other out, urged by a sudden desire to test our intimacy. In the sinister night encircling us, we wanted to affirm that our desires and actions were still free. During that period, we often made love with the desperate fury of the poor and oppressed, for whom it is the only means available to demonstrate their power. Each night might be the last we spent together. We might soon hear the knock at the door, and making love was a defiant act of courage. We could see the beautiful June sky and the stars through the open window. At moments like those, we felt neither weak nor humiliated.

THEN CAME THE time when we ate only boiled potatoes. Rumors of Francesco's misfortune circulated and everyone avoided us. Even my mother-in-law saw us only reluctantly, and she disapproved of us, using Signora Spazzavento's words. I knew that all the accusations she made against her son were aimed mainly at me—and she was cheered by the fact that her husband had died before getting caught up in this disgraceful matter. After each harsh utterance, she would sneak a glance at me to be sure that I had got it. She sat in a rigid armchair and we sat in two chairs across from her. She spoke to us sternly: I smiled, instead. I felt that Francesco was no longer her son but my husband. I remembered the first time I had entered that house, when he had sat on the arm of his mother's chair and I on the chair opposite. Now, though, he was sitting beside me and she was alone. Francesco had also lost the small afternoon job with Alberto's relative.

"You understand," the relative had told him. And Francesco had understood. My student's mother, too, had said to me, "You understand," when the news appeared in the papers.

My mother-in-law asked us how we would manage to get by; she expected to get her revenge with the question, which she had deliberately saved for last—hoping, perhaps, that we would ask her for help. I said that we still had my salary and that I was counting on some hours of extra work. Once more, my modest independence aroused obvious dis-appointment in her.

"You see, Signora?" I said. "It's good that women also work and men aren't forced to accept humiliating conditions just to support them."

"So you approve of your husband?" she said, angry at not having found an ally in me. "You approve of him? You encourage him?"

How absurd those words seemed and how dated her house, with its red curtains and black furniture, how pretentious the maid in her apron. I left there for the last time—that much was clear. I would never again hear any mention of Signora Spazzavento. Yet I remembered the night when Francesco had been sick, and I spoke gently.

"Try to understand, Signora," I said. "It's much more than that. I love him."

"She was always a liar," she said later. "A hypocrite and a liar, even while she pretended to be sweet and docile. But I knew that immediately." And she drew a portrait of me in which I honestly don't recognize myself. She went so far as to say that I was envious of her home and her china.

"Oh, that's not true. Why do you say that, Signora?" I wished I could convince her, but I was silenced.

She also said that I didn't love Francesco. She was the only person to say so, and I forgave her since she was surely, after me, the one who suffered most. But I thought back to our feeling of solitude, Francesco's and mine, coming out of her house that evening into Piazza di Ponte Sant'Angelo. It was no longer the sweet solitude of our first meetings: it was an icy emptiness, animated by her voice, condemning us. I wanted to tell him that nothing mattered more to us than our love, but I knew that he would have nodded without conviction. He wasn't happy, and so he wasn't happy with me, either; in fact, the courage I had to have confirmed his unhappiness.

Now and then, he seemed annoyed that it was still possible for me to work. He barely said goodbye when I left to go to the office. He became grumpy and sullen, even saying, "Always potatoes!" We had

received a sack of them from Abruzzo: Nonna was the only person I
didn't mind asking for help. She couldn't believe me grasping or lacking in courage, since she knew I had renounced the farm and couldn't
even get potatoes. The little money we had went on cigarettes, which
Francesco smoked one after another. It wasn't easy to find them; a
colleague gave me his ration and the office porter sold them, but he
didn't want to sell them to me because he didn't agree with Francesco's
politics. He had hung a large map behind his desk, and during the first
months of the war the little flags advanced enthusiastically. He smiled
and was jovial, and boasted about having a son in the army. But little
by little those flags disappeared, and on the map behind him we saw
Eritrea lost, Libya lost. Since Francesco had been banished from the
university, the porter, Salvetti, had begun scowling at me as if the flags'
retreat were my fault. Despite that, I showed up every day, knowing
that he would be able to provide me with cigarettes, and he answered
haughtily, "Well, what do you think, that I'm on the black market? Don't
you know my son is a soldier?"

I pressed him. "Please, Salvetti."

Again, he answered no, and cast a knowing glance at the map.

Once, in the office, I felt ill. Everyone huddled around, insisting
that I must have eaten some spoiled food.

"Impossible," I said. "All I had yesterday was potatoes." With some
discomfort I watched my colleagues look at one another, and then someone quietly asked if I was hungry. I said no; I didn't want them feeling
sorry for me. It would have been like siding against Francesco. I said I
often ate meat and beans from Abruzzo: I had honestly never gone hungry. I then saw them looking pityingly at my arms and my flat chest, but
I thought it unfair for them to blame Francesco for my normal thinness.

"I'm just fine," I said aggressively. "We're just fine." A young woman
suggested a collection, and I thanked her but stated that I couldn't
accept it for the precise reason that my husband was out of work for
political reasons. Then some of my colleagues approached and, hands
in their pockets, advised me not to be too proud. We were on the verge

of an unpleasant quarrel, which saddened me because they had been my work friends for a long time. I was speaking to the women, for the most part; but I felt that they were at last expressing the distrust they had always had of me: it created a distance between us.

Only Salvetti asked as I left, "Will you accept a pack of cigarettes from me, Signora Minelli?" He absolutely would not let me pay him: he turned his head and hid his hands like a child. "I like a woman who defends her husband," he said.

I thanked him for the gift, shook his hand, and, as soon as I got home, gave the cigarettes to Francesco, telling him the story.

He let me finish and then he jumped up, insisting that he didn't need handouts. He took the cigarettes and crumpled them up. I started, feeling it was an insult to Salvetti. In the end, he announced that he would see to everything himself: he would sell the rug the next day. It was the first time I had heard him speak in that tone—the way he'd spoken to the bellhop in Florence.

"Where's the rug?" he asked brusquely.

When I didn't answer, he persisted. "Alessandra, I asked you where the rug is."

I had to confess I had already sold it.

"When?"

"Three months ago."

"But why? What are we spending the money on? All we eat is boiled potatoes, thanks to your grandmother's kindness, and I can't even smoke without asking the office porter for charity."

Shocked, I said nothing. I had also sold the pin that Aunt Violante had given me, and pawned the sheets from my trousseau at the Monte di Pietà.

"Let's sell the armchairs," he said.

And I burst out, "No! never, not the armchairs."

"Ah, because they're yours, right? Because you paid for them with your money?"

How distressed Francesco must have been, to say such things. I made a move towards him, to take him in my arms and make him understand why I didn't want to sell the armchairs. But he went on.

"I won't sell your chairs, I'll sell my books. How about that? Am I entitled to sell my own books?"

I suffered, seeing him in such a state, but I left without saying anything. In the kitchen we had only boiled potatoes and a piece of cheese. Francesco was right: it wasn't fair for him to suffer like that, but I had no more resources. I sat next to the sink, as Sista had in our kitchen on Via Paolo Emilio. Sista always said that a man has a right to eat. She bought meat for my father and we ate soup and salad.

"It doesn't matter," my mother had also said. "As long as he has everything he needs." In fact, at the table she would say politely, "No, thank you, Sista, I'm not hungry."

I would have to find a solution; surely I would. I thought about walking to the office, but that wouldn't have helped. I would have to ask Nonna for a sack of flour, even though I wasn't good at making pasta: I would have learned better if I had paid attention. I was afraid it wouldn't be enough, and I despaired. *Oh Francesco, Francesco*, I said silently, the way one says *Oh God, God!* I didn't want him to sell his books. Better the armchairs, just one for now. As it was, I had so little time to sit down. I hurried to his study to tell him.

I found him trying to straighten out one of the twisted cigarettes. He hid it when he saw me come in.

The first bombardment of Rome took place a few days later. Antonio, Aida's brother, was among the dead. Like Francesco, he had been unable to work. Released from internal exile, he had been forced to abandon his work as a typographer and adjust to unloading goods at the San Lorenzo freight yard. He lived nearby with his sister, now married, and they had a view of the cemetery from their window.

"It's sad in the daytime, if you're not used to it," Aida once said. "But at night it's beautiful! You can see all the lights. My baby always claps his hands when he looks out." Antonio was hit in the stomach, and he had held in his guts until they came to take him to hospital, where he realized right away that nothing could be done for him. He said, "I'm sorry." He went on repeating it, and he died that very evening. "I'm sorry." To his companions on the ward, who were encouraging him, to his sister, who was crying, to the priest, who was suggesting that he resign himself to God's will, he had at last explained: "I'm sorry to be dying now, because we're so close . . ." Aida said that everyone there thought he was delirious, but he went on speaking with tremendous effort.

"I've been waiting for ten years: in prison, in internal exile, and I'm leaving now, just when we're nearly there," and he repeated it till the end, even with his dying breath: "I'm sorry . . . I'm sorry . . ."

I was in an old cellar on Via Venti Settembre throughout the bombing. The other women were really frightened, screaming and calling on the Madonna. I was very frightened and I called Francesco. I didn't know where he was, and supposed he must be at Tomaso's house. The most absurd news was circulating: the whole city had been bombed; our neighborhood, and Tomaso's, too, had been destroyed. When I came out of the shelter, I ran to call.

"Tomaso," I said, weeping, "is Francesco there?"

"Yes, he's here with me."

"How is he? Tell me!"

"He's sitting here smoking."

"Oh please, don't joke. Give me Francesco."

"Here he is," and he added jokingly, "Let me reassure you: I'm fine too!"

I apologized, blaming my agitation. He laughed.

Francesco said Tomaso was always joking. He said it that same evening, too. We were on the terrace looking at the red smoke from a fire. He also told me—without stopping to think that this contradicted his previous opinion of him—that Tomaso had been very worried about me while the bombs were falling.

"I was calm, though," he asserted. "There aren't any military targets around your office, and you're always so prepared, so practical and decisive. Tomaso was afraid you'd be out in the streets trying to get back to me."

I smiled faintly.

"Why are you smiling?"

"Because Tomaso knows me well."

"What do you mean?"

"I did leave the office, in fact, to come home, but I was stopped in Via Venti Settembre and forced to go into a doorway."

A couple of days later Tomaso and I went to see the neighborhood that had been bombed. We were in Piazzale del Verano when we caught the odor of dead horses, so penetrating that we had to put our handkerchiefs over our faces, and Tomaso took my arm. A stable had received a direct hit, we were told—the one where the black horses for funeral processions were kept. Those who came to help heard the high, desperate neighing. But they couldn't hear the voices of the men buried alive in the cellars. The horses had whinnied throughout the work of rescuing them, and when at last they were silent, surely the last human cry was also extinguished under the debris.

The neighborhood of San Lorenzo was deserted. Next to the houses, in gashes left by the bombs, mattresses, portraits, and articles of clothing were hanging, and the silence weighed on courtyards suffocated by plaster and dust. The sweet, nauseating odor was everywhere.

"Tomaso, what is that smell?" I asked, pale. And he gripped my arm.

"It's the horses," he whispered.

We met an old man carrying a bucket on his way to fill it at the fountain. "I had just come into the street," he told us, "and the house collapsed behind me." He went on repeating his words. I wanted to ask him about that awful smell, but Tomaso stopped me.

"It's the horses, right?"

The old man nodded and repeated, "I had just come out into the street when the house collapsed behind me."

Two soldiers also said it was the smell of the horses, as did a thin woman wearing men's shoes and wrapped in a black overcoat. "Yes, yes, it's the horses." She turned to Tomaso and said it wasn't the place to bring one's wife.

"Let me stay," I said to Tomaso when he insisted on taking me away. I saw my mother walking ahead of us through the deserted streets; she watched, she looked at the doors, shocked by a death she didn't know. She moved gracefully, with her light, airy step, not getting her feet dirty in the dust. I saw Nonna Editta, too: she was walking slowly and majestically, her face powdered under a big feather hat. And it seemed to me that theirs wasn't a real death like Antonio's: Antonio, who held his guts in with his hands, white with mortar; like the death that might take us; death was everywhere and left the odor of dead horses. "I'm sorry," Antonio had said, "because we're so close." I was still a child when Aida told us that he wasn't happy. Now Aida was married, her baby was entertained by the lights in the cemetery, and I was waiting for Francesco to be happy. Later, we could go back to walking like my mother, like Nonna Editta. "We're nearly there," I said to Tomaso. I was restless, upset. "Not long now, and then we'll be happy."

We went back arm in arm, and I kept my handkerchief to my nose because there were dead horses in every cellar and every street. I quickened my pace. I was afraid, even fearing that the planes would come back now that it was getting dark. I didn't want to say *I'm sorry,* like Antonio; I was yearning to get back to Francesco, to wait with him, to save ourselves now that we were so close.

"Yes," Tomaso said, "but now I won't be happy like you or Francesco . . ."

I stopped. "Why not?" I asked, in amazement.

Tomaso looked at me and I took the white handkerchief away from my face. And so at the same moment, I was smelling the sweet odor of dead horses and hearing his voice as he confessed, "Because I love you."

IN THE NIGHTS that followed, I stayed awake behind the wall of his shoulders. The heat assailed our bed and I would run my hand over my forehead to brush away the hair and banish Tomaso's voice: *I love you*. Francesco would wake up and go to drink on the terrace: barefoot, naked.

"Are you awake?" he would say.

I would ask him, "Is it true, Francesco, that we're nearly there?" and he would reply that it might be only a matter of weeks. We needed that day to come soon, so Francesco could go back to being what he was before: I had been seized by the irrational fear that it wouldn't come in time for me to be happy with him, because of Tomaso's voice. So when he came back to bed I embraced him and said, "I love you." It was hot, and Francesco begged me, "Sorry, can you move over a little . . ." It was because of the heat, but I felt abandoned—or, rather, rejected. I turned over in bed to shake off Tomaso's words, which were tightening around me, winding around my neck like a ribbon—*I love you I love you I love you*—forming an endless spiral. We stayed awake, lying on our backs, in the dark, looking at the window.

By this time we were carrying our boiled potatoes over to the radio, and we ate them sitting on the floor. Francesco ate them willingly, and the next Saturday the flour I had asked Nonna for arrived. On Sunday morning I started making pasta as soon as he went out. I was happy to be alone in the house; my one fear was that the doorman might come up. Seeing Claudio's letters arriving so often, he had asked me considerately if I had a relative in prison. I replied that it was a friend. From then on he had started handing me the letters with an air of understanding, almost secretly.

Once he even said, "It arrived this morning," letting me know that he hadn't thought it opportune to give it to my husband. I told

Francesco about it: he said it was wise to let it go and to foster the idea, since we were afraid of being reported or investigated. I worried that the doorman knew my thoughts and could blackmail me with them, come into the house and ask me harshly, *Where are the professor's papers?* I thought I might have time to run to the bedroom, get the revolver Francesco kept in the nightstand, and shoot. I was afraid I would be forced to shoot, which is why I bolted the door as soon as Francesco went out and started making pasta.

I liked sinking my hands in the soft dough: the pleasure rose from my fingers up my arms to my throat, to the corners of my mouth, the nape of my neck. *I love you*, Tomaso whispered to me, and I tried to take my hands out of the dough, but I was held there. *Leave me, Tomaso, leave me.* My mother circled around me and looked out the window: *What a beautiful Sunday!* I begged her, begged Tomaso: *Leave me. Leave me alone.* My arms ached with the effort. *We're nearly there*, I moaned. *Leave me alone.* I rolled out a wide sheet of dough, smooth and resistant, feeling I had won a challenge.

Francesco couldn't use his key because of the bolt. He knocked insistently, hurriedly. "It's me, Alessandra. Open up, Alessandra." I liked hearing him call me anxiously. He gave me a hug as soon as he came in.

"What's going on?" I asked, following him as he headed for the radio.

"We have to listen all day long."

"But why? What happened?"

He hesitated. "It seems like—Well, someone said we have to listen to music." After a while, I wanted to go back to the kitchen, but he said, "No, come here. Don't go away."

We listened for the entire day, sitting on the floor. We ate cheese and bread; he said he wasn't hungry. Now and again I thought about the rolled-out pasta and said, "Too bad." Even when the radio was broadcasting nothing, we stayed on the floor, I in his arms, lulled by the hum. Oh, it was a hopeless Sunday, a lovely Sunday. We were tired, our bones were broken, our nerves frayed: but we kept listening. When the phone rang, I ran and Francesco said, "Hurry!" Tomaso called to make sure we didn't miss the music program. But that day the arrogant voice seemed to be speaking with growing insistence, an almost furious bravado. I looked questioningly at Francesco.

"Let's wait," he said. "Let's wait some more."

Even Fulvia called to say that she was listening to the music.

"Thanks—we are, too," I replied. We heard that in the apartment next to ours and the one below, they were spending the afternoon listening to the radio. Francesco was hoping to talk to Alberto, but the phone lines were always engaged. Wary voices quickly passed from one receiver to another: "Listen to the music'" Darkness fell, and I began to believe that this Sunday, too, would end without hope.

"Francesco, it's late." I whispered, at a loss.

As he did every evening, he said, "Close the window now." Every evening at that time, while I was closing our window, I saw the women in the building across from us closing theirs, even though the heat was suffocating; we looked at each other for a moment. That evening we looked with greater intensity. I went back to Francesco's side and, putting our ears against the cloth that hid the speaker, we heard muffled knocking, as if telling us to have faith and wait.

But that evening we knew that the comfort of the forbidden station would no longer be enough. Francesco turned the dial and we surrendered willingly to the arrogant voice we had been listening to for years, waiting silently. Our protest expressed itself in that silence, in our patient way of waiting. In the patience of Antonio, who had waited in prison and then while unloading goods at the freight yard, never yielding; in Alberto's fear, Francesco's fear, which they endured, never yielding; in my own great fear, because I loved Francesco, which I endured, never yielding. In the patience with which we always ate boiled potatoes, waiting. In the patience with which my childhood friends left, and Claudio waited silently behind fences; the patience of the entire city, the entire country, which closed the windows every evening because it was afraid, and yet every evening preferred being afraid to forgoing the broadcasts from people who were free. We knew that remaining silent, being afraid, and waiting was the most stubborn form of protest. But a sudden weariness seemed to have manifested itself in us that night: I was pale and worn out, and with the windows closed the heat was becoming oppressive. But Francesco didn't say, "Can you move over?" He took off his jacket and our sweaty arms touched. *We'll wait the whole night long, we'll bring the mattress here, we'll wait lying down, exhausted. We must never get tired of waiting.* We knew that the entire city would stay awake with us, waiting.

All at once there was silence behind the yellow cloth of the speaker. It was a long and frightening silence, longer and more frightening than the one established between us and the names of the prisoners; in that silence, instead of the breath of the sea, we heard the breath of all who were listening, faces barely lit by the lamp. In fact it no longer seemed that we were listening but rather that the radio was listening to us. I jumped to my feet and moved away from it, ready to scream. It was the first time I had been really afraid.

"Francesco—" I took his arm—"we won't open the door if they come, will we? Let's not open it!"

At that moment, a new voice spoke, not arrogant but serious, sad, and sombre. Because I didn't recognize it, it aroused in me at first a fear much greater than the fear I was accustomed to. We knew that the arrogant voice would never speak again. And I should have been happy, if Antonio, who had died only six days before being able to hear this new voice, had repeated over and over, "I'm sorry," and Francesco, upon hearing it, had recognized it as the cherished voice of a friend. But I was alone with that wise, humble voice, and even though I was glad not to be afraid anymore, I burst into tears, humiliated to think that the arrogant voice had truly been the voice of my time and my age.

. . .

FIRST THING NEXT morning, Francesco unpicked the lining of a suit-case where he had hidden copies of the underground newspaper. He folded them and put them in his pocket, then went to meet his friends coming out of prison, as if he were going to meet them at the school gate. I called my office but they replied with a laugh that Mantovani had gone on vacation—they didn't know where—and the office would be closed for several days. So I called Lydia and found her distressed. She said, weeping, that Mantovani had left for health reasons, and she used the same wary tone that we had when we said we had to listen to the music. I understood that he had left because he was afraid, but I had hoped that no one would ever be afraid now.

It had been lovely the evening before. Francesco had held me in his arms while I cried, saying, "Calm down, Sandra, calm down." And with those words he, too, grew calm. Then we went to open the window onto a clear moonlit night. In the silence, instead of the voice of the radio, we heard the voices of the crickets. We looked out, and as I con-templated the night sky I was flooded with a luminous peace. I realized that from the time I was born there had always been something pre-venting me from stopping to listen to the song of the crickets. But that night all the windows were opened, one by one. Across from us was a large white apartment block, and all the people who lived there looked out their windows hopefully, came out onto their balconies to enjoy the starry night and the song of the crickets. And although they knew one another, they didn't greet one another or speak from one windowsill to the next. Over the years they had got used to being silent, so they were content to open the windows and listen to the crickets. For some time, no one had considered the importance of the crickets' voices in summer.

Side by side, Francesco and I looked out in silence and watched the people in the building opposite. I had always liked looking at people's faces and imagining their stories and thoughts. But when I was on the tram I felt sad and uneasy because I saw they were preoccupied, worried, and I knew they were tired of working, and were thinking about all the troubles in their lives: money they didn't have, relatives who were in the army or in prison. I knew they were always waiting for something: the mail, the end of the month, the end of the war. That evening, though, it was a pleasure to see people who seemed calm and serene, as if they had no sad thoughts, only rosy hopes for the future. You saw wives talking quietly to their husbands, and I imagined they felt as if every happy dream were about to be realized that night, everything for which they had waited in vain since childhood. Surely they all thought they would always be happy, the poor couples thought they would become rich, and those who were barren thought they would soon have a child; the weary thought they would be able to rest and the children imagined a world without punishment or exams, while the young girls smiled as if they had just had a proposal of marriage. The ones who had relatives at the front believed that when they woke up the next day those relatives would be at the door smiling, home at last. Surely the ill slept secure in the thought that the next day they would be cured.

And I, too, having endured nights both distressing and melancholy, experienced a sweet night of uncertain hope. It was even sweeter than the nights when, just a few days after meeting Francesco, I had stood at the window looking out at the river; maybe I had been happy like that only as a child, awaiting a gift on the eve of the Befana.

Francesco came to look out, too, and he spoke to me as he hadn't for a long time. When we went in a little later, I went straight to the kitchen to get his manuscripts from on top of the sideboard and put them on his desk.

Oh, that was a turning point. Until then, every step we heard on the stairs had forced us to hide those pages and look around, for fear of forgetting something. Francesco was insecure as he worked, as if he were engaged in some shameful business; and, copying his pages, I had the feeling that I was writing vulgar and obscene words. Yet that evening, in the circle of lamplight, those pages found their honest place, white against the dark wood of the table. Arms around each other, we studied them: Francesco slowly skimmed them and, in doing so, retraced the days we had been through: our anguish, our hunger and fear. Our life, after all.

Nevertheless, starting the next morning we couldn't be together for long because Francesco was constantly busy. I couldn't go with him, since women, he explained, could never take part in those meetings—except for comrade Denise. As it happened, I wasn't eager to go out in the next few days, since there was shouting in the streets, and I didn't like to hear all the people who had been silent for so many years now yelling; even our porter was shouting. Everyone at work treated me deferentially, as if I had grown old overnight, and they showed an ostentatious satisfaction with what had happened. Only Salvetti remained trapped in a bleak melancholy: he rubbed his bald head and said that, from that night on, he hadn't been able to sleep.

"I'd give anything," he said. "The position I've attained, this desk, the house—anything." I would sit and talk to him. I was sorry that he wasn't happy, and, to comfort him, I wanted to confess that I wasn't, either.

I no longer saw Francesco; I often ate by myself. There were many phone calls for him, and when he came home and I told him about all the people looking for him, he had to spend what little free time he had on the phone. At night he was so tired that he fell asleep as soon as he went to bed, not reading and often forgetting to turn off the light on his nightstand. I would get up to turn it off, looking for some time at Francesco's face, the thoughts behind his eyelids. I kissed him softly: he didn't notice. Then, sighing, I would go back to lying behind the wall. I still wouldn't admit that I was suffering. Francesco neglected me because of his work, but it must have been so exciting for him to go back to working and talking openly. He had proof of his students' affection, and his byline often appeared now in the papers. One evening a publisher came to collect the manuscript we had hidden for a year in the kitchen sideboard. When he left, there was a check in place of the manuscript. It wasn't for very much, but it was reasonably significant for us, since we'd always been poor.

"Eat now," Francesco said. "Buy yourself some meat." When he didn't come home, I ate the meat by myself in the kitchen.

Mantovani had returned. He seemed older and less brusque. "Happy, eh?" he asked, for the first time without his usual cordiality.

Everyone was asking the same question. "You must be happy now?" And every day it became more tiresome to answer "Yes." Some hinted at the fact that my husband must now be earning well precisely because of the work he had taken on, which was keeping him away from me. The question offended me, since it allowed people to assume that Francesco had done everything calculatedly, although now he was earning what everyone else had always earned: a modest sum, barely enough for us to eat if we watched our spending. With the publisher's advance, I got my sheets back from Monte di Pietà. But I felt as if I'd stolen them when I went past the doorman with my package, and I blushed when I paid our account at the grocer.

I was always alone. For some time I hadn't even enjoyed Fulvia's friendly complicity. When I went to her house, she immediately tidied the room and put away the stockings on the chairs; I felt it was because of Francesco's new situation.

"Is it true," Lydia asked, "that he's becoming a member of parliament?"

One day when I passed by, the porter on Via Paolo Emilio she humbly asked me to put in a good word for her son with Francesco.

Francesco laughed. "Remember when no one would say hello to us? You know who phoned me this morning? Lascari. Lascari, who was always in a hurry when he bumped into me. He even said, 'Remember me to your wife.'" He confessed that he had treated him coldly.

"Oh no, Francesco. You shouldn't have. He was the one who introduced us."

He laughed, eating hurriedly as he had to leave. So I said, "Francesco, look. We never get a moment to ourselves. We don't talk anymore . . ."

"Excuse me, but what are we doing right now?"

"Well yes, of course. But you know what I'm trying to say. You said that we'd be happy afterwards . . ."

"And aren't you happy now? Would you like to go back to the way it was before?" He wiped his mouth. I liked the way he moved, even the way he wiped his mouth.

"Oh, no, not at all! But I'm always alone . . ."

"Why don't you go out with Fulvia? Go to the movies?"

"To the movies?!" I exclaimed, on the verge of getting angry. "And you think that going to the movies with Fulvia and spending an afternoon with you would be the same?"

"I know. But just to pass the time . . ."

"I don't need to pass the time. I have my job and I've always got things to do in the house . . ."

"You could maybe hire a woman to help for a few hours . . ."

"But that's not what I'm complaining about . . ."

"It sounds to me like that is what you're complaining about, though."

I couldn't make him understand, and he was already looking impatiently at his watch.

We couldn't part like that, and I delayed him. "Please, don't go, just one more minute." I waited up for him, tried to talk to him when he came home. One evening he fell asleep while I was talking.

I was alone, horribly alone, like all people whom others believe to be happy. I read a lot of novels and after each one I was more in love with Francesco, with an even greater yearning to be happy with him. I stopped reading novels and began to study once more.

Francesco said, "Well done, well done," in my father's distracted tone. It wasn't my fault if I didn't enjoy walking and looking in shop windows or going to the movies. When I was melancholy I called Tomaso and he was always ready to comfort me and restore my faith in myself. Tomaso, too, asked if I was happy and I said yes in an obviously unconvincing tone. I felt that he was the only one with whom I could be sincere.

A wall was going up between Fulvia and me. One evening Dario had said to her, "I'm coming up. I have to talk to you seriously." So she had phoned me, exultant, and asked her mother to come home late. She dressed simply, barely putting on lipstick. But the next morning she called me, agitated.

"I'm coming to see you at work. Can you get out for a moment?" We went to a café and she confessed to me that she had actually waited in her old room, expecting him to offer to marry her. "I had spent the whole afternoon in church," she added.

But it turned out to be an evening like all the others.

Afterwards, Dario had lit a cigarette, pulled the sheet up over her, and said, "It's better if we don't see each other as much. I've met a girl I'd like to marry."

Tears ran down Fulvia's face as she recounted the story. The waiter looked at us, curious, and I remembered how bold Fulvia was as a girl, the day she took off her nightgown. She said she had humiliated herself to the point of asking him, "Why don't you marry me?" Dario had told her he couldn't because he already knew everything about her, including the lies she told her mother when she wanted to receive a man at home: he couldn't trust her.

"You might do with me what you did with your mother," he said. His words were so humiliating that I cried with her. Dario condemned her precisely for having given in to him—for loving him. I remembered the sarcastic way my father had described his outings with my mother in the boat during their engagement. He had openly dared to make fun of her uneasiness in front of me.

Fulvia continued. "It was so hard for me to say 'Marry me,' more difficult than it would have been for another woman. It was as if I were trying to persuade him to marry me because of what we've done, not because I love him. Oh," she sighed, "it's so difficult for us to make ourselves understood as women!" He promised that they'd see each other often, though they would have to be careful. He would tell his wife he had to be out on business, and he would come to her.

"Ah, he'd do that to his wife?" I asked her.

And Fulvia replied, "Yes. He smiled and said wives always believe those stories. He told me I could call him at the office to let him know when my mother's going out. I said those weren't the only times I wanted to see him—they didn't matter at all. But it was difficult to talk wearing nothing but a sheet . . ."

Two young men had entered the café, and they eyed us mischievously, with inviting looks.

"Disgusting," Fulvia said resentfully. "Let's go. It's so disgusting." It was August and the sun bit at our backs and our legs, and she was crying behind her dark glasses, but as we passed a shop window she said, "I could use that fabric." I tried to tell her how lonely I was, but she shook her head, saying that I was married to Francesco, so I should be happy.

I insisted. "Try to understand me.'"

"No, I can't understand you."

Another time I said to her, "Maybe it's better this way. Let him eat with someone else, sleep with someone else, and find the time to take you for a walk, to go to bed with you." She was offended, and we didn't see one another for several weeks.

I never loved Fulvia more than in those moments, however. I was with her the way she had been with me on the night before my wedding, when she called Francesco to ask him to take me the gardenias. I had also disapproved of her then. I felt sorry for her, because she knew nothing about men. She had received a man, in the evening, in the room we used to play in. But she had never slept behind the wall, and only by sleeping behind the wall does one get to know men. And this experience separates married women from those who aren't married, women who have had lovers from those who have had husbands.

So I remained really alone. Added to that, it was the month of annual vacation that I was granted by Mantovani's firm. I wanted to refuse it, afraid I'd get lazy, but Mantovani said that he, too, was leaving, and the office would be closed. The truth was that everyone was leaving because they were scared of the bombardments.

I had reluctantly begun studying again, feeling that I was doing something that should have been over at my age, not only because I hadn't finished on time, but because I was no longer interested in a degree. I preferred to read with no order or plan, although only regular, methodical study drew Francesco's attention. I wanted to stay at home with him, he with his books and I with mine, but he was always busy these days, nervous and easily irritated. I once heard him talking on the radio, and when I heard him say, in our rooms, things that had nothing to do with us or our affairs, he seemed to be truly lost. He was always seeing people and pursuing interests that were distant from me. He was locked in his world, finding life and passion in it: everything that had been our world no longer interested him. "Lovely times," he sighed when I mentioned the Villa Borghese or the Janiculum. Everyone told Francesco that our house was really nice, and he smiled, pleased to have a welcoming house and a pretty wife.

"Francesco," I told him, "I'm afraid you're becoming ambitious." He had no sympathy for me just then. I always told him the truth, and maybe that was a mistake; I should have flattered him. When he came home, I would emerge from the shadows in the house, as when my mother had come home. I had so many things to tell him, and I had underlined passages in my books that I hoped we could read together. I asked just an hour for us. Once, before going out, he squeezed my chin and lifted it towards his face. I thought he wanted to kiss me on the mouth; he hadn't for months—forever, it seemed. I waited anxiously for his kiss, as I had the first time. Instead, he said, in the solicitous tone of someone much older, "My dear, wouldn't you like to have a baby?"

He was proposing a child lightly, as if it were a pastime, in the same way he had once suggested that I go to the movies with Fulvia.

For some time now he hadn't drawn near me at night; and yet if I had said yes, perhaps he would have turned towards me that very night in order to give me the opportunity to distract myself later by sewing, knitting, nursing, and playing with a baby. He was a very intelligent man. Everyone knew his name, read his work; but I was an ordinary woman. No one knew anything about me outside my close circle of friends, beyond the street I lived on or had lived on. Yet, of the two of us, it was I alone who realized the significance of giving life to a child.

"No, thank you," I replied with courteous irony. That night, I cried behind his back, conscious of how nice he smelled.

"Sleep, my dear," he suggested. "Sleep. It's really late."

The following day I said, "Listen, Francesco, couldn't you stop working at so many things? We could live very well on your writing and teaching and my job."

"Well, sorry, but why?"

"You always say you're too busy, and that's why we never have time for us, to talk . . ."

He looked at the clock and then sat down. "Come on. Let's talk."

It was mean of him. How could we talk after that? I looked at him, trying to get him to comprehend what I understood a marriage to be. It wasn't easy to express oneself hurriedly in few words. "Sorry," I said. "Thank you, sorry."

I felt calmer when I came to realize that I could speak to him through Tomaso.

I UNDERSTOOD IT fully for the first time on my name day, the twenty-sixth of August. Tomaso called me every day, and we spent a long time talking. For a while now he had been speaking to me openly about his love, and as he talked, I would look at Francesco's portrait. My eyes intense and imploring, I would say, *Listen, please, listen to how Tomaso loves me.* I was on vacation and Tomaso called me in the morning, while I was still in bed. He had a pleasant voice, and besides, because he was in love, he had the unmistakable tone of sincerity. Listening to him was like looking in the mirror to discover that I was very beautiful.

I refused to go out with Tomaso as he asked me to do at first, and then he didn't ask again. When he came to our house, Francesco was always there, and I gave all my attention to my husband alone, forgetting the intimacy of our daily phone calls.

The following morning Tomaso called me earlier than usual. "Is the boss there?" he joked. And when he knew that I was on my own he changed his tone. Distressed, he asked, "Why did you do that? Tell me, Alessandra. You didn't talk to me once yesterday evening. Never looked at me. You're always looking at him."

"Him? Who?"

"Well, yes, him . . . Francesco."

"Oh," I replied coldly, to make him understand that he had to use Francesco's name. "Did I look at him? Maybe. I always look at him. You know very well that I love him."

I liked talking about him even though I knew that Tomaso's friendship with him had never been sincere. Francesco was on a different level: more serious and intelligent. I have always said that he was the best man I knew; I told Tomaso about Francesco's courage, his dignity, the success he was having. And Tomaso, who had never loved him, loved him even less because I belonged to him.

Francesco didn't remember that the twenty-sixth of August was my name day. I myself reminded him at lunch; he was upset. "I'm sorry," he said, and he also said that he had written it on the calendar and then forgotten to look at it. But I smiled serenely. Tomaso had called me and asked shyly, "Isn't today your name day, Alessandra?"

"Yes, thank you. How do you know?" I was amazed. He explained that some months before, he had looked carefully at his calendar. "Oh, thank you!" I said with emotion, just as I later said to Francesco, "It doesn't matter. We have all evening for us. We'll go and sit on the terrace. I bought a gardenia—it smells good." But that was a lie: the plant had arrived that morning shortly after my call from Tomaso.

He replied, "I can't—Tomaso will be coming soon. We have to go to a meeting."

"Make some excuse, darling. You know—it's my name day."

He vacillated and then decided: "No, it's impossible."

Cruelly, I said, "Send Tomaso to the meeting."

He explained. "It's chiefly for Tomaso. It's about a new newspaper, and it's important. We've been talking about it for some time and tonight we have to finalize things. I'm mostly going for Tomaso because he doesn't have a steady job."

But Tomaso still wasn't there by ten o'clock. "Maybe I misunderstood," Francesco said. "Tomaso went straight there." He hugged me as he left, adding, "We'll celebrate it formally tomorrow, dear."

I went back to our room. I was looking with sharp disappointment at the gardenia I had put in my hair and the cushions set out on the terrace when Tomaso rang the bell.

"Is the boss here?" he asked. He was dressed in white and smelled of soap.

"No. He waited till now and just left. If you run, you'll find him at the tram stop."

He took my hand, kissed it, and turned to go. But he stopped. "And you'll be here by yourself?"

"Oh, yes, but that doesn't matter. I'm a little tired, to tell the truth, and besides . . ."

"Alone on your name day?" Tomaso interrupted, coming back in.

I didn't want him to stay. I didn't want him to be better than Francesco. I persisted, telling him that the meeting was really important for him; that it might mean a job. But he said, "And what if I were ill? If I had a high fever? They would wait, no? They can all wait, when it comes to you."

THE NEXT DAY Francesco came home with a purse to celebrate my name day. It was a lovely one made of red cloth and I opened and closed it, admiring it. We compared it with the other purse I had and thought it much prettier. Everyone said it was difficult to find purses then, and I mentioned as an example one that Fulvia had wanted to buy. We hoped that soon, when the war was over, the difficulty of finding purses would also come to an end. He confessed that after all—just between us, he could say it now—he thought he had made a good deal. And I confirmed that yes, he had. I embraced him and he patted me on the back. He then set to work, I thanked him once more, and that was how my name-day celebrations ended.

I went to the bedroom and hurled the purse to the floor. The thud made me jump—it felt as if I'd hit Francesco's face. I knelt to pick it up, dusted it off and put it on the bed. It was truly a lovely red purse, and I wished I could be happy with it. I softened at the thought that he had spent a lot of money on me. It wasn't the first time I had been touched by that thought.

It hurt me that this was the only way he could express his love to me. I wished he knew how to express himself—like Tomaso, for example. And it really upset me to realize that someone else knew how to do something better than he did. *But if you don't succeed* . . . I heard Nonna's voice in my ear at night, in the silence of our marital bedroom, the same heavy silence as in my mother's. It had frightened me ever since I was a child.

Tomaso had stayed for nearly two hours the night before: he had sat in Francesco's armchair, without taking his eyes off me. I had talked to him eagerly, and it was thrilling to be able to tell him, again, the things I couldn't keep telling Francesco since he had heard about them more than once, and he often good-naturedly reminded me of it. Tomaso found them extraordinary. I had also shown him a few old photos I had excitedly taken out of a drawer, rummaging around and messing everything up. I had shown him the photo of my brother and later, he looked at me attentively before he said, "One might have taken you for twins." I blushed, and he asked me what was wrong. I confessed without looking at him that it was always Alessandro who awakened temptation in me.

He was quiet for a moment, and then he said, "I don't want to know Alessandro. I want to know you." As was always the case when we were together, time had a special, very rapid pace, and with regret I saw the moment arriving when I would be alone once more. But it was I who sent him away, brusquely. We stood at the door in silence, some distance from one another. I hesitated to give him my hand; it seemed like a commitment. He had held it in his, kissing it devotedly, and I felt happy and innocent.

Francesco always said that we couldn't be happy yet, because more difficult days were coming, but it seemed to me that his apprehension disguised his indifference to me, and his ambition. Of course, his work was an attempt to improve himself through the improvement of the society we lived in. But at the time it was hard to see it. He was surrounded by a lot of petty, low-minded people, and the cold practicality that was driving him seemed in opposition to the ideals he was fighting for. Whenever I offered to help him, he smiled but refused. Maybe he felt I was less intelligent than Denise, whom he was happy to work with.

One day she came to lunch. She had by then dropped her habit of asking if I was expecting a baby, but she let me serve her as though I were a maid. After lunch I went to the kitchen to wash up while she talked to Francesco. They went out later and Francesco barely said goodbye, he was so taken with her. She was already aging and she looked shapeless in her skirt suit. And yet Francesco seemed to prefer her to me.

I was jealous and I called Tomaso right away. "I want to see you." I was short with him, the way I had wanted to be with Francesco about Denise. I met him in the center, knowing that I wouldn't even have to lie to Francesco since he never asked me where I'd been. We started walking close together, and people looked at us amiably, as they never did when I was alone, or with Francesco. Maybe they were amazed to see us locked away on our lush, tranquil island despite the anxiety of war, the heat and dust. I didn't know where Francesco might be walking just then, beside the heavy, awkward gait of comrade Denise.

We were in a lonely little street near the Pantheon when I suddenly stopped. "Tomaso, who is Casimira?"

He looked at me in surprise, and smiled. I was suffering terribly. "Who is Casimira?" I repeated.

He replied as Francesco had. "A girl."

We began walking again, neither looking at the other. So Casimira existed. "Are you in love with her?"

"Me? No!" he answered quickly. "Absolutely not."

"Were you thinking of marrying her?"

"I wasn't, but she might have been. She was always calling me at the paper in the evening. She's an affectionate girl."

"Do you see her often?"

"No . . . I don't see her now."

I sighed with relief. "A pity," I said. "You should marry her. Francesco told me Casimira is a nice girl . . ."

"Francesco did?" Tomaso was surprised.

"Yes. Why?"

"I don't know. I didn't think he liked her . . ."

"On the contrary. At least I hope! He always says she has my personality . . ."

"Francesco says that?"

"In a manner of speaking."

Tomaso brusquely confessed, "Sorry, but I've never thought Francesco deserved a woman like you."

We were walking slowly, and he spoke about me as if I were someone I didn't know very well. I recognized myself in the affectionate portrait sketched by Tomaso. Why did Francesco say I was like Casimira? Tomaso knew a lot of things about me that I had never told him: the commitment with which I lived, my struggles, my concerns, the path I meant to follow. I was afraid that he also knew the wall I slept behind.

People hurried past the island created by our steps, apparently more preoccupied than usual. Tomaso said he had to go to the newspaper, and then forgot. I thought Francesco might be at home waiting for me. I hoped he would welcome me with a smile and embrace me when I told him about seeing Tomaso. Why couldn't it be like that? I welcomed him happily when he returned from his work, which, though it kept us apart, confirmed his value as a man. I served him when he ate with his comrade Denise, and I had to enjoy his splendid successes—no longer ours but strictly his. Loving me as he did, why couldn't he be happy if I, too, had some acknowledgment of my worth? I wanted to tell him everything Tomaso said.

"It's late," I whispered as the sky grew dark.

"So?" Tomaso replied. People were passing us quickly. A few huddled to talk and then, hearing a radio broadcasting, gathered around a shop. I was frightened when people gathered to listen to the radio; it was always a bad sign. In Abruzzo they were spread out over the countryside, whereas here they lingered in streets still light in the summer; they were at home, at the table, some were working, some were in love. They seemed detached and protected, yet they had to interrupt whatever they were doing and run meekly to hear what the radio was saying. No longer a miraculous invention transmitting music or distress calls from ships, it was an unstoppable power: the course of our lives depended in large part on what the radio said.

"Wait," I said, hoping that at least the two of us would have time to save ourselves. But Tomaso took my arm, like Uncle Rodolfo. We got there in time to hear the final words, and then we stood, pale and quiet, while the soldiers threw their berets in the air, cheering the signing of the armistice.

AT THAT POINT began the long day in which I could never rest. In truth, it seems to me that I didn't sleep for a moment, or eat, or smile, didn't rest until I did so in here.

The news didn't elicit any comment: for years now, though they didn't say so, people understood whether the news from the radio was good or bad. And in those days people forgot a lot, but not their well-established habit of understanding. Everyone began walking again, wrapped up in their thoughts, not hurrying back to their families or locking themselves in the house with them as they had done when they heard war had broken out. They knew, now, that houses were not enough to defend them, nor were their affections, so they walked calmly, showing that they were already used to long, dark days, to hunger and the smell of dead horses.

I walked beside Tomaso: he was only a little older than me, and surely even he did not remember very well what it was like to live calmly, without fear of what the radio said. A small boy went by asking his father, "They'll put on all the streetlights now, won't they? I don't remember what it was like when the streets were lit." And then I, too, turned to Tomaso.

"Tomaso, what's it like when the streets are lit?" He made no reply but took my arm, and I thought about the lighted streets crossed by girls like my mother, who were studying for a diploma in piano, and girls like my grandmother, who were studying to perform Shakespeare. "This is a difficult time, isn't it?" I asked him.

"No," he answered, but he was thinking *yes*.

"Could something happen to Francesco?"

"I don't think so. It's something we've looked into."

I wished I could calm down, but after a pause I asked anxiously, "Tomaso, what's going to happen now?"

We were no longer secluded on our happy island but walking along with all the others on the street, now getting dark. And yet from that evening on we had the impression that no one in the city was unknown to us anymore. We looked at each other with no curiosity or interest, like people in the same family, although we didn't speak to one another, just like family members.

Tomaso took me home without asking my permission. We walked in silence, squeezed onto the crowded bus in silence, among many other silent people; an oppressive and suffocating silence hovered over the city in blackout. Tomaso left me at the door: I didn't ask myself what Francesco would have thought about seeing us together. We separated in silence. But I had only climbed a few steps when I heard Tomaso running after me, panting. His white suit looked ashen in the light of a bluish bulb, and once more I see the intense passion in his eyes when I stopped and he caught up with me.

"Listen, Alessandra," he said. "I have to confess something to you. I'm going to do everything I can to take you away from Francesco. Sorry. I wanted to tell you the truth tonight. Do you understand?"

I looked at him and didn't even have the strength to respond, react, or protest. *Yes*, I nodded. I was already moving up the stairs, but he took my hand and he kissed it. As I heard his steps moving away I felt calm, resigned to the voice on the radio and also to his.

Francesco came home very late and immediately said, "Didn't I tell you that we couldn't be happy yet?" I wanted to tell him that ours was an age in which one had to adapt to being happy for only a few hours, an afternoon, a night: as soon as one could. Tomaso had been able to spend a happy afternoon with me before the radio spoke. But as I looked at Francesco, I understood that it was only with him that I could truly be happy: he belonged to my life, and my suffering for him belonged to me, too, like the long day that was just beginning, and which I couldn't refuse to live through. Francesco repeated, "What did I tell you?" and his voice held a reproach, even though my only fault was having tried to be happy together, whatever the cost.

We went out onto the terrace to sound out the night, the air, the wind; they were stronger than we were. My mother had taught me to befriend the trees, the sky, even the rain, which leaves behind the rainbow. Everything about that time was over, yet it remained in me like the faded memory of a fairy tale.

It was a menacing, sleepless night; the sky, swollen with clouds, pulsed with distant rumbling as if threatening a thunderstorm. I clung to Francesco, hiding my head in the hollow of his shoulder. I felt that this was our last night: both of us knew that the long day was about to begin, in which men and women would not be able to lie together in bed, speak to one another, love one another. The wind that rose lasted for three days, and seemed to accompany every difficult hour of my life, as my mood often kept pace with nature's. A warm wind swept the terrace. Francesco looked south, apparently listening, as when, beside the radio, we expected to hear knocking on the walls of our prison.

"They won't get here in time," he said. I, too, felt they wouldn't make it in time, and it was good that it was like that, that we found help in ourselves alone. That's how I knew that I wouldn't accept Tomaso's help, even if to get through difficult moments I'd think of him, just as we had supported ourselves for years by listening to the knocking on the radio.

We were alone again, Francesco and I; no one could help us, and this, our sentence, was also our desperate strength. Oh, I will never forget the bare terrace, the white sky and the two of us, also white in that light, amid the white houses with their windows closed and the high, deserted terraces. From up there you could see the whole city, alone in the desolate bleakness of its surrounding countryside: defenseless on the eve of the long day, as were the two of us. And I felt it was necessary to speak just then, to break the reserve that had constrained us to that point, because it was necessary for two companions to speak on a night like that to renew their feelings, their instincts and memories, the only things we could count on, as the city counted on all of us, on our houses, on the weapons hidden in cellars, and on a tradition that somehow had to be respected. I waited all night. At dawn, a comrade called to relay news of a landing being attempted to bring us help. It wasn't true. I knew there was no help. I heard again what Tomaso had said on the stairs, and the distant rumbles announcing a storm. We had to gather our strength, and not ignore the fact that the two of us were in danger; it wasn't just the city. He talked with his comrades: they called each other, suggested where they could find help and weapons, and I sat on a stool next to the telephone, waiting in my dressing gown. I wanted to help, too.

"Speak to me," I said to Francesco, following him as he prepared to leave.

"Dearest, does this seem like the right time?" he replied, caressing my forehead. And yet it was necessary to speak at those times; all day long, the churches were packed with people praying in order to reassure themselves that something remained, something was certain, even if the rumbling was coming closer and closer, and we knew now that it wasn't a storm.

Francesco picked up the pistol, pocketing it as he headed for the door. But he turned back. "No, I'd better leave it with you. You never know. Hide it somewhere within reach. Are you afraid?"

"I don't think so. How does it work?"

"It's all ready—all you have to do is press here."

It was terrible to hold a cold, heavy pistol in my hands.

Seeing me grow pale, Francesco asked again, "Are you afraid?"

"No. It's just that I don't want to be forced to shoot."

"Of course. You won't need to, but sometimes you have to defend yourself."

"Where are you going, Francesco?"

"To Alberto's for now. We'll see after that."

"Don't leave me like this!" I said on the stairs. We embraced: as he hugged me, he was already distant, already speaking with friends. I went back in, and shortly afterwards Tomaso called; he didn't believe, either, that they would make it in time to help us.

"I want to see you," he begged, "even if only for a few minutes."

I said no, I was staying at home to wait for Francesco. I had the pistol in my hand: I put it in the drawer of the nightstand and then

HER SIDE OF THE STORY

spent the morning on the phone responding to friends who were looking for Francesco. Tomaso called again later and told me there was
fighting outside the city.

"Where's Francesco?" I asked anxiously.

"I don't know," he replied. "I have to go now. I'm leaving with the
others. Listen: I want to tell you that I love you."

I needed to reach Francesco somehow, to prevent him from going
with Tomaso. I went out, but the porter detained me.

"Signora," he asked, "what does the professor say?"

I looked at him for a moment, already feeling hatred rising in me,
an old hatred I'd got out of the habit of feeling. But behind him were his
wife and his daughter holding her little brother. They were all looking
at me with anguished faces.

"Will they make it in time?" the porter insisted.

"No. I don't think so."

The woman looked at the string bag over my shoulder. "The shops
are closed, but I can give you a little of my bread."

Many things had changed overnight. People who didn't know one
another spoke in the streets. I looked everywhere for Francesco: I
looked for him in the trucks going by crammed with sad, tattered soldiers, among the lost men sitting at tram stops in civilian clothes, still
carrying their cartridge cases. There was no transportation, there
were no cars. Shaken, I kept going on foot. I walked alongside small
groups of pale women for part of the way, walking and walking, and
also trying to reach some man they identified only by his first name.

The wind was still blowing, muggy and oppressive. Fifty or sixty
people were gathered in two rooms at Alberto's listening to the radio.
Young boys arrived on bicycles carrying messages written in pencil.
Then comrade Denise arrived; she, too, carried a message, and she
looked me over with some irritation.

"Go home, Signora," she said. "Your husband would not be happy
to find you here."

She knew him very well. In fact, when Francesco arrived, he wasn't happy to see me there; his look told me so, and the optimism sustaining the comrades was destroyed by his severe aspect. The one o'clock broadcast hadn't mentioned any fighting.

"We've been abandoned," Francesco said. "Every one of us is alone with his comrades."

I was alone, too, since when he spoke he didn't address me. Once again, I looked at him and I chose him, even though he wasn't looking at me. There were a lot of other men there, some his age, others elderly; only a few were younger. They were serious, gathered in groups, and yet it seemed to me that even at those moments men found it very difficult to communicate with each other: they were held back by an innate reluctance and the shame of appearing weak. Their faces revealed the effort they were making in order to accept suffering; an effort unnecessary for women, who are so familiar with it. They were weaker than we were, even though they held rifles and said serious, uncompromising things, to which I now knew it was almost impossible to be faithful.

A message came from Tomaso, who was in an outlying neighborhood where there was fighting. At the end, he recommended, "Call Signora Minelli and tell her that her husband has gone back to the city, and she should stay calm."

Everyone looked at me, and I blushed. Then Francesco came over and advised me to go home and get food in view of the difficulties that would come the next day. I saw some women pushing carts along the street with their children in them and some of their furniture. They said they were coming from neighborhoods where there was fighting, and they went on pushing their carts, neither crying nor complaining, knowing that it had begun, the long day on which there was only suffering.

From that night on, we had to be home early because of the curfew. The siren would sound and we would go down into the shelters. During the day, I lined up at the baker's, and trucks passed along the streets continually, packed with Germans; they looked at us, weighing us up like animals. I never saw Francesco before evening; sometimes he didn't even call me. Tomaso, though, called often and gave me news, using an agreed code, because once more we were afraid of that arrogant voice. When we started hearing it again, we got shivers down our spines, but by now we knew it wasn't an inevitable part of our lives, as we had believed for so many years.

My father wrote inviting us to stay for a while in Abruzzo. I told Francesco about it, suggesting that we accept. Tomaso turned pale when he found out about this possibility.

"Don't go away!" he said. But then, reprimanding himself for his selfishness, he added, "I wouldn't be able to go on if you weren't here."

Francesco said, "Yes, you should go. But you, by yourself. I've thought seriously about this and I've decided to send you to your father." He was talking about me as if I were a baby, or a piece of furniture. I understood from the conversation that there was something to worry about.

"And you?" I asked.

"I'll have to leave this house tonight or tomorrow. It's not safe for me to stay here."

"So why don't we go to Abruzzo together?"

He paused before replying. "No. I've thought a lot about this, and I was tempted: I'm so tired. But it's not possible. I need to stay with my friends now that we've started to work. I don't think it'll end quickly. There may be two months left. I'll go to Tullio's brother's house tonight."

"And then?"

"And then I'll move, if necessary. But I want to feel calm about you, to know that you're safe, that you're sleeping well, eating—"

"Ah, right. . . ." He had failed to notice that none of that had ever meant much to me; now it meant almost nothing. "So then, if something should happen to you, I might survive, naturally."

"Nothing is going to happen to me."

"But if it should . . ."

"Of course, I'd feel calmer knowing you were safe."

I stopped talking, and then said bitterly, "It's something that's always made me think."

"What is?"

"This concern men have to save women from two things alone: hunger and death, two things women fear, as most of you do. But you never actually think about saving them from all the other things that are much more terrifying, whether around them or inside them. I don't want to be kept safe." I begged him again. "Francesco, let me work with you." I was sitting at the foot of the bed, and he was stretched out, his head sunk into the pillow; from there, he lifted his cold gaze towards me.

"No," he said after a moment. "It's better for you to go to Abruzzo."

I was irate. "You're afraid I'll talk, right? that I'm not cold-blooded enough, that I'm a woman like Casimira, right?"

"No, that's not it."

"Yes, you value the least of your friends over me, because I'm a woman."

"Calm down, please, Alessandra . . ."

"That's not possible. This is a momentous day. If you don't want to come with me to Abruzzo, let me follow you. You've done everything you wanted till now, but now I'm afraid. I'm afraid that everything is ending—do you understand? And the only thing that's important is you and me."

He tried to convince me. He said some things I knew to be fair but didn't want to believe because I loved him. If he had also talked about us, about our love, maybe I would have understood. But he didn't.

"And all of that is more important than us?" I asked when he finished.

"It's more important than anything, yes," he replied. "You always say that we mustn't betray our plans, right?" I did say that, but he had a way of repeating my words that made me blush at having said them. "And this is just the moment when we shouldn't betray them, do you understand?"

"No," I said coldly, "I don't understand."

Soon afterwards Tullio and his brother came to tell him that it was best to leave immediately. He left them waiting in the study and came back to the bedroom to announce that he would leave before the curfew. It was over; he was going. There was less than an hour before the curfew. But maybe in an hour we had time to talk.

"I'm not leaving," I told him. "I want to stay here, close to you, so I can hear news about you. Do you understand?"

"No," he was the one to say it this time, "but you're free to do what you want."

"I love you . . ." I said, lost, and abandoning the fight. We still had half an hour. We could still save everything. I got out a suitcase, put it on the bed and started to fill it. "Which suit?"

"The one I have on."

"Only one? That's not smart."

"Right. The oldest one then."

Shirts, socks; I was still hoping he'd say, *No, Alessandra, I just can't leave.* I was certain he would say something before I finished packing.

"Anything else?" I asked.

"No, thanks."

I was waiting for him to say, *Your picture, the one on the night-stand.* Maybe he would say, *You come, too!* before I locked the suitcase. We still had a few minutes, but Tullio was hurrying him. The lock clicked. At least he would say, *Forgive me, I can't help doing this, but I'm desperate about leaving you and I love you, I love you!*

Instead, all he said was: "Stay calm. I'll send news." And going on about these details, he made for the corridor. He embraced me in Tullio's presence and I, too, acted nonchalant.

When he had gone down the first flight, I called him back. "Francesco!"

"What is it?" he asked, stopping. Tullio and his brother also looked up.

"If you need anything, let me know." And I ran to the terrace to see him. Three men moved off, talking as they went. The tall one dressed in gray was Francesco.

A FEW DAYS later, Tullio brought me a note from Francesco. He stood there, watching me as I read it.

"It's all right," I said. In his note, Francesco suggested that I reply to anyone who asked that we had separated and that I didn't know where he was; that I supposed he had moved north.

"That note must be burned immediately," Tullio said. He was about forty, a bachelor, blond and severe. He gave me an icy look from behind his glasses, and I sensed he was hostile to me and the weakness I represented for Francesco.

"Please." He asked me to give back the note so he could burn it. "Francesco would also like to have all his things," he added. "Don't forget anything, Signora—from the bathroom, the wardrobe. Put everything in a suitcase. I'll wait."

He rummaged through the desk and took all the papers. He was calm, precise, relentless. I wrote a few reassuring words to Francesco, so I could cling, more than anything, to what he had written. But when Tullio left with the suitcase his goodbye was cold and respectful, as if I were no longer the wife of his comrade Francesco.

It was dangerous to embark on that game: we had all assumed new identities and we had to convince ourselves that those were the only real ones. Tullio was no longer an archaeologist; his identity card described him as a timber dealer. I was a woman separated from her husband. Sometimes I regretted having accepted that, as if I had fallen into a trap. I went so far as to think that Francesco was using this as an underhanded way of leaving me. It was very difficult to remain attached to everything that had happened before the long day. We wore the memory of our past as we would a scapular. There were times when even Francesco's face became confused in my memory. He didn't like being photographed, so all I had was a small snapshot of him taken at a university conference. He was wearing a hat and coat and he looked serious, not like the person who came with me to Villa Borghese. Yet it seemed to me that the photo had captured his true appearance. I always imagined him like that, with Tullio and the others: dark and severe, coat and hat on. The features of his face and the sound of his voice were getting lost, just as my mother's had been.

Tomaso's face was more familiar to me. In fact it had become the only familiar one in my life. I had to try hard to forget it, and sometimes I myself recalled it to ease my loneliness. Loyally, he kept track of my life, which was now unknown to Francesco. He, too, moved constantly, but he called me anyway several times every day. He would announce himself by saying, "It's me!" I began to wait anxiously for his calls. During our conversations I resented the judgment of the telephone censor, but later I reassured myself with the thought that I was pretending to be a single woman separated from her husband, and that would serve to confirm it.

The empty house and the sight of Francesco's clothes and books had initially filled me with an excruciating sense of yearning. I paced the rooms, calling him, and spent my evenings in the armchair so that I could feel his arms around me. For that reason, I felt a sharp relief when his clothes disappeared. I went to work, came home, ate the pitiful food women eat on their own. I thought I would numbly fill the hours between then and Francesco's return. But the truth is that all day I was waiting for Tomaso to call.

I could think of nothing else: I felt that I was constantly struggling against the feelings I was starting to have for him. I recalled his clear, open face, the way his eyes crinkled when he smiled. I often thought about nineteenth-century novels in which the strong, courageous female characters struggle to banish their guilty emotions and return to their wise and lawful love. But, remembering the books I had read, I noted that such struggles were always contrived and useless. Every attack served to move the heroine toward her beloved adversary, and the struggle exhausted her, bringing her closer to surrender. The inevitability of that end terrified me.

So I mustered all my forces and decided not to see him anymore. For several hours, I felt confident, determined, and genuinely glad about my decision. Then I thought how impossible it would be to disappear: he would call, then come and find me at home. I would have to give him some explanation, after all, and see him once more to get him to understand the feelings that bound me to Francesco. I thought that I would do well to call him the next day to arrange to meet. Perhaps even that evening. Or maybe immediately. Better immediately: that way I would feel calmer afterwards, and everything would be definitive, finished.

"Hello, it's me, Alessandra." I enjoyed introducing myself to him, politely, for the last time. "Aren't you afraid?" I asked.

"Very, but it seems they're not looking for me. They're looking for the people who matter— Francesco, for example, Alberto, or Tullio. If they arrested me, someone else could easily take my place. Not everyone can take Alberto's or Francesco's place."

All the while, he was gradually trying to take Francesco's place with me, and it was precisely his persistent devotion that dismayed me. He treated me as if I were a girl; he asked, please, if he could kiss my hand or take my arm. I worried about the happy innocence of our meetings, my certainty that I was doing nothing wrong.

Before long, I didn't even have my work to distract me. Mantovani had taken on a lot of important jobs that obliged him to move north. He had gone back to being decisive and abrupt. He put a radio next to the desk and he would turn it on every so often, if only for a moment, to reassure himself that the arrogant voice was still speaking.

"You'll come north, won't you, Signora Minelli?" he asked one morning.

There was a smooth space between us on the table, his leather brief-case, the beautiful writing materials I had wanted since I was a girl. By now, when we had the table between us, despite the generous kindness of my boss, or maybe even because of it, I felt that he was rich and I was poor; he very strong, and I extremely weak. That day, however, even though he had regained his confidence and Francesco had been forced to flee, I felt myself to be much stronger than he because I had always been poor, and without his help I would surely have gone to my grave, like his mother, never having had an armchair. But I wondered what he would do without that lovely table, the telephones, and Salvetti's bow when he opened the door. Above all, without the arrogant voice on the radio, which reassured him. Francesco and I were used to a life of uncertainty.

"Thank you," I said. "Trust me: I'm truly sorry not to be able to continue working with you, but I have to stay here."

"Because of your husband?"

"No," I said after a pause. "I've already told you that we're sepa-rated. It's because I'm afraid of losing the house."

"Right, I understand," he replied. It was easy to understand each other, even if we resorted to conventional language; that way we didn't feel we were lying. Lydia announced that she would be doing a lot of travelling between Rome and Milan. I went with Fulvia to the town hall, where we read all the notices to find out when Dario was getting married.

IT WAS TOMASO who told me to go to Francesco the next day at lunchtime.

"What happened?" I asked, dismayed.

"Nothing. He wants to see you."

I realized that Tomaso was jealous. Perhaps he wondered whether his love was stronger than Francesco's rights to me. But I wanted him to understand that it wasn't about rights; I was happy to go to Francesco because I loved him. I went up to Tomaso to tell him, to try to comfort him—which is how we happened to embrace for the first time. I hadn't been hugged like that for years, and I was surprised to feel pleasure in arms that were not Francesco's. I realized that until now I had confused Francesco and Tomaso, but I couldn't continue to do that. I had a specific feeling of intimacy with a man who wasn't my husband, and so I felt betrayal, and guilt.

"Go away, please," I said. All the same, the memory of that embrace stayed with me even while I was talking to Francesco.

I had taken the long way around for fear of being followed. Tullio's brother, Luigi, had a wife and four children. Francesco was pretending to be Luigi's brother-in-law, part of the family. They lived on the fourth floor of a house on the Aventine hill, and you had to climb a wide, sun-drenched staircase. Luigi's wife came to open the door. I didn't say anything, and she looked at me, weighing me up, and then smiled.

"Come in and sit down."

Francesco was sitting in the dining-room listening to the radio with a baby on his knee. When I appeared in the doorway, he turned and put the baby on the floor so he could embrace me. The baby started to cry, and the older children looked at us. His embrace was different from Tomaso's. Luigi's wife gazed at us, touched, and smiling: she was plump, and had a friendly face.

I wanted to be alone with Francesco but she showed no signs of leaving us. Maybe she thought that the things that a husband and wife say to each other can be heard by anyone. In fact, we said, "What are you doing? How are you feeling? Are you eating?" I wanted to take Francesco's hands, I wanted to cling to him, to rediscover his way of holding me, the scent of his neck. But instead I sat at the table, which was already set, among those strangers Francesco had made friends with. There they told me about things that had happened, still trembling with fears I hadn't shared. They showed me a small door hidden behind a bookcase, leading up to the attic. Meetings and conferences took place in that attic room, and Francesco and the others could hide there in case of danger. I felt like a stranger.

After lunch Francesco said, "Come and see my room." It was the oldest son's room. He was twelve years old, and the walls were covered with pictures of famous soccer stars; on the shelves were adventure books and tin soldiers. I was sorry he was sleeping in that room; I wanted to go back to sleeping behind his back, whatever the cost. Through the glass door you could hear the children playing.

"Come home, Francesco. I'm sorry—I know it's impossible, but I can't be without you any longer." We stayed in each other's arms, and I loved him with all the strength with which I defended myself against Tomaso.

He said to me, "Take off your jacket. Aren't you warm?" And then he went to the door and turned the key. A child came and tapped on the glass with two fingers. I thought about Luigi's wife, who could surely imagine why a husband wanted to be alone with his wife after two months.

"Fix your hair," Francesco said a few moments later, straightening his tie in front of the mirror. You could still hear the children's voices— one calling its mother, whining. There was a silhouette of Snow White stuck to the mirror. While I combed my hair, Francesco came closer to speak to me; his presence brought me such profound happiness together with such acute pain that I wanted to leave there as soon as possible so that the conflict would subside.

"Sandra, I wanted to tell you that I'll be leaving this house tomorrow. I'm going to a small village in the country where we also have a transmitter. We have to start working: we've assembled men, weapons, explosives—"

"It's very dangerous, Francesco."

He hesitated a moment, as if banishing an idea, and then he said, "No, I don't think so. But you must understand that I can't do otherwise.

You must understand me. I'm begging you to understand. I know we'll have to go for some time without seeing each other. Do you need money?"

"No," I said harshly. I reddened: I was putting on my jacket and felt that he was trying to pay me.

"Listen, Alessandra," he went on, taking my hand. "I want you to be brave."

"I'm not at all."

"I know. But as it happens, I also feel stronger when we're apart. Maybe a man's reactions are very different from a woman's at such times. But I hope, all the same, that you understand everything that's happening. Until now, we've had little time for us. I've never been what you wanted me to be. But I didn't feel free yet. I felt . . . I knew that we had to pay for this, too, in order to be happy at last." The room was cold. Francesco had thrown on his coat, and he looked just like his photo. "Soon, perhaps, you'll understand, but I already understand you, even if you don't believe it. We must free ourselves."

I said nothing; I was thinking that I wanted to free myself of my love for him.

"Let's go out now." He was, again, cold and distant with me as he had been just before. I could never get over the wall that divided us. Luigi's wife was waiting for us in the corridor, smiling, and I blushed, afraid we had left the room untidy. I didn't like her benevolent complicity and I barely said goodbye. Francesco hugged me with a child clinging to his leg.

"I love you. I'm scared!" I whispered in his ear. And I quickly disappeared down the stairs.

A FEW NIGHTS later I was on the phone with Tomaso when I heard persistent knocking at the door. It was past the hour of curfew and that frantic beating aroused my suspicions.

"Sorry, but there's someone knocking. It could be them. I'll call you back right away. Bye!" It was the porter's little girl, looking pale.

"They're coming! Watch out!" she said before going up a few more steps and hiding among the water tanks. I ran to the bedroom, took the pistol, and pushed it down the back of an armchair in the study. Already I heard heavy, hobnailed boots ascending the stairs; they were the steps one heard in the streets at night, steps seeking Francesco, now on my threshold. *All you have to do is press here*, Francesco had said.

Their knock was like their footsteps and their harsh gaze. There were three of them and they greeted me as they entered. I wasn't afraid. I felt locked, numb, frozen. I replied to their questions by saying that my husband hadn't lived with me for some time; that we were separated and I supposed he had settled in Milan. I spoke calmly and confidently, wishing that Francesco could see me. They looked at me with suspicion and I stared back at them, imagining myself pulling that trigger with a sort of bitter glee. They were tall and blond, and we had our height and the color of our hair and eyes in common. I knew them well: my mother had always spoken to me about my grandmother Editta's character. We were like four people from the same family, which is how they must have known that I wouldn't say anything. I wondered only if I would be able to withstand physical pain. They proved to be respectful and courteous.

"After you," they said, going into the study. I sat on the arm of one of the chairs. They looked carefully through my papers, and I worried needlessly that they would find something. But the precision of their method actually reassured me: if they weren't wrong to search, then I must have been right to destroy. *In the chest,* I thought, *you have to shoot at their confident, triumphant chests.* I was very apprehensive about the pistol; I felt that the armchair was transparent.

The soldiers left the study and I made a move to follow them. The officer said, "Please, Signora," giving me to understand that I had to stay with him, while the others rummaged through the rest of the house. He invited me to sit down, and I found myself a few centimeters from the pistol.

"Do you read much?" he asked, eyeing the bookshelves.

"Yes, it's my favorite thing to do."

"Good," he said, and he began to pick up books—searching, of course. He leafed through them. I disparaged his futile pretense.

"You won't find anything in them," I reassured him.

Surprised, the officer turned around. "I'm not looking," he said. "After all, I've already realized that we're not going to find anything. It's hard to find something in the home of someone who reads a lot of books," he added with mild irony.

I was scared. I worried that he knew me too well; maybe he knew that I would not be able to bear physical pain for long. *In the back,* I thought, *while he's getting another book.*

"Sorry," he said. "If I'm bothering you, I'll stop."

I shrugged to show that it didn't matter to me.

"Thank you. It's a long time since I've seen any books—since I left home. Now my house has been completely destroyed; the books, too. It's a shame. You can't buy a lot of books all at once, only gradually. I hope you won't lose yours."

I looked at him but made no reply. I wasn't sure what he was trying to say. I heard the soldiers walking around in the bedroom, heard them moving about, shifting a piece of furniture. Maybe he was trying to help me forget what they were doing, or maybe he was looking for the best way to get me to talk. He came nearer and I stared at him. He was young, perhaps a little older than I was.

"I often go into houses in this city," he said, his voice uneasy. "But I don't find many books, as you do in all the houses in my country. Sorry," he added, thinking I was offended. "Why do you have so many?"

"I studied literature."

"Me, too," he said seriously. "I was writing my thesis on this poet and then the war forced me to leave." He showed me the book he was holding: it was Rilke's French poems. He sat opposite me in the other armchair while I heard the soldiers turning the house over.

"Do you know these poems?"

"Yes, of course."

"Read one of your favorite poems, please." He offered me the book, and as I took it, I tried to guess where, in all of this, the trap was for Francesco.

"Which one?" I asked, staring at him, hoping to guess.

"Whichever you want to read, please."

I had never imagined reading a poem with my hand so close to a gun. I thought about people who had heard the car stop at the front door, about the news circulating in our short street, the apartment block awake with terror, the few remaining men taking refuge in the hiding places prepared for them. Perhaps even reading a poem could be a way of helping them.

"Yes, I do have a favorite," I said. I leafed through the book while he waited, stiff and alert.

Tous mes adieux sont faits. Tant de départs
m'ont lentement formé dès mon enfance . . .

I kept on reading, looking at him every now and then, worried that he would in some way take advantage of my sincerity. He shouldn't believe I hated him less because I was reading a poem.

"*Tous mes adieux sont faits,*" he repeated.

I heard the soldiers coming down the hall. It felt as if they were bringing Francesco with them. I was sure I had been the one to deliver him to them with that poem. *Tous mes adieux sont faits*, I thought, moving my hand towards the pistol.

They came in and showed the officer two photos: one was the photo of Francesco and the other was of Tomaso, laughing. I kept it hidden in my lingerie. They spoke but I didn't understand them; surely, that photo would lead them to Francesco. Inside me was a dog looking to bite someone.

"Please, Signora," the officer said, not looking at my hands, which still held the open book. "You must tell me which of these two is your husband." He showed me the photos. My blood froze in an instant—and then melted in a boiling stream.

"This one." I pointed to the photo of Tomaso.

"Thank you. And the other one?"

I reddened. "He's a friend."

"I understand." He nodded slightly, took the photo of Tomaso and slipped it in his pocket.

After the others had gone out, he said at the door, "I know these visits aren't welcome. I hope I won't have to come back. I don't want to ruin your memory of Rilke with my presence."

I heard their steps on the stairs; the building resounded with them and surely all the inhabitants were afraid that they would be stopping at their door. I heard the main door slam and then the car start up and move off. When the noise stopped, I ran to the study, took the photo of Francesco, and burned it. He was no longer there. I had removed him, I had saved him.

I headed for the phone to call Tomaso, feeling agitated, and only then did I realize the gravity of what I had done. It was a vile, abject act: Francesco would have despised me for it. I wanted to alert Tomaso right away, and I dialed his number frantically, but there was no answer. I redialed it in a frenzy: the phone ringing into emptiness made me certain that he had already been arrested. I convinced myself that it was impossible, all the while thinking desperately of his face stuffed into the officer's pocket.

The porter came up to get his little girl, who had stayed hidden among the water tanks the whole time, in the cold, trembling. Doors opened and my neighbors emerged in their bathrobes. "Thank goodness," they said. They asked why the soldiers had come and I responded vaguely. At last we were alone, the porter and I.

"Signora," he said quietly. "They showed me the photo and I said yes."

I blushed violently as he continued. "That man is outside, waiting to come in."

"Where?"

"Yes. He saw them leave, and he wants to come in. I signaled to him to wait, but maybe it's better now . . . Best not to leave him in the streets . . . because of the curfew."

"Yes." I didn't look at him.

He added, "They won't come back. But just remember the room with the water tanks: the last one on the right. It's empty."

A short time later I heard Tomaso's step on the stairs, coming closer, lightly, quickly. He came in panting, closed the door and we embraced feverishly in the dark entrance.

"Alessandra," he said, and I replied, "Tomaso," in a desperate tone. I was thinking about the photograph—"Tomaso, Tomaso . . ." I held him close. Then he leant over and kissed me on the mouth. We kissed for a long time—it was wonderful to kiss each other and to feel his warm, live mouth, his body young and free.

"I love you," he said. "I was afraid. Straight after your phone call I left to come here."

"What about the curfew?"

"Who cares? I hid behind some trees just across from here. I saw the car stopped at the door, and they just wouldn't leave . . ." All this time he was kissing me, holding me close. "Oh, Alessandra, how frightening! You're here—it's finally over. I kept thinking: *If they take her away, I'll shoot.* There couldn't have been more than two or three of them. My love . . ."

And I replied, "My love." We spent the night in the study; I sat in the armchair and he sat at my feet. I stroked his hair. I looked at a curl of burned paper, the photo of Francesco. We talked all night—about Francesco, too.

"Do you love him so much?"

And I nodded, a desolate, mute yes. I said nothing about the photo. I wanted him to leave before daybreak. We lingered, unable to separate. We kissed again in the shadows of the deserted stairwell.

.   .   .

THERE WAS NO more calm, no more rest for me in the weeks that followed. I couldn't shake off the remorse I felt for having exposed Tomaso
to such grave danger, which meant that I couldn't stop thinking about
him. I knew that whatever I told him about my despicable act, he would
not only continue to love me but also understand and love even that act.
Which is why I wanted to see Francesco, to take comfort from him. To
this end, I asked if I could speak to Tullio, and he gave me an appointment at Luigi's house. I wasn't happy about going back there, chiefly
because of what had happened in the boy's room. Luigi's wife opened
the door; Tullio was waiting for me in the dining room, and the children
were quiet, intimidated by their uncle's presence.

"I have to see Francesco."

Tullio replied that it was impossible: after the visit I'd received I
might be followed, and that could endanger not only Francesco but the
other comrades. Francesco was fine, and, as usual, Tullio handed me a
letter from him which I read in his presence. It was a truly beautiful
letter, in which Francesco reassured me about his fate and instilled
courage in me, always referring to higher sentiments, to duties we
needed to fulfill. It really was a noble letter, like the ones that revolu-
tionaries write to their families before being executed, and which are
then published in anthologies. After reading it, I was ashamed to
entrust Tullio with my muddled letter, expressing to my husband my
need for his love and his presence. Tullio bowed his head and smiled as
he took the letter. I asked him to tell me where Francesco was hiding:
he corrected me.

"He's not hiding, Signora. He's working." He was unwilling to
reveal where that was.

I was always at my worst with Tullio: my eyes filled with tears,
my lips trembled, I expressed myself uncertainly. "Please . . ." I tried
to insist, but his refusal was decisive, even if he seemed regretful.
Surely he would tell Francesco that I was a nervous, weak woman.

"Even so," I added as I was leaving, "I really needed to speak with my husband."

As he said goodbye, Tullio added coldly, "If you're questioned when you leave here, say that you came to see my sister-in-law. Her name is Maria."

I didn't meet anyone. Towards evening I joined Tomaso at a café. He was nervous. "Since they came to your house the other night, I've been afraid whenever you're late that I won't see you again," he told me. We were now seeing each other every day. He knew what I was doing, hour by hour, and how much money I had left. It was he who found me a job—a translation from French for an underground publisher. I told him I wasn't sure I could translate that well, but when, blushing, I gave him the first few pages to read, he was astonished and looked at me in admiration.

"I thought I'd have to revise the whole thing," he said. "But it won't be necessary, and I'm sorry. It's impossible to do anything for you. When someone gets close to you, he always ends up taking even if he means to give. You'll end up revising my articles," he concluded with a smile. That evening, I wrote to Francesco, telling him about the translation. I wanted to write him a nice letter explaining what Tomaso had said, but whenever I addressed him, the strength of my feelings overwhelmed the calm I needed to write.

It seemed impossible to join him now. I knew nothing about his daily life, and he didn't know about mine. I hadn't dared confess that I had swapped his photo with Tomaso's, even though I secretly blamed him for having driven me to that contemptible act, dictated by my love for him. Gradually, I came to suspect that my marriage had been a mistake, and that I truly belonged to the loving, devoted man with whom I was now sharing the most demanding time of my life. Perhaps neither of us was worth as much as Francesco, but our day was a gentle and harmonious circle. We would talk animatedly and often then work together under the light of the same lamp, on either side of the table. At those moments, life seemed so perfect and beautiful that when, as so often, he looked up from his work to gaze at me, I blushed and felt like crying. We were always connected and in unison. He would warn me when he went out on some risky job, and would call me just afterwards to let me know, in code, that it had gone well. Everything he did was very straightforward.

"No, I'll never be a hero," he said with a smile. "Fate will never give me the chance. Or maybe I'll never be dedicated enough to get that chance."

At the time, the city was full of people who would never have the chance to become heroes. And yet there was a solidarity circulating among us so profound that it often amounted to heroism, though it was through fear. Maybe that's why we easily understood one another: a nod or a glance was enough. We opened up our homes to the suffering, welcoming them to the poverty that was already there, as if we had finally resolved to reveal ourselves to one another. Yes, it was truly a time that made even those who had no ambition to become heroes better, those who simply felt an obligation to be true to themselves. It may seem strange, but I sensed that even the tall, stiff soldiers who were responsible for instilling such fear were driven by the same inescapable obligation. I couldn't believe that it gave them satisfaction to instill fear in women and men they didn't know; contrary to what some thought at the time, I realized that they felt their rationale was weakening all the time, and so they tried to sustain it through terror. Maybe my thoughts were influenced by my mother, who, although she lived during times very different from ours, had taught me to be merciful toward those who become instruments of war.

I understood, too, why Claudio hadn't written to me after the armistice. I couldn't forget what he had said when we were still children: at the time, he had condemned Antonio's courage, which I had so admired. He judged him as not having the courage required to submit to the humiliations particular to the times, those of living quietly and anonymously with your own family, from which you are inevitably estranged, with your own duties weighing on you, your only satisfaction the awareness that you are obeying.

In other words, you had to accept that you couldn't be a hero or play a leading role. And I would have to accept my marriage, the loneliness it brought with it, its decline, the end of the romantic plan through which we had invented ourselves. I had to have the courage to live behind the wall, as Claudio lived behind barbed wire. But I didn't have that sort of courage, just as Francesco didn't have the courage to accept the annihilation of his own moral freedom. Our inability to adapt to models suggested to us from all sides created an indissoluble bond between us that transcended our very different characters and the pain we caused one another. The letters we exchanged may have been exalted and rhetorical, yet, although they referred to different feelings, they spoke the same language, expressed the firm intention to resist surrender.

In the evenings, I would wrap myself in a shawl and pace the freezing apartment, with no light for hours. In the cold, silent darkness of the house, I thought about how tempting it would be to give up: the hours spent with Tomaso were so sweet, when he questioned me about my thoughts, about my past and my plans, and then asked: "Do you love me?"

"No," I always answered. "I don't love anyone but Francesco." And in the moment I didn't even believe it was true. I had nothing to sustain me beyond the memory of the night my mother died. I would beg her—*Help me!*—but, instead of seeing her with the dazed expression she had when she left the house to go to the river, I saw her once more in her blue concert gown. *Help me!* I pleaded, but she didn't reply. She kept on walking, flying down the stairs to meet Hervey. *I hope you will succeed*, I heard Nonna repeating, and meanwhile I imagined her looking dubiously at my slender figure, as she had when I first arrived in Abruzzo.

I often told myself I shouldn't see Tomaso again, but it was very difficult to be alone at my age: I was barely more than twenty-one. It was easier to resist when I was sleeping behind the wall at night, and when intimacy with a man felt like something filthy and humiliating. But it was more difficult when Tomaso sat at my feet, looking at me with loving eyes and saying the words I had always wanted to hear. We were always at home, and, young as we were, giving in to our amorous desires would have appeared not only innocent but natural. Sometimes the siren went at night, and in the morning we heard about the bombed houses. In the paper, next to the names of the victims were the words "fifty-eight years old," "sixty years old," but often you read "thirty years old," "twenty-one years old," and you wondered whether it was right that all a twenty-one-year-old woman should carry to her grave was the memory of nights sleeping behind the wall, or days standing in line, washing the dishes, and hiding in the cellar.

"It's not fair," Tomaso thought as he left me. Maybe it was the last time we'd see each other, since he could be arrested at any moment. "It's not fair," he had repeated ever since the first time he had asked me to let him stay. "I won't leave anymore," he said. "I'll go and talk to Francesco. We won't have any trouble understanding each other. People who've risked their lives together understand one another easily."

"No," I replied. "Please, don't take away the calm I need. You know very well that I won't leave Francesco, and you know very well that I love him." I said, "Would you really like ours to be the usual pathetic story of the wife who's away from her husband, who's alone on vacation, who—"

"That's all it would be?"

"Yes. That's all," I answered, avoiding his gaze. I hoped he would say, *That's all right, let me stay anyway.* I was begging him, inside, to do something that would give me a reason to look down on him. But he moved away from me, gasping as if he were coming back to the surface.

"I'm sorry," he said, and he kissed my hand. "Ciao."

I stayed behind the door, defeated. That night, I hugged the hot water bottle to keep from getting lost in the expanse of the bed. The siren sounded, and I went down to the shelter, where I could hear the thud of the bombs, the dull blows of the anti-aircraft artillery. I wasn't very frightened, but I was thinking, *thirty years old . . . twenty-one years old.*

Yes, at such moments it was difficult to go on.

THERE WAS NO one to help me.

It was very painful to accept that my friendship with Fulvia was over. We had nothing left in common besides memories of our childhood. I was always saying that I wanted to return to live in that neighborhood with those people, but maybe it wasn't true. In fact, all I meant was that I wanted to go back to being what I was before my mother died, before the war started and I met Francesco and then Tomaso. But that wasn't possible. Nor was it possible for me to keep up a sincere friendship with Fulvia, and that made me feel tremendously desolate, because her warmth had always been comforting to me, and now not even that comfort remained. There was nothing left to bind us together, neither interests nor people.

Dario was now married; his wife was the daughter of a wealthy grocer. They lived near there, and Fulvia and Lydia had got into the habit of lingering at the window, hoping to see them go by. Once I saw them, too. She was fat and rather vulgar. When she walked, she leaned on her husband. Dario had also put on weight, and I didn't understand what Fulvia continued to see in a man who had chosen to live with a woman solely because she was rich. Fulvia and Dario saw each other twice a week, always in the afternoon; he told her he preferred that time because of the curfew. Lydia arranged to be out of the house on those days.

The last time I went to see them, we had sat on Fulvia's bed to talk. I told myself I shouldn't go back there, not even to preserve the memory of the room where we used to play.

"It was an enchanted room," I told Tomaso. "The furniture threw huge shadows on the floor and we took shelter in them. The bed with the green bedspread was a vast meadow . . ." When Fulvia let Dario into that room for the first time they were just children, and it still seemed like a risky, forbidden game. I didn't want to imagine that pudgy young man now, so full of himself, undressing there and lying in bed beside Fulvia, who made herself so docile and pleasing.

They said I had been lucky to marry Francesco and I agreed. When they asked if I was happy I sensed their question was their last hope of undermining Dario's contentment with the grocer's daughter, using the example of my misfortune. Sharing with them my disillusionment would be the only way to be comfortable together again, but I couldn't confide in them because by that time we had completely different ambitions. In fact, they were in conflict. So I answered yes—and, to make Fulvia forget my earlier confession of disappointment, I said one had to get used to marriage because although it might be disconcerting at first, it becomes the ideal state: perfection. They looked at me as they did when the grocer's daughter walked by, and, from that day on, I felt as if I legitimately belonged to the building where everyone was happy.

"Yes," said Lydia, and Fulvia went off to pour some vermouth that she absolutely wanted me to try, "it's sad being a married man's lover. When the war is over I'll send Fulvia to her father in Milan. It's easy for women to find husbands when they're new to a city."

"But she won't want to—" I objected.

"Oh, I know." Lydia nodded with a sigh. "I'm hoping to convince her. I don't want her to end up like me. When you're young, everything's fine, but then . . . I don't know how to explain it, but I'm sure you understand. You're educated. You read lots of books. It's odd—there are so many things I feel I can't tell her, and quite often I don't even know how to describe them, so I don't find them that troubling. Then I read about them in novels, and that's when I really understand, and I feel like crying. I recently read a novel that talks about a woman who's the lover of a married man. I don't remember what it's called, this book—I'm always forgetting titles—but it explained a lot about me, my life. For example, at a certain point the married man wants to go see her, but he's detained by his wife, so he calls her, and he says, 'Sorry, I can't come tonight, Commendatore.' The first few times you both laugh at these tricks. He, too, often does that with me, calls me 'Commendatore.' It's silly, right? But then you feel really bad after you hang up. Now, for example, I'm writing to him care of one of his porters, very loyal, a certain Salvetti. All for his wife, of course. The doorman pretends they're his. I'd say it's nothing, right? And yet—I don't know how to explain it—this correspondence with the doorman . . . it's sort of humiliating."

"I don't think so . . . The main thing is to write and receive those letters."

"Right. That's exactly how it seems when you're young. But it's not how it is. When you're young it even seems wonderful to meet in a furnished room or a hotel. It's like an adventure. But then, in fact, you go home alone, and he goes back to his wife, goes to the theater with her, sleeps next to her . . ."

"And maybe he doesn't even look at her, doesn't talk to her . . ." I was afraid I had admitted everything with that and was about to take it back, but Lydia continued.

"Yes, I know. I know what you mean. I was married myself for many years, and we separated in the end because of Domenico's stubbornness." I didn't understand how she could call what had happened with the Captain "stubbornness." She continued. "I know. You aren't happy even when you're married, but it's different. Your husband is your husband. I can't explain it. In any case you might not understand. Not even Eleonora would have understood. But I know what Fulvia feels when she stands at the window for hours and hours and then says, 'She's so fat!,' laughing at Dario's wife . . ."

I said goodbye to Fulvia by the front door where she had once hugged me as a child. She asked me to come back soon, but I felt that we had nothing more to say to each other now that Dario was married.

"Remember?" she asked, looking over the banister while I slowly started down. Yes, I nodded, recognizing that we would never be as happy as we were before we knew Dario and Francesco. The stairway my mother had descended lightly was in blackout; the entrance area was partly blocked by sandbags. Tomaso was waiting for me nearby, just as the Captain used to wait for Lydia, hidden behind the newspaper kiosk.

A FEW DAYS later, I began working with Tomaso. It was the end of March, and the city was terrorized. In every house, the people were simply waiting for the moment when someone would come to take them away: entire families, worn down by hunger and fear, sat silent in the darkness of houses that were still cold, waiting to hear the footsteps that would put an end, finally, to their anguished waiting. The streets were increasingly deserted. People passed by hurriedly, head down, as if fleeing an epidemic. Fulvia called to tell me that my classmate Natalia Donati had been taken away with her baby in a swaddling blanket, because she was Jewish. I remembered going to sit in the gardens and hearing her read the letters she thought Andreani had written: I didn't remember that she was Jewish. She was a girl like me. We had the same childhood, the same teachers.

"They took them away in a truck," said Fulvia. "Screaming."

I hadn't seen Natalia since our school years, so I saw her in her little green coat, her long red braids and heavy glasses. That's how I pictured her climbing into the truck, still a child, carrying a red-haired child. *They were screaming*, Fulvia said. And I thought how oppressive women's lives had become, if they weren't even spared the cruel death that men claimed as their glorious privilege in peacetime as well.

I started one evening when Tomaso had messages in his pocket to take to the radio and was afraid of being stopped at the entrance to

Tullio's house. "I'll take them," I said. He objected; I insisted, serious. "I want to take them."

"Francesco will find out," he objected, but I could tell that this complicity was tempting for him.

"Even better," I said.

We were walking along the Lungotevere, not far from my mother-in-law's house. She had come to ask me for news about Francesco one day. I told her that we were separated. She gave me a cold stare; she had never been sure about me and found it hard to believe me. Nevertheless, she was easily satisfied by the proof I was providing of her shrewd judgement.

The shadows of other couples could be seen between the plane trees. Tomaso asked, "How shall I pass you the messages?"

"Kiss me," I replied. "And while you're kissing me . . ."

We stood close, feeling each other's warmth under our spring clothes. Tomaso gave me a long kiss; his hand moved to my neckline, found my bare skin, and let the slips of paper slide into my bra. I had never kissed a man in that momentous way. We started walking again, arm in arm, and though Tomaso hesitated, we separated a short time afterwards.

I was very frightened on my own. It felt as though everyone could see those slips of paper. I wanted to button up my jacket, but I worried that the gesture would be enough to betray me. I had never been so afraid, and I feared that I had overestimated myself. My legs nearly gave way every time a car approached. I wondered if Francesco got this frightened, and I convinced myself that he did. But I acted relaxed, bought my ticket on the tram, and said, "Excuse me, after you." Francesco would finally realize that I wasn't like Casimira.

An elderly woman answered the door at Tullio's house and said no one was there. I insisted, and she looked at me fearfully. Comrade Denise then came through a glass door partially opened onto a dark room, and said to let me in.

"You have to ring six times," she explained. She looked at me, unsure, and delaying me at the entrance, added, "Don't worry; your husband is fine."

"Thank you, but I haven't come to ask for news. I've come to bring messages. Tomaso was afraid he was being followed."

After she saw what it was about, she said, "Good. But why did you come, Signora? Your husband wouldn't be happy, and—"

"I no longer care whether he's happy or not," I said brusquely. "It's important that certain things get done, and Francesco can't stop me from feeling the need to do them."

I spoke harshly, and she looked at me as if seeing me for the first time. In fact, a couple of evenings later she came to shelter in my apartment before curfew. She said she had dared to ask for hospitality not only because Tullio had suggested it but also because she had wanted to come and talk to me ever since we had had that brief conversation.

"I'll leave early tomorrow morning," she said. "These are very difficult days." Together we buried some papers in the pots on the terrace, under the roots of the jasmine, and I thought back to the day I had bought those plants. Some of the branches had blossoms on them, and gave out a faint scent. We talked. I told her not to worry: the porter was trustworthy, and there was always the room with the water tanks.

"I don't think they'll come," she said. When she took off her beret, I saw that her hair was gray—the color of iron—at the roots. "We often overestimate danger, and, going from house to house, we're only looking to escape our own restlessness. Sometimes I think their fear of finding us is equal to ours of being found. The struggle rests on the possibility of enduring this fear for a fairly long time."

"Yes," I said, "and maybe the suffering they inflict on us is no less than what we inflict on them by forcing them to be cruel and inhuman."

"But it's easier to bear cruelty than to be cruel," she added. After a pause she went on. "And we'll win, precisely because cruelty is contrary to every natural law of life. In the end, right is always on the side of the patient and the weak."

"I don't believe that," I replied. "And in any case I will never resign myself to being patient and weak."

"I've noticed." She shook her head. "I'm much older than you are—I can use the familiar *tu* with you, right? I once thought the same. But maybe it's wrong."

As she was speaking, she took off her man's shirt, which hid her large, heavy breasts. "When I came to visit Francesco," she went on, "I liked seeing you moving around him, always so charming, with your feminine kindness. I hoped you weren't intelligent. Women should never be intelligent if they want to be happy. It's different for men: they never give their whole lives over to love. They don't consider it a very important feeling, and they sometimes believe that it's even less important than ambition, that it's a weakness, really. They might be ashamed of making a mistake in their career, or only in some financial dealing, but it doesn't even occur to them that they shouldn't make a mistake in love. When they're very intelligent, though, women understand that no sentiment is more important."

"So?" I asked, dismayed.

"So they realize that the relationship between a man and a woman is essentially the root of life, which continues through them. All other feelings are less important—and often they don't even originate in us but are created by the particular society we live in; we can't conform to them fully except through an awareness of love. But men don't love women who understand these things, who know what moves them, what leads them to act. They prefer to be closed up in themselves, refusing to be judged because of the risk of being condemned."

"So?" I persisted.

"Well, if you're intelligent and can't resign yourself, you have to adapt to being alone."

In the dim light I could barely make out her profile; she had bags under her eyes. She fell asleep quickly, and I was frightened by her body slumped next to mine: sleep walled her off in a bitter and resigned solitude, which made me feel irrepressibly rebellious. *She's old*, I thought with a sneer. *She says those things because she's old.* And yet, looking at her carefully, I thought that she might be only around forty, and that her appearance might simply be the result of her resolve. I was relieved to see her go early the next morning. Before she left, she entrusted me with several jobs, and her voice was different from the one she had used when she asked if I was expecting a baby.

I immediately wrote a long letter to Francesco, asking him to help me see myself clearly, along with the relationship we had put so much effort into from the start. He always replied the same way—affectionate, reassuring—and essentially my letters remained unanswered. I felt that the only means of reaching him was to work together, even if from a distance, and so I followed comrade Denise's instructions to the letter. She never again spoke to me as she had that night but as she did to men, and certainly as Francesco spoke to her.

On the other hand—and partly because of the fear that remained after her conversation—I felt increasingly reluctant to avoid seeing Tomaso. His way of working in the clandestine struggle was different from that of the other comrades. The others were serious, solemn, closed off in a habitual melancholy. Tomaso didn't act with Francesco's cold, methodical precision but with a spontaneity that I, too, had in completing my assigned duties. When we finished our work, we went to relax in the countryside around the city's outskirts. We lay down on the grass like students and, despite our dangerous day, felt the cheerfulness of youth circulating in us, the fervor of a new season.

"Do you love me?" he would ask.

And I would always jokingly reply, "A little." The truth was that, even in those moments, I knew I loved only Francesco. Yet to be with Tomaso, to hear him talk and laugh, to see him look at me was a joy—youthful, happy and wholesome—I couldn't remember having felt before.

We often went home together. As long as we were in the street, I felt I wasn't doing anything wrong; but then all at once I would read my guilt in the deferential eyes of the porter. I lived alone, Tomaso was a young man, and he stayed in my house for hours. Besides, the porter knew the story of the photo and that made me nervous in his presence. I wanted to stop and talk to him, convince him that the young man wasn't my lover, as he imagined him to be. But he wouldn't have believed it. No one would have believed it, seeing us returning arm in arm, enclosed within the boundaries of our island. And, to tell the truth, I didn't believe it, either. I felt that we had much more in common than physical intimacy: an intimacy of thought and feeling. All the same, when he asked me if I loved Francesco, I was completely sincere in answering yes.

Sometimes, afraid that I had already become like Comrade Denise, I undressed and looked at myself in the mirror. *Francesco*, I said, but I heard Tomaso's voice saying, *Why don't you want to, Alessandra?* I wandered around the apartment like a crazed person, hounded by the word *adultery*, which was constantly in my ears. I recalled my mother and her love of the story of Emma Bovary. I saw the book on her night-stand, the pages dented in the margin by her fingernail. Perhaps she would read it at night, awake behind the wall. If so, the struggle she had endured was added to mine, and it seemed that she had entrusted to me the responsibility for winning the battle for both of us. Yet I sometimes convinced myself that I was a slave only in my conventional fear of the word. *I'll give in*, I said to myself. *Give in, and free myself.* I would take a breath, relieved, but only for a moment, and then I was gripped by a cold, unbearable desperation. Yes, giving in was perhaps one way of becoming free. After that, I would throw myself from the terrace. It seemed to me, too, that, if I called death with such insistence, almost begging, it would in the end come to my aid spontaneously. But it didn't. I was often carrying manifestos in my purse, putting them in letterboxes, sliding them under gates, onto deserted front desks. I sometimes expected to hear the blast of a machine gun behind me.

I saw Tullio and gave him a letter for Francesco. It was both proud and despairing. I told him, among other things, "There are many ways to achieve mutual understanding: I've chosen the most dangerous and the most difficult. It's really extremely difficult. Help me." Tullio told me that Francesco had made a clandestine trip to the south by boat and had just returned the same way, having accomplished a bold mission. Such strict secretiveness with me at such a dangerous time seemed less dutiful than distrustful. However, Tullio's look had for some time now been less distant, if equally cold.

"You're a good worker, Signora Minelli," he said, "but we thought it best not to tell your husband until today, so as not to disturb his peace of mind."

So he was organizing us, just as I had suspected. And yet I, too, felt the unavoidable need to respect and obey him. He was thinner, but his look was as keen and energetic as ever.

When I got home the next day, the porter looked pale and his wife was sobbing.

"What's happened?" I cried out.

They told me that Francesco had come home and had been arrested at the front door.

I SAT FOR hours on the terrace in the evenings: waiting. I did nothing but wait, and the evenings then stretched out interminably. The porter's daughter came to see me sometimes, a frail, white child who wore her hair in two braids, as I had at her age. She barely remembered a time before the war had started, which was perhaps why her eyes had a permanent expression of dismay.

"What are you doing, Signora?" she would ask, settling beside me on the little bench.

"I'm waiting for it to end," I told her.

"When will it end?" she asked, and when I made a vague gesture she whispered, "I'm afraid it will never end." She had run downstairs after me on the evening of the arrest, had taken my hand and kissed it to comfort me. She really was a pretty and delicate child, and it saddened me that she had to know these things.

Tomaso had called a few hours later and we had spoken the language of difficult times. He asked if he could come and see me. I wanted to say no, that it was dangerous. I kept thinking about the photo I had given to the officer, but the porter said it was the same one who had arrested Francesco. So it was clear to me that he had known at the time that I was lying, and I understood what he had said to me at the door about his visits and Rilke. Of course, he, too, had presumed that Tomaso was my lover, and seeing me indicate his photo so confidently, he must have thought me a cruel, heartless woman even if I read Rilke well. But that didn't matter now. Nothing mattered since Francesco—having just learned that I was working for him and that I understood him— had come to tell me that he loved me and that he, too, had at last understood everything. But we didn't make it in time then, either.

I welcomed Tomaso in silence. He sat opposite me and we didn't say anything for some time. I must have been looking at him resentfully, because he said softly, "I know: you blame me for being free."

In fact, he looked guilty. He ventured to ask if everything would stay the same between us and I said yes, he had always known that I loved Francesco. And he looked at me as if I had become much stronger during those hours; but, on the contrary, since Francesco was arrested I had felt completely defenseless, because if he had been forced to surrender how would I have the courage or the motivation to keep going? If Tomaso had asked me at that moment, *Do you want to, Alessandra?*, I would have taken him to my room and lain down on the bed. If Francesco was lost, nothing mattered anymore. Betraying him would have been a sordid little thing, like all the other sordid things I had been through.

I didn't go out for days. The doorman's daughter went to buy me bread and I ate it with potatoes, as we did when we were waiting for the arrogant voice to stop talking. It all seemed a long time ago. One of the unusual things about that period was the way in which things that had happened only a few months earlier seemed very distant. It gave young people the sense that they had lived enough.

Tullio got word to me that he wanted to see me and would wait in a café on Viale Giulio Cesare. Tomaso wanted to come along. Viale Giulio Cesare is one of the principal streets of the Prati neighborhood, and we stopped to look over the parapet on the Risorgimento bridge. Heavy trucks packed with tall, upright soldiers were driving over the bridge, which, having only one arch, shook with their passage. Because of the bridge we were shaken, too.

"See?" I said to Tomaso. "That's where my mother killed herself. At the time, there was a pretty reed bed, the shore was grassy and the water a clear green, as if it were flowing over leaves."

I was certain that Tomaso didn't believe me. In fact, it seemed impossible that I had been happy living in that neighborhood, in those houses; or, rather, it seemed truly impossible that I had been happy. I felt as if I had suddenly come to know the truth; as if until then someone had tried to soothe me with merciful lies. The Tiber was a muddy river, and the Prati neighborhood low and flat—one of the saddest in the city. In me, every passion was spent, not only the acute hatred that for years had stirred me up against my father but also the memory of my mother. The river, the trees, and the glad fight of the swallows no longer kept me company during the day; it was the soldiers' marching, the dampness of the shelters, the dark, and the bridge trembling with the weight of the trucks.

Tullio was waiting for us in a small gray *latteria*. He was pale and emaciated, but his eyes exuded a fierce strength that completely sustained him, like armor. Nervous, wary, he gave us the most recent news as if he were sharing some precious booty. He thought it would be reassuring to us, but I told him that none of it was important to me anymore. I was waiting, and the day would surely come when he called to say that Francesco hadn't been in time to be happy; so I looked at him, waiting to hear him deliver the sentence I had always read in his face. Always unflappable, he answered that, on the contrary, he had good news about my husband, who, when he was free, would fully appreciate everything I had done. Tomaso was sitting beside me, and Tullio seemed to be alluding to the battle I had waged against myself, since it really was a difficult feat. As usual, a blush rose to my face, betraying my thoughts. On an impulse, I turned to Tullio, and my eyes showed him the landscape of my days. I said I wanted to do more, much more—not just the dangerous things but humble, painstaking things as well. I wanted to tell him that I had often gone to sit on a low wall in Via della Lungara and looked for a long time at the huge prison building as I had looked at Francesco when he was sitting in the arm-chair. The prison wall resembled Francesco's eyes, which never responded to me; it resembled his impenetrable shoulders, behind which I lay awake at night, crying. It was just like being with him, and it gave me the same desire to join him, the same sense of desperate impotence. Instead, I said that I wanted to go to the prison gates and take Francesco lunch as Aida had done for Antonio, standing in line with his mess tin for hours and hours. But Tullio replied that those things wouldn't help Francesco. I could help him only through my determination and my work.

That was why I said yes even when he asked me to do things he deemed very difficult, like the bicycle and the bombs. I had accepted instantly, and Tullio's gaze softened momentarily. When Francesco got out of prison, the comrades all talked to him about that episode, and I felt as if they wanted to humiliate and diminish me. I knew what they didn't: that I had accomplished a far more difficult task. But they wouldn't have judged it so, because of how differently men and women assess courage.

The difficulty had been something else, and afterwards it seemed I would be able to face anything without finding it difficult. The difficulty had been intensified by the season, because although the city was steeped in fear and men fought and hid, and women were alone, exhausted by their search for food and debilitated by the lack of money, trees still grew new leaves, flowers sprouted from old roots in gardens that no one had time to tend, and grass sprang up between the cobblestones even where the soldiers marched over them. The jasmine Francesco liked was flowering again on my terrace, in the pots where dangerous papers were buried. I've already mentioned that I was deeply influenced by the seasons, and so if I felt sad during the winter, I seemed to put forth buds and leaves in the spring.

On one of those mornings someone rang the bell, and as I hurried to the door I heard Tomaso's breathless voice. "Open up, Alessandra!"

He shut the door behind him quickly. He was pale. "I'm worried that I'm being followed," he said. "I have a message in my pocket for the radio and the new code."

"How many messages are there?"

"Four."

"Give them to me. I'll learn them by heart." I read and reread them, focusing my attention; meanwhile we headed for the kitchen, where we burned the paper they were written on. Then we hid the code in a crack in the top of the credenza.

"Look," he said, "this is my new name." He held out his false papers; in the photo he had a mustache, short hair, and glasses. He had actually looked like that for some time. I noticed that he had taken my maiden name: Corteggiani. His name was Francesco Corteggiani. "I'm your brother. Do you understand?"

"Yes." The close relationship between us already worried me. I didn't know how to remake myself in the false reality we were moving in. I started to repeat his name. "Francesco—" I broke off and asked harshly, "Why did you choose that name?"

"I don't know. It was the first one that came to mind, maybe because you so often repeat it. I'll have to stay here for a few days."

"Here?" I asked in dismay.

"Yes. Your house is the most obvious, and for that reason perhaps the safest: precisely because they don't think anyone would come here to hide since Francesco was arrested. In any case I wasn't the one who decided. It was Tullio . . ."

"Tullio?!"

"Yes. I even tried to refuse, to make excuses. But he was set on it and he insisted: 'I tell you, you'll only be safe in Minelli's house.' Maybe he was thinking about the adjoining terraces or the room with the water tanks . . ."

No, Tullio wasn't thinking about that. I said nothing and stood unmoving, leaning against the kitchen sink, not looking at Tomaso, now called Francesco. I didn't feel that Tullio could demand that from me as well; it was too difficult.

"I don't have any beds besides mine," I said.

"I'll sleep in the study on the cushions from the armchair. I'm sorry—it's not my fault. It was Tullio. I swear to you, I refused on principle. Yet it seemed to me that if I insisted too much they might have thought . . ." He stopped for a moment before adding quietly, "I didn't put up much of a fight, though, I confess. I was happy to have it clearly authorized, practically a duty to stay at your house. That's how I ended up taking his name—unconsciously—because of my desire to bind myself to your life, to be at once your husband and your brother. Anyway, you know very well that it won't be long now—and I don't want Francesco to come back to live with you. He no longer has any right."

"You're thinking about this now?"

"Yes, why? Because he's in prison? What does prison have to do with all this? He might be entitled to a medal, say, or a decoration. There's nothing left of him in this house."

"Me. I'm here."

"Not really! Think about it: you're not really here anymore. Just now, I came up the stairs two at a time, pleased that something bigger than us was forcing us to accept what I'd known for some time, and you had also accepted. It seemed that Francesco's right to come back here was at most equal to mine. I came upstairs joyfully, not even listening for footsteps following after me."

I was very afraid, though. I had never been more afraid in my whole life. Tullio didn't know, and he was amazed that I wasn't afraid that day with the bicycle. Even if they had caught me that day, nothing would have changed between Francesco and me.

"As I came upstairs," Tomaso continued, "I forgot the messages, the code, everything that will happen if we don't broadcast . . ."

"We'll broadcast," I said. "I'll go."

"No, that's impossible, but now that I'm here nothing else is important. The important thing was to come up the stairs, up to see you. Don't you see?"

Yes, I did. Just then I wanted to call Francesco for help, but he never came to me; I imagined him serious, as he appeared in the photo, hat on his head, wearing a coat, severe and impenetrable as the prison wall. I thought he had been arrested just when he was finally coming to talk to me, to tell me everything I wanted him to say. He hadn't made it in time, though, and his gesture, set against Tomaso's concrete presence and his words, remained intangible. I was so afraid that I hoped I would hear a car stop at the entrance to the building, followed by heavy steps climbing the stairs in terrifying silence. *They'll come*, I was hoping. *They'll take him away.*

"Alessandra," he called.

He sat at the marble table looking at me and smiling. His smile showed white teeth under the mustache that shadowed his lips. His eyes, like mine, were light; he was my brother. *They'll come*, I thought. *Surely they'll come and take him away.*

"Alessandra," he said cheerfully, "I'm hungry."

SO BEGAN OUR shared life. I served him because he had been assigned to me as my comrade, and his eyes followed me everywhere.

"How lovely you are," he would say, and whenever I went by he took my hand to kiss it. We could hear the explosions ever more clearly, but in the bright May sky they seemed no more worrying than a spring storm. "I like living in this apartment." Tomaso smiled as he looked around. He talked about the study as I had talked about Fulvia's room.

It was torture resisting the temptations of such a serene and harmonious life: I didn't know if I would be strong enough. I hoped they would eventually come to take Tomaso away. I was even glad that I had given the officer his photo. *They'll come, surely they'll come!* And with that hope I gave in to our day of happiness. I hoped they would come soon, because otherwise Tomaso would stay with me all night. *They'll come soon,* I said to reassure myself. Meanwhile, I secretly nourished the hope that they wouldn't come, so that the responsibility for Tomaso's being in my house could be attributed to carelessness or absent-mindedness. I imagined the dark, silent city in the tranquil order of the curfew, which seemed no longer a threat but, rather, concern for our well-being. The nights were long in that still silence. The code had to be delivered the next morning. "I'll go," I told Tomaso, and the resolution calmed me. *I'll go, they'll get me, they'll put me against the wall.* That's what would happen, I was sure of it. But at least I would have time to spend one happy night. I had a vague suspicion that no one would make it in time if he or she wasn't prepared to pay a heavy price for the right to happiness. Surely that was why Tullio had suggested to Tomaso that he come to my apartment; I understood the reason for the fleeting pity I had seen in his eyes. Tullio, too, wanted me to make it in time.

So I felt free to imagine the night ahead of me. I listened to Tomaso, to his words, his way of laughing, and, finally, everything was connected to being young, and was mine by right. I didn't want to go back to sleeping behind the wall. Tomaso would take me in his arms and let me rest. He had once said to me, "I want to see what you look like when you sleep, when you wake up in the morning. There are still so many Alessandras I want to love and don't know." Often, without asking for my consent and acting as if he were sure of it, he would describe how our lives would be when the war ended. He would say, "We'll leave Rome: we'd never be truly happy here. These days of anxiety will leave a scar in the streets and on the stones. We would always feel the urge to hide here, as we do now. We'll go to Capri, and we'll have a big table in front of the window and we'll work on translations together. I'd like to try writing a book. But I worry that I won't be able to. I don't write very well; I'm a passable journalist, that's all. We'll earn just about enough to live—we're used to not spending very much. And I don't have any ambitions other than to live with you." That day he said other things like that, and I listened, enraptured. In my mind's eye, I opened the window that looked out on the little port smelling of seaweed and I put flowers on the table we worked at. They hadn't yet come to get him, but maybe they wouldn't after all. The violent thundering of cannons came closer and closer, but it seemed easy to abandon oneself to happier dreams, as it had on the night the arrogant voice stopped speaking. *Not long now*, I thought. *Maybe it's the last night,* and I didn't want to die the next morning saying, "I'm sorry," like Antonio. We had to go on, to endure, as Francesco was enduring prison.

"Tomaso," I said. "You have to leave before the curfew." I was sitting in the armchair; he was at my feet and I was caressing his hair. Everything in me ached as I spoke.

"Why?" He turned, startled.

"Because I'm not strong, the way you think I am. There's only one thing in me that's very strong, even if sometimes it doesn't seem to be, and that's my love for Francesco. Everything would fall apart if you stayed here, you're well aware of that. Everything I've been from the day I was born, everything my mother was, that my grandmother Editta was—everything I've believed until now, and which expresses itself in my love for Francesco. So I'm prepared to do anything to defend myself. All day long I hoped they'd come and get you so I wouldn't be forced to be so strong tonight. It's always a difficult thing to be strong, and it's never been more so than now. Maybe that's what Tullio meant when he asked if he could count on me at any moment. I didn't think it would be so difficult; I didn't think it was possible to be more frightened than when I was carrying messages in my bra, or manifestos and a pistol in my purse."

Tomaso looked at me, pale, and asked anxiously, "What about me?"

"I don't know, I don't care. What I'm putting myself through is so ruthless I can't feel pity for anyone else." I barely heard him begging me, saying confusing, anguished things, *I love you*, repeating it count-less times: *I love you.*

Then he said: "I have nothing left."

And I don't know why, but it occurred to me to reply, "You have Casimira."

Tomaso looked at me, uncertain. All at once, I seemed to under-stand that she still existed, and it wasn't chance that I had said her name.

"You see her sometimes," I risked.

"Who told you that?"

"Are you denying it?"

"No, why? She often calls to ask for news about everything that's going on. She's weak, and she never knows how to behave in these times, whether she should leave or stay. She's really frightened. It's impossible to talk about such things on the phone. That's why I see her now and then."

"I see." I felt my heart contract the way it did when Mamma aban-doned me to go to Hervey. But I was also, as I was then, suffused with a sort of sorrowful bliss. "I'm happy," I said. "I always thought it would be better like that. She wants to marry you, doesn't she?"

"Yes," he replied brusquely. "But what does that have to do with anything? I love you. I don't care about Casimira."

I realized, though, that if I had been brave enough to send him away that night he would have ended up marrying her. "Does Casimira know that we see each other so often?"

"Of course. She knows we work together, but she doesn't understand a thing about such matters. She may imagine you as someone very different from who you are . . ."

"You mean like Denise?" I said, laughing with unbearable cynicism.

"Yes, more or less. She thinks the women who work with us aren't really like other women. She feels it's impossible that they think about love, for example. She's a simple girl."

"You care about her, don't you?" I smiled indulgently.

"Well, yes, exactly. I care for her. I feel tenderly towards her, sorry for her. Those feelings are a long way from love, you know."

"I know," I said. "I know that very well." I leaned my head against the back of the chair and looked at Tomaso, my smile fixed, angelic. "I suppose you had to see her the day you were in such a hurry to leave me and I didn't understand why."

"Yes," he confessed with an innocent smile. "I haven't seen her since then. It's been about a month. She was waiting for me in a café and was all excited because she was wearing a new dress—that's why she was so unhappy when I was late. But you know, I told her the truth. I told her I'd been with you till then."

I was smiling, all the while imagining how he would introduce me to her. He surely hadn't told her I was pretty, as he continually repeated to me. Maybe he had told her about my modest appearance and how thin I was. Casimira had to be one of those girls with wavy hair and a full bosom.

"Oh, Alessandra," he said, bewildered by my fixed expression. "I would have nothing if you left me." He took my hands. "I want to go back to the way it was before," he said at last, whining like a child. "Before you told me to go."

"That's not possible," I replied with an affectionate smile. "It was really difficult to say that: but I feel that a weight has been lifted from me. It will be even more difficult when you've gone and I'm here by myself. And probably also in the days to come. But it won't be long now, and Francesco will come back, and this girl will stop feeling so afraid. You mustn't take part in any more risky operations. Casimira would still be waiting for you at the café in her new dress, and you couldn't go at all that evening. How old is she?"

"Twenty," he replied distractedly.

"Exactly—she's very young." I spoke as if I'd left youth far behind. "I know very well that there are a lot of things you don't understand at that age. Tomorrow morning I'll take Tullio the new code."

"No, don't insist."

"It's easy for me, honestly. I pull back my hair and hide it in my bun. I've done that many times already."

"Oh, Alessandra," said Tomaso, "I don't want you to do that for me."

It was hard to explain to him that I wasn't doing it for him but for myself. He wouldn't have believed it.

"Let me stay," Tomaso asked. "I want to stay forever."

I shook my head and smiled, caressing his hair: because what I had chosen was really the best way to stay with him forever. I would always walk between him and Casimira. I would suddenly come into bloom beside them, when she somehow exhibited the misery and pettiness that exists in each of us. Yet sending him away that night was even more difficult than what my mother did to stay with Hervey.

"Alessandra," Tomaso said, "don't smile like that. I'm not leaving. I know you love me so much."

"No, not so much," I replied with the same distant smile. "A little. I don't love anyone very much except Francesco."

I went on stroking his hair to comfort him. I felt a sharp pain beneath the skin of my hand, in my fingers, in the bones. When the pain became unbearable I looked at Tomaso.

"It's late now. You have to go." A few days later, thinking back to the moment I uttered that sentence, I wanted to reassure Tullio, tell him, *Believe me, it was much more difficult than getting past the checkpoint.*

Tomaso looked at me and then asked slowly, as if weighing every word: "My going away tonight means something different from all the other nights, doesn't it?"

"Yes. It means something different."

"Why?" he insisted, his eyes full of loving anxiety.

"Because, Tomaso, you see, at a certain point you have to choose between giving up and defending yourself. You can't live with uncertainty and fear forever. That's what all of you have done. You hid at first, and then you started working."

"It's not the same thing."

"But it is. Some say it's more difficult to give up, and maybe it really is if I'm so afraid of giving up tonight; but I'm among those who, like Francesco, have no choice but to defend themselves. He'll understand when he gets back."

"Why hasn't he understood that," he said pointedly, "if he's been living beside you?"

"Well, of course he does, but—"

"No," he said, "he hasn't understood a thing, I know. And he won't understand even when he comes back. Look, Alessandra, I think there must be some reason for everything that's happening in the world right now, and maybe that's what people in the world understand. Yet many of them won't understand, and it will be a serious loss for them. This is what I'd like to write in a book, but I wouldn't know how. So others will do it; maybe Alberto, maybe even Francesco. And that's how even what happens between a man and a woman—between you and me tonight, for example—must also have a deeper meaning that escapes everything at first. Maybe this, too, happens because someone understands . . ."

I interrupted, not wanting him to go on. "It's late. It's best if you go."

"No, let me finish," he replied curtly and he took me in his arms. "Because it's not fair that your childhood friend—what's her name? Natalia, Natalia Donati—should be taken away in a truck with her baby in obedience to a law that is contrary to every other natural law. That's why it's not fair for me to have to go away tonight. Yet Natalia was taken away, even when she was screaming and holding on. So I'll go, even if I'm holding on to you now, and then I'll scream inside for the rest of my life, and maybe I'll hold on to Casimira. Maybe this, too, is happening so that someone will understand."

We were at the door and he kissed me and caressed my hair. Everything in me was pain, even my blood. *Any minute*, I thought.

"My love," he said sweetly, "I hope I'll be the one who doesn't understand." He hugged me again, and then stepped onto the landing so that the threshold was between us.

"Where will you go?" I asked quietly.

"I don't know. Somewhere around here, maybe Saverio's. It doesn't matter. Give me those papers."

"No," I said, as if frightened; I couldn't let go of those, too. "Go, hurry up."

"Close the door if you want me to go. Close it."

Any second, any minute, I thought. And then I slowly closed the door.

I went back to the study. It was almost dark. The imprint of Tomaso's body and an empty, crumpled cigarette pack could still be seen on the armchair. I didn't dare venture into that solitude. I dropped into the armchair and leaned my head against the back. A piano could be heard in the distance, rendering the silence around me even more desolate. At last I began to cry, and I cried, completely caught up in my tears, not even remembering what they were about. In that moment, crying was the only thing that mattered. *As soon as he goes, I'll cry*, I thought in order to endure as long as Tomaso was there.

The next morning I went to Luigi's house; Tullio was there. He was sitting behind a desk, calm, pale and severe as usual. However, he no longer aroused the fear I had felt at first. I would say, rather, that I felt a sort of relief when I saw him. I had cried until the first light of day, when I heard the windows of the building opening, shutters slamming. I decided to open my own window, letting out the scent of Tomaso's cigarettes, too.

"Here," I said. I sat across from Tullio and pulled the slip of paper out of my bun. "Tomaso—"

Tullio interrupted. "I know."

"—left yesterday evening before the curfew," I explained quietly, without looking at him. "I was convinced that he wasn't safe at my house, which is why, despite the advice you'd given him," I added, "I thought it was the best decision."

He was the only one of the comrades I addressed formally, and he also treated me with respectful formality.

"You did the right thing, if you were convinced he wasn't safe. It would have been terrible to lose him now, when we're nearly there."

Tullio's face never lit up, not even when he said that we were nearly there. Other comrades joined us right afterwards, and although they, too, looked grave and melancholy, their eyes, like mine, were shining. In order to speak undisturbed, we shifted the bookshelf and climbed up the dark staircase to the attic. The rumbling from the explosions came closer and closer. Perhaps because it was spring, they seemed like shots fired during country festivals. The trees on the green hill of the Palatine were framed by the window: as soon as the explosions stopped, I would be able to go back to the Palatine with Francesco.

During those weeks, a breath of confidence enlivened the city, and a happy reawakening was already circulating unseen in the streets and houses, like new sap rising in still bare trees. Everyone stepped onto the terraces and looked out from the balconies and sat there, waiting calmly for the long day to end. Girls went around in groups on the heights of Monte Mario. They would sit on the grass looking south and start talking about the future, something they hadn't done for a long time. The elderly came out arm in arm and they, too, enjoyed the view from various points. Large trucks passed by quickly, and soldiers, increasingly vigilant, walked the streets in pairs or groups, displaying an impassivity in their composure and their eyes that revealed a cruel desperation. They wanted the city, exhausted by fear, to beg for mercy, and they felt such an urge to be cruel and inhuman that they forgot themselves. But they couldn't do anything. They couldn't arrest women, children, and old people just for sitting on their terraces looking south.

I, too, sat on my terrace waiting. The porter's daughter waited with me. Sometimes she would ask, "What can you see?" because I was taller than she was. I felt very affectionate towards her. We were perhaps the only people in the building to be truly dismayed by waiting: she because of her age, and I because of my love for Francesco. Being together suited us, although I knew she would never again have the eyes a child should have. Perhaps before long children could once again have the eyes they are entitled to at their age; and then I would like to have a child. The porter's daughter could recognize the various types of planes and pointed at them with her finger. But she didn't know a single fairy tale or poem. I hoped my child would know fairy tales and poetry.

More and more people crowded the terraces. It was spring, and everyone, it seemed, just wanted to be outside. And the soldiers knew that young men stood behind the closed windows, watching as we were doing from the attic. And since during the long day each of us had accomplished the most difficult things life had asked of us, the soldiers knew we wouldn't hesitate to do more in order to defend our new and extraordinary sense of expectation. In fact, from time to time Tullio ordered something, and one of us went off quietly so as not to disturb our waiting comrades.

Tomaso wasn't with us. It was safer for him to stay in Saverio's house; Tullio had said so, and he obeyed. I felt a kind of relief in trusting completely in Tullio. The day came when we were all gathered in the attic and he asked if there was a girl who could ride a bicycle, adding that the steering would be heavy.

Everyone understood that answering yes or no was important. There was a silence that Tullio took for uncertainty: I was good at riding a bicycle, and I came forward. I saw that Comrade Denise wanted to hold me back.

No, it wasn't really difficult. Because the danger was outside of me, not inside: so I could face it with everything in me. I remember that I combed my hair carefully and put on a wide pleated skirt that Francesco liked. It was worn out by now but still had a fullness that gave me the feeling of flying.

At the time, women went to pick vegetables from the gardens on the outskirts. And since riding bicycles was forbidden, they had turned them all into tricycles, adding two wheels under a box or a basket. You saw long lines of women riding these bicycles every afternoon. As they passed the checkpoints going home, the soldiers looked in baskets and boxes. Sometimes they were happy just to look, but other times they would put their hands in, rummage around, and take a handful of peas.

On the way there, I felt as if I were going on an outing in the country. I pedaled slowly, and the box bounced around behind me joyfully. But on the way back I was as serious and purposeful as when I was lining up with other women in the early mornings while Francesco slept, because he wasn't allowed to work. At the time it seemed to me that every step might help him, and on that day each stroke of the pedals. There were a lot of us, and though we didn't know one another, we exchanged a few words, if only, "This bicycle is so heavy!" I had a really old bicycle that was already heavier than the others, and under the peas was salad, and under the salad the bombs. It was terribly heavy, and the handlebars were continually threatening to swerve. I have strong hands, but I still found it hard to hold on. Added to that, I had to summon my courage when I saw the checkpoint a few dozen meters away. The other women ahead of me were bent wearily over their handlebars, and, because we had to go through one by one, they were already forming a line. Inside I murmured *Francesco*, so I felt that I wasn't going toward the checkpoint but towards the man I pictured standing as he was in the photo—coat on, hat on his head, waiting for me. Maybe because of the emotion I felt going towards him, my legs trembled terribly; at one point I thought I didn't have the strength to keep pedaling. I put one foot on the ground, and there I was at the checkpoint. The soldier stuck his hand in my basket and took it out right away, disappointed.

"It's always peas," he said. We looked at each other, and I realized that he was tired of being there, checking all the women who went by with their vegetables.

"Always peas," I repeated mechanically, and it was clear that I, too, was very tired. So he gave my saddle a push, not knowing that I wouldn't otherwise have been able to get going again; I couldn't feel my legs anymore, and the bombs were heavy.

It was an old road near the Milvio bridge. You could hear the bicycles hissing over the packed earth in the silent twilight, a sound both uniform and comforting. We all pedaled together, not looking at one another but trusting in that hissing, which was like the faint hum of a workshop. *Always peas*, the soldier had said, sighing. I looked at the necks of the women as I had those of my classmates, and I wanted to caress them tenderly. Some women wore themselves out in the patient search for food for their children, in the search for the money needed to maintain them. They all worked, since their men were far away, and some of them had gone to steal goods from the freight cars that had been struck during the air raids; others went to bed with soldiers. Because there was no limit to what you could ask of a woman; you could ask anything. Tullio asked us to make up a bed, wash the underclothes of a comrade who needed shelter, asked us to cook at all hours, for everyone who came by; we had to serve them all, find food for them all, sometimes money; he even asked someone to take in Tomaso and then asked if we knew how to ride a bicycle. He asked the men only to ride bicycles.

I stopped as planned in front of a tinsmith's workshop near Luigi's house. Two other men in overalls were working with the tinsmith, and they had unusually fine hands for laborers.

"Here," I said. "I've brought the vegetables," and I handed over the bicycle. My overwrought appearance made them look at me suspiciously. But after feeling around in the box they were reassured. I then went through the door and started climbing the stairs; I remembered the first time I had entered that house to visit Francesco. I had hesitated, feeling emotional, and now I was going up the stairs easily, as I had gone down the stairs in the Borghese Gallery. On the day of my first visit, Francesco and I were still two people with little in common besides our encounter on a boy's small bed, surrounded by photos of soccer players. And one of us often said, "Women," and the other, "Men," and we'd both responded, "I don't understand." Climbing those stairs, I was sure that I really understood everything now: I had closed the door in Tomaso's face and I had carried vegetables in a box.

Luigi's wife embraced me when the door opened. Then we shifted the bookcase aside and I went up the steep staircase to the attic.

Everyone was there in the attic, even Alberto, whom I hadn't seen for some time. Those of us missing were in prison, like Francesco, or gathered at Saverio's house, like Tomaso—or they had gone out, like me, and we were waiting for them to come back. Some had never come back—a girl named Laura, and Pino, a young professor. That's why we all waited anxiously for our comrades to come back. "It's Alessandra," I heard them say, relieved, and their expectation was even more gratifying to me, because I had never been loved by my colleagues or my classmates. No one could guess how much love I carried within me or how much I wanted to express it to the people around me: now at last I saw that I was recognized, and so my appearance at the attic door was like my mother's coming home at night.

Tullio came up to me and unexpectedly called me by name. "Alessandra, it's so late! We were really afraid."

"Afraid?" I repeated. "Why?"

I knew I had overcome much greater dangers, and surely the others had overcome them, too, in the course of the long day. I didn't understand why they were placing such importance on my adventure with the bicycle and the bombs; at worst, I might have died.

"Don't exaggerate," I said. The others circled me in silence, and I was pleased to understand that that silence meant they cared about me. "You should know," I told them, "that these errands aren't that difficult." But I could see that they misunderstood what I had said, thinking me dismissive, perhaps, or overconfident. Tullio, too, watched me uncertainly, and they all explained my behavior by attributing it to my anxiety over Francesco. They assured me that he wouldn't be taken away, and that everything was ready to ensure his release.

"It won't be long now," they all said, looking at the window and listening to the cannons going off as if it were a holiday. I looked up at the sky, shrouded by the evening, and at the Palatine hill.

"I'm not afraid," I said. "I'm sure Francesco will come back."

Shortly afterwards I went home on my bicycle. Tullio had suggested that I stay and sleep at Luigi's house that night, but I had said I didn't see the need. I asked only that he let me go home on the bicycle. It was forbidden, and he objected, but I replied with a smile that for some time everything we'd been doing was forbidden. Tullio had said that it wasn't worth the risk for no reason.

"Believe me, Tullio," I insisted, "I feel there's a reason."

The tinsmith removed the box from the bicycle, and I left, nodding a cheerful goodbye. Relieved of that heavy weight, the bicycle ran easily. It was the first day of June: a light breeze lifted my hair and I pedaled rapidly, feeling again the youth and strength of my body. I rode along the river, which, in that green evening, had once more taken on the lovely color of water flowing over leaves.

I rode beside the river talking with my mother. She no longer passed by without seeing me as she had the evening when I was walking with Tomaso in the bittersweet odor of dead horses. I called her, she responded; we used the same language. No one would ever be able to prevent me from talking to her: I rode brazenly past the soldiers, a lettuce leaf between my teeth, taken while the tinsmith was removing the box. I pedaled quickly, moving my shoulders and twisting the bike this way and that as if in a dance.

The soldiers looked at me without suspicion, forgetting their orders, which no longer seemed valid if a young woman could allow herself the pleasure of riding a bike. They weren't as rigid, hostile, or sure of themselves now, though they tried to lend their fear some dignity. Maybe, before long, I would be able to write to Nonna again. I hadn't heard anything from her or my father for months. "I'm managing," I would write to her, "I've made it." I had even managed to close the door on Tomaso's anguished eyes. I heard his words again, and, inspired by those memories, I pedaled even more quickly, fearful of not making it in time to reach Francesco. Maybe since his return was near, he appeared clearly in my memory. He no longer had the severe look of the photograph, hat and coat on. We were at the Borghese Gallery on the eleventh of November and he was looking at me lovingly. With the rush of the bicycle, my skirt swelled in a circle, as it had when I ran down the stairs. I would go up to him as I had then and open the door to him: *You must regret having arrived so late*, I would say with a smile.

I COULDN'T TELL him that. Once again, it was chance: we were always unlucky. Over the past two days, I hadn't wanted to see anyone. I hadn't even wanted to have news. Some were amazed that I wasn't afraid for Francesco, but, in all honesty, I hadn't had the faintest doubt of his return since the day I had succeeded in sending Tomaso away.

At night you could hear the trucks go by, without a break at first, then at increasingly longer intervals, and, little by little, the last light of the long day vanished. Francesco would come home to sleep with me, every night. I tidied the house, happy, in short, to go back to cooking for him, plumping up his pillow. And yet the house seemed to offer resistance to my preparations. My clothes had started taking up all the space in the drawers, like my books in the bookcases, my things on the bathroom shelf. Francesco's table was crowded with my dictionaries, manuscripts of my translations. It seemed impossible that we had already lived together in those rooms, each with his or her own life. I made room for him joyfully, in the apartment and in myself, as I had done when we met and he had disturbed my solitude. I imagined the wonderful long conversations we would have. I wanted to tell him what had happened and then talk at length about myself. It seemed to me that if we didn't do this he wouldn't recognize me. I wanted to tell him right then about Tomaso, about the nights when I was alone and afraid, with the thought that they might be my last nights. *Do you understand?* I would say. I would confess that I had kissed Tomaso—a long kiss on the night of the photograph—but I'd get him to understand that I was seeking him, Francesco, in that kiss, wanting his life to be saved, free. *Do you understand?* I would ask. I didn't want him to hold a grudge against Tomaso. Francesco was the winner, and so it seemed that he should behave generously with his foe and, indeed, appreciate the nobility of his sentiment and his conduct. I saw him going up to Tomaso, his hand extended. *It's natural that you should have loved her,* he would say. *It's impossible to live with her without loving her.* Arms around one another, we would say goodbye to Tomaso, and I would ask him to introduce me to Casimira. As his step faded away on the stairs, we would remain alone in the apartment, the home that was ours at last, with room for both of us: our clothes mingled, our books, the big bed where we could lie down together, guiltless.

Tomaso called to find out if I needed anything. Before hanging up, he asked if I was happy.

"Yes, I'm very happy," I admitted quietly. I didn't keep myself from asking "Do you think he'll be out soon?" Later, I recalled his flat tone when he answered, "Yes, I think he'll be with you this time tomorrow." I wanted to call him back that night, but the lines were cut off and the electricity went out; the last trucks to abandon the city wanted to leave darkness and silence behind them. In that silent darkness, I heard Francesco coming upstairs, skipping steps as Tomaso used to do.

I was obsessed by his ascending steps. *Tomorrow*, I thought. I would put on my old grey skirt and it would swirl, encircling me, I would open the door with a smile. *You must regret having arrived so late.* I let my head fall backwards as I imagined the violence of Francesco's kiss. Again, there was an emptiness around my waist where his arms should have been. *Not long now*, I said to myself, *just a few hours.*

In the morning people went out warily. They cautiously inspected the streets and squares, now empty of trucks and soldiers with rifles levelled. At first they were dismayed by the squalor, and worried that it concealed a trap, a final trick. But it was precisely the melancholy desolation of the battered, humiliated streets which assured them that the city had been abandoned. In a flash, the houses emptied and people poured out, overflowing into the streets like water. The pavements echoed once more with footsteps and people calling. Everyone was speaking aloud, neighbors called to each other from their windows. Girls rode bicycles, their hair loose in the wind. From the terrace, I watched impatient people throng the sidewalks of the long boulevard near my house, waiting for the arrival of those who'd knocked tenaciously for years at the walls of our prison, while we scratched our nails on the other side. Slowly, the wall between us was worn down, flattened, and today, finally, we would get to meet one another. Trucks packed with tall, grave soldiers had just gone out the gates to the north, and other trucks were already coming in through the southern gates, loaded with happy soldiers in shirtsleeves. The grim silence of the long, harsh day now gave way to frenzied cries and applause. So this was the moment we had all been waiting for: I should have been happy, but I wasn't, and I wouldn't be until among the steps of those returning I heard Francesco's. Out on the terrace, I was dazed by the clear air of that lovely spring, the festive shouts exploding here and there like fireworks. Voices rose from the window below, disapproving of the boisterous enthusiasm, but to me it seemed easily understood as a way of congratulating ourselves—our courage, our patience—and erasing the hard days we'd been through. Clapping, shouting, yelling, proving that the long, dreary day was truly over. You would have to be devoid of empathy not to understand how all that repressed life—restrained and gagged—had to explode somehow. My entire life was concentrated on Francesco's steps coming up the stairs.

I waited for him like that for two days. I was beginning to feel afraid. I would linger at the entrance for a long time, waiting, and, with every hour that went by, my fear deepened. I didn't call Tullio for news; when the telephone rang, I ran to it and then didn't have the courage to pick up the receiver. The bell sounded shrill in the empty house, but the cold, inscrutable black device would not have jumped if it were bringing me bad news. "I don't want to know anything," I murmured, shaking my head and stopping my ears. "They won't be able to tell me." I would stay at home and wait forever. I wouldn't go out again, so as not to meet people who might announce to me that Francesco wouldn't return. *No*, I said inside, tormenting myself, *no. Francesco must return, he will return.*

I sat on a chair in the entrance, waiting. Daylight grew, waned, and the memory of the night I waited for my mother became increasingly vivid. All at once, I heard a lot of people coming up the stairs, and then the steps came closer and I heard voices, too. They were men's. The voices and steps kept coming—and then I thought stopped on the floor below. Instead they continued. No one lived up there but me.

Someone rang the bell. *I won't open it*, I said to myself. *I don't want to know*. In the meantime, though, I opened it.

Francesco stood looking at me and smiling happily. Behind him other people were smiling.

He took me in his arms, kissed my cheeks here, there, held me close. "Oh, my dear," he said. I heard other voices, those of our comrades, the same voices I had heard when Francesco wasn't there. So it seemed impossible that he was with us now. Impossible that his return should have come about so easily. I had waited months for him, and now he was here in an instant, and we had embraced in the middle of all those people looking at us. I didn't dare separate myself from him, didn't dare look at him. I was afraid he was someone else, had become different. Besides, the other people made me embarrassed. I didn't want them to witness my emotions. I hated them.

"No," I said, hiding my face from Francesco. It really was him. I recognized the shape of his shoulders.

"Calm down," he said. I looked up and saw him smiling at the others. They said, "Of course. The shock."

Francesco stroked my chin with a faint smile. It really was his rugged face, hard and unforgiving. I loved him. I went back to holding him. "Send them away," I whispered in his ear. He nodded, putting his arm around my shoulders, and we all went into the study.

Our friends hurried to find me a seat. Francesco looked around with satisfaction at the table, the bookshelves. He touched them slowly, delicately. I waited for those people to leave, so that Francesco would look at me the way he looked at the table, and touch me the way he touched the books. He sat in the armchair and the others sat in a circle a little distance from him, randomly recounting the latest developments. It was one of those moments when you should offer a vermouth.

"You're happy to be at home, eh?" said Alberto.

"Yes," he replied. "I thought constantly about one thing: the bathtub." They laughed and then Francesco began talking with the comrades, recalling his life in prison. He held my hand while he spoke and stroked my fingers, but he didn't look at me. I felt a violent fury rising in me. I wanted to send all those people away, to be alone again, waiting for Francesco. I didn't want to linger in that stupid, chatty atmosphere.

But just then Luigi interrupted the comrades, leaned towards Francesco and said, "Your wife was very brave."

"I know. She's always courageous and brave." Francesco nodded, stroking my hand affectionately.

"Yes, but you don't know—"

"Luigi, please," I interrupted.

The other comrades protested. They, too, wanted to talk to Francesco.

"No, really," I said. And turning harshly towards Luigi: "Please, Luigi," I repeated.

Dear Luigi. He wanted to talk at any price, but he ended up ruining everything. He talked about what I had done. Now that the difficult days were over, I had convinced myself that I hadn't done anything, and Luigi's generous praise poisoned the small amount of pride I'd taken in those endeavors.

"Well done!" Francesco said. "Were you really so brave?" He tipped my chin up and I gave him a fixed smile even as I wanted to run away and cry. I could no longer make him understand that above all, it had been a way to get to know about him even what made me suffer, what was naturally foreign and inimical to me, and include it in our love. I wouldn't be able to confess to him that when I was afraid I called out to him as some call out to God. Alberto also talked about the bombs and the vegetables. Francesco stared at me for a long time before saying, "Well done," and I felt ashamed. I had nothing left to tell him now.

They all started talking again, but I felt uneasy and I was red in the face.

"Where are you going?" Francesco asked when he saw me stand up.

"To the kitchen. I want to heat some water to prepare a bath for you."

There was no gas. I lit the flame and, with some effort, poured water from a heavy jug. I sat near the stove waiting for the water to get warm.

After a while Francesco came in. "What are you doing, Alessandra?" he asked. "They want to say goodbye to you."

I said goodbye to our friends at the door, and they made their farewells one by one, as at a wedding or a christening. I closed the door at last and leaned on it with my entire body. Francesco stood in front of me; I looked at him, and with that look I ran to him as I had the first time at the Borghese Gallery. Now he was truly entering the house: he would hold me in his arms, kiss me, and I felt my lips softly surrendering. He drew near and then, looking at me lovingly, said, "You should rest, my dear. You look very tired."

He said that, and I felt the tissue of my skin freeze: it was a sensation I hadn't had since he had left.

"No, thank you," I replied. "I don't want to." I stared at him despairingly, asking myself when he would decide to return. "Why did you come home with those people?" I asked.

"They came to get me, and—"

"I know. But I wanted to see you alone."

"We're alone now, dear . . ." He was kissing me. His hands were trying to undo my blouse: maybe he thought that was the most effective way of showing his joy at coming home. I wasn't used to his hands, and my muscles tensed instinctively, defensively. I remembered how I had imagined running lightly to open the door, saying, "You must regret . . ." I pushed Francesco away gently.

"Wait, my love," I said softly. "Please, not like this . . ."

But by then it was truly difficult to start over. I knew now that he had not considered it important to see me alone, that he had thought it natural to kiss me for the first time in front of strangers, on one cheek then the other. I was worn out by anxiety and my intention not to succumb to anger and bitterness.

I felt it was absolutely necessary for us to speak first. So many things had happened during those months. We had to find one another again, almost choose one another again. "Look at me," I said. "It's been months since we last saw each other . . ."

"It seemed that it wouldn't last long, remember? We always said it wouldn't be long. But actually . . . I was worried about you. They said there was no more food, that family members were being taken hostage. I was really worried."

"That was the only thought that upset you?"

"Yes. I wasn't worried about the rest. Look: one is afraid until one is forced to surrender. Afterwards, one acquires calm. Besides, we knew there were a lot of us. There were five in my cell. I'll tell you about it later. And we sensed other people around us: all it took was a tap on the wall or a look when we were out getting some air to feel that we belonged to a private club. Above all, there was an ineffable feeling of choosing your own thoughts, collecting them, since they might be your last. You can't understand, but—"

"But I do understand," I interrupted.

"Excuse me, dear, but I don't think so. These are things you can understand only if you've been in prison—even for just a day. I don't know if that's an advantage. Maybe . . . maybe it's not an advantage. But you leave totally changed."

"I also changed a lot . . ." I whispered.

"I hope not. You stayed out."

"Yes, but that's just it," I added. "There are things that only those who stayed out can understand."

He went to the window, not replying. "It's so beautiful up here," he said. "I didn't think a few bars separating us from the sun and the countryside were so important. And yet they allow us to understand certain truths we thought we understood but didn't, not at all. They're more useful than all these books. It's undeniable that, after leaving prison, one has the impression of having some essential perceptions that can be learned only inside." He spoke without looking at me, letting his gaze run over the landscape, the countryside and the big new houses. "Yes, you have to be strong, when you're inside," he went on. "I was only concerned about you and my mother. She's gotten older, but, over all, she, too, is well."

"How do you know?" I asked in wonderment.

"I went by her house briefly—it was closer to the prison. She's well."

"Of course, you did the right thing." I turned and started for the door.

"Where are you going?" he asked, holding me back by the hand.

"To prepare your bath."

There were three large pots. I used two rags to hold them since the handles were burning hot. I carried them into the bathroom, one after the other, moving unsteadily because they were so heavy and the water was sloshing. I emptied that boiling flood into the bath and steam rose to my face, making me slightly dizzy. I wished I could carry an infinite number of pots, unburdening myself as I poured out the boiling water in one quick stream. I longed to carry weights and drop them in order to feel at least a moment of relief.

"Why didn't you call me to help you?" Francesco said thoughtfully, before he exclaimed, "Oh! the bath . . ." I was touched by his delighted amazement. *Yes, the bath,* I wanted to say, *and our home, and the sun, free outside the windows, and me, Francesco, my love, me.*

I imagined that he would want to bring his gaze back to me, gradually, through everything that had accompanied us until the moment we were separated: the apartment, the books, the view from our window. But meanwhile, he had closed the door and left me alone.

I found his suitcase by the door. Maybe he would come to me from there, I thought, clinging to a faint hope. Inside there was only dirty laundry, a comb, and a notebook. I flipped randomly through his note-book; it was a diary. All at once it became clear, and I realized that Francesco would finally speak to me from those pages. I sat on the floor near the open suitcase and looked carefully for my name: it wasn't there. I read avidly, following the lines with a finger. It was a beautiful diary, a long letter from a revolutionary on the eve of his execution. How I loved him, finding him so superior to other men. I fell in love with him all over again. I felt bound, enthralled. We fluttered together like a large flag. But he never spoke about me, or feelings of love, in those pages. At one point, alluding to the possibility of his approaching end, he said: "I hope my mother and my wife will understand."

FRANCESCO WENT TO bed early. Slowly stretching his legs out, he said, "My own room, my own sheets . . ." I had put a sprig of jasmine in a glass on the nightstand. He cheered up at the sight of it, still alive and in flower. I had told him about the evening when Denise and I had buried papers in the pots. It was a miracle that the plants continued to bloom, having served that purpose.

All that time, I was looking at him lovingly, and, as I did, it was easy to imagine the hard days he had been through. The events had been such as to reveal the fabric of our characters, to change our way of living and judging, precisely because of the total commitment they'd demanded of us. Both of us had become much more generous, and in every sense better. So it seemed that our life together, enriched by experiences from which we had emerged victorious, was beginning for the first time. Moved by the delicate beauty of the moment we were experiencing, I lay down beside him and gently closed my eyes.

"I read your diary," I told him. "Sorry—I was indiscreet." And then I added warmly, meaningfully, "I wanted to tell you that your wife would understand."

He didn't say anything, so I continued. "It's very hard to under-stand everything that comes between love and us. But when you're very much in love, you always understand in the end. I started to understand you the night we left your mother's house, remember? and we were completely alone. Then . . . Well, I'll tell you everything gradually. We've come to the same conclusion by very different routes, but what we hoped would save us both was the integrity of feeling that brought us together. You've no idea how much courage I needed . . ."

"I know, dear. Luigi told me . . ."

"No, Luigi didn't tell you anything. Anyway, we have time, now, to talk. I would like my husband to understand, too. That's why I started working. It seemed like a way of speaking to you, reaching you. I wrote to you and—"

"Yes," Francesco interrupted, "which is why they arrested me. Of course it wasn't your fault."

"What do you mean, fault?" I asked in astonishment.

"I came to the house because I didn't want you to work with us. I knew the letters wouldn't have convinced you."

"That's why you came?"

"Yes. I meant to stay only a few minutes, just enough time to convince you. I didn't expect the door to be under surveillance."

"Ah. I see."

He kissed me as if to forgive me, and said we didn't have to think about it anymore—now it was time to begin again. But I couldn't start over like that. It wasn't enough to take up our tattered habits. I felt Francesco coming close to me, the way he did when he was asking what book I was reading.

"Let's not think about anything, Sandra," he said.

If I hadn't let Tomaso come to me when he understood everything and he loved me, I couldn't let Francesco just because he was my husband, or because he had been in prison. I was thinking all this as I welcomed him into my arms.

"Francesco," I whispered lovingly into his ear. "Francesco," I murmured during the night while, awake behind the wall, I listened to the monotonous sound of the clock, ticking away the hours of my loneliness.

BUT IN THE MORNING I didn't forget. I had managed to get some sleep towards dawn, trusting that the birth of a new day would bring some natural consolation with it. But when I woke up I found my sadness and regret intact. It was early, and the clock's ticking, its inexorable and inhuman rhythm, drowned out the cries of the swallows circling our house. I'd been used to sleeping alone for some time now, so I started when I noticed a strange, awkward shape lying beside me under the white sheet.

Francesco slept on his back. The heaviness of his sleep, the still firmness of his face didn't allow the slightest opening in him. I wondered why this man found it natural to sleep in my bed without providing me with some justification for it. This man, who demonstrated only the dull satisfaction of sleeping in my bed, couldn't be Francesco. Francesco, coming home after a long absence, would have wanted to take his place again by virtue of his love, not his right.

I continued to look at him, not daring to move. His clothes in the room disturbed the harmony with which I had consoled myself; his clothes were dark and his long, stiff socks hung askew from the back of the chair. I couldn't find the least sign in him that he belonged to our happy past. I rose up on my elbows to get a better view of his face. I followed the contours of his cheeks, his forehead, the shape of his eyebrows, his lips. But he was, after all, a stranger. I was afraid. In the fear now gripping me, I recognized the nature of the fear I had felt the day before, when Francesco returned. No, I said to myself furiously, and now I felt I knew how to resist an unwarranted invasion.

"Francesco," I called, but he didn't move. "Francesco," I persisted. "Francesco . . ." I was afraid he'd gone deaf in prison, and I would never be able to talk to him again. I would circle him with my stories, but he would be unable to hear them. Maybe he had gone deaf on purpose, so he could stay locked in his own world and keep me from breaking through to him. So far, he'd spoken only of himself; he'd taken no interest in what I said and didn't bother to answer my questions.

"Francesco," I called more loudly. All he had to do was open his eyes to make my skin flush with warmth and well-being. He pulled me towards him, and held me against his side.

He lay still and looked at the furnishings in the room, the pictures on the wall. Maybe he was worried about getting too comfortable with our old ways again and not measuring up to the feelings expressed in his diary. Of course he wanted to stay as he had been, during the long day that had forced us to hold out against surrender. I wanted the same for myself. But the long day was now over: we were still young, and sure to live for a long time. We didn't even know that a benevolent invasion had begun: Francesco had come home smiling and happy, and everyone was celebrating him, just as in the streets people were clapping for the friends who had knocked for so long at the door of our prison, via the radio, and were now crossing the city in shiny trucks: smiling and happy, and handing out candy. Meanwhile, Francesco had invaded my room with his dark clothing and my bed with his dull, heavy, hostile sleep. The city walls were hung with decrees imposing the death penalty, and the palaces and beautiful villas, the meeting places where we could finally amuse ourselves had also been invaded, with systematic bonhomie. We were like dogs, waiting outside the places where our friends were eating and enjoying themselves; we, who had neither eaten nor smiled for such a long time, were humiliating ourselves by asking for charity. I was a dog keeping watch behind Francesco's back, waiting for a loving gesture, a kind word.

I was pondering these thoughts when Francesco rolled over and stroked my shoulder. I turned to him with a smile, but I could see that his eyes were closed. Maybe he thought he was still in prison, waking up with his cellmates, all of them mute with the agonizing desire for a woman. His stroking was so insistent, so limited and pointed that it

was obviously driven by some obsession. I wasn't interested in satisfy-
ing that obsession; I couldn't reduce myself to assisting his fantasy. He
would call my name, he would say, "Alessandra," and, finding me again,
would bridge that nightmarish distance between us. But still he said
nothing, while his hand invaded the jealous territory of my body. "No,"
I whispered. "No, Francesco," I said breathlessly. But he didn't hear my
voice. We didn't know each other anymore, didn't remember anything
of what we had loved about each other. He knew my romantic nature;
how could he have forgotten all that, and remember only the vows the
priest had read to us? It seemed to me that there was also an intimate
code to be respected, one that both of us had wanted to keep faith with
until now. If we had lived during a time of slavery, he would have
claimed his rights as a man, he would have fought and killed to prevent
one man owning another, because no one is entitled to own the body of
another human. You couldn't buy the body of a slave, but you could enjoy
owning the body of a woman. You acquired it with the obligation to
maintain it, just as with slaves. But if I had decided to leave Francesco,
the law would have recognized his right to remain master of my body.
He could prevent my making use of it for years, for my entire life, even
if he were a bad man, or unfaithful, or had lived hundreds of kilometers
away from me for decades. A slave has greater freedom than a woman.
And if I made free use of my body, I would get not only lashings, like a
slave; I would be imprisoned and dishonored. The only way for me to
decide for my own body would be to throw it in the river.

EARLY THAT MORNING, Tullio returned to look for Francesco.

"What do you want?" I asked as soon as the door was open. He gave
me a faint smile, as if to remind me that I should instead have greeted
him with a *buongiorno* as he had me. He wanted to talk to Francesco,
but I objected, saying that he was in the bath.

"That's all right," he said. "I'll wait." I knew his fixed determination. But I looked at him once more, taking his measure: he was thin,

blond, and not very tall. His determination was expressed wholly in the strength of his hands. If he had fought someone he could have destroyed him easily.

I went to alert Francesco. I found him standing in front of the sink shaving, his torso bare, the foamy white lather giving him a playful look.

"My love," I said, and he turned around, smiling.

I hadn't seen a man living in my house for months, with his presence, his habits that could be symbolized by a shaving brush. Taking in the sharp odor of soap mingled with the strong scent of tobacco that lingered in the tiny bathroom, I felt my pores breathing, my lungs opening, and I rebelled at the memory of all the time I had been alone. I went up to Francesco and asked him quietly, "You're not really going out with Tullio, are you?"

I was released from the nightmare that had oppressed me during the night; in fact, when I recognized Francesco, I was proud that he was my husband. Suddenly, perhaps to spite the single woman I had been until that point, I felt a bold joy, an irrepressible delight.

Surprised, Francesco turned to look at me, his razor in midair.

"Will you take me to Villa Borghese?" I asked with a playful smile, and I drew close to his soapy cheek.

I APOLOGIZED TO Tullio for leaving him alone in the study. "Francesco's coming right away," I added. "He's ready."

Tullio stood up when he saw me come in, and as I went towards him we nearly collided. "Sorry," I said, blushing, and he, too, said, "Sorry." We stood opposite each other as we had on the day when he came to get Francesco's suitcase.

He said, "I'd like to bid you farewell, Alessandra."

Tullio almost never used someone's name unless he judged it important. Otherwise, it seemed like he shied away from familiarity as he might from the danger of softening up or surrendering.

"Why?" I asked quietly, a bit suspicious.

"Because in recent days we all believed that at least our struggle had come to an end. I thought so, too. There was a moment when all I thought about was the temptation of lying down and resting. But then I realized that I couldn't do anything but go and join those who still have to become free."

"Do you really think it's so important to become free?"

"No, maybe not," he replied after a pause. "Mostly because we're never free, and one invasion is followed by another. But it's important to feel the need to liberate ourselves, and to struggle for it."

"I understand," I said, looking down. "I have the feeling we'll never stop struggling, since territories will always be invaded and there will always be people who want to free themselves . . ."

Francesco came in and we stopped talking. Tullio was leaving that evening, so he had to make arrangements with the comrades. I was still hoping that Francesco would say, *Sorry, Tullio, but I can't: the most important thing today is to be with Alessandra.* But instead he said, "Let's go." He threw a glance at the window with the obvious satisfaction of someone who would soon be enjoying the fresh air. Only moments earlier, in the bathroom, I had said to him, "Believe me, nothing is more important than being together today, the two of us, and going to Villa Borghese." And he had replied, "Be reasonable. Why today, exactly?" I had tried to make him understand that only a slender thread tied us to the possibility of making it in time—and that it would soon break. He then smiled and consoled me with that way he had of treating me as if, following our wedding, I were a child again. He said we would always have time for us, and that these were surely difficult days, but they would soon be over. "What's important," he said, admonishing me gently, "is that I've come home." He had said the same thing the night before, and I realized that he was going to keep reproaching me for his return: as if in staying alive he had made a sacrifice for which I had to be forever grateful to him. He said that at first he would have a lot to do. He tried to convince me, his words and arguments echoing the letter of the revolutionary but adapted for teaching in schools. I stared, unable to find the tiniest fissure through which my love could make its way to him. As he spoke I was overcome by fury. *Get out of here*, my look shouted at him, *don't give me all this nonsense. I might have believed you before I carried bombs with the vegetables or read Rilke with my hand on a gun.* I had no pity left for him. I thought about what Lydia had said: *Just watch: they'll make him a member of parliament.*

Francesco embraced me at the door. Tullio shook my hand and said, "Farewell." I suddenly realized that after he left I wouldn't know whom to call for help. For months, Tullio had set our daily schedule and our daily tasks and, in doing so, saved us from the perils of our own impulses and reactions. I wanted to grab his arm and ask, *Now what should I do? Let me take some more bombs, more leaflets, force me once more to banish Tomaso, force me, force me to show my best side.* But he was already on the stairs with Francesco. I stood behind the door for some time, following their receding steps with my thoughts.

FORGIVE ME, FRANCESCO now says tenderly, *forgive me, Alessandra. Tell me, have you forgiven me?* How could you not forgive a man who speaks so lovingly? And since that man is Francesco, I immediately surrender, won over. *Forgive me*, he insists. *Yes: it was all a mistake after I came back. But maybe my return was the mistake. We all survived our appointment with death. Because if ever there's a moment when you draw fully on your ideals, it's when you're waiting, hour by hour, to be called to your death. I'd never been as pure, noble, or generous as I was during that time, and, precisely because I felt that way, it pained me to die. I didn't understand that it was actually that ultimate farewell that was prompting me to become the heroic embodiment of all my finest masculine ideals. And in fact when we knew we were free I hung back—maybe instinctively; I was the last to leave the cell. I wanted* to remain the character it seemed so easy to be inside. I was alone. I looked around and whispered, "Alessandra." Because every second of that time, and everything I'd achieved in myself, was dedicated to you. I didn't write about it in the diary: if I had so much as entered into the whirling vortex of your name, my every resolution would have been overturned. I would have written to you that I was desperate to die, and I might have asked you: Help me! I would have felt depressed and humiliated. But I was proud to be the only one among my comrades who didn't cry. If you had read that romantic desperation in my diary, you would have judged me a weak man who'd died full of turbulent feelings, hatred and resentment. But I wanted you to think of me as a man for whom loyalty to his own moral precepts was even stronger than love. I wanted to remain the same in your memory as I'd seemed to you when we first met. At the beginning of the bitter months of struggle, I was very often on the point of giving in. I didn't want to work with Tullio again after the armistice. I was afraid, too. And it was very difficult to accept losing that fear in the fight: if I did so, it was really for you, at the cost of appearing not to love you. I preferred you to imagine me like that, rather than to see me hidden in some cellar or dressed up as a friar in a monastery; you would have remembered what you said about me and my goals and you would have had proof that I was only a blowhard. Now, you see, I can speak to you frankly: in prison, I always feared being placed against the wall and executed, and I thought constantly about how I'd act at that moment, my demeanor, the last word I'd utter. I felt that my choice of word would be very important: I certainly couldn't have called out "Alessandra!" with rifles levelled at me. But in fact it was "Alessandra" I would have been saying when I shouted "Long live freedom!" I would have told you all this immediately if I had come home, in a single step, from the cell to our study. But the comrades came to get me and I went out with them—and that's how I noticed that the city hadn't changed a bit since I'd gone to prison. The first thing I noticed was a lady in white gloves, walking her dog on a leash. You know, these are minor considerations that those who've been outside may not understand, but when you're in prison, with bedbugs, you can't believe someone could think of taking a dog for a walk. These thoughts are often expressed, or taken for granted, I know that very well. But we really thought the city was holding its breath, huddled around the dying and the imprisoned. Then I saw a couple walking arm in arm, their stride demonstrating their love. I thought, maybe the way to utter a final word of love to you would be to call out Alessandra! alongside Long live freedom! That seemed the most passionate way of giving expression to love. Yet again, though, we didn't make it in time to express ourselves the best way we knew how. On the city walls there were signs in foreign languages, arrows, billboards. Other soldiers were going by in trucks, but they were smiling and had rosy, clean-shaven cheeks. When I turned into our street, I was amazed to find that our house had not been crushed or destroyed by suffering. I could see no sign of distress: not even a broken window or a scratch on the walls of the stairwell. I thought coldly that it would all have been like this even if I had died. Surviving was my mistake. My only hope was you: I believed you had remained safe from the cruel suffering, from the sad homecomings, and that's why I counted on you to restore me to what I'd been in prison and in my diary. You alone would recognize in me something superior. You would look at me, astonished, and I could tell you my story and you would listen in bewilderment and admiration, not realizing how easy it can be sometimes to embrace heroism. Only you could save me, and I convinced myself of that, finding you the same as ever, so beautiful, even though you were surrounded by things that are superfluous to a man's simple needs. Even though I soon noticed that you'd learned to say no sometimes, like Tomaso. When they told me what you'd done, I could hardly believe it, because I didn't want to know. But they made a point of it. And I noticed the vehemence with which you tried to get them to stop talking about it. It was actually your insistence that surprised me, because I recognized in it the hidden flaw of everyone who's been in prison or *carried a bomb in a shopping bag. Now, like me, you knew everything. You couldn't help me. That's why I asked Tullio if I could keep working with him, begged him to make me work like a dog. It hounded me, leaving you alone, but I kept doing it. I wanted to be really alone, properly alone as I had been in prison, in order to rediscover the confidence I'd had then. Gradually, however, I felt the moment of death moving off. The ideal of the manly hero had disappeared from within me. Yes, it's true: I told myself I'd be elected to parliament. And just as I hid my love for you behind dutiful feelings when I was in prison, so behind the unavoidable obligations I tried to impose on you I hid my miserable ambition to be more than just someone who had outlived the myth of the manly hero, exalted in death. Oh, forgive me, Alessandra, forgive me!*

I WAS NO longer forgiving, though. I was still alone, and, from the moment I sent Tomaso away, I hadn't had anyone to talk to or confide in. I rarely saw Francesco during the day. He often stayed in the city, and since he couldn't warn me, owing to disruptions in the phone lines, I'd end up waiting for him, heating and reheating his lunch. He was always busy with his friends, and seemed to want to keep me away from his interests and activities. Sometimes I asked myself why I still loved him: but the resentment, the spite, and all the bad feelings I harbored were ways of loving him all the same. One evening when he was home, I tried to talk to him about the time we had been apart. I noticed that he always avoided talking about it. I hoped that he would at least be interested in the work I had done with Tullio and that he was continuing. Francesco granted me his affectionate but distracted attention. I was reduced to talking about a new dress I wanted to buy. But my words no longer elicited an echo from him, and, if at night we were divided by a wall, during the day there was a book between us.

The comrades often came to see us in the evening to talk about Tullio and the work he was doing in the north. The long day quickly retreated from the city, and as soon as it vanished it took on the importance of a heroic legend, even in the eyes of those who had lived through it. Yet it had been our most beautiful time, and we had to refer to it, as we do to childhood, to explain certain things about ourselves. In fact, when we were talking, we would often say, "Remember?" as Fulvia and I now did. Then, too, I found nothing to say to the comrades now: the friendship we had feigned was contrived, and the fact was they had gone back to being Francesco's friends. When they brought along a new friend or comrade, they would briefly introduce me as Signora Minelli, and, drawing him away by the arm while he hoped to linger with a polite comment, they would introduce him to Francesco in an entirely different voice. And then they would describe my husband's now famous ordeals. I was glad that they didn't mention the humble missions I had accomplished, since their value for me was entirely personal, and it bothered me that others made free use of them. All the same, I started to suspect that the bombs I had carried weren't real; to wonder if only the ones the men carried were dangerous; I questioned the content of the fliers; remembered that the messages were for the most part inane sentences, like the ones you find in foreign language grammars. Maybe they didn't mean anything. I began to believe that they had been prepared just to mock me. But, even if they had been fake, it wouldn't have been important. I had carried them with the same fear, I had accepted an equal risk. And now we were all here, all safe, all survivors.

So I often stayed in a corner, silent and intimidated. Absorbed in his own arguments and surrounded by sympathetic company, Francesco would occasionally turn to me during the evening to ask, "Please, darling, would you bring us some lemonade?" I would go back to sitting there quietly, and I would remember the way Sista ironed my father's white shirt, her cruel persistence around the collar. It must have given her a sort of relief.

IT WAS LATE afternoon when Tomaso came. "Is the boss here?" he asked with a smile. I started at the sight of him. And hearing that phrase, which took us back to the period of our first encounters, I was worried that I would have to start everything over again.

"No," I replied quietly, "he's not here."

Tomaso had not yet seen Francesco, because he had had to go to Naples on business for the newspaper as soon as the city was liberated. I bought the paper every morning, and when I saw his name in it I folded it up and carried it home under my arm. At those times it seemed to me I was still a very beautiful woman.

He came into the study and immediately looked around, slowly, as Francesco had done. But I felt his passionate, melancholy gaze seeking me on the cherished walls, the features of my face.

"Are you happy, Alessandra?" he asked, staring at a vague spot where he had found my eyes.

I hesitated a moment before saying softly, "Yes." There was a serious, awkward silence between us.

"Right, I get it," he said. "I felt calmer when I couldn't leave Saverio's house, and later, while I was in Naples. I thought you were waiting for me and I'd find you when I got back. Now I won't have a moment's peace." He paused and then went on. "I should have stayed that night. I shouldn't have obeyed you. At the time, an order from Tullio mattered more than a marriage certificate. I should have taken advantage of those laws—for your good as well."

I didn't want him to speak like that. "Tomaso," I reproached him.

"Sorry," he whispered. Contrite, he was silent again, and I felt a vague but overpowering fear. With a couple of languid steps, I put the table piled with papers between us. As he leafed through a magazine, Tomaso asked, "Where's the translation?"

"Over there, because here—"

"I understand."

In a few days the table had meekly let itself be overrun by Francesco.

"What did he say about the translation?"

"Who?" I asked. Tomaso kept leafing through the magazine but didn't answer. "Ah," he said quietly. "He hasn't seen it yet . . . And he hasn't asked you to—"

I interrupted. "But he doesn't even know I'm working on it."

He looked up at me for the first time, and his gaze expressed a question. Now that Francesco was back, I felt defenseless. "What did you come here for?" I asked in a hostile tone.

"To see you. I called immediately, but the line was still disrupted. All the same, I felt I could hear the bell ringing in the house: I know its vibration, its echo. I know that you put your hand between your mouth and the receiver when you speak, as if you were ashamed of what you're saying." He paused, and I felt as if I'd suddenly stopped breathing. But Tomaso was afraid of hurting me, so he went back to perusing the magazine and said in a different tone, "I came to say goodbye to the boss."

I realized that I hadn't spoken for some time. Then Francesco came home, and he and Tomaso embraced. I was about to stop him: I feared that, as he did so, Francesco would become aware of everything. Maybe he would suddenly pull back his hand, look at it in shock, and murmur, *What's going on?* I shouted inwardly to warn him. *No*, I said, *no! Help me. Don't embrace him. Insult him. Send him away!* But Francesco didn't hear my pleading resounding in the room: he was deaf, and that was the only time when, watching him, I enjoyed the deceit, as I had with my father when I went to phone Villa Pierce.

"I came to say goodbye to the boss," Tomaso said.

"Finally!" he exclaimed with joyful reproach. "You're always joking." Patting him on the shoulder, he added, "I'm really glad to see you."

My thoughts were disturbed all night. *No*, I fretted, *I won't let Francesco reduce me to this.* When Tomaso was at the door, he had said, "Come back soon." Tomaso replied, "Thanks, maybe tomorrow," meanwhile staring at me as if confirming a date. I knew how tenacious Tomaso was and I felt that he would use that against my will. As I washed my face, I looked at myself in the mirror. *Yes*, I repeated, to measure how firmly I had replied to his question: *Are you happy?* Then I reassured myself that the phone was still disconnected and drew a sigh of relief. The next day I would stay out all day, but I didn't know where to go. This is how it became clear to me that my mother and I had never had friendships. Tullio, it seemed, was the only one to have intuited the fervent passion of my character. But it was now impossible to communicate with him. He had crossed the front, and Francesco regretted not having gone with him.

"Why didn't you?" I asked him.

"For you," he replied.

At that point I could no longer hold back a scornful, vicious laugh. "For my sake? To what end? We haven't once gone out together and we haven't spoken, not even for a moment." He protested, and, hearing him repeat that these were difficult days, I jumped up to sit on the bed and my face unnerved him. "Ah no, Francesco, no, right? Neither you nor I believe in those things anymore." He turned onto his side and turned off his light. In the small circle of light on the other side of the bed, I lay beside a dark abyss.

I could no longer control my thoughts. I saw Tomaso's look reach me across the paltry defense of the table. I didn't feel safe. He seemed to have sensed my weakness. Warned by the merciless ticking of the clock, I felt that the fateful passage of time would not allow me to linger in this conflict. Tomaso would surely come the next day. I heard him climbing the stairs, two at a time. I had imagined Francesco climbing the stairs to me just like that on his return. I felt it unacceptable to confuse them so freely. I didn't want them to greet one another affectionately. I preferred them as adversaries, but they would become friends. It was what I feared: that they would become inseparable. They would exhibit the same tastes, adopt the same habits. Tomaso would come more often to our house—every day. If he couldn't come one day, Francesco would feel his absence. Maybe it would put him in a bad mood. *No*, I said to myself, but my blood circulated to the rhythm of that step. Tomaso would ring our bell the next day, and after a few moments he would start ringing again. A little longer, longer still, never stopping: a pleading call. *It has to open*, he would say to himself, *it will open*.

It's not possible for someone in love to call and get no answer. Yet I called Francesco all night and he never answered. I strained my ears and I heard the mute sound of an insistent bell: Tomaso had already come and was ringing the bell. The sound rose, continuous, tireless. I made a futile attempt to distract myself, crushing my ear against the pillow so as not to hear it. It was drilling into my mind. *Soon, Alessandra*, Tomaso said that day. *I'm being followed.* The sound wouldn't stop, so I got up and went to the door, because when someone is in danger you must always reply. *Here I am*, I said in response to the sound. I opened the door but didn't see anyone. The stairs were dark, the doors were closed. The sound persisted ruthlessly. I worried that it was Francesco calling, and I ran straight to the bedroom. He was sleeping, his face still, arms clasped around himself as if in self-defense. *But if you don't succeed* . . . Nonna challenged me. I had given her a brazen answer: "If I don't succeed, I'll kill myself."

The next day I went out in the early afternoon, though with no idea of where I was going. I didn't have any money, and besides, unlike many women, I had never had a taste for buying things, which is a way to validate yourself. I begged Francesco to go with me, but he was busy. I went to sit at the Villa Borghese and took a book with me, as I had often done in high school. As the light faded, a somber fear took hold of me. I wished our house had a lovely window with a view of trees and swallows circling it in flight. Our windows, however, looked out on a sad landscape separated from us by a row of tall, untidy white buildings. As evening approached, the kitchens would light up, one above the other. When I was a child, all those lighted windows made me curious and I wanted to know the stories of the people who lived there. But now

I knew that there is always an unhappy story in those houses, and I no longer wanted to look.

I came home rather late, and the doorman handed me a note from Tomaso. "He told me to give it to you when I saw you alone," he said quietly. My first instinct was to refuse it, but I held back because of the complicity established between us on account of the photo. His was a delicate job in any case, in which one knows too many things that one must pretend not to know. By now, I knew he was a good man: he hadn't wanted me to be alone the night Francesco was arrested. I often reflected with some astonishment that many people are truly good. In fact, I had never met someone who was all bad inside. Even the officer who had arrested Francesco must have been good: I realized it when I heard him talk with such regret about his home and his books. It seemed to me that with so many good people in the world it should be easy to be happy all the time. But, on the contrary, things happened to prevent it, and, instead of reading Rilke, you were forced to arrest or kill.

As soon as I got home, I opened the note: Tomaso said he had come and had rung the bell for about half an hour. I hadn't wanted to open the door, but he would come back the next day and the next, until I decided to open it. He said all this lovingly, just the way he always talked to me. I had walked a long way, I was exhausted, and I had only troubled, rudimentary thoughts: *sleep hunger Francesco Tomaso.*

I went to the kitchen, took a piece of bread, and dipped it in water the way Sista used to do. I recognized the soft taste and I felt as if I had returned to the time when my mother was alive and we were waiting for her in the kitchen. Sista, too, was good. I saw her again, bending over to lace my mother's shoes. Everyone in the world was good, but we were all likely to show it at different times, so that we were never aligned. If Tomaso had had a telephone, I would have called him to say, *Don't ring at the door, please: don't do it,* I would have begged. *Because I'll surely end up answering.*

•   •   •

FRANCESCO AND I sat in the study after supper. He had come home in a serene mood and I immediately tried to fit in with him, hoping to be in time to spend a happy evening together. Outside the windows was the desperate expanse of summer air, yet the study was cozy and welcoming. Looking around, though, I saw everywhere the signs of the loneliness I had experienced between those walls. The cushions on the armchair, no longer proudly fluffed up, exhibited housewifely submission. Francesco was sitting in the armchair Tomaso used to sit in when he came to see me.

Tomaso's visits, I thought with a shudder, had also served to give life to the room. In fact, I felt that its intense character, which surprised everyone who entered it for the first time, owed something to the hours we had spent together there. "It's so pleasant in this room, Alessandra," people said. And I always answered the same way, so that by now it had become habitual: "You can feel that I live in it. The apartment is so small, and I'm forced to spend all day in here."

From the chair in which Francesco was sitting I saw Tomaso looking at me, smiling tenderly. "I don't know which you love more: me or this room," I had playfully reproached him once.

"Both," he had replied without hesitation. "This room is you: without you it would lose all its charm." I smiled and he continued. "It's your world. One falls for your world as soon as one encounters it. That's why one can't accept being with you for only an hour or a day."

I discovered a sort of heroism in the solid warmth of that room. It seemed to me that it had become intimate and welcoming at the cost of my suffering. The armrests on the chair were worn by the feverish rubbing of my hands when I couldn't overcome my anxiety for Francesco or the desire to call Tomaso. In a wave of gratitude, I went back in my mind to all the harrowing hours I had spent there the evening I read Rilke with my hand on the gun; and to my agitation, which was vented in the smoke from the bad cigarettes I rolled for myself when I was alone. It had been a prison, a cell, a torture chamber, but Francesco was now sitting opposite me, and I could watch him while he read. We would have to defend that room as we had defended ourselves from the temptation to surrender.

"Francesco, I'd like to talk to you."

Surprised, he looked up from his book. "What is it?" he asked, barely glancing at me before going back to his reading.

I studied his face, his fine figure, his hands, which made me feel an amorous longing as they moved. Oh, I loved him intensely! I sparkled as I looked at him, enhanced by sweet affection and knowing pride. I had never been as beautiful as I was at that moment.

"I'd like to talk to you," I began once more, gently, and Francesco put his open book on his knees and waited. "During these months," I went on, "first when you were hidden and then when you were in prison, someone fell in love with me. I was alone and this love, so devoted, so persistent . . ."

"Did you have a lover?" he interrupted, serious but calm, trying to conceal the import of his question.

"No," I replied instantly, victorious but shocked. "No . . . But the temptation was unbearable." After a pause, I added softly, "It was one of your friends."

Francesco didn't immediately ask who it was, which disappointed me. I didn't want him to imagine a second-rate rival, a mediocre man, easy to resist. I was waiting for him to ask me *Who?* Inwardly I formulated the question and suggested it to him, but his silence undermined my confidence.

For a little while, Francesco's fingers played contemptuously between the pages of the book. Finally he said, "I don't like these men who take advantage of a husband's absence to court his wife. Especially when the husband is in prison. They're not loyal and they're not good sports."

"But he was in love with me!" I corrected him, anguished, fearing that Tomaso would be misunderstood and humiliated.

"Oh, come on!" Francesco exclaimed sarcastically. "In love! . . . No, I don't like those men. I'm sure you don't, either."

That's what he said, and then he went back to reading. He hadn't asked me who it was, didn't want to know—as was the case with so many other problems he avoided with quick and easy judgments. Fear of such a judgment kept me from speaking now: if I had confessed to him how tempted I was, he would have mocked me, perhaps, or maybe he would have doubted my love for him. Besides, it was difficult to talk to him after hearing him say *in love* the way my father had said *amuse himself* when speaking of Francesco. I tried to stay calm, hoping to defend myself and also to defend Francesco and that room. It was necessary, therefore, for him to understand me; I wanted him to understand that fighting a war like that, trusting only in our conscience, hadn't been as easy as he thought. I wanted to talk to him about the nights I had spent lying awake, about the things Tomaso had said to me. He couldn't ignore the battle I had waged, the doubts that had assailed me, the desire I had repressed and forced myself to stifle. I had had to fight all that was beautiful, alive, and attractive. And though he had held out against the forces of brutality and evil, which it's natural to struggle against, I had held out against love.

"Francesco . . ." I called to him, bewildered. I begged him to understand that it had been very difficult, and that he shouldn't just say *wives* but *you, Alessandra*, a woman carrying the same anxious fairy tale that every woman carries inside her, one that is dearer to her than anything, dearer even than freedom. I looked at him, fearful, worried that he was no longer the man I had walked with on the Janiculum, if he didn't remember my romantic nature or how important certain feelings were for me. I was afraid he had forgotten everything that had given me ecstasy and joy with him, waiting for him, in his arms, I was afraid he had become a relative, my husband. What right did "my husband" have to sit in that room? "Help me, Francesco," I said. "Why have you never helped me?"

Again he put his book down. He stared at me in surprise, and also annoyance, it seemed.

"How could I help you, Sandra?" he said calmly. "There are moments when each of us knows very well what we have to do. A woman has to know that better than others; she has to carry it in herself. You knew, in fact. It seems pointless for us to dwell on this subject further."

Silenced by his strength, I didn't answer. It's not true that a woman knows very well what she has to do; she only knows in principle, and principles don't count. I didn't know at all, especially since he'd come back, and his person was at odds with the image of him I had formed in his absence, and had relied on. I wanted to drive him out of the study, wipe him from my thoughts, from my life; but I felt that I would never dare close the door after him. *Help me, Francesco*, I begged inwardly, since I loved him too much to beg aloud. I had got into the habit of calling him in silence, hoping he would know how to listen. *We still have time*, I told him, *only you can save me: Save me!* But he never listened.

My sobs tore him from his reading. He came over to me and stroked my hair. "Why are you crying, darling?" he said tenderly. "I'm sure you've done nothing wrong."

WELL, I ADMIT that from that evening my memories become hazy and confused. The feelings have remained clear in me, the whole exasperated tangle of them, but I wouldn't know how to place them on any given day or at any precise time, since they all seem to get lost in a dark, endless night.

It was after this apparently peaceful discussion that the terrible night began. It started with a heavy sleep in which I had a nightmare that often returned to oppress me later, during the rare moments when I slept.

I dreamed that I was a dog. In the dream, I was aware of this new state of being. I was an old dog, and although I couldn't see myself, I felt the weight of my old skin hanging on my shamefully thin body. It was night, and I was walking with my head down, maybe because my ears were dangling the way my braids had when I was a child. I was walking beside a wall, because it protected me from the cold; I walked and walked, hoping that the wall would open up, and I would be welcomed into a warm house where I would finally be able to lie down and sleep. I was exhausted, and my stomach was twisted by pangs of hunger. Now and again, I was surprised to see an open door and I would immediately ask for shelter: animated by a hopeful contentment, I would sit and watch the inhabitants of the house, promising to dedicate to them all the life that remained to me. I looked at them, promising a serious commitment that was visible in the way I carried my head, in my proud, noble muzzle. But immediately they all drove me away, harshly, and I found myself outside again, without having satisfied my hunger or, above all, having been able to demonstrate my loyal devotion. Mortified, I sat in the dirt under the shadow of the wall. I started over again, and again I was chased away. Sometimes I sat patiently outside the door for hours, waiting for them to call me back: it was inconceivable that no one wanted a good dog like me.

I woke up and struggled to shake off the sense of that grim humiliation. Little by little, I stopped being a dog, but I remained tense and upset, and my heart beat frantically. Francesco slept beside me. He could sleep even while I was a dog and everyone was chasing me away. The alarm clock didn't stop, never skipped a day, an hour. So the night never ended.

I woke Francesco, told him about the dog, and he confided that he often dreamed that he was still in prison. I think I was alone for a long time, because I have a memory of the doorbell ringing insistently, and I see myself walking back and forth crazily between the desolate walls, wringing my hands, plugging my ears, yet somehow finding the strength to resist opening the door.

Sometimes I didn't get out of bed for the whole day. Francesco stroked my hair, told me that I was too tired, that I should call a doctor.

There was a constant tremor under my skin, and my forehead and neck had gone as rigid as steel. Now I heard the doorbell ringing even when Francesco was home. He was deaf, or maybe pretending not to know what the sound meant.

"Stay with me," I begged him. But I was always alone, even when he stayed. And now I was afraid of being alone. I felt I was governed by a force that was sweeping me along. "Don't leave me," I begged. But he would point to the alarm clock, check it against his wristwatch, leap up, and a short time later I would hear the door slam behind him. I would run to look over the balcony: maybe if I threw myself off it and fell in front of him, Francesco would finally look at me. *Yes*, I thought, leaning over the windowsill, *just there, where the sidewalk ends*. Francesco went out the door and walked over me without realizing it. I felt his hard shoes on my face and on my supine body, inert in the slack posture of death. Nonna's words jabbed at me: *And if you don't succeed? If I don't succeed, I'll kill myself.* The words jumped around in me like a broken record. I never saw Francesco's face, and I would try so hard to picture it that my eyes clouded with tears. *My love*, I wanted to say, *I'm afraid! I fear that what happened to my mother might happen to me.* I had the distinct feeling that I wouldn't be able to control my actions. I clung to Francesco, so that, by holding me still, he could stop me from carrying out what I proposed to do during the day. My nerves relaxed only when I imagined the cold pistol against my temple. Then I would fall into a benign and refreshing sleep. *Sleep*, I dreamed Francesco was saying, *sleep in my arms. I love you so!* The night was lovely and cool and my mother moved around me like a breeze. I was a dog sitting in the shade of a tall tree in the garden at Villa Pierce. Happy, I laid my muzzle on the grass. Finally I could see the white peacocks opening their fantails, the orchids on the trees, the butterflies with colorful wings, and the great cedar of Lebanon inhabited by a horse. *Sandi*, my mother said as she came towards me with her graceful step, *Oh! you must regret having arrived so late.*

Then I fell asleep by the tree. Perhaps no one can understand what it means for a poor, tired dog to put its head down on a thick, damp, grassy lawn. Tomaso knelt beside me, ruffling my hair, and he told me I would never leave Villa Pierce. He would watch over me and stop anyone approaching. He stroked me gently, and once more I felt all the happy rush of youth beneath my skin. Contented, I raised my head to look into Tomaso's eyes. It was the first time a man had looked at me with such kindness.

I was always at home, and I heard Tomaso's voice on the telephone, which had been reconnected because Francesco was now an influential person, and some said that he would soon become an undersecretary. I decided not to answer, and then I worried that it might be a call for Francesco. To tell the truth, I knew it was Tomaso. I asked him, "Do you really love me? Then please have the paper send you on a reporting trip."

But Tomaso, who loved me so much, didn't want to help me, either.

Francesco and I looked at each other like enemies, or at least I looked at him that way, and the thing most bitterly hostile to him was my love for him. We had gone out together one night and I felt nervous and awkward, as if it were the first time I'd gone out with a man. I imagined we'd walk slowly, talking without looking at each other, as we had when we first met, trusting in the sweet complicity of the summer night. But he said he wanted to see some documentary at the movies. It was playing at a cinema near our house. We were sleepy and silent on the way home, and the streets between the white buildings were melancholy, deserted. A swarm of fireflies suddenly lit up the honeysuckle-scented air, and at the sight of them I wavered in my decision to die: I couldn't bear the thought of never seeing fireflies again, never catching the scent of honeysuckle.

We were in bed when I said to Francesco, "Listen, my love, I have something to tell you."

He turned towards the clock to object. "Now?"

"When else can I speak to you? We never see each other."

"So you're scolding me for working?"

"Oh, why do you say that, Francesco? Anyway, we can't work and do nothing else. We mustn't be reduced to that. I'm ready to give up everything except being with you, talking. I don't know what you think anymore. So I don't know where to start. And I worry about going in a different direction from you . . ."

"Oh no," he said, "don't torment yourself . . ."

"But I do torment myself. Our conversations, our intimacy come after everything else—that's just how it is. All it takes is the arrival of a friend, an important editorial to derail you. Do you see? To a friend, you'll say *Sorry, I can't see you, I have to go out. I have an appointment with Alberto*, but you'd never say, *I can't see you because I have to talk to Alessandra*. If you're called to a meeting and you have a previous commitment, you say, *Forgive me, I'm sorry but I can't*. But you accept instantly if that commitment was to spend the evening with me. You think we'll always have time for us, which means we never have time, so you talk to everyone else more than you do to me, and everyone knows you, knows what you think. I'm the only one who knows nothing about you."

"We had the entire evening to talk . . ."

"But tell me, how could we, at the movies?" I was so distressed that I made one last attempt. "Listen, why don't we go and live on Capri, you and I? You could write books, and I earn enough with my translations. And we're used to not spending very much."

I told him about the big window, and everything that Tomaso had described. But he shook his head like my father. "If only!" he sighed. "Maybe later." At his reply, I succumbed to an ugly feeling of resentment. Finally, after kissing me on the cheek, he stroked my hair. "Sleep now, my dear," he said, getting ready for sleep himself. It upset me terribly that the hand that caressed me burned my scalp like a branding iron.

"Sorry, but I can't sleep, Francesco. Keep me company. I'm so afraid that—" I was ashamed to confess my haunting obsession. I was afraid he would scold me, like a parent with a child. "Yes, well, I don't think I'll live much longer." I blushed as I said it, meanwhile thinking it was really over between us if I blushed when I confided my thoughts to him. He reassured me, saying I had a very healthy constitution, and he suggested thoughtfully that I go and stay with my father for a few days now that the heat was so oppressive. "I don't feel that well myself," he added.

It then seemed to me necessary for him to know. I felt a duty to reveal my desperate plan, so that he would come to my aid. "Listen, Francesco. I'm afraid I'll end up like my mother."

He seemed to give little weight to my words. "Nonsense!" he said. "You mustn't think such nonsense. You are very different from your mother."

"What do you mean?" I asked, ready to defend myself.

"You're calm, serious, rational . . ." I looked at him in amazement, wondering if he was actually talking about me. "Your mother, on the other hand. . . ." He hesitated, and now I wanted to press him to go all the way with his revelations.

"My mother?" I persisted.

"I don't know," he went on, uncertain. "I didn't know her, but—"

"But?! Say it! Go on."

"I think she was a bit excitable . . ."

"Ah," I said, and I froze. "I see."

Francesco tried to excuse himself. "I don't know. You might not like what I've said. Are you upset?"

"No, not at all."

"Well, that is what I really think," he went on seriously, "and in fact I'd like you, too, to be convinced of it."

"Right. I understand. But I don't think it will be easy." I was silent, overflowing with anger, like the smooth, frozen surface of a lake under which the water rages torrentially.

Francesco wound his watch and checked it against the alarm clock.

"Goodnight, my dear," he said. And after kissing me on one cheek, he turned his back to me, leaving me alone with my thoughts behind the wall.

Awake and unmoving, I remembered the time when we were courting and we went to kiss in the shadow of the Lungotevere, near the place where my mother died. I talked about her, and Francesco had seemed to be listening devotedly. Perhaps he had judged her harshly from then on. Anyway, he noticed that after that conversation I kissed him with increasing passion, and so he urged me to speak. We had looked over the parapet, into the wind, and I raised the collar of my old raincoat. At the time, he was a solitary man, and he was enchanted to discover the fantasy world of a young girl whose mother had killed herself for love. But now it involved his wife. Very slowly and methodically, he was proposing to alter my characteristics. He would have liked it if I took after his mother in my old age, with the tight white choker, the maid with the starched cap, the pretty teacups. He said I was calm, relaxed, rational. How could he truly think that of me? I was struck by the suspicion that Francesco meant, with these words, to suggest a model for me. He had once said to me, "I'd like to see you dress more elegantly." Maybe he was thinking of me as the wife of the undersecretary.

"So," I asked him, in one of the moments of that dark, foggy night, "so you think that we should resign ourselves, accept marriage?" I waited, trembling: my entire life depended on his answer.

He sighed and shrugged his shoulders. "It's the most ancient of institutions."

I threw myself on the floor beside him, clasped his knees, and begged him, "No, Francesco, no! No!" Hatred and love were so confused in me that I embraced him even as I wanted to wound him.

"What did I say? That's a general opinion. It has nothing to do with you and me. I love you, Alessandra. Our marriage is a happy one."

I heard the front door slam. I dreamed of being a tired dog walking behind the wall.

We had to accept our marriage. That's why he would never let me talk about Tomaso. I'd tried many other times. "I'd like to talk to you," I would begin. Francesco wouldn't look up from his writing, or the paper, or his book. "I'd like to talk to you," I would repeat, trying to make my voice heard beyond the wall. "Listen to me: I'd like to talk to you." But there was always a car waiting at the entrance, a friend in his study. I would end up not talking. Because adultery is an institution just as ancient, and I was too in love with him not to give in. I already accepted the notes Tomaso sent me through the porter and no longer avoided his collusion. On the contrary, once, saying "Thank you," I gave him some money. But I was awake for a long time that night. I couldn't forget Lydia, who wrote to Mantovani at the porter Salvetti's address. When I fell into an exhausted sleep, I dreamed of being a dog outside the kitchen doors. I relished the greasy smell of the food, and the servants threw me scraps. And I always found something in the trash cans, so I was no longer hungry, and I slept with a full belly and a sense of well-being. "Francesco," I called, waking up. "I've had a sad dream, a nightmare. It was a horrible night." I felt that he struggled to believe me.

"Sleep now," he said. "Don't think about it. Sleep."

Lydia said that when you're young it's lovely to meet in secret: you lie easily when you're young, she had observed. It's a game. Even meeting in furnished rooms seems like an amazing adventure. I was a grown woman now, so it was time I lost my habit of blushing so easily. Francesco was an influential man who had the right to ask his wife to dress elegantly. I would learn to be relaxed about going out. *I'm going to the dressmaker*, I'd say, *I have an appointment with the hairdresser*. He would make a fuss over me when I came back, the way Tomaso had with Casimira when she waited for him in a new dress. His silences would no longer upset me, I would no longer say *Help me* or *Stay home with me*. Then he would think, with satisfaction, that I had truly become calm, serious, and rational, as he wanted, and that women are happy only when they have a pretty new dress. *They don't want anything else,* he would conclude somewhat bitterly. Every day, Tomaso would tell me *You're so lovely* and *I love you* and all the other beautiful things he was always saying. We were young, and we would laugh as we looked around the furnished room. Then, while Francesco thought I was at the dressmaker or the hairdresser, Tomaso would start devoutly unbuttoning my new dress.

No! I protested furiously. I didn't want him to drive me to that. If my love for Francesco could spoil and turn bad, then everything about me could as well, I was certain. And I would lose everything by surrendering. I didn't want to surrender. Anyway, he didn't want to surrender when I had begged him to: he was the one who had provided the example of that costly intransigence. By accepting his motives, I had simultaneously reinforced mine. *We have to endure*, he told me. Nonna's monotonous voice insinuated itself into my sleep, disturbing the prolonged dozing that soothed my nerves. *And if you don't succeed? I'll kill myself*, I answered. *I'll kill myself.* The thought calmed me. I felt as if I were lying on the river's green bed, with the water flowing over my body: green, opalescent, clear. The trees and sky were reflected in me. Through the water, I saw Tomaso bending over me, calling me anxiously, distraught. But I could no longer hear anything, and I smiled without answering. Then I saw Francesco's face: harsh and sad, his eyes cold. *Alessandra*, he said softly, and his voice, like the water, encircled me. *Alessandra.* I immediately got up at his call. Francesco walked ahead of me and I followed him, but I was a dog as I followed him, a tired dog whose old coat was dripping with water.

I would never stop loving him, not even in death. My mother, though, was lying gracefully in the river. At that moment, I was gripped by a spiteful anger towards her. I wished she had fled with Hervey and they had lived together for years in the same house, the same bed. Maybe she would no longer be able to get up in the morning with the light step she had when she flew down the stairs to go to Villa Pierce.

"Francesco!" I shook his arm to wake him. "Francesco, listen." It was humiliating to reveal the bitter taste of my suffering, but I said, "Please, don't sleep. I'm too upset. I'm afraid."

He asked drowsily, "What is it, Sandra?"

"I can't bear to be alone tonight. Help me."

He answered, "Calm down, dear. I have to get up early tomorrow morning."

He might already have been at the door, hat on his head, wearing his coat as in the photograph. He said goodbye and I heard the door slam. He was a stranger though he shared my bed. I looked at his dark head lying on the white pillow. "Francesco," I whispered. I wanted to remind him of those nights at the beginning of our marriage when we stayed up late loving each other in the fresh scent that came through the open window. Afterwards, we would talk and smoke, our minds alert, our bodies young, free, and happy. Until the swallows came to chasten us and we hurried to turn out the light, as if caught in the act. Francesco often had to get up only an hour later; but he never resented the lost sleep. I wanted to say to him, *Don't sleep at all tonight. I'm afraid. Throw away one night for me, Francesco, please give me that.* But when I turned towards him I found he had already fallen asleep again. Maybe everything would have been different if we had had separate rooms and I hadn't seen him sleeping.

I rose up on one elbow and stared at Francesco, calling him desperately. My eyes were sweet names, passionate words of love. In the shadows, the precise features of his face got lost, consumed by the violence of my gaze. Sometimes his thin profile even seemed to assume the heavy strength of my father's. He resembled him, of that I was certain: it was him. Shocked, I ran my hand over my eyes to chase away that hallucination. I tried to calm myself by considering that they had nothing in common besides the shape of their broad shoulders. In summer Francesco slept without his pajama top, and his naked shoulders made a tall, unscalable white wall. Just seeing them I felt a tremor run through me, shaking me, increasingly violent. I was a rabid dog; I wanted to get my teeth into someone, to bite. Dismayed by that terrible sensation, I tried to calm down, to control the fear instilled in me by that malicious rage, to wear myself out in pain. But now I was a rabid dog: the rabid dog was inside me. In order to dispel the impression, I struggled to remember that aversion to water accompanies rabies in dogs, and I considered that I had drunk willingly the night before. But by this point thoughts no longer meant anything. I walked along an endless wall, my tongue dry, my head drooping. Beyond the wall I heard my mother's step, the light step of a young girl. *You could never walk like me*, she said mockingly. I heard her laughing but I couldn't see her. The wall separated me from everything: from warm, welcoming houses, from kitchens where I got scraps. Even from my mother's memory. Just beyond the wall she was laughing with Hervey. I kept on walking persistently, patiently, sniffing, looking for them. Finally I found them. All it took was one bite, and I saw them fall to the ground and lie down as in death: they were arrested in the flower of their youth, in the chastity of their love with no decline or guilt. I wanted to mangle and destroy them. With my paws I attacked my mother's face, her eyes, but it was like scratching the face and the eyes of a statue. I kept on scratching for hours, rasping. It was as if I were digging in the sand of the river, in the hard, gray mud. From the mud my mother's body emerged, untouched and dressed in blue.

I woke with a start. The first light, still cold, was coming through the shutters. By now I knew the routine of waking: the nightingale would sing first, alone and passionate, then the sparrows, and finally, with the sun, came the heartrending cries of the swallows. I hadn't seen the dawn glow for some time, and I was convinced that the long, foggy night, in which I had taken refuge, was on the verge of expelling me. I had to accept the implacable rhythm of a new day. Each day, I would hear the door slam behind Francesco, and then the telephone would ring and I would answer Tomaso. "No, no," I would say. *Francesco, help me!* My temples pulsed, the rabid dog panted inside me. *No, no*, my mother implored, running breathlessly to my aid. Her step was quick and soft, and she seemed to be descending a staircase. Nonna Editta slowly approached holding her skirt in her hand; she stopped by my bed, her face sad and expectant. Though I loved them dearly, I froze at the sight of them. I was afraid and I wanted to retreat, flee: I could no longer contain the terrible fear. Natalia Donati, too, slowly drew near, soundlessly. She was a little girl with her red hair in braids, her lovestruck gaze sparkling behind her glasses. *You will know all of this, too,* she promised, reading her love letters in Prati's dusty gardens. She seemed unchanged from that time, except that she was holding a red-haired baby in her arms, and her eyes were wide with terror.

The light slowly grew stronger, the swallows flew around my house as they had in the courtyard in Via Paolo Emilio, and the long night was over. Before long I would have to get up and start over. "Francesco," I begged, "please, Francesco." His shoulders were an endless wall of stone. My mother sat next to my bed caressing my hair, and her airy hand brought neither calm nor respite. She had caressed me like that when I was a child and we lingered by the window. I told her I wanted to see at least one of the peacocks at Villa Pierce. And to go back to the Janiculum with Francesco, go back to Villa Borghese. "Francesco," I pleaded, "let's go to Villa Borghese." I called him, my face softened by tears, but I couldn't make him listen. *But if you don't succeed?* I was standing in front of Nonna, as I had the first time I saw her. *If I don't succeed, I'll kill myself,* I whispered, no longer self-assured.

I opened the drawer and took out the pistol. It was cold and hard, and my arm, exhausted by its weight, collapsed to the side of the bed. My weariness and desperation subsided and even the rabid dog quieted down. It would be difficult, much more difficult than carrying bombs under the vegetables. Even more difficult than the night when I shut the door in Tomaso's anxious face. But afterwards I would never again sleep behind the wall. I would never go and beg for scraps outside kitchen doors. I was afraid. My mother and Nonna Editta were afraid, too. Moved by pity, they watched what I was doing, and my mother was pale in her blue dress. I called them but they didn't answer me. I thought once more of fleeing and taking shelter in the old house in Abruzzo. I would find Uncle Rodolfo sitting at the desk in his peaceful study, with the painting of the great family tree and my name trapped within its branches. Uncle Rodolfo was a man of my blood, and I could trust him. He was the only one who could take me in his arms, carry me away, and leave me to rest in a bed with white curtains. I had never met anyone in my whole life I could lean on, apart from him. *Uncle Rodolfo*, I repeated, *Uncle Rodolfo* . . . He didn't come. I was alone behind Francesco's shoulders, a dark wall in the faint light of dawn. Finally I felt the relief of the cold pistol on my temple. *Tous mes adieux sont faits*, I said, looking into my mother's face. *Tous mes adieux* . . .

"Francesco," I burst out desperately: "Help me, Francesco!"

He barely moved. "Go to sleep," he murmured. "Stay calm. Sleep. We'll talk tomorrow."

The rabid dog in me took a sudden leap. I threw myself at Francesco and emptied the pistol in his back. Instantly I saw the blood run down over the white sheet. My mind was a blank, and I called out, "Francesco!" shaking him softly, as I always did to wake him. "Francesco, I love you. Forgive me! Forgive me, I love you."

He didn't answer, so I shook him harder. "Answer me, Francesco," I screamed in terror. "Answer me!" I kept on shaking him, and when I stopped his body fell back heavily. "Francesco," I begged in a strangled voice. "My love, answer me! Answer me!" At last I jumped off the bed, calling savagely for help. I threw open the windows, the door to our apartment. "Help!" I shouted.

The neighbors found me kneeling at his side. "Do something!" I said. "He's not responding. Do something," I begged. They had all come running in their dressing gowns, with uncombed hair, and they stood silently around us, moving back, a circle of curiosity and terror. They left us alone. I caressed Francesco's hand. I looked at his still face, closed and inflexible, his strong jaw, and I talked to him with the heartrending love that had been in me since the day I met him. "Answer me! Don't do this, please, answer me!" I brought my lips to his hands. "I love you," I told him under the horrified gaze of the porter's daughter.

The police arrived.

ON THE DAY of the trial, all the women spoke against me. I was used to the silence and isolation of the Mantellate prison, where I had been for eleven months, and for the first time I was witnessing reactions to what I had done. Until that point, I had thought that the crime was a matter for me, my life, and the law. But when I entered the courtroom the women seemed pleased to vent a long-suppressed hatred. Some of them shouted and I saw their furious faces turn towards my bench, their eyes devoid of pity or anything remotely human. I was shocked: they might at least have understood, but, instead, they raged against me. Those who had been called to testify barely knew me, yet they assured the court that Francesco had been an ideal husband: the neighbors said he always brought me pastries on Sundays. Fulvia didn't dare look at me during her deposition. She was my only friend, and her testimony made a big impression. She said I had never appreciated how lucky I was to marry an honest, loyal man, and that, indifferent to such privilege, I was always accusing Francesco of various imaginary, petty inadequacies. My lawyer was agitated, and I listened astonished and pained, until I realized that she was testifying not against me but against the grocer's daughter.

It was then the turn of Francesco's friends. Serious and melancholy, they went to testify and they all judged me harshly but without resentment. They said little about me but spoke at length about Francesco. I liked listening to them and I was able to convince myself that I had been right to fall in love with him, that he was truly an extraordinary man. When Alberto spoke, the public listened with emotion, and afterwards the women again denounced me, so that the presiding judge threatened to clear the courtroom. I wanted to nod my thanks to Alberto—his commemoration seemed truly sincere and worthy—but he refused to look at me. No one gave me a friendly look. My past life, apart from the moment I pulled the trigger, had ceased to exist. And, hearing it interpreted in so many ways, I myself no longer recognized it as my life. Some witnesses also talked about what I had done during the hateful period of the invasion and unanimously agreed that my remarkable courage was clear proof, again, of my recklessness and cold cruelty. Tomaso and his wife were in England; he was the correspondent for his paper. His deposition was read aloud, and he spoke of Francesco with respect and of me with devoted admiration. However, this favorable testimony bore no weight, since it was clear from the porter's statements that Tomaso had been my lover.

After Francesco's mother, some of my relatives testified. They arrived late because my father had been ill. He walked in on Aunt Sofia's arm, and his height, his white hair, and his pitiful infirmity won the court's instant sympathy. Despite the painful reason that had brought him there, I realized that he was proud to appear, finally, as the person to whom he believed he had always been true: the rigidly uncompromising man who won't hesitate to sacrifice his daughter to the laws of the State. In fact, he said that I had been odd since childhood and subject to violent outbursts. He considered me, above all, cruel and scatterbrained. Because he was blind, it was easy for him to talk about me as if I weren't there, and so I came to know what he had thought over the years but never dared say to my face. All the same, he tried to exonerate me, stating that my upbringing had been misguided, owing to my mother's character. He hinted at her tragic end, and his grim resignation managed to accuse both of us, so that ultimately it was he, rather than Francesco, who aroused the compassion of those present.

Aunt Sofia seemed hesitant. She looked at me after each question, hoping I would suggest what she should say. She said I was a good girl,

even though I wasn't religious. She attributed to me many other quali-
ties I hadn't known I possessed, among them patience and tidiness.
She said that she had secretly been afraid of me during my time in
Abruzzo. She didn't understand me, and could only vaguely imagine
the violence of a rebellion in a character as solitary and patient as
mine. As an example, she mentioned the fury with which I had killed
the rooster, and the Court's attention lingered on this episode. She
spoke about my mother's mother, who had performed on the stage. I
didn't understand why they were dwelling on these pointless details.

Nonna's turn came, and a respectful silence fell over the courtroom
when she swore the oath. She had never been to Rome, had never been
in a courtroom. But she stepped onto the witness stand without the
least awkwardness and took her place with her natural solemnity.
From there she immediately sought my gaze, bridging the space
between us, and I hid my face in my hands. She was harsh in blaming
my mother for the example of weakness she had shown me; and then
she spoke about me at length, about the peculiar circumstances in
which I had lived, and, above all, about my character, highlighting its
hidden aspects, emphasizing my sweetness, loyalty, honesty, and the
acute sensitivity from which I suffered. I realized with some emotion
that she was the only one who had always understood everything. In
fact, she alone testified in my favor.

And so I received the harshest sentence possible. Francesco had
been an incorruptible man, had done nothing that the law condemned.
Throughout the trial, I didn't even try to defend myself. If I had found
it possible to reveal to all those people everything that had hurt me in
life, I wouldn't have been Alessandra but someone else. And then my life,
too, would have been different. I hadn't been able to speak since the
judge—harsh and hostile—had first interrogated me and then coldly
dictated to the registrar. I was taken to a small gray room in the Palace
of Justice that looked out on a street in Prati and reminded me of the
rooms of the house I grew up in. Inside, I took heart and started to

speak with confident spontaneity. But the judge had soon countered my sincerity with sarcastic disbelief, as my father used to. It was already so difficult to express in only a few words what had driven me to do what I had done and, more than anything, to refer to concrete facts. My mother used to say that women are always in the wrong when faced with concrete facts. I felt that the judge would be deaf to my motives, as he surely was to those of the women in his house. So from then on I preferred to say nothing, and accept my guilt completely.

Even my defense lawyer, an Abruzzese hired by my father, knows very little about me. He didn't know me previously, nor was I open with him during our infrequent meetings. So he had to stick to the traditional motives for appalling deeds like mine. He spoke of infidelity on Francesco's part and a jealous scene that had probably taken place the night before the crime. He even hinted at a sudden fit of madness. In order to exonerate me, he alluded to my mother's suicide and various hereditary characteristics. I let him speak, since it was his duty, and he carried it out zealously.

I believe it would have been easy for me to explain myself if my lawyer had been a woman or if I had seen a woman among the members of the Court. But though I realized that my obstinate silences provoked indignation among those present and prevented any impulse of sympathy or compassion, I couldn't speak. If I hadn't been able to make myself understood by the man who lived with me and whom I loved with all my strength, if I couldn't speak to him, how could I speak to anyone else? So I shook my head, acknowledging that I had no response to make, and calmly accepted the sentence, submitting to the long-established norms of the community. But as soon as I was here in prison, awaiting the outcome of the appeal, I wanted to write an accurate account of this tragic event, since it seems only fair that it should also be seen from the point of view of its protagonist, the person who experienced it. I don't know if those who are to judge me will have time to read this memoir. It is in fact a long one, because even the brief life of a woman is infinitely long—hour after hour, day after day—and rarely is it a single motive that drives her to a sudden act of rebellion.

It has been easy to recall my story in the harsh peace of this place, and writing it has been a great relief. I've tried to set it out objectively, so as to dispel the suspicion created by my reserve, surely one of the reasons my mother and I had so few friends. I believe that after reading this a man might more easily understand my crime even if it would go against his nature to justify it. In any case, if my sentence is confirmed and I have to serve it in its entirety, I won't regret being locked in a cell for years, even though I'm still young.

This cell, for example, looks onto a courtyard where the swallows swoop down at dusk. At that hour, the nuns take me out for some air and allow me to water the geraniums. Those who know these pages realize by now that sitting silently beside a window has, since the long-ago days of my childhood, been one of my requirements for happiness.

Then, too, Francesco comes to see me every evening. He enters, and I'm suffused with well-being at the mere sight of him. He has now lost that habit of seeming perpetually hurried and distracted which brought me so much suffering. He sits across from me in the armchair from home and looks at me. He never tires of looking at me. Every evening we rediscover the magic of talking together and revealing ourselves to each other as we did at the beginning. He is now just as I always dreamed he would be. And I wonder whether it was only my act of violence that allowed him to become aware of his love, and to recognize me as the person I aspired to be when loved by him.

AFTERWORD

WHEN I WAS very young, my goal was to write with a masculine tone. It seemed to me that all the great writers were male, and hence it was necessary to write like a real man. Later, I began to read women's literature attentively and I embraced the theory that every little fragment that revealed a feminine literary specificity should be studied and put to use. Some time ago, however, I shook off theoretical preoccupations and readings, and began to write without asking myself what I should be: masculine, feminine, neuter. And while I'm writing, I confine myself to reading books that serve not as entertainment but as solid companions. I have a modest list that I call books of encouragement. One of these is *Her Side of the Story,* by Alba de Céspedes, which is now available as a companion for English-language readers in this wonderful new translation by Jill Foulston.

I first read this novel when I was sixteen years old. As is often the case with books that influence us in our youth, we remember passages according to our needs. I'm talking mainly about the first hundred and fifty pages of *Her Side of the Story*, which is the story of a mother-daughter relationship and, more generally, a memorable catalogue of relations between women.

When I read those pages for the first time, as a teenager, I liked many things about them, others I didn't understand, still others annoyed me. But the point is the conflicted reading that developed, the fact that I couldn't seriously identify with the young Alessandra, the first-person narrator. Certainly I found the relationship between her and her mother, Eleonora, a pianist who is held back by a vulgar husband, very moving. Certainly, in the passages where Alessandra describes her deep bond with her mother, I recognized myself. But her absolute approval of the passion that Eleonora feels for the musician Hervey disturbed me: I mean, rather, that Alessandra's acceptance of it seemed to me sentimental and improbable, it made me angry. I would have fought a hypothetical extramarital love of my mother's with all my strength: the mere suspicion kindled my rage, incited my jealousy much more than her definite love for my father. In short, I didn't understand, I had the impression that I knew more about Eleonora than even her own daughter.

And it was precisely the pages about the dress made for the concert with Hervey that marked the difference between me, the reader, and Alessandra, the narrator. Those pages seemed brilliant to me, and I still love them today, as an important part of a novel that I now perceive to have a great literary intelligence. Let's look, then, at the story of that dress, whose development is complex. Eleonora has talent as an artist, but, dulled by her role as the wife of a vulgar man, she is diminished, and has the faded appearance of a sensitive, loveless woman. Her mother, Alessandra's grandmother, also wasted her life: she was Austrian, and a talented actress, but she married an Italian artilleryman and had to pack up the veils and feathers of her costumes for Juliet, for Ophelia in a box: she, too, was fated to give up her talent. But now Eleonora, nearly forty, going from house to house giving piano lessons, ends up at a wealthy villa where she is to teach a talentless girl named Arletta. She meets Arletta's brother, the mysterious musician Hervey, and falls in love. Love restores her talent, her desire to live, her artistic ambition, and she is invited to give a concert with Hervey.

It's at this point that the problem of the dress arises. What will Eleonora wear for her concert of liberation, in Arletta and Hervey's luxurious villa? As an adolescent reader, I trembled at every line. I liked the fact that love counts so much in this novel. I felt that it was true, that one can't live without love. But at the same time I understood that something wasn't right. The clothes in Eleonora's closet distressed me, I recognized something I knew. "They were all in neutral colors," de Céspedes writes, giving voice to Alessandra: "sand, gray, and two or three were made of raw silk, saddened by a white lace collar: dresses for an older person . . . Her dresses hung limp on the hangers. I said quietly, 'They're like so many dead women, Mamma.'" There: the image of the clothes as dead women hanging on the hangers perfectly captured my own secret feelings about clothes: I have often used it, I do still.

And there is another image, a few pages earlier, which refers to the vanishing body of Eleonora in love, and which I immediately inserted in my vocabulary: "She was so thin that her dress seemed to contain only breath." The dress animated only by a warm breath seemed so true. I read. I read avidly to see how it was going to end. What dress would Eleonora wear? She jumps up, goes to the dresser, takes out a large box. Her daughter, Alessandra, doesn't take her eyes off her mother: "The box was tied up with old twine, and Mamma tore it open at once. When she took off the lid, pink and blue veils appeared, feathers, satin ribbons. I had no idea she possessed such a treasure, so I looked at her in amazement, and she in turn looked up at her mother's portrait. I realized that these were Juliet's veils, or Ophelia's, and I touched the silk in veneration. 'How can we use them?' she asked me, uncertain." I trembled. The dress of liberation would arrive through the maternal line; the costumes of Eleonora's actress mother, thanks to the dressmaker's skill of their noisy neighbor, Lydia, become clothes for a concert performer, a garment enabling her to appear beautiful to Hervey. Eleonora puts aside the neutral clothes of her role as wife and uses pastel veils to make a dress that is the color of a woman in love, a lover. I was nervous. I couldn't understand Alessandra's joyful attitude.

Reading, I felt that things would not turn out well, and I was surprised that the sixteen-year-old Alessandra—a girl the same age as me—didn't even suspect it. No, I wasn't blithely blind, like her. I perceived the tragedy of Eleonora. I felt that the passage from dull clothes to bright-colored clothes would not improve her situation. Rather, when Alessandra exclaims to Lydia, "We have to make a dress for Mamma with Ophelia's veils!" I was sure of it, tragedy was near. The new dress made from the old theatrical fabrics wouldn't save Eleonora. Alessandra's mother—it was clear—would kill herself, would surely drown.

In fact that's what happens. Alessandra didn't understand, but I did. The need to offer her beauty to the man she loves seemed to me not liberating but sinister. Eleonora says, showing off her half-naked body to her daughter and the neighbor: "Every time I arrive and he looks at me, I want to be as beautiful as a woman in a painting." The passage continues like that, in the voice of Alessandra: "She got up and ran to embrace Lydia, Fulvia, and then me. she nearly flew to the mirror and stopped in front of it, studying herself. 'Make me beautiful,' she said, clasping her hands to her heart. 'Make me beautiful.'"

Make me beautiful. How I wept at those words. The phrase remained in my memory as a cry not to life but to death. A lot of time has passed since I first read this novel and many things have changed, but the need that de Céspedes's Eleonora expresses still, to this day, seems desperate, and therefore meaningful.

Let's return to those passages as I felt them at my first, long-ago reading, and still feel them now. Eleonora, impelled by love, decides to take off the clothes of punishment, of suffering. But the only alternative she comes up with is the costume inherited from her mother, the dress worn by the female body exploited and put on display. Lydia, the dressmaker, sews the dress, and Eleonora adorns herself as an offering to a distracted Hervey: a Juliet dress, an Ophelia dress, a dress that is no less humiliating than the neutral dresses, the self-annihilating dresses of the roles of wife and mother. This I knew, this it seemed to me I had known forever. I knew that both the demure clothes of Eleonora's domestic life and the ones meant for theatrical display are clothes that hang in the closet like so many dead women.

It would take Alessandra the whole book to understand this. Too late: like her grandmother, like her mother, she, too, emerges into death. I had perceived it, I don't know how, in my mother's clothes, in her passion to make herself beautiful, and that perception tormented me. I didn't want to be like that. But how did I want to be? When I thought of her, once I was an adult, once I was far away, I sought a means of understanding what type of woman I could become. I wanted to be beautiful, but how? Was it possible that you necessarily had to choose between dullness and ostentation? I was anxiously searching for my path of rebellion, of freedom. Was the way, as Alba de Céspedes has Alessandra say, using a metaphor perhaps of religious origin, to learn to wear not clothes—those will come later, as a consequence—but the body? And how does one arrive at the body beyond the clothes, the makeup, the customs imposed by the everyday job of making oneself beautiful?

I've never found a definite answer. But today I know that my mother, both in the dullness of domestic tasks and in the exhibition of her beauty, expressed an unbearable anguish. There was only one moment when she seemed to me a woman in tranquil expansion. It was when, sitting hunched over in her old chair, her legs drawn up and joined, her feet on the foot rest, discarded scraps of material around her, she dreamed of salvific clothes, and pulling needle and thread straight she sewed together again and again the pieces of her fabrics. That was the time of her true beauty.

—Elena Ferrante
Adapted from *Frantumaglia*
Translated by Ann Goldstein

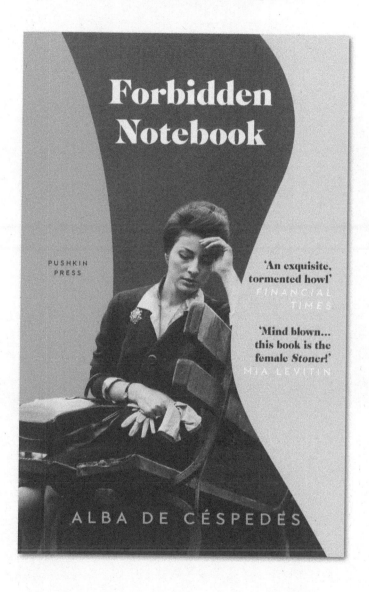

AVAILABLE AND COMING SOON
FROM PUSHKIN PRESS

Pushkin Press was founded in 1997, and publishes novels, essays, memoirs, children's books—everything from timeless classics to the urgent and contemporary.

Our books represent exciting, high-quality writing from around the world: we publish some of the twentieth century's most widely acclaimed, brilliant authors such as Stefan Zweig, Yasushi Inoue, Teffi, Antal Szerb, Gerard Reve and Elsa Morante, as well as compelling and award-winning contemporary writers, including Dorthe Nors, Edith Pearlman, Perumal Murugan, Ayelet Gundar-Goshen and Chigozie Obioma.

Pushkin Press publishes the world's best stories, to be read and read again. To discover more, visit www.pushkinpress.com.

THE PASSENGER
ULRICH ALEXANDER BOSCHWITZ

TENDER IS THE FLESH
NINETEEN CLAWS AND A BLACKBIRD
AGUSTINA BAZTERRICA

AT NIGHT ALL BLOOD IS BLACK
BEYOND THE DOOR OF NO RETURN
DAVID DIOP

WHEN WE CEASE TO UNDERSTAND THE WORLD
THE MANIAC
BENJAMÍN LABATUT

NO PLACE TO LAY ONE'S HEAD
FRANÇOISE FRENKEL